Joyful

The Love Affair of Joan of Arc

A Novel

By

Amy R Farrell

This Book is dedicated to...

*My grandmother, Hulda Cassow Oppermann,
who brought Joan of Arc into my family through the hands
of the sculptor, Richard W. Bock of Chicago, who used
Hulda's visage as the model for his 1923 work "Joan of Arc."*

*Hulda, pregnant at the time with my mother, named her only
daughter after The Maid of France, and therefore, this book is
also dedicated to my mother Joan (Jody) Oppermann Farrell,
who has been my personal Joan of Arc throughout my life,*

*And also, and with great love,
to Gilles, where he does dwell.*

Joyful

is Book One

Of

The Love Affair of Joan of Arc

for Cindy
a book warrior
from Amy R Farrell

ACKNOWLEDGMENTS

I would like to acknowledge the following people for their assistance in the production of this book;

My partner Mayra Sonam Paldon for her patient guidance in navigating the unknown territory of self-publishing and for her belief in my work;

Megan Jo Doyle, my friend and co-adventurer in all things Medieval and my copy-editor, who finds mistakes where I thought there were none;

Yvette Wolff, psychic, seer, and handy boatman, who first noticed Joan walking where I walked and suggested I stop and talk with her.

Flames, a prologue

It begins with flames and it ends with flames.

And all through it, flames have been there, keeping stride with me.

From the fire that burned in the King's grate on the day I first met him at Chinon, to my banner burning on *La Rue du Renard* to the flames which brought down Gladsdale at *Les Tourelles*, and the war-camps of a thousand campfires, and other flames both great and small.

My first memory is of a face and flames; my face, reflected in the still waters of the font at our little church in Domrémy, the reflection of my face ringed about with candle flames. I studied my face as one would the face of a stranger; for I had not seen my reflection before, or not that I had known. I was only three or four.

But the face and the flames fascinated me; I could not tear my eyes away, though my father's hand urged me to follow him and in the end pulled me away. But those flames, small, cheering, innocuous, had remained in my mind, as had the face; round, with a pointed chin, large catlike eyes, and a lip that trembled with fear or with wonder or with something else I have never been able to adequately name, but which has filled me since my earliest remembrance.

And here it ends with a face and with flames.

But it is not a reflection in water, though the heat

rising in quavering waves and the blue-black smoke whipping my body like a many-tipped lash and the tears stinging in my eyes give it all a watery aspect. And it is not my own face that I see, but yours.

You are here, as I prayed you would be.

I had wanted to see you one more time. We had been apart for far too long.

A monk had brought out a cross on a pole and raised it high above the crowd, that I might find it with my eyes to give me hope through my torment. Twas a blessed kindness and I asked my angels for a blessing upon his soul. I fixed my eyes on that cross and blinked away the tears that I might see it better.

But then I saw you standing there, not far from the cross, and that is where my eyes rested.

The flame-light was dancing across your chest and your face was downward-cast, your eyes on the stones of the street or on your own bare feet.

In an instant, I saw it all; your gaunt visage, your ragged clothes, your bruised cheek, the hair once ringleted and golden-brown blowing in a clean breeze, now matted and dirty from months sleeping in alleyways; and knew you had stayed as close to me as circumstances would allow, and suffered for it.

Perhaps now, after these next moments, you would be free.

I had taken everything from you, and you had paid it willingly, as if it was the best bargain in the world, and I still don't know what it is I gave you in return.

I had asked you for everything, and you had never denied me, well, only once denied me, and you had been right about that.

I had sworn to be your shield against danger, and yet I had taken you with me into the mouth of danger, over and over. And seen you hurt, and seen you suffer, and nearly seen you killed.

Yet I did it because I could not bear to be without you.

When I was taken, my first thought was for you, "Well, here is an end to it. He is free."

And such a relief I felt, that my selfishness would not be the end of you. You would hie yourself home, make peace with your mother, hunt rabbits in your native fields again, marry a good girl, have children and live out your natural life in God's grace.

Yet in my cell, I prayed you would not leave.

Not yet.

I prayed that you would be here on this day.

A day I sometimes deluded myself would never come, that I would be freed, that my King would come and wrest me from our foes, that my angels would intervene, that earthquake would strike and these walls crumble, and I walk out stepping over the rubble and through the dust into the open air and stride away.

Now the day is come, the flames my child's eyes foresaw in holy water have come, my death has come, and you have come. You who gave me everything. But even so, there is still something I need of you even now.

"Raise your eyes," I say.

My voice is not a voice; it is a rush of tortured over-heated air from lungs which are dry as tinder.

"Open your eyes, look at the light," I say, and you do, your head tilted back, your chin jutting upwards, and your eyelids, languid and soft as butterfly wings, flutter open.

Your eyes meet mine. Your eyes, they are a color that is

beyond color, more like light of varying degrees.

I have seen them dark and gray as slate, and as yellow, light and clear as clover honey, as blue as a summer sky, and as green as new leaves on the limbs of the birch.

Now, through a thickening veil of heat and smoke and, yes, of rising yellow flame, flying cinders, and ash, with the firelight full upon you, illuminating you, burnishing the planes of your face, accentuating your perfect lips, your high cheeks, your strong brow, and beneath that brow, those eyes are a clear gray-blue and as sweet and soft as the gaze of a rabbit as it hides from sight under a berry-bush.

They weep for me, those eyes, and blink the tears away, but they are steady on mine and unwavering as you have been, stalwart in your love of me, and never faltering.

"Thank you," my voice that is not a voice says, "thank you, and bless you, and God keep you, and my angels watch over you...."

Those in the crowd that day, my foes and my friends like, will all say the same of me, that my last words were to cry, *"Jhésus! Jhésus!"* to the heavens as I burned and suffered, but they will be wrong.

I did indeed call out our Lord's name, many times, but my very last words, my final words were, *"Joyeuse! Joyeuse!"* shouted to the boy at the base of the cross in the Old Marketplace at Rouen where they burned me to death.

+ + + + +

1, The Boy

Twas their deaths I saw, a gift of sight that was a gift I never wanted.

The archangel Michael had warned me of the gift when was I only thirteen, telling me it would be bestowed when I was ready. I was special among girls, he said, for I had the wonder of life and that God was in my eyes, seen first everywhere I looked.

He told me many things, among them that I must never know a man's body and that I must be good and kind always and have compassion for all beings and that one day I should know why these things were necessary for me to do, for I would know the pain and torment of all the world and see the deaths of all upon whom my gaze should fall and would therefore love them and serve them before I should serve myself.

How could a child of thirteen understand these things?

I was terrified and shook in fear whenever the angel

appeared to me; his was a light that was blinding in my eyes and I fell upon my knees and bent my face to the earth that his light should not burn me.

Ever would he say, "Lift your eyes, child, look at the light," and I would obey, and see through the light, his face, his beautiful face, burnished like polished bronze, his eyes bright as the sun and his golden hair in ringlets to his shoulders.

He had gleaming armor and a sword of blue flame, a shield of an azure sea and a cloak of the winds of the world. When he touched my face once to make me look at him, his finger left a burn that never left me.

On my right cheek below my eye, it could not be seen but I felt it evermore.

Tis with that burn that he bestowed on me my sight.
It is no surprise that when I first saw the boy, I mistook him for Michael. They looked so very much alike.

But I precede myself.

I should begin earlier, when I first heard my voices in the Oak Wood at Domrémy, under *l'arbre de fées*, the Faery Tree, or when I went to Vaucouleurs to find Squire de Baudricourt, or when I met the Dauphin whom I called the King of France.

But these things you may be told by any citizen of my country, any denizen of any hostelry upon any road may tell you of these things, a minstrel may sing of them at any wayside inn or public house, women at their washing will speak of them, and grooms currying horses.

Tis the things no one knows that I would tell of, the things never written in the Histories, and so I shall tell of the boy I first saw on the road to Blois, the boy who had come with all the others to see me pass on the way to my destiny.

Twas their deaths I saw, the ones who came out all along

the way to get a look at me.

They came from solitary farmsteads, from villages and from walled towns. They came from the fields and the forests, mills and shops.

They left sheep in the meadows, and iron cooling at the forge's side to hie them to the places where I would be passing. The King had given me men-at-arms and horses, knights of fame, warriors of fortune, two royal heralds, several squires, banner-bearers and varlets with wagons loaded with supplies. All a great spectacle on any day, but I was *La Pucelle*, and my fame had spread, though as of yet I had achieved nothing but talk.

Prophesy had spoken of a girl like me, long before my birth, and now that I was here on earth twas said great miracles would be made manifest. Or so the common people whispered amongst themselves.

He was a boy who sat on the roadside, one long bare leg folded up underneath him, the other extended out before him, the bottoms of his bare feet calloused and brown with the earth. A great dark beech tree rose above him, gnarled branches spread across the sky. A crossroads there, and the folk had come to see us pass, my contingent with the men, horses, arms, banners and wagons, and me myself, *Jehanne, La Pucelle*, the maid who would save us all.

He of all them seemed uninterested.

He sat, eyes cast down, his fingers tying up the lacings on the bag he held upon his lap. I did not notice him at first.

I was riding one of the two destriers, a white and a black, the King had given me, along with my kit for war, my harness of white gleaming steel made to my proportions, and my white banner made to my instructions depicting the Lord on His throne, two angels, the names of *Jhésus et Maria* overall

9

and a scattering of lilies that each had a tiny border of red silk, red for the blood of Christ, the *sangrail.*

The banner flew above my head, carried by my banner-man, a young good-hearted fellow, sent with me by the King, whose name I could not remember.

I did not wear the harness as we were in French-held lands, but I wore the padded gambeson and the jupon made of the same stuff as my banner and with the lilies of France upon the breast.

The white destrier was not truly white, but gray and speckled brown. He was an aged creature and steady and twas thought a good mount for me until I had learned to ride better. His large gray hooves thudded and clattered alternately on the road, as they struck first upon ancient cobbles and then upon soggy ground where the stones had been prized away or settled under shifting soil. His tackle jingled and clinked as his powerful old shoulders surged back and forth, straining at the strap around his chest that held the saddle steady in the charge.

The strap was red leather, wide and studded with polished and embossed steel plates, rusted at the edges and a few of them missing, for like the horse, it was old and worn. Other plates, lozenge-shaped and riveted to red leather, hung down from the straps and clinked together as they swung to and fro with the movement of the horse.

His long gray mane was twisted and tangled, yellow at the ends, and bounced on the right side of his long arching neck as he walked at the fast head-bobbing pace that was the way of the steeds of knights and mounted men-at-arms among whom I rode.

I sensed he was a good horse, a kind horse, and I could tell such things about animals. I could generally, but not always, tell such things about people too.

There was a dense forest to our right and, to the left broad green fields with the winding road betwixt them. It was morning. We had left Tours at sunrise, three quarters of an hour past, and the slanted sunlight on the young barley lit the fields like green fire and the darkness of the wood was a stark contrast to my eyes as I gazed from one to the other.

It was so beautiful and I could not fill my eyes with it enough, though I tried to see it all, to let the beauty fill me, like a breath deep-taken.

I wanted to be the beauty, have the light shine straight through me and illuminate me the way it illuminated the young green grass, the barleycorn, and the leaves on the trees.

The people stood at the place where the smaller road connected to the broader way. As my eyes lit upon them, they became part of the beauty, for they drew breath in and out, their blood sang through their bodies, and they were living in their own precious lives.

They were a group of perhaps ten and five, perhaps a score, simple folk, mostly women, children and a few older men. Farmers and crofters, they were as familiar to me as my own family or the neighbors I had left far behind in Domrémy.

One of the women, her hair covered in a linen cap tied under her chin, wearing a gown of rough homespun, a shawl over her shoulder, and with hands stained with dyes made of plants and flowers, was the first to see me as the riders ahead of me passed the group, and twas she started up the cry, *"La Pucelle! La Pucelle!"*

They stepped forward into the road, close to the lumbering horses and the men with weapons that were in front, heedless of the danger of trampling, their eyes raised to me, their arms outreaching, their voices imploring. I legged my horse on the left side and the gray side-passed to the right, closer to the people.

Raising my right hand, I held it out above their heads, my fingers spread as though I could drop blessings upon them from my open palm. As I saw each face, their deaths flashed in my mind and though I tried to blink the images away, I could not.

The woman with the cap (twas she I knew, who had brought the people here), she would die under chimney stones toppling. The old man with one eye had only two months to live and would die of a wasting illness that was even now settling into his organs. The smallest child, held in the arms of its young mother, would not live out its first year of life but would be buried before summer. And the girl who was a few years younger than myself would grow and be married and die in bloody childbirth, losing the child as well.

I saw it all in an instant as my gaze fell upon each in turn, and I wept, the tears springing to my eyes, welling in the lids and spilling down my face, hot and salty; tears for their precious lives, tears that they lived them not knowing how precious they were, and tears that they were all to be lost.

I had been born with the gift of seeing the beauty of life, the realness of life, and then I had been given the gift of seeing the end of life.

I had the gift of wonder and now, this gift that the archangel had given me with the touch of his finger on my cheek, the gift I had never wanted, was the gift of compassion.

For in seeing their deaths and knowing the fate that

would befall them in days that would come upon the heels of this day, I wept tears of sadness for them and my heart loved them and felt pity for them and wanted to serve them in such a way as to make the days remaining to them happier, safer, and more blessed.

Fourscore years of war had been waged upon this soil, borders had shifted and governance had changed from hand to hand, and the people that belonged to the land had suffered.

Twas peace that I wanted to bring them and an end to fear and uncertainty.

That was why I had been born. Though I said it often, I had a difficulty in believing it myself. But I was *La Pucelle* and the act of saying it was the act of making it true.

I held my hand over their heads as my horse carried me by them, with the tears streaming down my cheeks. The boy under the beech had by now stood up, with a graceful motion he was suddenly on his feet, the little bag still held in his fingers by a slender strap.

He was looking at the horses and the men, quickly taking in the banners, the armor and accoutrement, and all the equipment of war that hung from every saddle and from the shoulders of the men riding and marching. They seemed to be things he had never seen this closely before and he was interested. The others were crying, *"La Pucelle!"* and finally he looked at me.

Those eyes, pale yellow-green like the light of the sun on the young barley, saw first the bridle-bits in the mouth of my gray, the slobber running down the chains to patter on the ground, and then rose to stop upon my face, and I saw a movement of his brow as he recognized the fact of my weeping.

13

I gasped, for he looked so much like Michael with the morning light on him, turning his cheeks bronze.

His linsy shirt was open at the throat, two little strings hanging down with which to tie it closed, and his tunic over that was a faded brown and stained at the underarms.

He had a singular hat, made of two skins of rabbit sewn together, the four ears bobbing at his crown, and the front legs with their pads and claws hanging down, two on either side of his face and down his chest, the hind legs hanging down over his shoulders in the back, the weight of the legs holding the hat firmly on his head.

Twisted cords of golden hair escaped from the hat on either side and framed his face, so much like unto the archangel's ringlets that I had to deny the impulse to dismount my horse and drop to my knees.

He stood there, his bare feet only inches from the great clopping hooves of the gray, and looked up at me, his chin with a light stubble on it and his pretty mouth pursed slightly and his brow quirked as he stared at the tears on my face, his eyes lit by the sun and squinting at me.

My hand passed over his head so close that if I had dropped it a few inches I would have touched the rabbit ears of his funny hat. I could've snatched it off, and would have if I had been a girl, a simple country girl, who wanted to tease a boy, a boy of her own age and whom she thought she might like to marry one day.

But I was not a girl, I was *La Pucelle*, and I was never to know a man.

As my gray surged past him, I turned in the saddle, my eyes still on his, my hand still outstretched. I took in the whole sight of him, the bare feet, the short trousers that were unlaced around the knee, his strong legs with the light brown hair curling on them, the narrow hips and broad shoulders, and his face and hair and that hat with the dangling rabbit-paws, his arms and the hand that held the little bag, the strap hanging down onto the road.

He was not an angel; he was only a boy, a boy almost as beautiful as an angel. In truth he was surely a man, but his heart was that of a boy, and would be that of a boy forever, I was certain.

Twas only after I had passed and had had to turn away, for the tall saddle-bow had not allowed me to turn any further, that I realized I had not seen his death.

Of all the people, he was the only one whose death I did not see.

I saw his light, his life, and his joy, but not his death.

Twas in seeing their deaths that I wept for them, that I loved them.

I did not see his, yet I loved him even more.

2, A Girl

I am only a girl, and a maid who is never to know a man.

Never to pick a man or a boy to love, to walk with by the millpond, or meet secretly by the Tree of the Faeries, and to be courted by, not even a maid who shall be bargained away by her father into a marriage she might or might not find joy in.

As I was growing up in my little village of Domrémy, I thought I should be a normal girl and live a normal life. I often thought of the boy who would grow to the man who would be my husband, and he would be kind, and comely, and a good man to me and our children.

He would tend his flocks, or his fields, or his cooper's shop or whatever his trade might prove to be, and he would hold my arm as we stepped up the steep stairway into our bedroom at night, for surely he would be a prosperous man and our home on two levels.

He would be respected and other women would envy me

my good fortune in marriage.

But then my angel came. He broke all my daydreams to shards.

He was in the form of a man yet not a man.

He came in the light.

In fact, he was all light, the first time I saw him and heard his voice, all light and blinding, blinding both to my eyes and to my mind. But as he appeared to me again and yet again, the light became less blinding or perhaps my eyes grew accustomed to the light and my mind became accustomed to his presence.

He was bright and strong and powerful and dangerous.

I could see these things about him; how terrible his wrath could be were he to become wrathful; and yet, with me, he was gentle as a lamb. He was beautiful too, and when he stood near me, like any girl, or perhaps any woman, I felt the unspeakable things within my body that might be the result of a man and woman, wed and in God's grace, being in close proximity, and I felt shame.

But when he came near to me, I trembled so and my knees weakened, so that I fell upon them and my heart quailed, and he had to ask me to look up at him.

Tears came to my eyes as I beheld him, not only from the light, but from my love for him, that seemed to be born there in my heart at the moment I saw him. A love my heart had never known or could know existed. And sinfully, I wanted him to touch me, as a man might touch a woman but he only touched me the once, and that only upon my cheek.

And that touch burned, for he was an angel, not a man.

Then he made it known to me that I should never know a man's touch, a man's love, a man's body. Never have the pleasures of a hearth and a home with a husband and children and all the things a girl dreams of, which are all part of the wonder of a normal life, part of the beauty of a normal life, and which I could see in other people; my parents, my neighbors and friends; as clearly as I could see the blood flowing in the delicate vessels under their skin.

I wanted those pleasures, I longed for them.

I wanted to live a life to the fullest, to feel everything, to have love and joy in the simplest and most tiny precious moments of life.

But my angel would deny me that, for he said that I must travel away from home, and leave my mother and my father and friends behind, and journey with strangers far into the land of our enemies.

He told me that the truth must be fought for and that I must lead the men who would do the fighting, that I was the only one that could lead them, and whom they would follow, bearing the truth with them for all the people of the world to know.

Twas a duty, he said, that I could not shirk, for I alone was born to do it, and I must do it for *Jhésus*, and *La Magdalena*, and *Maria* the Mother of God, and for the truth to be known.

All I wanted was the tiny little simple truths, not the great important one, but angels are not to be denied. So here I was on the road to Blois to bring provisions to the King's army.

I had already traveled far, to Vaucouleurs, and with much difficulty, convinced Squire Robert de Baudricourt to support me in my quest to join the Dauphin, whom I called King Charles though he had not yet been crowned, and he did give me a few men and boys and some horses, some boy's clothing to wear and an old sword he no longer had need of. De

Baudricourt did not like me from the first and told me I was a foolish girl and was more like to get myself ravished by baseborn soldiers, my belly filled with a bastard-child, and ruined for any honest purpose, than to ever be granted an audience with Charles, much less be given an army to take against the English.

It was only after I told him that the French had lost a great battle against the English near Orléans, news that caused him to laugh in my face, and three days later the news arrived to him from the lips of a fast-mounted royal messenger that indeed this battle had taken place and indeed the French had lost many good men, that he looked at me with a different eye.

I think at that point I frightened rather than amused him. He was glad to be rid of me and that was the only reason he rendered me assistance.

It was, of a certainty, not for love of me nor belief in me that he did so, though his men that did offer their service to escort me, the knight Jean de Metz and the squire Bertrand did look upon me with a kind of awe, as did the royal messenger Colet who would guide us through enemy-occupied lands to reach the King.

Along the way, a messenger from Lorraine met up with us and insisted that we detour to Nancy to attend upon the Duke. I did not wish to be delayed in this way but de Metz suggested that mayhap an ally such as a Duke would be a good thing, and that, being as he was my liege lord, it was not mete that I should deny him, and so we went.

The Duke of Lorraine was an old man and very ill.
He bethought me a miracle worker and wanted me to render him a healing but I told him I was only a girl and that like any good girl, I would pray for him as he was a man, and one

who suffered, and that was all that I could promise.

More than that, I said, he should beg God's forgiveness for his sins, and there were many, for I could see in his eyes that though a man of high station he had lived little better than a rogue's life, and that if he truly wished to ease his way, he should render some assistance to France and the King in his last days.

He promised his son to join my retinue though the young man didn't jump at the chance and in fact absented himself on the day I rode forth from Nancy, though I would later meet him, long after my successes at Orléans.

Further on, near Fierbois, I learned that we were close to the Lost Chapel, which mysterious place had been hidden from the eyes of man for centuries, with the woods having grown up around it and through it, and only rediscovered and cut free from the primal forest some years past.

I was filled with such a desire to see this holy shrine of Saint Catherine, as were many of my companions, and so we traveled there. The ancient walls of the chapel were hung all about with the chains and fetters of slaves and prisoners who owed their freedom to the saint. We heard mass there three times a day and I remained upon my knees in prayer for the better part of those three days.

During that time, I received visitations from Saint Catherine herself, and several angels who gave me succor, wetting my lips with honeyed water, as I prayed on my knees before the alter, crying uncontrollably, whether weeping for myself and my lost life or for the ruined lives of others, I could not tell you.

Like the prisoners whose fetters decorated those hoary walls, all I wanted was to go home, to be free to return to my garden and my beasts in the field, my quiet days in meadows, fields and the Faery Wood.

But Saint Catherine, in her goodness, did not release me, and neither did the bright angels who came with her.

And finally, the voice and visage of the archangel appeared to me. The blue fire that was Michael in his glory, the fire too hot for me to withstand, compelled me onward and we left Fierbois and the sanctity of the Lost Chapel and found the road towards Chinon again.

My tail grew, those that followed me, men and boys and horses and cattle pulling wagons and folk who followed out of curiosity.

Did they want to see what would happen to me when and if the King granted my request and sent me to challenge the English?

Did they want to see what chance one young village girl stood against a foe that had occupied French lands for eighty years?

Did they expect to see me ridiculed and laughed out of the Dauphin's court, perhaps run out of town on a rail, painted black with pitch?

Well, I was not.

I knew the King out of thirty men, though he hid his face and placed another richly dressed man upon his chair. I picked him out as easily as I picked a ripe melon from a field of green ones and they all were astonished at my feat.

They were even more astonished when after all the jeers and laughter had abated, the King stated that he would grant my boon. There was many a high-flown mouth agape at his pronouncement and then later when he had seen fit to set me up as well and richly as any noble-born liegeman, there was the dry rasp of jealousy upon many a tongue.

But then, they do not know what came to pass to turn

the Dauphin's mind away from good humor at my expense and tilt it gently but firmly in the way of prudent, thoughtful Kingship.

Twas when I asked him to speak with me privily and we went alone, just him and me, into his private chamber.

A fire burned in the grate within that chamber and I went to stand near it and gaze a while into its flames, those flames of King Charles' which warmed me and which I would long remember and think on with joy in my heart for they would remind me of how he listened to me and how the look in his eyes changed from one of incredulity and skepticism to one of amazement and belief.

As we had passed through the doorway to enter his room, a man-at-arms standing against the wall who had joined in the jocular speech of all those others after I had made my appeal, and whose booming laughter I had heard above the other voices, now made a comment both ribald and presumptuous to the Dauphin: "The girl is pretty enough for a Dauphin, perhaps after the Dauphin has had her, a man-at-arms might try her on?"

His wide and leering mouth with its broken teeth in the front and the laughter issuing forth did not deceive me, for I saw it all in an instant; the same mouth, open, would be flowing water as they dragged his body from the moat, the head would loll lifelessly and the eyes, now filled with mirth, would be dark and dull as stones.

"Seek more pious and proper thoughts," I said to the man, "for twould be a shame to meet God with lust in your heart, you who are so soon to lose your life."

His mouth clapped shut and his eyes looked at me with resentment for having quashed his mischief but I did not mean him harm, for I only spoke in compassion and with the tears springing to my eyes.

It was not meant unkindly but as solid advice from knowing counsel as I had been availed of knowing counsel by my angels, for in gazing in his eyes I saw his fate, that which would befall him in a few hours' time, and which did in fact come to pass.

The seeing of the death of the man-at-arms was the first seeing that I did have and it shocked me and made my head to reel and my heart to pound, though I had been told by Michael that my sight would come upon me first in the presence of my King and thus, I should have been prepared for it.

Those tears of knowing were drying in my eyes by the heat of the Dauphin's fire when Charles said to me, "So, girl, what would you have me hear of you?" and I turned from the flames to peer up into his face, not yet even knowing why I had asked him here, away from the others.

But then the words came into my mind as I spoke them.

"You, Gentle Prince, carry in your veins the blood of our savior, *Christ Jhésus*, Son of God, and His blessed Wife-companion and First Disciple *Maria La Magdalena*. Do you know that The Church has lied about her? Do you know that she was a Princess and that They were married? Do you know that They had children? Do you know that Their blood lives even now in you?"

I did not wait to hear his answer. He seemed dumb-struck and I had more to say, though I do not know how the words were formed, they simply sprang complete and perfect from my mouth and even I who spoke them did not understand their full meaning.

"Do you know that the Church Militant wishes to deny this Truth and destroy all who believe in it? Do you know that it will do all in its power to destroy the bloodline of Christ? To see that it disappears from the earth? I have come to run the English out of France and deliver the country back into the hands of its rightful King, he who bears the *sangrail*. That King, gentle Charles, is you. The time is short, my King, for in a little over a year's time, my mission must be completed or never at all. So use me soon, and well, or give France over to men of unholy blood forever."

He stood, did the King, as a man dumbfounded, his mouth hanging open as if it were a basket ready to accept picked cherries. I could see my words terrified him, because of what I had said about The Church, but also excited him because of what they meant, about him, about his origins.

His heart was racing to catch up with his thoughts.

And then I added, suddenly, "I see the deaths of all who fall under my gaze and in that I am both blessed and cursed. An you did command it of me, I would tell you your death, that you might understand that all things are temporary, even and especially our lives, and then mayhap the urgency of my quest might better be known by you."

He clapped his mouth shut and turned from me then and walked the room up and back, up and back, glancing at me now and again and muttering to himself.

Was he frightened?

I bethink me so, though I was a country girl and as out of my place as a fish is upon land, and he was a King and in his palace, with his knights and soldiers and priests just beyond the door.

The words to describe the crown that he would wear came into my mind and I spoke them just as they came.

'He stopped his pacing and stared at me, his jaw hanging down. He knew the truth of my words, for he had seen this crown, and I, of course, was a simple girl from the country, and could never have seen it.

His face began moving slowly, muscles shifting under skin, and before my eyes, he seemed to become a different man, and then without a word, he flung the door open and rejoined his court, leaving me to follow after.

I glanced once more into his fire and was loath to leave it, as it warmed me and gave me hope, like his Kingly heart, which only now was beginning to beat as a King's heart should, with the fervor and desire of a King, and would soon come to love me as a King's heart should love his loyal vassal.

But that heart, being changeable like fire is changeable, in time would burn me, though I did not know it then.

He had left a wind in his wake which moved the flames, and seeing this, I left the fire burning in the King's grate and followed him.

3, The Road to Orléans

The next time I saw the boy he was suddenly at my knee, one hand clinging to the chest strap of the gray, and running alongside the horse.

The rabbit-skin hat was hanging down his back, the two sets of front legs tied in a loose knot under his chin, and his eyes, urgent and worried, looked up at me and his breath was quick as if he had run a long way to catch me.

The mercenary captain known as *La Hire* was riding on my left, knee to knee with me, his huge brown destrier prancing and tossing its head, constantly fighting the bridle-bits, and the man I called the dark knight, but who is known as The Bastard of Orléans, was on the right of me, not as close as *La Hire* nor so far as to have made it easy for the boy to squeeze himself between the great steeds to speak to me without being in danger of being trampled.

I looked down into his eyes and he spoke to me between

panting breaths, telling me that we had passed Orléans; that I should know that the city was now in our rear.

The dark knight raised his gloved fist and brought it down upon the head of the boy, who fell between the horses to the road and was left in our wake, the other riders and marching men having to part around him.

Looking behind me, I saw the boy, who had picked himself up onto one knee and was cowering there between the passing horses, holding his arm over his head, one blue-green eye peering from under his arm to watch me go. I turned to the dark knight and said, "He is only a boy, why did you strike him?"

The knight flexed his big hand within the worn leather glove, which had some rusted rings of maille still sewn to it, though most of them had long since come off, and said, "He is a peasant brat who speaks out of his place."

Am I then, in your mind, *Le Batârd d'Orléans*, as much a peasant brat who speaks out of place? I wondered, but I did not say it.

I pulled back on the reins of my horse and the gray flung its head twice, making the chains of its bridle jingle, but it came to a lumbering halt, which caused *La Hire* and The Bastard to have to rein their destriers to a standstill and the men behind us to clump together or to leave the cobbled road so as not to pile up upon us.

I turned the horse sideways that I might look back and see the boy raise himself to his feet, rubbing at his scalp with one hand and shaking the hair from his eyes.

"Is what he says true?" I asked of the dark knight, whose impatient mount was snorting close by my ear. "Have we passed Orléans?"

I had wanted to ride straight at the enemy, to take them

by surprise and, piece by piece, roll up their siege-works, making French what had been made English, like a tide rolling over a beach.

Though he had greeted me warmly when we first met, face to face, on the bluffs above the River Loire, saying, "I praise God that you have come," The Bastard now showed his contempt for my station as he made answer, "The wisest captains of France have decided to bring you by this route, and deemed it safest that you not engage the enemy outright but until we have brought the supplies into the city and had a chance to make council with those within who are besieged."

I snorted, much like unto his horse, as I remember it now, and stated, "I am not here for my safety, Sir, else would I have stayed in Domrémy. I am guided by wiser counsel than a hundred captains, an I were not, I would have preferred my flocks in their fields to this field of war. I am here to relieve the city of Orléans, and bring it back to France where it doth belong, and see to the return from English hands its lord, your brother Duke Charles, whom you have failed to ransom in twelve years."

The dark knight's face grew darker with rage and he pulled hard on his horse's head at the same time as he spurred it and the beast's eyes rolled back and it flung its head into the air, throwing a line of drool from its open mouth onto my jupon at my breast.

My gray turned its aged head and snapped long yellow teeth at The Bastard's horse, causing it to take a step back, which the knight didn't like, he spurred it closer to me and said in a voice sinister as a demon's, "Give not that shrew's tongue to me, girl, I care not for it, though my cousin, the Dauphin, be charmed by your comely form and pretty promises. You are but a shepherdess and I am a man, a knight, proven in battle since the age of fifteen, and have forgotten more about war than you'll ever know."

The mercenary captain *La Hire* now gave tongue, begging for a council here upon the road. Prudently, we all dismounted and had the horses drawn away, while we retired to a copse of trees and all the leading men who were with us joined our circle. The soldiers and varlets were strung out behind us down the way, a long line of milling people and animals settling themselves in for a respite from hard travel, awaiting the command of their leaders.

I kept glancing about, searching for the boy amidst the throng, but did not see him.

Little did I know how close he was, he hid behind a nearby tree as quiet as a hiding rabbit. In fact, he was so close that I might have heard his breathing, had not the voices of the men been so very loud and interruptive of one another, their voices over-laying in a rising chorus like monks in chapel though not harmonious.

They argued about things I did not understand, and, not for the first time, I felt what a poor choice of the angels I must be for this great enterprise.

These men were not like the men I knew, hardworking humble farmers, craftsmen and merchants; they were hard brutal men, warriors and killers, butchers of human flesh, and men vying for greater power in a world in which they already held much over the heads of lesser folk.

They seemed creatures of another breed, different from me as a leopard is from a goat, a wolf from a groundhog.

The one called *La Hire*, whose sobriquet meant "the Anger," or "the Ire," a man volatile in his rages, who cursed in every sentence he spoke and who wanted beyond anything to secure for himself the most spoils of war as he could gather, like a raven spends its days gathering up silver ornaments and shiny pieces of things to line its nest with; he was loud and bold-speaking, always laying his rough tongue over the voices of the other men, shouting them to silence, trying to gain advantage. With his long unruly hair flying everywhere around his fierce face, he laughed as loud and as often as he talked, making my ears ache with his every dogs-bark of a laugh, and with his every booming argument, I wanted to cower.

The dark knight, arrogant as a bishop, let *La Hire* have his say and then, in a matter of a few words, told him how it was to be, and to my astonishment, the mercenary backed down. The look in The Bastard's eyes is what gainsaid any true argument, I bethought me, as I watched the men; The Bastard would kill you as soon as look at you and *La Hire*, a violent man himself, knew it.

The Duke of Alençon, a close friend and confidant of the King's, was there as well, though he alone of all the leaders, kept his words to himself. The other men, lesser captains, all had their say, regarding the forts and battlements around the city that the English had erected in the past year that they had held Orléans besieged.

There was only one gate, I came to understand, that was not in the hands of the enemy and through which, with luck and perhaps a diversion somewhere else to distract the besiegers, supplies could be brought inside the walls.

This was *La Porte de Bourgoyne* or Burgundy Gate, as it was known now, but had used to be called the *La Porte de Saint Aignan*, or the gate of Saint Aignan, and lay on the north side of the city and across the river. It had long been the only way the people of Orléans had received succor and they were hungry and in a state of suffering for lack of basic needs being met.

The Bastard claimed that it was to reach this gate and to bring me into the city secretly that he had marched us by this route, a plan he had not told me of, and of which I was unaware until the boy had run up to tell me and been punished for it.

He spoke of me as if I were yet another commodity to deliver to the city, like sacks of peas, or casks of wine, and so I sat upright from where I had been leaned back against a tree, and said, "The warriors I have brought with me are shriven and have prayed with me, and they are ready to do battle, eager to do battle. Tis my wish to heed the angels of my council and bring war upon the English where they stand, this day, the 28th of April, Fourteen-hundred-twenty-nine."

The men ceased their discordant discourses and stared at me, for all the world as if a mouse nibbling crumbs at their board had suddenly spoken up, declaring itself to be the Archbishop of Rheims.

As I looked around at their faces, faces whose names I would came to know in the days to follow, I saw in each man's eyes the death that would befall him and I struggled not to let my compassion overflow my own eyes, for they were wicked men to a one and would see my love as a weakness and have no pity on me.

"I would have had this city today if you had not deceived me, thinking yourselves to be greater than the angels of heaven, but I will forgive you this and we shall proceed. Let us cross the river in a small party and in secret and enter into the city before nightfall and let the main army camp here and rest while we make our plans from within the walls. Tell the captains of my men that *Jehanne, La Pucelle* shall soon rejoin them and lead them to victory and that in the mean while they are to remain in readiness, body and soul."

As I spoke these words, I caught a movement in the brush and saw a blue-green eye peering out at me from the tightly-grouped leaves of a shrub, only feet away. It was my boy and my heart gave a sudden jolt, like it had received the sharp bite of a fly, and against my wishes, my mouth quirked at one corner.

We rose from our seats upon the ground, each one brushing the dirt and dry leaves from his clothing, and the deep voices rumbled as each man decreed what role he would play in the unfolding pageant of our entrance into Orléans; one would ride back along the line and give orders to the soldiers to return along the road to a certain place and to make a strong camp there; one to ride ahead and secure boats for our smaller party to cross the river; one to secure passage ahead of us to let the city fathers to know that *La Pucelle* was on her way and would be with them this night and require lodging; and other things that were needful.

I stood and rubbed the dirt from the seat of my breeches and saw the boy in the bush, watching me.

I smiled at him and gave a little nod and stepped away with the men to where the pages held our horses.

My page, Louis, held the gray's head as I mounted and we rode down the road, leaving the large body of our army and supply train behind.

It had begun to lightly rain and the wind was blowing into our faces as we rode eastward, but the excitement of being close to the enemy warmed me as if I were wrapped in a warm cloak.

The Duke of Alençon, whom I had met at Chinon and whom had taught me the fundamentals of the joust on the tourney field at that palace, now rode up beside me.

I believed I might come to like him, though at this time, I did not think that I could trust him, and I wondered if I only felt I could like him because of his handsome face, his lilting laughter and his snapping bright blue eyes, even though he was surely just as wicked as all the rest.

My angel had told me I should never know a man and so I was wary, because this duke seemed far too familiar, as if he perhaps thought me an innocent country girl whom he might deceive with flattery or gifts of fineries.

I was not such a girl and if thus was the way of his thoughts, they would soon be turned.

Alençon's steed was jigging in place, rising and falling, turning sideways, capering and dancing as if in performance, and the Duke sat in a blue velvet saddle as if in a chair by his own fireside, as perfectly relaxed and sedate as if going up and down and sideways was a natural state for him.

"*Jehanne, La Pucelle*," he said, pleasantly. "You have not yet ridden the horse I gave you. Do you prefer this old nag to my finest-bred, my finest-schooled?"

I looked at him, his smiling face and teasing expression, and I reached my hand down and stroked the neck of my gray, where the misty rain had settled.

"This one the King has seen fit to give me is as fine a mount as any I have ridden," I said, as blandly as I could manage, determined not to take his bait.

He laughed his high bright laughter.

"And you, *Pucelle*, have ridden a great many, and thus are a qualified judge of horseflesh, are you not? I shall have you to my next purchasing and take your opinions before I open my purse."

I nodded and rested my hand, my fingertips wet with the

dew, back upon my thigh.

"I should be pleased to be of assistance," I said.

He laughed again and quietened his horse, and it was plain that the animal was trained to dance and prance and trained also to leave off doing so at a cue from its master.

We rode together for a while without speaking, *La Hire* and his friend Xaintrailles before us and the dark knight and some others behind.

"In truth," he said after a while, "I bethought me you rode quite well at Chinon, as I watched you tilt the rings and run the courses with lance against quintain. I did not think shepherdesses got in much tilt practice, but perhaps things are different in your country of Lorraine."

I glanced over at him. His eyes were front-facing, watching the road ahead of us and the backs of the mercenaries. I thought I saw the hint of a smile on the corner of his mouth. He shook a damp lock of hair from his face.

"Or perhaps," he said, "not in Lorraine overall, but just in Domrémy."

I stroked my horse again and gave tongue, "Yea, tis true that in Domrémy, we girls practice archery, run footraces like Grecian women, and tilt at quintain every Sunday after Mass."

I said it as mildly as I could, just to see his reaction.

One blue eye flicked at me and his lips curled again, so that I laughed and said, "Nay not, Sir, I am teasing. In Domrémy, we are as ordinary as anyone."

He looked full at me then and said, "Jehanne, you are far from ordinary."

I think I blushed then, I felt the heat in my face and I looked away from his eyes and fixed my gaze on the point between the ears of my horse where his forelock emerged from under the broad red-leather strap of his headstall.

"You ride as well as any squire, notwithstanding you have chosen the most staid old campaigner of your stable as your favorite," he said, indicating with a tip of his head my old gray destrier. "You have a composure which would be expected in a Prioress, the courage of a seasoned man-at-arms, and the flippancy of a tavern-maid, if you'll excuse the comparison."

Not knowing quite how to answer that, I said nothing and the Duke said nothing, not for another mile or so, and then rather suddenly, he side-passed his horse closer to me, leaning from his saddle, and said into my ear, "The King has asked me to keep an eye on you, *Pucelle*, and not only because some among the clergy still think you may have come from the devil, but because there are some among those here," and he lifted his chin, gesturing at our companions, "who may think you a threat and wish to see harm come to you, or at the very least, not wish to see success come to you."

I looked at him then, astonished, because I could not understand why any Frenchman would not want to see me succeed when all that I assayed to do was free Frenchmen from the unjust rule of foreigners.

Suddenly chilled now, and feeling the rain water gather at my neck, I said, "As regards my origins, I have been examined by the very clergy you speak of and found to be unstained by the devil's touch; for a fortnight and more at Poitiers did they question me. My body has been examined by the King's own women relatives and found to be pure and un-breached. And as I have no other intention than to fulfill my mission and retire quietly to my village once again, when I have served France and King Charles, why should any man fear me or wish me ill or wish for my failure in these, my honest tasks?"

I would not speak to him of angels and decrees from God. I had explained all of this to the King and been queried harshly and at length about all of that by a host of clerics, from simple brown-frocked friars to the Archbishop of Rheims, with a smattering of academic theologians thrown in for good measure, and been found not wanting.

Alençon himself had been present for much of it.

Now here in the road, in the field of battle, mere miles at last from the enemy, by soldiers, mercenaries and rough warriors, I was still doubted?

Still doubted, even now?

The Duke looked at me, pity in his blue eyes.

"These men," he said, "are each fighting their own wars. Each has his own idea of what victory is and who should win it. You will find that all is not as simple as your so-called angels have led you to believe."

I think then, maybe I did begin to trust him, just a little bit, even though he had broken some hope within me, that now, after all the waiting and all the preparations and all the challenges to my character and my intentions, the war could be joined, fought, and won and I should be free to go home.

He glanced around once more to make sure we were not overheard. "And as far as your body remaining pure, *Pucelle,* it is imperative for your credibility and for your success that it remain so, but may be not easy, surrounded as you are by men, men who do not all wish you well. Your innocence is charming, but pray, do not be innocent about that. Men are used to taking what they want and only think about the consequences later."

He nodded his head slightly, the whisper of a bow, and said more loudly, "*La Pucelle d'Lorraine*, I am not to enter

Orléans with you this day. The King has made me commander of his army, and as the army is remaining here for the time being, so shall I. You have asked to be brought here, and so we have brought you here. I wish you joy of it. And I for one, wish you success."

He reined in and turned his horse sideways, facing me and looking me in the eyes.

It was raining harder now. We were at the place where the boats had been brought in. The others left the road and leapt their steeds down a short steep embankment onto the strand.

"We shall meet again, very soon," the Duke of Alençon said quietly and spurred his horse away back down the road, a group of his knights and squires following him, mud flying back from their hooves.

4, The Beach

They took my horse from me at the beachhead and lead him away with the other mounts to a barge upon which, they assured me, it would be safe for the horses to cross the Loire, and the mercenary known as Xaintrailles stepped into one of the boats and held his hand out to me to guide me onto it.

I looked about me.

La Hire and the dark knight were standing beside me, waiting. They would board after me and The Bastard waved his gloved hands at me to say, "Go on, you foolish girl, don't be afraid of a little boat ride," but that was not why I hesitated.

I was looking for someone, as I stood upon the shingle, hearing the river lap at the small round stones, smelling the water and the mud, feeling the cold air against my cheeks, and the rain pattering on my head, and casting my gaze up and down the shoreline and back up the bank to the road.

I was looking for the boy who had followed me from the

crossroads on the road outside of Tours, the barefooted boy in the rabbit hat, the boy who had been hit upon his head for telling me that the captains had led me beyond the city, the boy who had hid in the bushes to be near me during my council with the men.

The boy, the only person around me whom I truly knew that I need not fear.

And there he was, standing at the edge of the river, one bare foot reaching out to test the water, as though he might try to swim across it if there was no other way to follow me. Then he looked right at me and there was bald-faced terror in his eyes.

I stepped towards him out of the ring of men, a step and another.

"You," I said, "please, come here," and I extended my hand in his direction.

He came slowly and tentatively, as if *La Hire* and the dark knight were ravening dogs and might take him down and rip his face from his skull like dogs unchecked will do.

I dropped my hand to my side as he approached me, so that I did not touch him, fearing he would bound away and disappear if I did so. He came close enough to stand before me and for me to look into his face.

He was just a little bit taller than me, which is to say not very big (these men towered over me) and slight-built like myself, though with the very narrow hips and the broad shoulders of a growing young man, a small young man but very strong, and we stood for a moment just looking into each other's eyes.

I watched the breaths flare his nostrils as he breathed, fast like a frightened animal, and wanted to calm him, as one would calm such an animal, with quietness of spirit and with a gentle gaze.

I heard, behind me, the heavy boots of the men shifting impatiently upon stones. I heard their muffled conversations.

It was late in the day by now and while it was raining here, it was cloudless to the west. The lowering sun was over his shoulder, lighting his golden-brown hair from behind.

A glow of light was on one side of his face and shadow upon the other so that he looked like a man of two faces divided down the middle and pieced together.

His eyes never left mine.

One eye, the one on the sunlit side, was the color of honey and the other in shadow was dark slate blue. It was only a trick of the light but I felt like I was being stared at by an angel on the one side and a demon on the other.

I felt a thrill in my heart at that strange thought.

I took a step back from the demon I imagined even as I wanted to step closer to the angel.

Whatever spell we had woven was broken then and he looked away from me, looked at the stones of the beach, looked at the boats, looked at the water, looked at the men, looked back at me.

He seemed so young and lost then, far from home, like I was, lonely, like I was, scared like I was.

Had I known him before?

It seemed I had, though my mind knew this was impossible for he was from a village on the other side of France from the one I belonged to.

Yet there it remained, a familiar feeling like we were instant confidants, or very old friends, or even strangely, two halves of the same person.

"You shall go in my boat," I said to him, and saw in his face a change so small as to be barely noticeable but which told me of his relief that he would not be left behind to find his own way over.

"There in the bows," I said, pointing to where he should ride, "and we shall be in Orléans tonight."

I turned from him and faced the dark knight and *La Hire* and the others that stood about.

"This boy," I said in a loud voice, "will go with me to Orléans."

I stepped to the boat and gave my hand to Xaintrailles to help me in.

The boatmaster rushed over from the barge where the squires and pages were preparing to load the horses. He went straight for The Bastard and made a great show of obeisance as if he feared he would be struck.

"Great lord," he said, "forgive me, but the wind is against us. It has blown contrary for days and weeks, we shall not be able to make passage without oarsmen and there shall be none until the morrow, as they have all been dismissed."

I turned and caught the dark knight's arm as he raised his fist.

He glared down at me but held himself in check.

I looked at the little boatmaster, thin as a wraith, seamed and lined as men of wind and water ever are, with a bushy head of gray-white hair that blew in all directions. I saw him, his years of service upon this strand, his skill with ropes and sails and oars and poles, his dead sons and no one he favored to learn the secrets of his craft.

I saw the good years and the bad years in his eyes, and the years since the besiegement of Orléans had all been bad ones, and I saw his death, one of chains and the stocks and starvation and cold in an exposed square. Some great man would be displeased with him and for that he would suffer and die.

But not today.

I turned away from the boat and stepped up to the man. "Boatmaster, tell me of this wind."

He looked with dread from the dark knight to me, seemed as much afraid of me as of The Bastard of Orléans, and said, "*Pucelle*, by sail is the best way to cross the river, though it is possible with oarsman, especially if the boats be not too heavy-laden. The wind generally changes direction twice in a day; during the day the winds tend to be favorably blowing towards the city, by which I mean sou-west to nor-east, which is when we may usually bring supplies and people in; by night they shift and blow away, or nor-east to sou-west, and we usually return the boats to this side in preparation for the following day. These last weeks, *Pucelle*, I grieve to say, the winds have proven contrary to their habit. We have had ill winds, blowing almost constantly away from the city, and been forced to rely on oarsman for whatever loads we carry. As you can feel at this moment, the winds are blowing in our faces if we try to make a crossing."

La Hire was mumbling curses at my left shoulder, Xaintrailles, still standing in the boat, was chuckling at his friend's bloody vocabulary, and the dark knight, The Bastard of Orléans, was livid with rage and wanting to strike the poor boatmaster, as if the winds were the man's own invention and he had got it wrong.

I gave a little nod to the boatmaster.

Turning to The Bastard, I remarked, "You wisest captains of France voted to bring me by this route. Well, I say that you shall know that not all is subject to man's wisdom, but to powers greater than man."

I turned and held out my hand towards Xaintrailles.

"Help me on, Poton, if you please," I said.

Poton de Xaintrailles cocked one eyebrow, glanced over my head into the faces of his comrades.

I waited, counting away more seconds of my life, as I had been counting them away, it seemed, for months, waiting on men to decide.

An unspoken conversation went on over my head, the men discussing with their eyes whether I was a lunatic or a pawn of the devil, or less than either; a mere foolish girl.

I measured my breaths, in and out of my breast, a count of seven, my eyes fixed on the mercenary's scarred cheeks.

Seven breaths I could ill afford to waste, I who would be used up in a year start to finish, as I had told them before.

Told them so many times before.

Xaintraille's face was as harsh and sharp-planed as a gyrfalcon's. His eyes, that showed all the tiny red vessels crisscrossing the whites, had the look of a man who had seen and caused so much death that he laughed at everything, because if nothing, not even life, was of importance then all things must be humorous. His mouth, ever set in a brutal grimace, pursed as if to say something, then gave it up.

Instead, he chuckled and gave a shrug.

Then he reached out his hilt-hardened hand and, gripping my fingers hard enough to hurt me, helped me into the boat.

5, The Boat

I looked for my boy, thinking that during these last proceedings perhaps I had lost him.

In the blink of an eye, however, once both my boots had hit the deck-planks, he vaulted the gunwales and was crouched in the bows, his bare feet standing on the great coil of heavy hemp-rope that was stored there.

I looked at the men, saying not a word.

Finally, *La Hire*, with an explosive oath, stepped into the boat and in a moment, with a curse, The Bastard followed him. Their banner-men, bachelor knights in their service, and my heralds, all clambered on after them, until the boat was filled with men and boys and me.

The boatmaster stood dumbstruck upon the rocky beach staring at us.

"Boatmaster," I called to him, "please, raise your sails and have your men cast us off," and as I said these words, the wind, which had been blowing into our faces, suddenly shifted and was beating against our backs.

Even the rain lessened, for it was driven by the winds and as it was cloudless to the west, whence the wind was now coming, it was now was being driven away.

The little master felt the change immediately, though it took *La Hire* and the dark knight and the other landsmen a moment longer.

The boatmaster climbed in and, with nimble old bony fingers unwrapping the sheets from the clews, he quickly ran up the canvas.

With a shout and heave, three river-men grasped the gunwales and the stern of the boat and pushed us deeper into the lapping river waters, one leaped in after to take the sheets controlling the yard from the master as he stepped to the rear to grasp the tiller.

Then with a pop! the wind filled our sail and the boat gave a lurch and the shore waves crashed hard against the bows, causing the boat to shiver, cold river water roiling over the lip and splashing into the bottom, wetting my boots. But with another shiver, and a shake like a great dog ridding its coat of rainwater, the boat shook free of the shore breakers and plowed out across the choppy current of the river.

The men, of whom some were standing and some sitting on the benches, gave exultant cries and broke into nervous laughter. I glanced back over my shoulder and looked into the face of the boatmaster.

His mouth was open in awe, showing his lack of teeth, and his eyes fixed on mine and the look in them told me he believed that a miracle had taken place. He knew this river as no one ever had and he knew what things were within the normal realm of possibility and what were unheard of.

This had been unheard of.

I nodded at him and gave a smile, and he nodded back, and pulling hard with gnarled hands against the rough wood of the tiller, guided the boat at cross-angles over the river waves, the bows rising and falling, rising and falling, the slap of the water loud against the planks.

The Bastard laughed uneasily and grabbed my shoulder, forcing me down onto the bench as if he feared he would lose his prize overboard and mayhap be blamed by the King for having lost *La Pucelle* in the River Loire.

He and *La Hire* and Xaintrailles remained standing, as if it were a matter of pride to them to ride the river upright on their feet, though all of the other men had by now sat down, clinging to the gunwales and to each other and to their weapons.

I sought my boy then, who crouched in the bows, his little bag slung over his shoulders, and his hands wrapped firmly around the big rough rope that ran through the clews at the front.

Water sluiced from time to time over the rim of the bow and drenched him, running into the back of his tunic and down over his shoulders, but he ignored the water and clung fiercely to the rope, rising up and down, and I could see his lip tremble with the cold or perhaps with fear.

I willed him to look at me, as I sat there on the bench, the hard wet wood under my buttocks, my boots side-by-side on the decking with the water in the bottom swirling around them, and upon my shoulders the hard hands of the dark knight on one side and the mercenary captain on the other, holding me down.

My sword in its scabbard was across my knees, my hands wrapped tightly around it.

It was the sword found behind the alter stones at the

chapel of *Saint Catherine de Fierbois*, the one I had sent a man to retrieve for me as I waited at Tours for my harness and my gear to be prepared; the ancient sword rumored to be secreted in the Lost Forest Chapel but that no one living had ever seen or could vouchsafe its existence.

It bore five crosses upon its blade, not engraved, as it first appeared, but integrated into the very steel which the craftsman had forged and folded, forged and folded, scores of times, creating a fine layering of black and silver steel so intricate that it took my breath away with its beauty, the forms of the crosses built right into the steel itself.

I had said where the sword was to be found, that they would know it by its crosses, and that it would be found rusty.

It had been right there where I said it would be.

The rust had simply fallen away with the first touch of a cloth, revealing the five crosses in their beauty. Though I had stayed there on my way to Chinon and it was from that holy place that I sent my letter to the Dauphin asking him to receive me at Chinon, I had no inkling of the sword's whereabouts while I prayed for three days within a few feet of its hiding-place.

It was only afterwards, after I had met Charles, spoken those words of the *sangrail*, those inexplicable words, and gazed into his living fire and been taken to Poitiers and there examined by all the clerics, high and low, of France, and made to explain myself a hundred thousand times, making sure to mention nothing of the bloodline of Christ or of the marriage *Jhésus* and *Maria La Magdalena*, it was only then that I knew, knew! where the Sword of Saint Catherine was and that it was to be the one I carried into battle.

And that, carrying it, I could not be defeated.

Holding my sword now, my sword which would bring me all victory, I willed my boy to look at me, through his fear and his trembling, to look at me, and in a moment, he did. It was as if I had called his name, and he hearing it, had turned to the sound.

But I did not know his name, had not yet been able to inquire it of him. I thought of him only as "my boy," but of course that was not right nor fair, to treat him as if he belonged to me.

I decided that I would ask his name.

At some time soon, I should know what to call him.

He did look at me as I so strongly willed him to; turned his head to the right and met my eyes and I tried to look kind and reassuring, so that he would feel as if he could continue to look at me.

The eyes that met mine were that of a wild animal, trapped and helpless, and they quickly looked away.

The crossing was long, the river so very wide, and in the center of the river, a fog gathered around us so that I could not see and we passed through ribbands and veils of it and it was cold against my face and the mist wet me all about as even the rain before had not.

Around me, men and boys laughed uneasily, and the hand of The Bastard tightened on my shoulder as if he feared I might simply vanish in the mist. Then finally we were free of it and the great walls, spired towers and slate roofs of Orléans came suddenly into view.

The English held the city in thrall and their fortifications were all about, ugly structures and diggings, and heaps of trash and piles of building materiel, their fortresses and siege engines, old and new, in states of construction and disrepair.

I gasped as I saw what they had wrought.

And there were men upon those battlements as well, lewd Englishmen leering down at us from their high places.

We passed close enough that arrows, if loosed, might have struck us, yet none flew.

Soon we were well past the danger-point and coursing hard into a small inlet where a tributary found ingress into the River Loire.

The boatmaster pushed upon his tiller and banked the boat at a hard angle to the stream and I felt under my boot-soles, a vibration caused by the gravel of the river-bed, and I heard the crunch of the stones under the hull. The boat lurched to a sudden stop and then began to rock quite fiercely from side to side, as the waters pushed full against its flanks.

I stood then, shaking the hands of my minders off of my shoulders.

I looked at the boy, whose eye was now upon me.

To him I gave a flick of my chin.

He understood me instantly and springing from his place, vaulted over the pointed prow of the boat, bringing the rope with him.

As I walked forward, I could see the boy upon the strand, bearing back hard upon the rope, his bare feet scrabbling for a hold in the loose gravel of the beach.

The waters surged around his feet and the stones pushed out from under him and he fell back upon his bottom into the waves.

He looked up at me, the cold making his chin tremble, as the water swirled around his legs to his waist. The river-man who had manned the yard jumped over the side, jerked the boy to his feet, and lent his aid.

Together, man and boy, they brought the boat, riding

upon the next wave, securely onto the beach.

My boots sounded on the planks as I walked the length of the boat to the prow, holding my sword in my hand, the belt wrapped around the scabbard, to disembark.

He looked up at me, my boy, with his clothes soaked with river water and wet sand upon the seat of his breeches, and slowly, with the dignity of... of what? ... of an angel? ... he reached out his hand to me and I placed my hand in his.

It was then, with his smooth cold fingers in mine, that I saw his death.

6, A Shield

We had to wait for the barges with the horses to make landing. I belted my sword on and strode up the bank to the bluffs where I could stand and watch the rest of the boats come in.

My feet were wet, and water squelched inside my boots, making little bubbles appear at the seams. They were new boots and hastily made but no matter; they did not need to last more than a year.

As I scrambled up the narrow path, I heard the boy behind me, following me.

When I reached a good spot to stand, I turned and looked down.

The men were milling on the riverbank and the first barge was struggling through the water, laden with unruly horses. My old gray campaigner, I noticed with pride, was the only one that stood calmly on the roiling flatboat, as if rough river crossings were every-day affairs.

I turned from the sight and looked at my companion.

He was watching me and his eyes were squinted against the day's lowering sun.

I suddenly felt shy.

I, the country girl who, but a few weeks ago, had argued theology with the most learned men of France, who had told them straight into their faces that they might not wish to waste my time with questions, when what was needed was swords, men and horses for France to be freed and me invested to lead them.

I had not been shy then. But I was shy now.

I had thought that I should know what to say to him at the moment when we would first find ourselves alone, as I seemed to know just what to say to Kings, and to dukes and bishops.·

I had thought I should turn to him and say, "I am Jehanne, daughter of Isabelle Romée and Jacques Darc of the village of Domrémy, and who are you and where are you from?" but instead I looked at him, and said, "What do you have in your little bag?"

His brows beetled and he turned half away from me, his hand on the bag, clutching the top lacings closed. I felt instantly ashamed, as if I had said something perfectly rude and intrusive.

"Forgive me," I blustered then, with all the poise and grace of a milk cow in a market-stall, and I looked at my hands and at the river and at the men and the barges and at my sword-hilt and at my wet boots and at everything but his face.

There was a bit of a breeze and the wind rustled the tall grasses that grew all around us on the bluff. Green young grasses were growing up through the taller dry yellow grasses of last year.

It fell into my mind suddenly that these new green grasses would at this time next year be the tall dry yellow ones and other new green young ones would be growing up between them.

I would not be standing here, nor would this boy.

And where will I be in a year? I wondered.

Where will he be?

"I really..." I said, "... I really ... only wanted to know," and I looked at him then, "...what your name is? And where you are from?"

I smiled, or thought I did, though it felt more like a grimace on my lips.

He gave a little laugh, like he was surprised and amused that I was stumbling over my tongue, and because of him, and he pushed the bag on its shoulder-strap so that it hung in the small of his back, in the graceful curve of his spine above his buttocks.

He took both his hands and ran them up his face, shoving the wet ropes of tangled hair back away from his cheeks and forehead. He looked at the sky with those unusual eyes of his, the colors changing within them as if lit from inside by a lamp.

I could see the soft down of new beard upon his jaw and down his throat and a little dimple in the center of his chin. He clenched his teeth together and looked at me, his lips making a shape like a bent bow.

I could not take my eyes off his face, as if I had to study it well because someone would be expecting me to render a drawing of it and I wanted to do justice to the task.

The ridge of his brow was pronounced and his forehead high and square and he looked more like a grown man than a boy at this moment, and his look at me was manly too.

But then he smiled and cocked his head to the side and the boy returned and put me at ease.

"You are *Jehanne, La Pucelle*," he said in a quiet voice.

"Yes," I said, "yes, I am."

"You will save France?"

I felt the redness rise to my face, in a way it had not done once in the hundred times I had been asked this question since coming to Chinon.

"Yes," I said. "Yes, I shall."

He nodded at me and seemed quite satisfied with my answer, in a way I wish the Archbishop of Rheims had been.

"I would see you save France," he said.

"Well, then you shall see it," I told him, "since you are coming with me to Orléans and to wherever else we shall be going thereafter. One place you shall see is Rheims where I shall be taking the Dauphin to be crowned King. And you shall see Paris, which we shall be taking back from the English within a year."

He nodded again; quite happy with these plans.

"So," I said, "if we are to save France together, my friend, perhaps you would, please, to tell me your name?"

He looked at me then, a curious expression upon his face, his eyes seeming now very green and very deep, like the river, and he said, "It is you will save France, *Pucelle*, and I who shall watch you do it."

I laughed. "And this is why," I said, "that you have followed me... from... from?"

"Le Moineau," he said. "That is what we call our village. It is a small place, like the sparrow it is named for, you will never have heard of it."

"Le Moineau," I repeated. "It is to see me save France

that you have left Le Moineau?"

He shrugged.

"Then why?" I asked, thinking this much like a game that we were playing, he and I.

Looking at me, he pinched his lower lip between his teeth. "That is not the reason," he said, "at least, not the only reason."

Now I cocked my head at him.

I was going to wait. I was not going to ask.

Instead of speaking, he reached out his hand towards my face. Abruptly, I pulled back, avoiding his touch. I did not want our flesh to come into contact, for I knew, by touching him, I would see his death, and I did not wish to see that sight again, or feel its terrible coldness, its darkness and its silence.

He looked away from me, as if his feelings were hurt, as if he thought that I thought that I was too good for him, that he was only a peasant brat and I had been elevated and now was better than him. But I had no such thoughts and tried to say so with my eyes.

"Well, anyway," he said, embarrassed, "it is because you were weeping," and he looked at my face almost as if he still saw tears there, "you were weeping, when you saw us at the crossroads, and I just wanted to know what it was that made you sad."

I believe I stood as if struck dumb, staring at him, for it was hard to understand how a person would leave all of life behind; mother, father, family, fields and village; and follow an army, and be terrified and be struck upon the head by cruel men and almost trampled by horses and cross a dangerous river just because he was curious about why a girl cried?

I wanted to say to him; boy, girls cry all the time!

You don't follow every crying girl across France.

But as I thought about what I truly should say, my attention was drawn to the riverbank, where the horses had been unloaded. The men and squires and pages were sorting them out and starting to lead them up the narrow trail to the bluff where we stood.

Louis, my page, was first to come, leading my big gray by the bridle-reins, trying to not fall under the great hooves as the horse powered its way up the steep trail upon the lad's heels.

"What is your name?" I suddenly demanded of the boy from Le Moineau. I had only a few seconds before our conversation would be over.

The Bastard was right behind the gray, leading his own horse, and I knew that in the presence of the dark knight, the boy would not speak. He saw them coming, and his brows came together when his eyes lit upon the dark knight. His body braced suddenly, like a wild animal before it flees.

"*S'il vous plait,* what is your name?" I asked again.

He looked back at me. "Gilles," he said softly and then he vanished into the tall grass.

I smiled, tightening my hand around the hilt of the Sword of Saint Catherine. I have a sword, I thought, and I have a shield.

For the name Gilles means shield.

7, The City

The Bastard of Orléans grabbed my boot at the ankle and lifted me from the ground.

I swung my leg over the high cantle of the saddle and settled upon the back of my destrier. Nodding at Louis, I gathered up the reins in my hands and the page let go of the bridle-chains.

Men and horses now surged around me, trampling down the tall dry yellow grasses.

My ears were filled with the sounds of horses stamping and snorting, leather creaking as heavily-armored men dragged themselves into saddles, a jingling and clanking as they adjusted their maille-coats and their armor and made their swords and weapons to hang just right.

I noticed then, that most of them had taken the time to put on their armor if they owned it. They had wisely crossed the Loire without its burden but now had donned it, albeit hastily, leaving many buckles and pins unfastened.

Then I remembered that we were close to the English fortifications and therefore in some danger of attack.

"Wait, my harness!" I cried and flung myself down from the horse. "Louis, take him," I said, tossing the page the bridle-reins. "Raymond, help me arm," I said, "and you too, Poton, if you please."

Xaintrailles had not yet mounted and his brigand's face twisted into a malicious sneer at my request, but he left his horse to graze on the tall grass and came to help Raymond with my armor.

Raymond was one of two pages the King had given me, lads of about thirteen, sons of noblemen sent to court to be trained to knighthood. Raymond was dark-haired and shy, I might even say sullen, where Louis was yellow-haired, cheerful and ebullient.

When my suit of white harness was in place, and I made sure every buckle was properly fitted and each pin correctly through its eyelet, I bent and turned and squatted and kicked my legs forward and back and swung my arms as if to fight.

The harness, made to my exact proportions, fit me as if it were a metal skin. It moved with my body fluidly and gave only the mere whisper of steel on steel, a musical ringing, almost like a harp. Aided now by Poton de Xaintrailles, I mounted my gray and kicked him to stand between the steeds of *La Hire* and *Le Batârd d'Orléans*.

The Bastard wasted no time then.

He spurred his horse and our column moved swiftly away from the river. The road was a good one and well-traveled. We passed through the village of Chécy and on to *La Porte de Bourgoyne*, which had used to be called *La Porte de Saint Aignan*.

The sky had darkened by the time we arrived outside Orléans and there was much shouting to and from the men in my company and the men in the gate towers, as to who we were and what our purpose was.

It had been The Bastard himself, as the acting governor of the city during the imprisonment of his half-brother, who had laid down the law that the Burgundy Gate stay closed between sunset and sunrise and now that he himself wanted to enter, he found himself denied.

The Bastard was angry that he was not instantly obeyed but there had been some bloody skirmishes in the past few days and the guards were taking no chances in the dark.

It was only as I removed my helmet and *La Hire* took up a torch that had been tossed down to us and caused the light to shine upon my face and upon my gleaming armor, that the guards believed that *La Pucelle* had finally come.

The gates were unbarred and flung open.

As we rode in under the guard-post, the dark knight shook his gauntleted fist at the men and shouted, "I am *Le Batârd d'Orléans*, you fools, and I was the one who went to fetch *La Pucelle* and bring her here!"

Then we were swept through the gates like a stream that speeds up as it is forced through a narrow channel.

My horse broke into the trot with all the others and we moved like a tide down the street between the many-storied houses. I looked down and saw my boy at my knee.

His hand was wrapped tightly around the red-leather chest-strap of my destrier, and he was running apace with the big lofty trot of my gray.

In the dark, with the glaring and bouncing light of a score of torches, and with a gathering crowd of townspeople all taking up the cry, *"La Pucelle! La Pucelle!"* he was unnoticed by all but me.

In fact, as our party entered the city and began to make its way down the avenue, people came from the houses like bees from hives and began to move along with us and they all seemed to want one thing; to touch me, or failing that, to touch my horse.

Therefore, my boy... Gilles I should call him... was not even seen by The Bastard, whom he feared, nor did it seem strange that he should be running alongside me, for many were doing so, and the atmosphere was that of a celebration, with joyful voices ringing out and lights and torches dancing in the streets and alleyways and our banners fluttering back from poles as we surged through the city.

Even the church bells of the city began pealing, a sound which always brought me joy. The happy cries of the folk were as songs in my ears, and for a short time, as we went from the *La Porte de Saint Aignan* to *La Porte du Renard*, it seemed when I looked on people I did not see their deaths but only their joy, their light, their beauty.

It was as if a weight had lifted off of me, if only for those few moments.

For those moments, I felt only joy.

I looked down and saw the bouncing curls of Gilles' hair and I almost put my hand out and touched him but I stopped myself.

That would end my joy, I knew.

Seeing his death again would end my joy, even though it was many years in the future, and even though, I somehow knew... knew! that I myself would not still be alive to see it.

There was a sound of alarm, and I looked up from Gilles to see bright yellow flames blossoming from my standard. It was being carried near me by my banner-bearer and he had born it too nigh a flaming torch.

The silken fringes had caught fire and the banner was alight, though even its bearer had not noticed, others in the surging crowd had seen it. I reached out my hand for the pole but could not reach it. My impulse had been to leg my horse closer but Gilles was on that side, so I could not.

As it was, it was the hand of Gilles that reached the pole and he grasped it high and pulled it towards me.

The flaming standard whipped about my steel-clad shoulder and I grabbed it in my bare hands and patted out the fire.

I did not even feel the flames, though I wish I could say that was true in all my life.

When the people saw me extinguish the flames, they gave a great cheer of approval, as if I had accomplished a marvel, and on this renewed surge of joy, the crowd bore us away down *La Rue du Renard*.

8, *La Maison de la famille Boucher*

Within sight of the Renard Gate there stands a house of four stories, made of brown and black mortared round stones and owned by the family of Jacques Boucher, the treasurer of the imprisoned Duke of Orléans.

Twas to this house I was brought to be given lodging while in the city. We rode straight up to the door, the great crowd of us, with a few hundred singing townsfolk making our tail.

Now it seemed I had become very popular among my wisest captains, for they all; *La Hire*, Xaintrailles, the dark knight and several others; all leapt down from their horses and vied to be the first at my side to lift me down.

The Bastard of Orléans won the contest, by the fierceness of the glint in his dark eye. Even the cold-hearted killer Poton, who had begun to enjoy my attentions paid him, stood back with deference as The Bastard brushed him aside.

Even in my armor, I was light enough that the dark knight, a big man, lifted me as if I was mere child. He set me lightly on the stones of the street and his hands lingered on my steel-clad waist. His eyes looked down into mine for the briefest moment before he let go of me, and I felt the change in him.

He who had treated me as a foolish girl, whose charge he had been burdened with against his will, now seemed to think there might be something to me. The shifting of the river wind had shifted the ill wind within his heart as well.

Or, mayhap, and probably more likely, he was looking at me as he looked at all things, to see what, if any, the value to him I might be. His was a heart, I suddenly knew, whose depths even the most skilled of river-men might fail to plumb and whose shifting currents might not be navigable.

The door to the house swung open and I was hustled inside. I could hear the clattering of the horse's hooves upon the cobbles as they were lead away and in a moment I was in the narrow foyer of the house being introduced to Madame Boucher and her daughter Charlotte.

I looked behind me, wondering where Gilles had gone, but all I could see was the fronts of men as they followed me inside, their maille and armor raising a clangor in the tight space.

There was a strange sound behind me as the men striped off their gauntlets and dropped them all along the foyer to be picked up upon their exit.

Soon, we were in a small hall, seated at two large tables, and being fed a humble fare that Madame kept apologizing for.

Not knowing that we would be under her roof, she had not, she explained, been able to make arrangements in advance for meat and fruit and a better grade of wine.

I smiled to ease her trouble and offered that a city under siege is expected to be careful with its stores, to make sure none of its citizens should starve. If it was not strange to her to be feeding twenty fully-armored men at her board, I pointed out, it should not be strange that she would not have meat to feed them with in time of war.

Once the siege is lifted, I assured her, life as it should be in France would be restored.

On that day, I said, I would be pleased to deliver to her door such victuals as would grace a Dauphin's board, to give her repayment for her generous sharing of her house and her table during this time of duress.

When we had done and the spurs of the warriors had raked the floorboards as they leaned back to settle in their chairs, pushing away their trenchers, Charlotte lead me up the narrow wooden stairs to her chamber on the floor above, where I would take my rest while residing in Orléans.

She lit the lamp and showed me the chamber pot and then went away, as quietly as a mouse, to share her mother's room.   Louis and Raymond carefully removed my armor from my body, piece by piece, and, wiping each segment with an oiled cloth, stacked it neatly in the wooden trunk in which it was carried, the one painted blue with the golden *fleur de lys* painted on the lid.

Then they, too, went away, to sleep on pallets outside my chamber door, or perhaps, as it was not yet too late in the evening, to join the men in the rooms downstairs.

I paced the room up and back, looking at all the little things belonging to the girl who lived there, the hair brushes and hair ornaments, some jeweled brooches and necklaces, a tiny ornate box for personal treasures, a few delicately-carved figurines, and aged childhood toys.

I bethought me; how nice it would be to be such a girl.

A strange thought, since this girl lived in a besieged city, with foemen all around her, and never knew from one day to the next what her fate would be.

Like me, in a way, because I didn't know from one day to the next what my fate would be either, though I had said over and over to any ears that would listen, that I would raise the siege of Orléans and see that the Duke of Orléans would be set free from captivity, defeat the English and drive them from France, take the Dauphin to Rheims for his coronation and return the great city of Paris to French rule.

And all in a year's time, though two months of that year had already been wasted with questions; with examinations and with argument and with men's pride.

I sighed. Men's pride.

I could hear them now, a bunch of them below me in the foyer, their boots ringing loud and their voices penetrating the floorboards. I pictured them picking up their gauntlets and filing out the door.

Stepping to the window, I looked out, and yes, they were leaving, not all of them but most. I did not see The Bastard, nor *La Hire*, nor Xaintrailles, and I assumed that these, my minders, would be staying in *la maison de la famille Boucher*. Suddenly very tired, I laid myself down upon the bed, not even taking off my boots.

I fell into a dream, though I can't say for certain that I was even asleep, for it seemed that simultaneously with dreaming, I was aware of my body on the bed, and the fact that I should not be sullying the bedclothes with my boots.

I was aware that my sword had been laid upon the bed when I first unbelted it and that it was still there, its hilt jabbing into my shoulder, though its presence was more of a comfort to me than a discomfort.

I was aware, once in a while, of the men's voices downstairs and a rumble of loud laughter from time to time.

I was aware of all of this, and at the same time, dreaming.

9, A Dream

I see him now, in a forest of broad-leafed trees with thick dark trunks, spangled with shadow and sunlight. He stands at the edge of a clearing, and in the clearing, meadow grasses grow in the sun, alight with tiny blue and pink flowers, and he is as still as a sapling growing straight towards the sky, only his eyes, his beautiful eyes, move slightly from side to side, as he watches.

There is a sound and, at the edge of the meadow, a thin tree bent over now springs upright and from the string tied to its top there dangles a rabbit, caught by the hind legs, kicking and bucking and trying to free itself.

He darts from his stillness and bounds across the clearing, catches the rabbit in his hands and with one quick movement, ends its struggles.

The limp warm creature lies upon his hand for a moment; he strokes its soft fur and runs its velvety ears through his slender fingers. In a while he slips the snare loop from its legs, bends down the young tree and resets the snare.

Reaching in his bag, he draws out a long leather strap which he slings over his shoulders, and adjusting it as he likes, he pulls the legs of the rabbit through one of the many leather loops on the strap, snugging it tight.

Then he turns and runs, leaving the clearing for the dark shadows of the forest, his bare feet thudding on the narrow path betwixt the low leafy shrubs, the body of the rabbit bouncing against his hip.

And he goes, faster than I can follow him with my mind's eye, the golden-brown curls dancing on his shoulders, the forest swallows him within its voracious darkness.

He is so wild, I think.

Will the world ever tame him?

10, Awakening

Now I really am asleep and waken suddenly with a start.

I am in a dark room and cannot tell where I am. All is silent, and the air is cold around me.

There is something hard under my shoulder and when I shift over and reach for it, I find the Sword of Saint Catherine.

Then I remember where I am. I swing my booted feet off of the bed and sit up, rubbing my face.

The room is still and dark, though some light is coming through the window.

"Hello?" I say softly, testing to see if I am alone.

My mind tells me no one is in the room with me and yet I feel like I was just with someone.

It is then that I remember the dream of the boy in the forest.

My boy.

The boy who had followed me all the way from Le Moineau.

Because I had wept.

"Gilles?" I say softly into the dark room.

But no one answers.

11, Gilles

I had a desire then to know where he was.

The last I had seen him, he was running alongside my horse as we approached the Renard Gate. When I was lifted down from my horse outside the House of Boucher, he was gone, vanished in that way he had of vanishing.

I stood and walked to the window.

The street outside was empty, the well-worn stones gleaming in the light of a torch someone had left burning in a sconce outside of the door to the house across the street, for some late-home-comer to find his way.

Then I looked straight down and saw a foot.

Pressing my forehead against the glass, I peered down.

Yes, a dirty bare foot, which then disappeared as its owner pulled it up onto the stoop.

Directly below my window was the stone stoop of the doorway of this house. I remembered stepping up onto it and into a shallow enclave before coming in through the door.

Turning my head sideways to get my eye closer to the glass, I looked down and saw the rabbit ears of his funny hat and a golden curl of hair.

The poor boy must be very cold, I thought.

Going to the bedchamber door, I opened it and looked out into the corridor.

My two young pages slumbered on narrow pallets along the wall. I carefully stepped by them, walking on the toes of my feet lest my boot-heels wake them up, and to the head of the stairs. I went down slowly, as the stairs were steep and wooden and I did not wish to alert anyone.

Below, I crossed the foyer to the front door and, lifting the great iron latch, I pulled the door open.

He was sitting there, his back upon the door and he toppled almost onto my feet. His eyes, widened with terror, narrowed to relief when he recognized me.

I think he thought the master of the house had come to drive him from his door, or worse, that the dark knight had discovered him and come to beat him bloody.

Without thinking, I reached down and took his hand.

His cold slick wet death slid into me, invading my mind, causing my heart to clutch around itself like a fist.

I gasped, and closed my eyes, but the images were inside me, not in my eyes, and so I was not freed of them. I felt him rise to his feet, still holding my hand, and I could sense him watching me, sense the concern he felt; the knowing that he had that something he did not understand had gripped me.

For his sake, then, I opened my eyes.

I smiled at him, or tried to, with the death still in my

head, his cold wet death, his body which would bob in the river course and become food for fishes and that no one would know what had become of him or even that he had drowned.

I gave his hand a squeeze and let go of it, like a girl would do that liked a boy and thought that someday she might like to marry him, and he cocked his head and looked at me, the rabbit feet tied under his chin and a little smile playing around the corners of his bow-shaped mouth.

Twas a strange juxtaposition, the flirting of the boy and the girl; which I saw almost as if I was standing nearby, a separate person; and the deathly vision in my mind of a time far in the future, the boy having become a man with gray around his temples and a thick muscular body from the pushing of a plow and the swinging of a scythe; things he had not wanted to spend his life doing but had happened to him anyway; and when he would sink away into dark waters, and the last breath of his life would explode from between his lips and he would watch it break as bubbles upon the surface high above, his hand reaching up into the receding light, the hand I had, but a moment ago, held in mine.

"Come," I whispered, and I stepped past him off the stoop and led the way to the side of the building, where a passageway ran alongside it from the street to the alleyway behind and from it a steep stone staircase went down to the kitchens.

The door was unlatched, thank God, and I preceded him inside. It was the basement of the house, with solid stone walls and a large fireplace where a warm fire was banked and an iron pot of soup was hanging.

A fat woman with a food-soiled dress rose to her feet from a bench and began to tell me that we were not allowed, but then she saw that I was *La Pucelle* and she changed her tune.

"This boy," I said to her, "shall sleep here by the fire, and you shall feed him."

To show her that I was serious, I reached out for a loaf of bread that lay half-eaten on a trencher and handed it to Gilles.

He took the bread in both hands, biting into it ravenously. I bewondered me, when was the last time he has eaten something? It had been eight days since I had first seen him outside of Tours. He had been following the army that many days, had he eaten nothing?

I put one fingertip near his shoulder and waggled it, careful to avoid touching him, trying to ignore that cold slippery death, and with the force of my eyes, pushed him down onto the bench close by the warm fire.

He chewed his bread and his eyes, overflowing with gratitude, looked up at me.

I wanted to say to him, "Gilles, you are under my protection. I, *Jehanne, La Pucelle*, will care for you," but I did not know how to say that without sounding presumptuous or pompous or proprietary.

So, I gave a stern look at the cook and walked across the kitchen to the inner door, which I assumed and was correct in assuming, gave entrance to the rest of the house.

And I went back to bed.

This time I took off my boots, undressed, and got under the covers. I slept and did not dream of boys, or rabbits, or snares, or forests.

I did not dream of the watery death of a man who would grow from a boy whom I knew.

I slept without dreams.

12, *La Pucelle*

When had I become *La Pucelle*?

I had been a girl, a simple village girl, then I had been a girl who had an archangel for a friend, then I had become a girl with a mission, a girl with a mandate from Heaven, all of which translates to a girl without a choice.

I went from a girl everyone loved and bethought them was so gentle, obedient and tractable to being a girl that inveigled others to do her bidding, deceived and kept secrets from her parents and left things out during confession, and finally, who insisted to everyone she met that she was chosen by God to do great things, as if she were the most haughty and vapid girl in creation.

Who would listen to or believe such a girl?

How could I tell them about Michael?

Who would believe I was visited by angels who told me that I must go and lead the army of the King?

In time of course, certain persons were told of Michael and my visits by him and other angels, but in the early days I keep these visitations, these apparitions as I bethought me of them, to myself, a burden no young innocent girl should have to bear.

Why should I speak of them?

Truly, twould seem a fancy or a lie to justify the wantonness my father feared. My father said that he had dreamed I would run away in the company of soldiers. His dream would not come true if he had any power to prevent it, he determined, as he would not allow the family to be disgraced by his daughter becoming a soldier's trollop.

Yet, when in my life had I ever been any but a dutiful girl who was clean in her habits and good in every way?

Why should my father fear I should become a wanton? But how else might he understand his premonitory dream? It was not a usual thing for girls to become soldiers.

So, knowing I should not have my parents' help in this, I snuck away and convinced my uncle to bring me to Vaucelours that I might meet the Squire there, de Baudricourt, and I convinced de Baudricourt to aid me in my bid to meet the Dauphin at Chinon, and I convinced several men in the service of de Baudricourt that to accompany me and provide my protection upon the road would give them an opportunity for glory and recognition as the first followers of *La Pucelle*, those who knew before all others that her cause was true and her mission Heaven-blessed.

I had to convince them that I was God-appointed and instructed by angels, that I was pure and virtuous and that I would do all that I claimed, without a doubt.

Yet, even as I heard my own voice saying the words, I myself could not believe them.

To convince these men, I had had to become a zealot for my cause.

By saying it over and over to this one and that one, I came myself to the beginnings of belief. But only the merest beginnings. I was still only a village girl, with a village girl's view of the world and a village girl's hopes, plans and desires for herself.

And beyond Vaucelours, and beyond Nancy, and beyond Fierbois, and all the way to Chinon, I still only had the merest beginnings of belief, though I had convinced my uncle, and several townsfolk, the Squire of a town larger than my own, many knights and soldiers and finally a Duke, and at Chinon, the King and his court were convinced, and thence to Poitiers where I had to convince with my growing zealotry, the clerics.

Worst of all, the clerics, with their heavy robes and dour faces, their absolute belief in their own sanctity and their watchful suspicious eyes always searching for heresy, a heresy that I knew that I myself did bear in my heart and must carefully hide from them, the clerics, whom after fierce questioning, I did manage to convince.

Through all of that, I really only believed myself a simple ordinary girl.

What's more, after all my insistence that I was to raise the siege of Orléans and take the Dauphin through English-occupied France to be crowned King at Rheims, all I really truly wanted to do was go home to be an ordinary girl again.

I had insisted to everyone that I was, like the girl of prophesy that many spoke of, though I myself was loathe to believe in such things as prophesy, a girl who could and would, save France, and yet I had myself only the merest beginnings of belief.

So, when did I become *La Pucelle*?

There was a moment at Tours, after Poitiers and the examinations, when I had been fitted and refitted and my harness was being beaten out and my military attire was being tailored and my standard was being stitched in another shop and I saw it laid out upon a long table, I felt, suddenly, seeing it, like the maid who would save France.

For the first time, though I had been proclaiming it for weeks to all, Dukes, Kings and Bishops, who would listen, I felt that I was The Maid.

Seeing my banner coming together in all of its elements just as I had envisioned it, with the names *Jhésus et Maria* emblazoned upon it, I finally believed in this thing I was doing, believed in myself as the one who could do it, the only one who could do it, just as my angels had said, just as I had been telling them all.

So finally, the act of saying it had become the act of making it true.

Now that I believed it and my banner was flying over my head proclaiming it to all the world, I had come to be glad that I was chosen for this mission and glad that my life was not to be ordinary, that for some short time, a year or a bit more than a year, my life should be extraordinary and I should have this time to look back upon in later years and remember with pride.

I was *La Pucelle* and wanted to be *La Pucelle*, an extraordinary girl.

Not by any means a wanton, which my father feared, but the exact opposite; a pure girl whose body and mind are chaste and the perfect vessel for God's grace and the instrument of France's redemption and release from bondage.

I finally felt that the things I was expected to forsake in order to fulfill my destiny were worth it, that I would rather be The Maid than a simple village girl, that this was something I wanted to do and would not regret.

And then, leaving Tours with that belief in my heart, what happens to me?

I meet a boy.

13, The Kitchen

I lay there thinking of that boy.

I had slept soundly for a while, several hours, I suppose, but then had awakened. I stretched my legs in the bed, the comfortable bed of Charlotte, the daughter of Boucher, the bed whose linen sheets and woolen blankets were of the highest quality. When I had turned down the bed earlier, I had run my hands over the sheets and gloried in the silken smoothness of their weave.

Never had I felt any so fine and smooth, not even in the King's palace at Chinon. I had decided then to sleep unclothed, a thing I never did.

Was this a sign of wantonness, I had to bewonder me?

But I did not care.

I was as chaste and virginal as the day I was born and sleeping naked would not change that.

But then I woke up thinking about that boy.

I thought about his mouth, the little smile that bent it into the shape of a bow about to shoot an arrow. I thought about his eyes, the beautiful colors that the light made of them. I thought of his golden-brown hair hanging in tangles and curls as if just waiting for the hand of a girl to run gently through it and work free the twists and twirls of it. I thought of how it would feel between my fingers.

I thought of the sunlight and shadow on his face and the angles and planes that they revealed, the brow and cheeks and chin of him and what they would be like to touch, if it was possible to touch him without seeing his horrible wet death.

Could I touch his hair without seeing it, I wondered?

Might be that I would try that, next time I was with him.

I moved my legs back and forth under the covers, enjoying the smoothness of them on my skin.

I felt such a feeling. It made me smile but at the same time, it made me feel as if there was something wrong with me.

Was there something wrong with me?

Aside from the fact that I was *La Pucelle* and was never to know a man, and here I was, lying in bed, thinking about one? If I was not *La Pucelle*, would it be all right to think about Gilles in such a way?

And since I was *La Pucelle*, what was I now to do with these thoughts?

The house was still and silent; it breathed deeply, as if sleeping itself. In fact, I know that in all that large house, I was the only being awake, except for perhaps a mouse.

My mind whirled with thoughts; the one about touching his hair was primary. I wanted to try it now, and I should not be able to sleep unless I knew.

I slipped out from between the warm covers, my feet hitting the rich carpet over the hard planks of the floor. The cold air wrapped my nakedness in its clutching embrace. I shivered and almost retreated back into the bed. But I stood, and, using the faint light that came through the window, found a chemise that Charlotte had laid out for me, pulled it over my head and pushed my arms into the sleeves.

It clung to my body and fell to just above my ankles, its fabric cool and slick against my skin but not so cold as the night air.

Again, I went to the chamber door, opened it and stepped into the passage.

I felt my way past the sleeping pages, down the steep stairs and, feeling along the walls, I found the stairs that led down to the kitchens, where I had left Gilles to be fed and to sleep. These steps were of stone, not of wood, and were cold under my bare feet.

There, a door at the foot of them stood open, allowing the heat of the ovens in the kitchen to flow upstairs into the rest of the house. I put my hand on the door jamb and stepped down off the last step. The fire was burned down to mere coals in the great fireplace and the big table stood cleared of all food and utensils, not even a crumb for that mouse that was awake.

I could hear the old cook snoring from her pallet in the corner, and there on the hearth lay the form of Gilles.

He lay upon his left side, his left arm curled under his head creating a pillow, his right arm wrapped around his little bag, his back to me. The last light of the glowing coals limned the curve of his hips and of his shoulders, and glinted softly in his golden hair.

I leaned in the doorway and ran my gaze over all of him.

His two bare feet were nestled one atop the other like slumbering kittens, his knees, pulled up into an angle, were practically against the iron dogs of the fireplace, so close lay he to the fire for warmth.

His hips rose, with a line of red-gold light upon them, from the curve of his buttocks, and then dipped away to his narrow waist, where the tail of his tunic was rucked up, exposing the small of his back.

I wanted to step over there and pull his clothing back into place to keep the air from his skin, but I dared not wake the cook. It was warmer in the kitchen than in the passages behind me or even in the room I slept in but he had no bed and no blanket and even the clothes he had come away with were meant only for a Spring day in the fields.

How I loved him!

I realized it suddenly, like a bolt to the breast.

I had never been in love before and it hit with such force it staggered me.

As if it were the most important and permanent thing in my life, as if all other things were not important and had never been, though they had been all of me until this moment. Now, everything that had gone before seemed as naught.

He was all that mattered, all I wanted, and all I needed was for him to feel the same of me.

I felt panic then, like I had never felt it.

I was trapped, in a cage, and would die ere I could escape! Was there any escape?

Could I take him and get away from here?

Could I dress and sneak away from my minders, take him and go?

Could we slip away this night, he and I, saddle and mount my horse, my faithful gray, and ride off before the sun?

Could we get out of the city?

And where could we go?

Would he even want to go?

And what of Orléans? The King, and France?

What of Michael?

Michael!

My archangel would be angry if I ran from my cause, if I threw Heaven's mandate back into the face of God. My archangel would unleash his wrathful nature an I were to betray my destiny. If I were to know a man.

The door jamb was hard against my shoulder as I wiped the tears from my face. I was leaning against it, one hand gripping the carved wooden molding around it, and my legs were weak, my knees feeling like they would collapse upon themselves and fling me to the floor.

I did not know when I had begun to weep, but the tears were all the way down my throat into the neck of the chemise, so many that my hand was wet with wiping them away.

Mayhap my archangel was truly a devil, to bring me to this pass. Mayhap even now, the angel laughed cruelly at my plight.

Mayhap twas the angel Lucifer that I knew, not Michael at all. Twas said that the devil is a master of deception.

I was only a country girl, how was I to know what powerful forces were coming to play in my life?

And Gilles, he lay there on the hearth, the dying firelight outlining his form in the dark room. He was an innocent, and not part of any of this push and pull that had become my life, this tangled bramble of events that I had walked into and now knew not how to escape.

He lay in his simplicity, in his dirty, threadbare clothes,

with soot upon his shoulders and ashes in his hair, and despite this place and time, this house in this city he would never have come to if he had not been following me, I could feel his wild spirit like a tingle in my heart and I could smell the forest and the fields on him.

And I loved him so.

I had come to the kitchens wanting to touch his hair.

To sneak quietly in, and waking no one, to reach out and finger a lock, just to see if I could do so without being flooded with his far-flung future watery death. But I knew I could not do so, not now, for if I did come so nigh him in my current state, I should want to touch him, more than his hair.

I should want to wake him, roll him into my arms and kiss his face, move my lips over his brow, down the bridge of his nose and across his high cheeks, and finally to his bow-shaped mouth. I should want to pull him up into my arms, hold his body against me, breathe deeply into his hair for a few moments and get the smell of the forest in my nostrils.

I should want to pull him to his feet, see his beautiful light-filled eyes upon mine, take his strong slender hand and then run away with him.

Run as fast and as far as we could, to get away from my destiny, to get away from this war I had come to fight, this war I was supposed to be winning, I who knew nothing of war, to get away from angels who were all-powerful and all-seeing and from whom there was never any escape.

Foolish Jehanne!

Foolish me! To let a banner in bits upon a seamster's table convince you of your grandness, only to fall for a farmboy and throw all your grandness away.

What are you really, *La Pucelle*?

I had no answer for that.

I took one last longing look at the boy in the ashes, and with great effort vanquished my imaginings of the taste of his mouth and the smell of his hair and stole back to bed.

I dreamed of flames.

Flames, smoke, and ash.

And of a single glowing face.

And a strong hand holding mine, pulling me away.

14, Awareness

They threw him from the kitchens early the next morning, upon going down to break their fast and finding him asleep upon the hearth-stones.

I was dreaming it all, though I could not wake and go myself to put a stop to it.

I seemed to be chained hand and foot by my slumber, feeling myself upon the bed, my limbs luxuriating in the smooth bedclothes, under the warm blankets, seeing even through my closed eyelids the early gray light of dawn stealing into the room, yet unable even to open my eyes to the new day, and all the while dreaming of what is taking place downstairs.

They clattered down the stone stairs in their heavy boots and spurs, pushed open the door and crowded in, Xaintrailles first, calling for the cook to warm wine for them and bring them fresh-baked bread and cheese, The Bastard next and *La*

Hire behind him, with some other knights and all their squires coming in after.

Xaintrailles shouted out, "Well, now, see who is here!" and the dark knight looked over his shoulder and saw the boy before the fire.

Gilles had heard them coming and had sat up, pushing his hair from his face.

"Peasant brat!" The Bastard said, shoving his way around Xaintrailles, knocking the killer against the big table, causing the scar-faced man to utter a curse.

Gilles got a leg under himself and smoothly bounded back away from The Bastard's kick.

"Run, Rabbit Boy! Run!" shouted *La Hire*, barking with laughter like a bulldog, and Gilles did run, finding the door by which we had entered the night before, drawing back the bolt, flinging it open, enduring a kick to the backside by The Bastard's boot, clambering, with hands and feet, up the steep steps from the kitchen to the passage on the side of the house.

The chill air of the morning slapped him in the face as he rose to street level and the chorus of "Run, Rabbit Boy! Run!" (for now it was a chorus of several voices, knights and squires together) rang shamefully in his ears.

All this I dreamed and was helpless to wake, rise, go and stop it.

I was aware, of my own presence in this room, of their presence in that room, and now of Gilles' presence in the cold morning air of Orléans outside the House of Boucher.

I was even aware of the mouse, which last night had been the only being awake and which now was sound asleep in its tiny room where a brittle stone had once crumpled, creating a neat little space inside the wall behind the great slab table used for butchering meat, its right front paw curled around its nose.

I was aware of Gilles, his bare feet cold on the flagstones, looking up and down the passageway, trying to decide which way to go, whether to the front of the house, where he might be seen by the men when they left, for surely they would leave by the front door when they did, as knights and squires would be sure to do, or to explore the passage and see what lay in the alleyway behind *la maison de la famille Boucher.*

I was aware of the kitchen and its occupants; the cook, ingratiating now and not rude as she had been to Gilles, pouring wine for the men and placing food before them; the squires, whispering to themselves on the benches against the wall, waiting for their turn at the food as their masters took their choice of all the best offerings; *La Hire* tearing bread from a loaf and dipping it in his wine and filling his mouth with it; Xaintrailles making a joke about the look on the rabbit boy's face when he saw The Bastard standing over him; The Bastard saying (and I heard it as if I sat at the table beside him), "I will be grateful to any man who makes that peasant brat think better of his journey to Orléans."

I was aware of the taste of the wine-soaked bread in the mercenary captain's mouth, and of the broken teeth in the mouth of Xaintrailles as he laughed, the feel of their sharp edges against his tongue and I was aware of the thoughts that roiled in the mind of the dark knight, thoughts about the boy from Le Moineau, that no good would come of allowing him to trot on the heels of *La Pucelle* like a puppy, that there was trouble in having such a person about, someone not under the control of the captains, someone loyal only to Jehanne, even if he was a lout.

I was aware of the shape of Gilles' body impressed into

the gray ash that lay upon the hearthstones and of his body heat which had warmed those ashes and those stones, body heat now fading, and of a stray strand that had fallen to the floor as he woke and ran his fingers through his golden-brown hair.

I saw it all as if I stood there.

And I was aware that Gilles had decided to explore the passageway and, passing a mound of horse manure dropped there the previous night, had realized that this may be the way the horses had been taken.

I was aware of him entering the alleyway and seeing there a wide stone ramp by which horses were taken to the basement stable at the rear of the house, just as the kitchens were in the front, and there housed underground.

I was aware that he went down the ramp and within the stable, found the stalls filled with the steeds of the men, their saddles and tackle hanging upon rows of racks, and found also, on one side of the stable, the stalls where my own horses had been bedded down, and that he leaned against the rail and that splinters of wood poked through his shirt at the elbows where some other horse had chewed at it and that he had looked at my gray for a long time and that the gray had stepped towards him, reached out its great head and blown through its nostrils into his face.

In the kitchen, *La Hire* and The Bastard had commenced a discussion about whether or not, now that the city had been re-victualed, to start a fight with the English enemy straightaway from within the city walls or wait until the army of the King could be brought up to encircle the besiegers, and if so, how would it be decided by what means and in what order the various strongholds of the English would be attacked. *La Hire* seemed to favor the most aggressive tactic while The Bastard wanted more men before acting.

I was aware of the words they spoke, hearing them as if I was looking over their shoulders, and yet I did not understand all the issues at hand.

They rose, brushed the bread crumbs from their clothing and retired from the kitchen to their quarters to ready themselves for the day. The Bastard maintained a house within the city; he had only spent the night in the House of Boucher because of the lateness of the hour that they all had had their fill of Madame Boucher's hospitality.

He would gather his things and go there, now, open his house, and make certain his servants had cleaned and readied it for his habitation. That house would be the headquarters for the war while we were within the city precincts. I was aware, through his mind, of the house he lived in, its distinct smell and the way the light played across its walls and floor.

I was aware even of the carnal desire he had for his housekeeper and his plans to satisfy his desire soon upon returning to the house, if she did not hide herself away somewhere, for she was a married woman, upon hearing he had returned.

All the while, I was aware of myself in the bed of Charlotte Boucher and of the deep slumber that held me in its grip, so that, though I tried to move my arms and legs, they were as if pinioned. I was aware of the fact that I was dreaming all of this and that because I was dreaming; it may or may not be true.

I was aware of the light of the rising sun persistently pawing at the closed and curtained windows. I was aware that Gilles had ducked under the rail into the stall of my gray horse and had laid himself in the straw at the destrier's feet and had fallen fast asleep.

I was aware that Xaintrailles was thinking profanely of The Bastard and of what he might like to do to the man with the haft of his war-axe, and that his dislike of the half-brother of the Duke of Orléans was a fire that was daily being fed. He glared, his eyes with their crisscrossing tiny veins narrowing fiercely, at the man's back as The Bastard preceded him up the stairs to their rooms.

I was aware that under the slab table in the recess of the crumbled stone, the mouse uncurled its paw from around its nose, stretched and yawned. It drew its tail up between its legs, stuck the tip of it in its mouth and sucked, never opening its eyes.

And in my dreaming awareness, I saw its death eighteen days later, struck twice by the fire-poker wielded by the hand of the cook, as it ventured out unwisely in daylight.

15, *Le Batârd d'Orléans*

The Bastard in his own house was as arrogant as a King in his palace. He strode his dark floorboards, where the carpets, once fine, had years ago worn through to the warp, and terrified his servants with shouted commands. On the second story of the graystone house, the windows looked out upon a great tree whose buds were tight and green upon her boughs, preparing to bloom into flowers and bright green leaves.

He paced back and forth, his hulking form silhouetted against the light coming in those windows, moving objects from one part of the room to the other, as if in his absence they had become misplaced and he could not commence to order his affairs until all was as it should be.

I was more interested in the affairs of the King and of the nation than in the placement of The Bastard's statuary, books, and his quaint baubles; spoils of long-ago battles, I supposed, and said so. He stopped his pacing and lowered his bristling brows over his dark eyes.

"What did you say to me, *Pucelle?*"

My mouth quirked in a wry smile; at least he called me by my title, the title I had appointed for myself to remind them of my virginity and the holy calling vested in me by that purity.

"I did say, Sir, what matter the disposition of your trinkets when the disposition of the English is the great matter of the day?"

He thought me an impertinent child and his mouth began to form those words, but he changed midstream and said, "You are... perhaps correct in that, *Pucelle*, but you see, I have been in Chinon with the Dauphin and I have been in this place and that for many weeks now and must needs reacquire some semblance of governance over this place. This city is mine to govern in the absence of my brother Duke Charles. You see, the business of this besieged city has piled up while I have been away."

I looked about me at the shadows cast by the heavy furniture across the floors.

I looked at the surfaces of the tables and writing desk, where dust had collected and where no piles of unfinished business presented themselves.

I looked at the face of the man before me, saw his death behind the sheen on his eyes, an old man's death, a death preceded by a lifetime of war, captivity, defeats and triumphs, the friendship of Kings and the mentoring of princes, chaste and courtly loves as well as base debaucheries, the loss of wives and sons, friends and enemies, and said, "I should like to attack our enemy this day, Sir, and do wish to know how you think we should begin."

He stopped in mid-stride, holding a tiny painting of a

woman, and stared at me.

"Begin?" he said. "I think we should begin with you returning to the House of Boucher and waiting a day or two, doing whatever young maidens do, perhaps a bit of needlework or lute-playing, or have Charlotte braid your hair with ribbands, while I gather up our captains and hold a council or two and bring up the King's army from downriver where we left them. If we can cross them at all, which is doubtful, considering the contrary winds."

I broke in. "The winds shall blow fair, do you have no fear of that."

He had let his impatience with me show, with his comments about needlework, and lutes, and girlish pastimes, and I determined to let my own impatience show as well.

"I have waited long enough, longer by two months than the English should have been allowed to sully our land with their presence, their consuming of our wines, and eating of our cheeses, and their belching and their farting into the pristine air of France, and I shall start a fight if you will not."

His dark bristling brows rose high at my words and a smile curled his lips.

"*Pucelle*, you surprise me," he said.

"*Pourquoi?*" I asked. "Because I know how to speak frankly? I am, as you like to call people, a peasant brat. Under these trappings of nobility, these silks, this gold braid, that is what you think of me, is it not? You all, French or English, may paint me as you like," I continued, my eyes drifting to the tiny miniature of his wife or his lover, "as witch, devil, whore, or virgin of impeccable purity and virtue, whatever suits the needs of the day or of your ambitions, but in the end, I am still a peasant brat from the wilderness of Lorraine, and thus, might as well speak frankly."

He looked down at the portrait in his big hard calloused hand, set it on the table beside him, turning it just so that the light from the window caught the woman's face, illuminating the delicate strokes of the artist's tiny brush, and looked at me again.

"You are more than you seem, *La Pucelle*," he said, as if it were an admission he made only grudgingly. "I will grant you that. But I and the other captains shall not pick a fight with the English until the Dauphin's full army is arrayed upon the north side of the river."

I knew then that he feared a defeat, had had one in the not-so distant past, one that cost him dear and had badly crippled his reputation as a fighting man and a brilliant captain. Twas the battle lost that my voices had told me of while I was at Vaucouleurs, the knowledge of which had swayed the mind of de Baudricourt. He was frozen with fear of another such; his eyes told me this and the way his mouth turned down at the corners as he said the words "shall not."

I was inclined then to agree with him but he had to add a last jab.

"So, *Pucelle*," he said, "find your rabbit boy outside my house and let him take you back to the House of Boucher and, when I have put my affairs in order and brought the army into position, mayhap I shall send for you." He had seen in his pacing before the windows, looking down into the street, below the spreading mostly-naked limbs of the great tree, the boy from Le Moineau holding the bridle-chains of my gray.

I had told Gilles to try to remain out of sight if he could, but now I knew he had been unable to. I had a strong desire then to move quickly into The Bastard's reach and strike him on his leering face.

To strike him hard in return for kicking Gilles and driving him from the kitchens where I had brought him, where I had placed him under my protection.

My new boots squeaked as I shifted my weight from foot to foot upon his floor.

I held myself from moving, thinking that I must act slyly and thoughtfully, without impulsiveness. Not like a country girl, whose every thought shows upon her face, every thought is spoken out loud. My own brows knit together, none so impressive and fierce as those of The Bastard of Orléans, but to my face they felt as angry.

"I can start a fight as easily as you, Sir," I informed him.

He gritted his teeth, stopping himself from saying something, and I saw things swimming in his mind, things he had worked hard to keep secret, deals and private meetings and messages and money. There was more than one reason he was delaying.

He had long-laid schemes in the works.

Well, I was *La Pucelle* and my time was short.

Better today than tomorrow and better tomorrow than the next day.

"*Oui*," I said again, "I can start a fight."

Now, I felt as arrogant as a King in his palace.

I turned upon my heel and went out.

16, Bees

The sounds of the city were not the sounds of the countryside, not the sounds of the winding roads between orchards of blooming trees or fields of grain or wild untilled meadows, nor were they the sounds of the river with its particular musical notes; water lapping on the bank, ripples and rivulets of the moving current, splashes of fish, reeds whistling in the breeze, and birdsong.

The sounds of the city were of cobblestones pounded under horses' hooves, the creaking of wagon-joints and rumbling wheels, the squeal of a barrow pushed by a street-sweeper, the scrape of his shovel on stone, the ringing of steel made by the hammer on the anvil of the blacksmith, the singsong voices hawking wares or voices in ceaseless chatter, the clash and clatter of windows opening and doors closing.

As I rode through the wending ways of Orléans back to my place at the House of Boucher, my rabbit boy jogging

barefooted at my side with his hand upon the gray's harness,
I heard all these sounds in my ears only faintly, as if they
were heard from a distance or as if I were under water.

What I heard most distinctly in my head was a sound like
the whirring of a bee hive.

It was the sound of my anger, a sound I liked not at all.

In the yard before the house, Louis stepped up to take
the reins of my horse as I jumped down. The look on his
usually bright face was gloomy.

I did not miss the look he gave Gilles as the boy from Le
Moineau held the off-side stirrup for me so that the saddle
would not slip as I dismounted. It was the look of one who
feels his place has been usurped, of a page sent by a King to
be a page for me who now sees that the place beside me has
been filled by another.

Louis had his own hive of bees working, I could see.

But I had other concerns to worry on.

Raymond stood leaning lazily in the doorway. He seemed
to not care if there was another boy in my entourage, in fact
he seemed to care nothing much about anything.

"Raymond, the horse," I said as I strode briskly for the
door. "Hold him here," I said. "Louis, and Gilles, put me in
my harness."

I went in and quickly climbed the stairs.

The bees in my head were still busily humming away as
the parts of my armor were being put on me, the anger that
was my purpose thwarted, the anger that was my need
unmet, the anger that was me being held back by men who
seemed to have all the skill to fight but none of the will to do
it, men who had all of the ability to act but none of the
desire; that desire which burned in me, hot in me, but which
they seemed not to feel.

The window was open with a light breeze coming in.

A strand of my hair blew across my check, long and wavy. I could see its red-brown color and the way it glinted in the light. It tickled my face but my arms were outspread while the boys fastened the tiny buckles of my rerebraces so I could not sweep it away.

Below, the dark-haired boy held the gray.

The animal tossed its great head and blew hard through its nostrils, spraying the page with horse-snot. Raymond responded by whipping the bridle-chains hard against the horse's muzzle.

The old campaigner bared his long teeth and snapped at the boy, missing his nose by a hair.

Raymond jumped back in alarm, giving the old horse a furious but more respectful look, and then set to wiping the snot off of his tunic.

I smiled.

The whirring of the bees was slowly subsiding.

I breathed in and out and felt my ribs expanding and contracting against the enclosing steel of my cuirass.

I liked the little sound of the leather straps that held the front and back plates against each other, that creaking sound as I breathed deep, and also the tiny hiss of steel as one plate moved over another, just soft and gentle as a bird wing on the wind.

I liked the feel of the armor, the way it encircled me, strongly and decisively, like an embrace. I liked how it felt when I moved; the pieces, neatly fitted together, that slid over each other just enough to allow me to move with reasonable ease while still covering me in such a way as to protect me from harm.

Over his hands, as he tucked the tab of the last leather

strap under its holder, Gilles saw my smile.

His brow wrinkled as he wondered at the expression on my face. The wrinkle was just under a small curl of golden-brown hair that had laid itself gently over his forehead when he had bent to pick up the rerebrace from the armor-chest.

Over his strong slender hands and below that wrinkled brow and that pretty curl, his eyes were very light blue, the green of meadows having made way for the color of the sky outside the window.

I lowered my arms and rolled my shoulders, making sure the armor was secure.

The bees were silent now and into the silence, I said, "I shall take the sights of Orléans this day. I should like to visit the English in their dwellings. Any who wish to go with me are welcome, but I shall not wait for them to ready themselves or tack up their mounts."

And with that, I left the room.

Going down the steep stairs, I heard the whisper of bare feet upon the planks just behind me.

My boy. My constant companion.

17, Visiting the Enemy

My gray moved quickly through the streets of Orléans as if he wanted as much as I did to visit the enemy. It was as if the old seasoned warhorse knew his business entirely, for he took me straightaway to the closest of the English fortifications without any guidance from me.

I did not know the way in any case and trusted in my angels or in the hand of God or in my horse to take me where I needed to go. Alongside me, keeping stride with the old destrier was my constant companion.

Those words, "my constant companion," seemed to fly into my mind each time I thought of him now, even when we were apart, for I knew somehow that he was constantly thinking of me even when we were apart just as I always seemed to have him with me even when he was not.

Bare feet upon the cobbles, he ran at my side, close enough for me to touch him if I wanted.

I did want, but did not want.

Wanted because I wanted to touch him, hold him, be held by him so much my heart was afire for it, but did not want for that I knew what cold grim visions I should have if I did so. For this moment, I had to be content to see him there beside me.

I had to be content knowing that he wanted to be near me. The sound of his feet on the stone was a music fair as church bells.

Englishmen stood upon a battlement, their cannon mouths gaping black and fierce against a blue sky scattered with clouds, their coats smudged with the soot of powder, and their faces dark from smoke.

I stopped below them, an simple arrow-shot for one of the infamous English longbow-men, and hailed them.

"You are far too easy, leaning on your walls," I called, "you men who should be making for your homes in England. Did you not hear that I have invited you all to leave now, before your blood is shed in this foreign land?"

A man took off his basinet, set it on the wall, and ran a hand through his shaggy hair.

"God-damn," he said, "is it the cowherd herself? Where are your cows, little one?"

The others gathered close and more came from nearby, until there was quite a contingent of Englishmen looking down at me. Several of them began to make moo-ing sounds at me and gestured with their hands the movements of milking.

I smiled gently and placed my hand upon my sword hilt.

One man, white-headed under his helmet and with a lined face and a scar from his jaw to the collar of his hauberk, pushed his way to the fore.

"Tis indeed the cowherd," he observed.

I could tell by his accent he was not English but a Burgundian, though it mattered not to me, he was the enemy just as surely as he had been Henry VI himself, since the Burgundians and the English slept in the self-same bed. I looked at him and said, "I thought all you Burgundians had gone home. Deals made and monies paid, I thought your services were no longer required at Orléans." I knew not what I meant by that, but the words just came out of my mouth.

The scar-faced man gave me a look of surprise, then laughed heartily. He said, "Some of us Burgundians don't give a rat's arse for the deals of highborn men, we just like to kill French. We would rather stay here and do that than go home and twiddle our thumbs."

I frowned at him. "I am sorry for you," I said, "for that choice shall cost you your life."

He laughed again and said, "I am glad you came to see me. You are very amusing. I was getting a bit bored this day, spending cannonballs through the walls of French homes. You have made me laugh; something French people do not do very often unless their guts are spilling out. I find that amusing also."

"You are a sad man to find joy in such things," I said. "What is your name, Sir? I will pray that you find God."

He ignored my question and only laughed at me again.

"Is this your army, little cowherd? A sizable army you bring, and so formidable," he said, leaning on the wall and feigning a broad yawn that showed his back teeth.

It was only me, the gray, and Gilles.

His comrades like this thrust and they widened their eyes and looked about, as if casting their gazes over an immense host.

I smiled benignly at him and his fellows. "It is never the size of the army that wins a war," I said, "but the rightness of the cause."

He spat a glob of phlegm over the side where it slapped on the stones.

"Now you really make me laugh!" he said. "You have fought no battles, girl, seen no wars, as I have done. Yet you think you know? You talk like a cleric, like a bishop in a manor house far from battle. Just wait until your little army is chopped to bleeding bits on the ground, and see if you talk the same horseshit."

I thought, as I watched his crude words form in his mouth and heard them spoken and saw his death, the dark blood boiling from his nostrils, a river of it finding the crease of his neck scar and following it down inside his clothing, but I have seen angels, heard their words, as you have not.

There was a sound to my rear, and movement, and Gilles, beside me, turned and looked behind us. Observing his face and the flickers at the corner of his mouth, I knew what he saw.

They were coming up to join me, warriors of France, and people of Orléans, a small army to be sure but more than one girl and one boy and one old horse. I saw too, on the face of the scarred Burgundian, a look of chagrin and of disdain.

"You see, they come," I said loudly, without looking back.

The man looked down, coughed into his fist. "I have fought on this ground more years than you have lived, girl, and I have yet to see the French army that could set my heart to beating fast. These beauties are maybe enough to add a pretty face or two to my fancies while I whank off, but that is all." The men on the wall with him guffawed at this.

"Time to open your eyes, then," I said, feeling my face flush and hoping it was not seen at this distance. "When you keep them tight closed, you see nothing but the inside of your own head. You do not see what I see, the deaths of you and your men here, who could live and see their families again."

He did not laugh now, but bared his teeth like a bulldog, showing no teeth at all in the bottom front of his mouth.

"My eyes are wide open," he said. "All I see is a country mopsie dressed up in a knight's full kit, a cowherd in silk and steel. I could dress up my harlot in the same and be as frightened."

His comrades laughed at this and he lifted his hand to silence them and they were instantly silenced.

I knew from this that he was a man of power.

"You are the captain of these men?" I asked him, as my horse pawed once, twice, raking its iron-shod hoof over the street stones.

"I am called the Bastard of Granville and they do my bidding."

"Then, bid them this, Captain Granville," I said, the tears already escaping from my eyes, "bid them march in good order from this place and return for their home countries, for I promise you," and I wept now, though I tried not to, hot tears splashing down the steel upon my breast, for I saw each man's death in the faces, whether jeering, lascivious, hate-filled, or merely curious, that looked down on me, "I promise you, that if you abide here, within a week and a day, I shall kill you all."

I lifted the rein in my left hand, spurred the gray on his right shoulder, and he reared up and flashed out with his two front hooves as he pivoted on his hinds, and with a bound, he broke into the canter and we left those men to think on that.

The French parted around me, and my rabbit boy was beside me, his hand on the gray's harness, undaunted by the airs of my destrier. He had floated like a bird on the wing when my gray performed his stunt, his bare feet rising from the paving-stones and landing sweet as a dancer's, ready to race away with me.

I heard the Burgundian holler at me before I rode away.

Turning in my saddle, I looked up at his scarred face; saw his hatred and his fear writ large there. He leaned over the ramparts, jutted his lower jaw forward like a dog whose teeth have been broken off in a half a hundred fights, and shouted after me, "Have this for your troubles, cowherd," and with a flick of his fingers he caused the man beside him who stood at the side of the great gaping gun, to lower his hot-match and touch the cannon's hole.

I quickly reined in and my gray's four hooves struck the cobbles at the same instant and he stood like a stone statue. There was a pop and a boom and the cannon spat a mouthful of sparks, black smoke and pepper-shot, which flew high over us.

Gilles, unprepared for the blast, dropped and cowered under my horse's neck, trembling.

In seconds, I could hear the sounds of the shot as it struck houses, windows, roofs and streets and people some blocks away.

My compassion which was always present, now made room in my heart for anger, anger at the cruelty of men, at their pride, at their indifference to the sufferings of others. Together, compassion and anger, biding there, shared common room in my heart, elbowed each other for space and eyed each other with suspicion, and finally, somehow came to an uneasy peace.

I touched Gilles lightly on his hair, my fingertips only just brushing his scalp, and thankfully felt only a slight chilling of my fingers. He looked up at me, his eyes wide and dark as a shadow on the sea.

I carefully wheeled my horse about and gazed up at the men on the wall.

I would not speak with Granville again, he who had ordered the shot, but I spoke to his followers.

"You Englishmen, you Burgundians their allies, listen to me, you fighting men for whom there is no reward but death. I warn you now, abandon your forts and depart in peace, home to your mothers and fathers, wives and women, your sweet and innocent children. Go now, else I shall raise such a war-cry against you as shall be remembered forever. I shall not speak with you again. Our next converse shall be of swords. Swords and arrows."

The gray knew I was done speaking and without a cue, he spun and leapt into the canter, the boy from Le Moineau at his side.

As we rode through the mob, I saw Louis coming on his palfrey, and Jean de Metz and Bertrand, who had been in my train since Vaucouleurs, and some of the other knights and squires of our company. Their faces showed their keenness to follow and soon I heard their hoof-beats as they got their horses turned in the crowd of people and came after us.

What I did not hear was the insults hollered by the enemy after me as I rode away, the words whore, witch, trollop, and ditch-bank doxy that were fired at my back like more random cannon-shot, though I heard about it afterwards.

18, Water for an Ox

We had gone but a few streets over when I was forced to rein in my horse to wait for an old man and his son to back a heavy wain out of the roadway after the ox that was pulling it had been unhitched and was lying exhausted in the street.

Shopkeepers were standing about, yelling at the drayman to clear the street that commerce not be interrupted. Times were hard enough, several were shouting, without the road to their places of business being blocked by dying cattle and unmovable wagons.

I swung from the saddle and left my reins in Gilles' hand as I walked over to peer into the eyes of the brindled ox.

Twas a massive animal, bigger by far than my destrier.

One front leg was folded under it and the other, with its great knobby knee as big as my head, was extended before it. Its horns were cut off at the tips and bronze balls affixed to them that no one be gored by the horns as the animal moved through the crowds and that the animal could never chose to stick a horn through the body of a human handler. Its great dark eyes lolled from side to side and drool slid over its lower teeth and its black drooping lip and made a puddle on the cobblestones.

"Water, someone," I said, as I knelt before the massive head of the poor creature.

My eyes searched the beast's body, looking to see if perhaps the enemy's pepper-shot had wounded the creature. But of that I saw no sign. A blacksmith brought a wooden bucket, dirty water slopping over its lip, and placed it next to the ox's extended leg.

I pulled a glove and dipped my hand into the water, dribbling some over the wide flaring black nose of the beast. The huge pointed tongue reached out and caught the droplets, the nostrils inhaled and exhaled fiercely, and the animal swung its head from side to side.

My hand braced against the brindled cheek.

I moved so that its head not strike me.

The firm thick meat of the ox's jaw against my hand brought an instant vision of the animal's death, a slaughtering by pole-axe and by glaive to the throat, a gout of heavy warm blood splashing over those knees, legs and cloven hooves, a great groan and thrashing and the blood pouring out like a torrent, a stilling of the great pounding heart and a final exhale of red-vapored air.

The vision stunned me and rocked me back on my heels more than the movement of the animal's head in my direction had done. But that vision was not of this day, no, not today, but a day in the future when the City of Orléans would be free and in French hands again.

I was not even sure where I would be on that day, but not here, no, not here.

The ox had found the bucket and was drinking all the water. I pressed my palm upon its rock-hard forehead betwixt the great curved horns with their ball-tipped ends and felt the life in it, felt the impulse always to press forward against the collar, the pleasure of the taste of fodder in its mouth, and satisfaction in the power in its own straining muscles, the joy found in a bed of soiled straw and dried manure at the end of a long day of toiling.

I saw the beauty of its pure and simple life.

"He shall live," I said, standing. "Watch out, now he shall rise." I stepped a few paces back.

The blacksmith retrieved his empty bucket. The people had all gone quiet now, shopkeepers, by-standers, the old man and his son whose wain was now in the alley nearby, and all the pages and knights and people who had been following me at the time I had to stop for the ox. Even more had gathered, curious, and the words, *"La Pucelle, La Pucelle,"* were being spoken by all and sundry.

The ox gave a moan and its tongue moved in and out of its mouth a few times.

Its dark gentle eyes fixed on my face and it stared at me for a long while.

The crowd stood as if breathless, not a word from anyone, not a stirring of a single shoe on a single stone. Then the ox pulled its one leg back underneath of it and rose slowly to its huge flat knees, its hindquarters straining and its back hooves scrabbling on the cobbles. Soon it gave another moan and got a forefoot under it and then the other and it stood straight up on all four feet.

The crowd gave a cheer.

The old man came forward, and gave a bow before me. He tried to speak but found his tongue would not form any words.

I looked into his face, trying to ignore his death which was writ large there, for he would die sooner than his ox, though comparatively bloodlessly.

"Tomorrow is a Sunday," I spoke loud enough for all to hear. "Take this poor creature out *La Porte de Saint Aignan* and halfway to Chécy. There are fields there full of grass. Let this stalwart beast have his day of rest midst the meadow flowers. And you rest there too. Praise God upon His day in the beauty of His creation."

The old man's eyes widened.

I read his fear there, fear of roving English bands.

"No harm shall come to you there, I give you the promise of the angels," I said and went to mount my destrier.

Gilles stood there in his ragged clothes, in his bare feet, his golden-brown curls swept back from his face, holding the rein. Speaking of angels, I thought. He could be the half-brother of the archangel.

My eyes met his; they were now green as chipped emerald and as bright and twinkling. His mouth had a tiny quirk at the corner, a hint of a smile, the smile of one who is a familiar, one's constant companion, one's love in all seasons.

I reached out to take the stirrup and I felt him at my side, heard his whispered words.

"You are a wonder, Jehanne, a wonder of the world."

I glanced at him and could not hide a smile of my own.

I had dropped my glove. He picked it up and held it to me as I settled into the saddle. I took it from his hand and slipped it over my fingers. He handed me the reins.

"*Merci*, Gilles," I said, and did not mean for my glove.

I meant for all his love, which I could see in his eyes, winking there in the hues of yellow and green, moving there to and fro like fishes under water.

I meant for his presence by my side, his hand upon my horse, his wild spirit that he was slowly, somehow, and for some reason that I could not understand, chaining to mine.

For his being here, I was so grateful that tears stung my eyes as I cued the gray to walk on.

When I rode away past the revived ox and down the streets of Orléans, I had a tail of hundreds behind me. Church bells began to ring again as they had when I had entered the city and people opened their windows and threw down favors; fresh and dried flowers and scraps of colored fabric too small to sew.

They fluttered down all around me like butterfly wings.

19, *La Porte d'Orléans*

My horse, so very wise, so sure-footed and so strong, now carried me to the Orléans Gate, which the gatekeepers unbarred and swung open for me, and I rode out upon the long-unused river bridge close to the Gatehouse of Saint Antoine to visit the enemy there.

An arch or two of the bridge, which had been the primary entrance to the city before the siege, lay in ruins between the Orléans Gate and the fortress and I rode my gray right up to the edge without fear. His big iron-shod hooves stopped mere inches from the open air. He planted them squarely and, like a stone statue, stood.

La Guérite du Saint Antoine loomed across the gap, built upon the mid-river island called *Belle-Croix* that the bridge spanned before the gate, and beyond the island, extending towards the south shore, was the long snake-like bridge of multiple arches leading to the high towers of the southern gatehouse known as *Les Tourelles*, or The Turrets, separated from the beachhead by a drawbridge, operated from within the gatehouse.

Destruction was everywhere.

Arches of the ancient bridge had been demolished, the huge gray lichen-covered stones lying half-buried in the river with water swirling around them, and the trash and debris of English occupation and the detritus of their construction of the fortifications lay all about the riverbanks and the beaches of the island. It stank of urine and rot and the feces of men.

Their minds had become as putrid and rotten as their fortresses for their commander Glasdale called down to me, thusly, "Leave that rabble of French cowards behind and come over here, girl. My men are hungry for a taste of French tart and will gladly share you about, bite by bite. Your men are but limp fish, every one of them, and cannot raise their mackerels enough to give you the *firking* you deserve."

I was not familiar with this English word but I knew from the reactions of my following that Glasdale had offered ravishment and rape should I be taken by the English.

I answered him plain-spokenly, "You English have had your way with France already for far too long. That rapine has come to an end. If you desire to keep your parts, all of them, intact, and live to use them another day, flee now for England, where the women, being English and used to the stench, may welcome your advances, as we French women do not."

My people burst into laughter and cheering at this bold *riposte*.

But Glasdale and his English were hotly insulted and threw stones and a few crossbow bolts our way. I reversed my destrier and rode slowly away, knowing that no bolt would strike me, not yet, and I may ride off at a measured and unhurried pace.

The last I heard of Glasdale, he had shouted these words, "I shall catch you, *firk* you myself, and burn you for a witch."

I reined my horse in and looked over my shoulder. The image of flames danced before my eyes. Flames hot and yellow, blue at the base and roiling with black smoke at the tips. Heat rising like quavering waves, whipping my body like a many-tongued lash.

Surely, he did not believe me a witch for he would not have offered to violate me if he thought me so, would have been too afraid, so I had then to wonder if he meant to burn me as a witch unjustly?

Surely that was case: An excuse to execute a prisoner of war in violation of all the rules of civilized combat.

I must, surely then, avoid capture at all costs.

I looked back at the man.

Ironic, I thought, he speaks of burning me to death when in truth and in but a few days, he shall die by drowning and only because he wishes to avoid dying by fire. I marked well his face and let myself feel pity for him, not because he would die, for all of us shall die, but that he had wasted so much of his life here in a country not his own when his wife and children in England suffered for his absence, and unlike me, would never see his face again.

I visited many of the English that day, making the rounds of all the besieging fortifications which were close enough that I might call and be heard from the walls of Orléans, one after the other until after night's darkness fell.

At each, I invited the foreigners to leave peaceably and soon, else would I see them all dead. I had already seen them dead, in my mind's vision, but I could not tell them that, and even as I offered them an escape from their fate, I knew in many cases, that they would not heed me, for I saw how they would die in the next few days, here at Orléans, by sword-thrust and axe-chop, and pinned by arrows or crushed by mace-blows, dying in the confusion and press of battle, in falls from towers, tramplings by horses, and in raging fires and by cold unrelenting water.

On my knees in Charlotte's room at night, with the Sword of Saint Catherine in my hands, the sword that would give me all victory, held tip-downward so that the hilt formed the cross of Christ's crucifixion, I prayed that the men I had seen today would heed my heartfelt word and leave this country behind and in peace, but even as I prayed, I knew that they would not, for my vision given to me by the touch of the angel had shown me the deaths to come.

20, Council of War

I **did** cause the captains to meet with me in the hall at the House of Boucher after morning mass the following day. The leaders of the men of France gathered there, in their roughness and in their insolence. They had seen how the folk of Orléans did embrace me, did follow me, cry out my name and cheer for me. Their faces were hard and their tongues worried at the insides of their cheeks as they crowded into the room.

These men, the captains of France, were they jealous of the faith the people had vested in me, that was no longer vested in them, or were they still doubtful that I could do the things my angels had promised me that I could and would do?

Perhaps I should never know all that weighed in their hearts or nibbled at the edges of their minds, but that was neither here nor there, the things that they felt or that they believed.

I would have them do my bidding, beginning now, whether they would or nay.

Doing my bidding was all that mattered from here going forward. It was time.

"*Batârd d'Orléans*," I said and all eyes turned towards me, all mouths stayed their whispering and their chatter. The Bastard's dark brows came together over his fierce eyes and his lips pressed into a hard line between his beard and the hair that covered his upper lip.

I looked him straight in the eye and spoke as Michael the archangel had always spoken to me, soft and slow but clear and precise, each syllable carefully pronounced. "You shall leave this day and hie thee downriver to bring the King's army to us, here at Orléans. Find *Le Duc d'Alençon* and bring him to me."

As I spoke, I knew that there was an obstacle to the army's movement, an obstacle in the shape of a man, but which man I could not tell. It was no one here, that much I knew. It was one sent by the King and not a man of war.

It was a man whose authority I would have to challenge, this I knew, in order for me to bring war to the doorstep of the enemy and see them routed.

"I shall withhold battle upon the enemy until you have returned," I told The Bastard, "but tarry not, for battle must be meted out before five days have come and gone, else our cause be lost." This also I knew, though I knew not how. "But if we strike them, and in good time, they will not be able to stand against us."

Every face turned now to the dark knight, for every eye wanted to see what the great warrior and leader of men would do.

Would he take orders from this mere girl, this peasant brat?

Each ear cocked to hear his retort, he who was famous for his bluster, renowned for his arrogance, infamously unmovable except by his own ambition.

He stared down the long table towards me, his eyes burning with some kind of fervor.

Was it fervor of hatred for me, or of disrespect of me? I could not tell.

But it was of no matter, all I required was his obedience.

His beard seemed to part once, twice, and thrice as his mouth opened and closed, forming words and then letting them dissolve. He shifted from one booted foot to the other.

I stood easy in my own skin and watched him settle himself to his task, like the great ox did settle itself into its collar every day of its life and begin to pull.

Shortly, he spoke.

"*Pucelle*, whom would you have me take?"

I said, "Take with you whomsoever you need, my lord. As many as you need. Your judgment is better than mine in this matter. Orléans shall be safe until your return. And when you return, we shall have war."

With that word, War, the fervor in his eyes revealed itself for what it was.

Finally, his reticence and all his little reasons had stepped aside to reveal what stood behind them; the fervor to kill the enemy and drive the foreigners from this land and to redeem his reputation and to slay as many English as he could find within the reach of his sword.

The fervor of belief that it could be done.

His dark eyes blinked once, slowly.

"*Pucelle*," he said.

And that was it.
Le Batârd d'Orléans bowed and left.
And all the captains of France filed out behind him.

21, In the Stable

The place Gilles and I always found to talk was in the stable, in the stall where the gray was kept and where Gilles had made his camp.

We had spoken of our homes; me, my town of Domrémy, where the river Meuse ran through the rugged hills and rolling meadows and where the forest of great trees stretched away in three directions and where I had hung garlands on the limbs of *l'arbre de fées* as a girl; he, the tiny village of Le Moineau or The Sparrow, where his father had a turnip farm and his mother was a wool-dyer, where he was the oldest son (there was one other, a four-year-old) and expected to follow in his father's trudging footsteps behind a plow and where his five sisters were already learning to gather plants and flowers for the dyes.

All he did that he enjoyed, he told me, was to hunt for rabbits in the fields and along the streams and in the breaks at the edges of the forests, for he felt free in those places and loved the silence and the peace that filled his mind when he was alone with only the furred and feathered people and the leafy ones.

He considered them such, he told me, in his quiet way, as I looked into his eyes, marveling at their color, a lovely yellow-green.

"I only kill the rabbits," he had told me, "because my parents would never allow me to while my hours away for naught. I can help to feed the family, I can make things of the furs, and my father is glad for fewer of them in his crops." Even so, he seemed a bit sad about it, the killing, and I saw the tenderness of his heart, the pure unstained beauty of his heart.

When he spoke of the forests and the meadows, his joy of them animated his face, and glowed in his bright eyes. Twas this joy I had beheld in him when I first saw him on the road outside of Tours.

The joy of a person as one with his own nature, untroubled by choice, or by self-doubt, or by expectations, or by destiny.

I sat there now, in the bed of straw, leaning against the rough wood of the wall, with Gilles facing me, his back against the other wall, and the great gray horse slumbering on his feet over us.

The Bastard had been gone two days, having taken most of the main men with him, *La Hire* and Xaintrailles included, and we had had two days of processionals about the city, two days of exchanging insults with the English, two days of church ceremonies and visits from clerics who now all wanted to be seen at the side of The Maid, who at Poitiers had wanted only to berate and challenge me, trick me and trip me up.

For two days I had acted the gentle pious shepherdess, the pure and holy vessel, the figurehead of righteousness at the prow of France, hours upon hours, when all I had wanted, in my heart of hearts, was to lie in the arms of the rabbit boy.

So I came here, into the stable, where no one suspected to ever find me, and sat with him. I put it out to my confessor, Father Pasqueral, that I was in Charlotte's room, praying, and he put it out to the populace, and then I snuck down to the stable to be with Gilles.

I did not lie in his arms, could not lie in his arms, but wanted to lie in his arms.

Instead, I sat near him, near enough to feel him breathing, feel the air stir with his breaths, near enough to gaze into his eyes, those eyes of many colors, and feel him probe my mind, gentle as a butterfly's wing, probe my mind for the truth to be found there, that I was in love.

In love as I never had dreamed to be in love, for I had not, in my all girlhood fancies, known what love was, what it felt like, what it tasted like, what it did to one's mind, to the heart beating in one's chest, to the place at the root of the body.

What it did to the place at the root of the soul.

He was so good.

He did not assay to touch me.

His foot might be inches from mine, his long leg stretched out across the stall, the straw and horse manure piled up against it, yet he did not move it an inch to bring it closer to mine, though an inch or two would have been enough to touch me.

His eyes told me how much he yearned to.

My eyes, presumably, told him not to.

"You are a wonder, Jehanne," he said, as he often did.

I smiled and said, "I know, a wonder of the world."

I picked up a straw and broke it in my fingers and put a piece of it in my mouth. It was sweet to the tongue and smelled like the fields outside of Chécy.

"I have never known a girl like you," he said.

"There are no girls like me," I told him.

We had played this game before, several times in the past few days, as we sought for ways to be with each other and things that were safe to say.

He sighed deeply and looked at the spider-webbed ceiling.

His hands were in his lap and he laced his long fingers together and steepled the forefingers, tapping them together.

His brow wrinkled as if his mind was chewing something over.

Before he could speak, for I feared what he might be about to say, I said, "I have never known a boy."

He looked at me and the wrinkles relaxed from his brow. "Like me?"

I blushed.

"Any boy," I said, trying to put meaning into the words.

His eyes lit up with understanding and he bobbed his head. "*Oui*, well, I knew that," he said. "You are *La Pucelle*. It is expected."

I inhaled deeply, smelling horse urine and manure and sweet hay and dust and mildew.

"*Oui*, it is expected," I said, relieved, in a way, that we had come to it at last. "And so..."

He smiled, and unsteepled his fingers and tapped his thumbs together, then spread them wide. "And so... it must remain. Even though..."

One golden-brown eyebrow cocked above an eye that

seemed so blue, as blue now as the sunlit sea, and he waited for me, waited for me to speak the truth that lay between us, had lain between us since the day that I first saw him under the beech tree on the road outside of Tours, when I had mistaken him for an archangel, then seen that he was only a boy, a boy as beautiful as an angel, and had thought to snatch his funny hat off, as a girl might do to tease a boy, a boy whom she thought she might like to marry someday, and, turning in my saddle to see him recede behind me, had known that I loved him more than all the rest of the vast ocean of humanity, more than all of them put together.

"Even though," I said.

It was all I could say.

Being *La Pucelle*, the girl who was to save France, the girl who could never know a man, what else could I say?

It was enough.

Gilles nodded his head once and a smile as broad as the River Loire spread across his face.

He lifted his right hand to his lips, kissed his fingertips and then reached out and touched them to the toe of my leather boot.

Mon Dieu, what that did to the place at the root of me!

22, *L'avant-poste de Saint Pouair*

I was not pleased to see Regnault de Chartres, the Archbishop of Rheims, riding beside the dark knight when the army came up the river. He had not been pleasant to discuss theology with during my fourteen-day-long ordeal of examination at Poitiers and I did not expect him to be more pleasant company here in Orléans.

Seeing the Duke of Alençon again, however, was a pleasant thing, and good as his word, The Bastard of Orléans brought him straight to me.

I had mounted my gray and ridden out *La Porte de Saint Aignan* to greet my army as soon as the messengers had come to *la maison de la famille de Boucher* to announce that it was in sight.

Traveling north and then west, my small contingent and myself, with Gilles running at the side of my horse, his hand as ever upon the breast-strap, we met upon the plain near the Outpost of Saint Pouair, which the English like to call

"Paris" since it guarded the road to that great city, which they proudly considered <u>their</u> great city.

I met the army of France in plain sight of this and the other English outposts on the northwest side of Orléans.

Seeing me, my men, and my banner trailing in the breeze, Alençon spurred his rose-red steed to the gallop and with The Bastard of Orléans right beside him, covered the ground between us in seconds.

Doffing his hat, the Duke reined up in front of me.

"La Pucelle d'Lorraine!" he shouted with evident glee.

"Le Beau Duc," I said, and saw him beam his bright smile at my new sobriquet for him. "They do call me *La Pucelle d'Orléans* now, though I think not that The Bastard of Orléans is fond of the nickname."

The Bastard glowered, holding his steed in tight with the reins so that it flung its head and rolled its eyes wildly.

"They have called me The Bastard of Orléans most of my life," he said. "What matter if they call you The Maid of Orléans for a few days?"

The Fair Duke cued his horse into a series of graceful airs, as he sang out in a lilting voice, *"La Pucelle et Le Batârd d'Orléans!* It sounds like a song sung by troubadours the world over."

Looking to the army progressing over the plain, and the Archbishop riding in the fore of it, I asked Alençon, "What is his business here?"

I admit I feared a repetition of the examination I had suffered at Poitiers. Perhaps what Alençon had whispered to me during our ride towards Orléans had been true, that some clerics, including this most high one, still believed me to be come from the devil. Or mayhap the King had been convinced I needed to be watched over by more learned and highly-placed men than Father Pasquerel or by those innumerable men of the cloth who had flocked to Orléans as if it were a holy site on a pilgrimage.

The Duke stilled his cavorting horse and spoke in a low tone. "The King sent him to oversee the army, religiously-speaking. To see to the army's spiritual needs just I was sent to see to its temporal needs." The handsome face twisted into an unhandsome grimace. "All it resulted in was delay and dissension. I do not believe the man is fully committed to defeating the English in battle, I think his allegiances run along other than purely national lines. I cannot prove it, however, but I bethink me he wishes an alliance with the Burgundians, who to my mind are simply English who cook better."

He threw his head back and laughed gaily at his own wit.

I frowned. "Well, there are still many Burgundians here," I said. "Even after they were all bribed and paid much to leave."

Alençon looked at me shrewdly. "What do you know about that?'

I glanced at The Bastard, who was pretending not to listen to our conversation. "I know more than I am told by men. I have other councilors."

The blue eyes of the Fair Duke widened in surprise.

He wanted to ask another question of me but in that very moment, Regnault rode up to our party, his eyes hard and cold though he affected a smile as he greeted me, calling me by my given name.

I dipped my head before him.

"Your Excellency," I said.

I would not dismount to approach on foot and kiss his ring as I would have done a month ago. I saw his old man's death in his face, a death in bed with his emaciated body lying in its own waste and his attendants in a flurry to clean him and change his bedding, his last rasping breath bearing to the air the smell of internal decay.

My eyes filled with tears, for it was not in me to not feel compassion, even for those I knew to be my enemies.

The Fair Duke asked me would I like to see the soldiers, how they had transformed under his care, and I said I would, and so we all rode back along the lines, as the army marched towards past the Paris Outpost towards the Saint Aignan Gate. The men were well-armed and had gotten some better clothing and armor, brigandines and hauberks and tabards of the colors of the houses of the captains who led them, and bore aloft flowing banners.

Those that rode had schooled their horses to rear and strike and to turn and knock down a standing foeman. They showed off their airs to me as we passed them.

The army's size had increased as well and marched with good discipline.

"It is wonderful, my lord," I said, "how good they look. In five days they seem transformed."

Alençon gave me one of his most brilliant smiles and capered his horse. "Five days was enough, *Pucelle*, given the freedom to treat them as French soldiers not cowardly serfs, getting them out of Chinon, away from the King's ministers, and allow them to be men."

I nodded my agreement.

"You have done well," I said.

Alençon beamed at me. "It is your doing, Jehanne."

"Mine?" I said. "I have done nothing. I have been here in Orléans."

"You have given them hope," Alençon said. "Your hope is

the hammer. They have hardened like iron into steel under the pounding of your hammer."

I smiled at him. "If I am the hammer, what is the anvil? Your schooling of them?"

"Destiny," he said.

"Hmm," I said, "...or God's will."

"It is not the same thing?" Alençon asked.

"Is it?" I wondered aloud. "If we fail to do God's will, is that not our destiny also?"

He looked at me then, his smile fading from his lips. "You shall not fail to do God's will, Jehanne," he said and paused, his bright blue eyes searching my face. "Surely you are not afraid you shall? Not you, the milkmaid who jousts and rides and bears the sword of the saint at her side?"

I would not tell him it was my greatest fear and that, like Gilles, that great fear was my constant companion.

I was *La Pucelle*, the maid who would save France, the conversent of angels and the chosen of God. I could afford no fear, could not have nor show any uncertainty.

He, the Duke of Alençon, seemed newly converted to belief in me. When we had met before and parted on the south side of the river at the boat landing, he seemed, despite his devil-may-care mien, cynical and a bit jaded. Now he seemed, like the men of the army of France, renewed and transformed.

Or was he only teasing me?

Was he only riding this capering steed as far as it would take him, to see where it would end?

After all, it was a life that we were all living, and no escaping it, what choice did any one of us have but go along for the ride?

"Nay, not," I assured him with a toss of my head. "I have

no fears. I am in God's hands."

Alençon smiled at me, then gave a nod to the wall.

"There, we are at the Paris Outpost. This is the main English strongpoint on the north side of the city. It prevents any access to the city through the Paris Gate. It will have to be taken if we are to lift the siege."

I looked up at the formidable structure, with the great guns and the trebuchets and the piles of round stones for projectiles, the multitudinous arrow slots and the sharpened spikes to ward off attack, and the men-at-arms that clustered upon the ramparts.

"We shall not touch it," I said, with instant knowing. "The English will empty it upon their own two legs."

Alençon gave a laugh, then turned to look at my face.

When he saw the seriousness there, he cocked his head and said, "Which of your angels, Jehanne, tells you this? Michael the archangel, he who is the protector of the righteous warrior?"

I bethought me upon Michael then, the fierceness and the gentleness of him, his power that radiated out right of him and made your very bones ache, made the blood in your vessels quiver and almost seem to boil like water in a pot. Michael, who blinded your eyes with the blue light of his love, the red-gold light that was his anger.

Michael, about whom I knew, in his presence, that I belonged to him, the deepest inner workings of my soul were his to command, more so than God, a faceless, un-seeable, unknowable God.

Michael was seeable and knowable and touchable, though his touch burned. His face was seeable, and beautiful, the most beautiful face, save one, that I had ever seen.

I thought on him now and thought of when I had seen

him last.

It had been at Fierbois.

At Fierbois and not since, though I had seen his blue fire light in the sky over Chinon and I had seen it at Tours over the house wherein my standard was being stitched. And I had seen it around my standard, the first time I had unfurled it from its staff and lifted it into the wind.

But since I had seen the boy on the road outside of Tours, neither my archangel nor his light had appeared to me.

I looked down at Gilles, walking beside my knee. He picked his barefooted way carefully, watching for the spiny goat-headed seeds in the grasses, his little bag, as ever, slung over his shoulder and riding in the small of his back. I bewondered me then, as I often did, what he carried in the little bag.

"Saint Catherine does tell me," I answered the Duke. "She whose sword I carry."

Alençon looked at me with as much wonder as had ever replaced the mischief in his face, but he said nothing.

We had come nigh *L'avant-poste de Saint Pouair* and sat our horses within an easy bow-shot. The English at the gate crowded the ramparts to get a look at us and at our army. Six score of faces peered over the walls.

I rode within hailing distance and waved at them.

"How do you find the army of France?" I called to them.

Several shook their fists at me, one called me a foul name, someone asked who I was.

"I am *Jehanne, La Pucelle*," I answered.

"Are you the whore of the Armagnacs?" a man called down. Armagnacs was what some called we who were for the Dauphin to rule and against the rule of England.

"Nay not," I called back, "I am the child of God, the page of Christ, the soldier of Michael Archangel, he who recruited me with a touch of his finger upon my cheek. And you, I see that you are a good man and should not die here in this land unknown to you."

He laughed and looked uneasy, casting his eyes from side to side to see the faces of his comrades. A few of his friends slapped him on the back and shook their heads, as if to say, you are in this one on your own.

To spare him having to think of what to say, I went on, "We are all good Christians, would it not be better not to fight one against the other but to join together and march against the infidel in the Holy Land, where in a massed army of God, we might redeem the Holy Sepulchre? You and I might then find ourselves as boon companions, good friends and comrades-in-arms rather than blood rivals, vying for the chance to kill one another before the other kills us."

His friends laughed at his discomfiture and to impress them, he leaned far out over the wall and shouted down to me, "I might but for the fact that you are not my boon companion, you are the whore of the Armagnacs, and I would spit on you before I should take your hand in friendship."

I turned my horse in a circle, with Gilles moving deftly with us, his hand on the breast-strap and so close to my armored knee that I could almost nudge him with it if I was so inclined.

"That gives me grief," I said to the man on the ramparts, "for I know that your fair-haired wife Lizette, whom you call Lizzie, would far rather if you must spill your blood in combat, that it be in a worthy cause, not in this affair of Kings and wealth and possession and power. She would have something to tell your new son (whom she has named after you) other than that your life was wasted as a playing piece in the games Kings play. Why don't you go home, Tom, and see your son? His eyes are green like yours."

I turned and rode away and did not wait to see the look of astonishment upon the Englishman's face. The man did not know that his Lizzie had born him a son in his absence.

The Archbishop of Rheims eyed me warily as I galloped to join the milling group of riders that was himself, Alençon, the dark knight, *La Hire*, Poton de Xaintrailles, and other captains of rank, plus their banner knights, squires, pages, and standard-bearers.

"Have you had your fun now?" The Bastard asked me.

"I have spoken my heart," I said to him, "which is my office to perform."

Xaintrailles smirked, his killer's face more narrow even than I remembered it, a face like a blade honed for slaughter. He liked to see The Bastard challenged, even by a soft parry of words.

The Duke of Alençon touched a forefinger to his hat brim in a gesture of salute to me and followed it with a wink.

"We will ride hard now," The Bastard said, "so we may enter the city at the head of the army." He frowned down at my constant companion. "You must leave that rabbit boy to hippety-hop his own way back to the gate, for he will not keep up on foot."

He yanked his horse's head around and spurred its flanks with a jingle of rowels and he and his following, including the Archbishop, took off in one great clattering and clanging mob.

When he had said this thing about my rabbit boy, I saw the wicked intent in his eye; that if I should leave Gilles to come in by himself on foot, the dark knight would make it mete that some accident might befall him and he perhaps, never been seen again.

The Duke pulled back on his reins and his horse obediently held his ground. Alençon looked at me, a smile playing at the side of his mouth.

"Your boy may ride with me, if you like," he said kindly.

"*Merci*, Sir," I said, "but that will not be necessary. Gilles will ride behind me."

I kicked my foot free from the stirrup and looked down at Gilles.

He looked up at me, one hand on the gray's neck and the other on the strap so close to my knee that I could have nudged him. I did nudge him, just a bit, so that he would see that I was serious. His eyes were a dark unreadable gray.

Then, without a word, he moved, put a foot in the stirrup, and grabbing the back of the saddle, he sprang up behind me. The gray, anticipating a gallop, reared back a bit and danced in place.

Gilles, fearing to fall off behind, placed his hands upon my hips to brace himself. His hands grasped me below the maille skirt of my armor and I felt him through the fabric gambeson.

A cold dark merciless death swept over me, blackening my sight and making me reel in the saddle. Gilles felt me fall back into him, he pushed me upright, then took his hands from me.

I came back to myself, the dark cold tide slipping off me like a veil fallen to the ground. Taking a deep breath, I gathered my reins well in my hands.

"Now," I said to the Fair Duke, hoping he had noticed nothing, "we are ready."

I let the gray have his head and he broke smoothly into

the gallop. Gilles, his long fingers looped into the barding on the horse's side below the leather of the saddle, rode there easily, although his mind at first had clenched tight as a fist against the notion of riding. I had known that he and the gray had become friends.

And I had thought that if the boy from Le Moineau was ever to ride a horse, it would be this one.

I was right, he would ride a horse.

By himself he would ride one and sooner than I had thought.

23, The Black

They say that I was sleeping when I dreamed of French blood being spilled and awakened to shout angrily at my pages that they had not told me battle had been joined.

They are wrong.

I was not sleeping and I did not blame anyone but myself for not knowing that brave Frenchmen had assaulted one of the English forts. I may have yelled angrily but it was at myself for not knowing, not feeling the pain of those who were getting wounded, not seeing the deaths that were taking place not far from me.

As for sleep, in truth, it was the army that was asleep after their long ride in to Orléans from where they had been detained at Blois by the King's man, Archbishop Regnault.

The coming of *Le Batârd d'Orléans* had rousted the army from its inactivity and put it on the road to me before the day had broken and it had marched hard. Arriving at

Orléans at midday, the army had swept like a living river through *La Porte de Bourgoyne* and men and horses had filled every market circle and broad avenue, park and courtyard in the city. They had collapsed to refresh themselves with wine, water, and food brought to them by the grateful multitudes of townsfolk, and eventually they had fallen into a midday slumber.

And me?

I had ridden in at the head of that army and was in my chambers at the House of Boucher, not asleep, but in prayer.

I had my army now, had it with me, had it in sight of the enemy, not left behind me somewhere on the road and detained and dilly-dallying at the command of the King's man. The obstruction now cleared from my path like a boulder dragged out from a river, I was free to act, to make war, but how?

How does one make a war?

How does one strike the first blow?

How does one who abhors killing, go forth to kill?

Those around me who knew would not speak to me. The captains of France, those great and fearsome warriors, they were keeping their own counsel.

Well, I had my council too, or at least I had had. Would they come to me now, tell me what to do?

Or was a country girl chosen of Heaven supposed to simply know these things?

So I prayed.

I prayed to Michael, that he would appear to me, not abandon me, that his bright blue light would again blind my eyes, burn me, remind me that he was real. He had made this war my burden and without him to help me bear it, I was not sure that I could. Without him to show me how, I was not sure I could do all that I had promised.

Was the act of saying it the act of making it true?

Now was the time to find out.

I kneeled in my room, my knees in the steel knee-cops upon the hard wooden floor, and I leaned my forehead against the hilt of the sword that would give me all victory, the Sword of Saint Catherine, as against a cross.

They say that, when the alarum came, I called for my people to arm me, but in truth, aside from my helm and gauntlets, all that I had removed from my person was the steel arm protection, those things I could easily remove by myself. I was yet in my breastplate and back-plate, my legs and feet still sheathed in steel and so it was that I kneeled in my steel knee-cops on that hard floor.

I knelt and, forehead against the cross of my sword, I begged Michael to come to me again.

I pictured Michael, imagined him, his beauty and his power. As I tried to hold his visage in my mind's eye, the visage of the boy kept overlaying it and taking its place. I could not for long hold steady upon the archangel but that the boy would take his place. Finally, I succumbed and let my mind drift over every angle of Gilles' face.

Deep in my imaginings, which to satisfy History, I admit, was much like a sleep, I heard a sharp clink against the glass of the window.

I raised my head.

I heard another clink. A pebble tossed from the street below.

Gathering one foot under me, I rose, the armor whispering softly as I strode to the casement, my sword in my hand, the blade trailing on the floorboards. Down below, barefooted upon the worn cobbles before the House of

Boucher, stood my rabbit boy.

My heart took a leap and I flung the window open.

"Jehanne," he said, breathless. He was as beautiful as an angel, his golden hair all-a-tangle around his cheeks.

He had been running. He flung his arm to the east and pointed a finger. There I saw them, coming in to the space in front of the house, bloodied and battered.

They were not soldiers, though they had been to war. They were the common people of Orléans, armed not with weapons but with tools and with will.

And now broken and bleeding.

Twas then I called for Louis and Raymond to ready my horse. Not the gray, for he was tired from the long ride to meet the army, but the black, whom I had not yet ever ridden.

Charlotte and Madame Boucher, hearing my angry shouts, came in to fasten upon me my steel arms and to buckle my sword-belt around me.

In the stable below the house, the black was rearing and snapping at the boys who were trying to saddle him. He had been too long kept like a bird in a coop, he was in a bad humor and dangerous. He struck out hard with one great iron-shod rear hoof and left a deep mark in the oak of the stall, which caused the old timber and stone house to resound like a beaten drum. He dumped the saddle from his back into the straw and stepped on it, tangling his legs with the barding.

Perhaps I did get angry at the boys then, for their ineptitude, or at their King who had given me boys too young to know how to handle destriers. Finally, after much ado and many kicks and nips, the black was saddled and bridled.

I could not mount while in the stable for he was rearing.

The boys brought him out into the air, holding his head between them on ropes pulled tight in their hands so that he could not bite them. Even before I rode him, his black hide was flecked white with sweat.

A crowd was gathering, of excited and wounded people.

The horse snorted through his flaring nostrils, smelling blood, and spun in circles, tangling up the boys with their ropes, knocking Louis to the cobbles and nearly walking over him.

Suddenly Gilles was there, catching up the rope that had pulled out of Louis' hand. Under the black's jaw, with eyes like dark gray slate, he stared down Raymond, who flung his rope into the rabbit boy's face and stalked off. Gilles walked in a circle slowly, pulling the black's head around firmly as he made the animal follow him, flicking the tail of one of his ropes at the horse's heaving flanks, making it step under its body with its near hind leg.

The beast calmed.

I was not very big and the black was huge. There was no great man here to help lift me up.

"Bring him here to the cross that I might easier mount," I said to Gilles, and he lead the horse to the pedestal of the cross, where I climbed up the stones and was able to then throw my leg over the saddle. I caught the stirrups with my feet and gathered the leather reins in my hands. I looked down at the top of Gilles' golden-brown curls as he worked to unfasten the ropes from the black's headstall.

Once freed of the ropes, the black flung his great head up and down, slinging slobber from his teeth into the air.

I paced him in a couple of big circles, trying to avoid trampling the people underfoot, while I thought about what it was I was missing.

"My standard," I said.

It was in my chamber.

I spurred the horse to below the window and called up. Charlotte leaned out. She was, perhaps, still there to lament over the state to which her beautiful chamber had been reduced, like a barracks room for soldiers rather than a chamber for a young lady of worth.

"Charlotte, *mon ami,* hand me out my standard," I called out and she did, pushing the draperies aside with the staff and letting the rolled fabric slide through her fingers as the banner lowered into my grasp. But I saw right off that it was no good.

As the white silk unrolled and fluttered, the black shied and reared, nearly throwing me out of the saddle.

Gilles ran forward to take the staff from my hand.

Both hands on the reins once more, I brought the black under a semblance of control. I wheeled him about, and aimed his forelock to the east and gave him my leg. He bounded straight up into the gallop, his hind shoes skittering on the stones before he found purchase and we flew along the street, his forehand popping up with every stride, his thick black mane whipping my face. I gathered my reins in each of my hands and tried to bring him into collection.

His head swung from side to side as he tried to get behind the bit.

The chains were jingling, the blue and gold barding around his chest was ringing with tiny bells, and his shoes clattered loudly on the stones. Beneath me, he was a torrent released from a dam. All the strength of my body could only barely hold him back.

He was five times the horse the gray was!

But like the gray, he was a warhorse.

Without my even guiding him, he found the sound of the cannons in the distance and he raced in that direction. The buildings rose to either side of us, stone and timbered, like a narrow canyon in which we, the torrent, ran.

A different flood ran in the other direction, a growing flood of people, dirty and bloody and bruised and dead being carried by the living. They parted, but barely, as my black galloped down the street. I had to jerk his head to one side or the other as a person appeared before me, too slow to get out of our way.

Soon, I began to hear the cries, *"La Pucelle! La Pucelle!"* behind me as people recognized me, and soon the cries preceded me, erupting in the street before me, and rather than the people streaming past me, they were stopping, stepping to the side and watching me pass, raising their hands and their voices, *"La Pucelle!"*

And then some were even following me, running alongside my black, holding up their hands to touch me or touch the horse, trying to keep up with our fast pace and falling behind but still running. I came around one corner close to *La Porte de Saint Aignan* and almost collided with three men, two of them carrying the third between them.

Striking sparks on the stones, the black skittered to a stop and I looked down into their upturned faces.

The man in front, carrying the legs of his fallen friend, was a leather tanner, this I knew, though I knew not how. Mayhap because his hands were stained. Mayhap because of the strong smell of urine about him. He was short in the legs but big in the shoulders, with a large head stuffed into a barbute helmet which I knew, though I knew not how, was the property of the wounded man.

He had picked it off the head of his friend, ostensibly to

carry it, though he hoped by so doing he could claim it as his own if his friend were to die.

The man in back was smaller and was a cobbler, and I wondered why he was carrying the shoulders of his friend, the heavier portion, when the tanner should have been doing so. The carried man, a tinsmith, was wounded in the belly, his middle wet with blood and dripping on the stones, his face ashen and slack and drool running down his stubbled chin.

I knew his face, had seen him in the crowd the day I raised the ox. He had cheered and smiled at me in a fatherly and approving way and I had seen in his eyes his death, this death, for he was dying now, here, in front of me as I looked down from the back of my heaving horse, just as I had seen it.

The only thing that was different was the breathing I was hearing was not the heavy labored breathing of the stricken ox, but the strong rhythmic breathing of the black horse.

The tinker's eyes suddenly opened, wide with terror, and looked into mine. They were pale gray-blue, like my father's, and they recognized me. He drew a hard breath, shuddered, moaned, and died, just like that, looking into my eyes.

The tanner and the cobbler felt him shudder and laid him down in the street in his blood and looked down at him.

The tanner raised his big dark hands and pushed the helmet more firmly onto his head and the cobbler crossed himself and looked sadly up at me, and the sight caused a chill to run down my back and the hair at my nape to stand up.

I shook it off, gathered the black in my hands. Giving him my spurs, I was off again.

Down the street the black carried me.

To the Saint Aignan Gate he bore me and through the gate, with the multitudes of people streaming in, leaping aside from under the pounding hooves and some stopped and staring at me and some turning and following me back out of the city. Out and out into the open rolling lands he carried me, and on and on towards the sounds of the booming cannons.

As he bore me out of the city, to the place where I had recently ridden with the Duke of Alençon, I remembered that this horse, this most magnificent and most powerful horse, was not the black one the King had given me, but the one the Fair Duke had gifted me with at Chinon, after watching me on the jousting field.

The one from the King I had lent to a young knight in my train, Joseph Cadieux, who, with his twin brother Pierre, had followed me from Nancy. Their father, a knight in the service of the Duke of Lorraine, had only had one horse to give them, a black, which he had given to his eldest son, Pierre, who had been born three minutes before Joseph.

I had lent Joseph mine from the King, that he and his brother both might ride and upon matched blacks. I thought of the boys then and of how proud they would be to see me upon my black: Twould make it seem as if they rode blacks because I did, as if they had the wealth to choose.

24, The Field of Death

In the recently tilled and planted land before the English fort at Saint Loupe, I found, already in full bloom, a field of death.

The fort's guns were firing, spitting balls of lead and sprays of small shot across the gentle rolling farmland, where the people of the city had gone to taunt the soldiers with news of the arrival of the French army. As the army had laid at rest, the folk had gone forth, in a celebratory mood, and full of wine and happy spirits, had shouted at the walls and brandished their makeshift weapons and warned the occupiers of war in the offing.

The English and Burgundians had not found their comments amusing and so had commenced to fire their guns upon them. Some of the army, hearing the reports, and being eager for the fight, had charged to the fray and assayed to take the fort by its main gate. But the fort was strong. Its back was to the river, the field before it open and without cover.

As I rode out across the battleground, I saw townspeople, and French soldiers, and some mounted French knights, many killed already, many more wounded and most fleeing. Some were trying to rally the fleeing, and all was in turmoil and confusion.

I rode out, the black splendid in his speed and his grace, and showed myself to the people. The cry went up, *"La Pucelle! La Pucelle!"* and those fleeing turned and followed me, like a rag-tag procession. I heard shouts and cheers and felt their lives behind me, those pulsing, glowing, full-flushed lives shifting from terror and dismay at once to hopefulness and jubilance.

They ran, through the fields and along the banks of a small water-ditch, holding their weapons high, to follow me back into the fray. Joining them were the ones who streamed back out the city gate, all those bright lives, those hearts full of hope, those mortal bodies racing out to the exposure of cannon-shot and barbs and arrows.

All along the walls of the fort the guns roared, belching smoke, showering sparks, and sending balls to greet me. The young grain in the fields was just showing green on the brown earth and was now being trampled by horses and men and destroyed by shot.

And now by me, I thought, as the great iron-rimmed hooves of my destrier pounded and churned the deep soft soil, lifting up the newly sprouted seeds.

And the folk who followed me?

Many of them would spill their hot blood into this dark fertile soil. The labor and lives of men and women was once again being laid waste by war.

Oh France, I thought, dear beautiful France, when will this pain and suffering end?

Please, God! Let it end!

Please, *Jhésus et Maria!*

Please, both *Marias,* the Mother of Christ and the Mother of Christ's Children, I beg You, let it end with me!

25, The Headless Horse

I guided my black towards a man trapped under a fallen horse.

The horse was a rust-colored brown, with a flaxen tail that had a darker streak down the center of it, and as I rode closer, I saw that it had no head. It had fallen onto its hocks and knees, its neck down and the bloody end of it in the dirt, without its head. I glanced left and right and did not see a head anywhere. The man who rode it was sitting sideways off the saddle, one leg caught up under the horse.

I could see the long pointed toe of his sabaton, the armor of his foot, sticking up from the opposite side of the horse's belly. My brother and I had once laughed upon seeing a knight wearing such long pointed toes upon his armor, we had thought it a foolish fashion then and I could see now how very foolish it was.

He was a knight, a wealthy knight, in a yellow and red

weasel-trimmed tabard that covered his cuirass, and he had a yellow-plumed helmet with an open-billed gilded duck as a crest and a visor that swung open like a window on a hinge.

That visor was open now, his face peering out, red and angry, and he was yelling at some men on the ground around him to get him out from under this horse. The visor was swinging on its hinge, opening and closing, and making a squawking sound.

I almost laughed at his predicament and his comical helmet and the way his visor slapped shut on him and swung open as he was yelling at the men and tipping his head from side to side to get the visor to swing out of his face.

A gun boomed from the ramparts of the fort.

The blast of air that buffeted my cheek told me a ball had been fired in our direction. I turned and saw the ball strike the ground, sending up a plume of dirt, and then bounce away, almost striking a group of townsfolk.

Looking back at the scene around the fallen horse, I could see the men were running away, trying to get as far as they could from the target that was made by a knight in a colorful jupon and a sun-glinting golden duck upon his helmet trapped under his headless mount.

I spurred my black after the men and reached to pull my sword from its scabbard. The sword would not release from the cloth-of-gold-covered scabbard the monks at Fierbois had made for it.

It was beautifully ornate but completely impractical.

One-handedly, as I had one hand on the reins, I tugged and yanked and finally freed it. I charged after the men, brandishing my sword and admonishing them to return and help to free the brave knight of France.

One of them I spanked with the flat of the Sword of

Saint Catherine as a mother might spank a child with a spoon. The man stopped on his heel, spun, and looked up at me.

"*La Pucelle!*" he cried, and then he waved his arms and shouted the names of his friends and, *"La Pucelle!"* and the men all stopped running and turned to stare at me.

When they saw who I was, they came back and they gathered about the dead horse. The knight fumed at them, calling them lowborn cowards and slink-away dogs, but I silenced him with a hard look, and he, realizing suddenly who I was, stopped his complaining.

The English on the gun were fast reloading. I could see them swab down the barrel and begin packing in another charge.

"*Dépêchez-vous,* you men of France!" I said, and the men grabbed parts of the horse and began to tug and push, trying to roll the horse. The knight screamed in pain and cursed them for fools.

His long pointed toe was sticking up, wrapped around the horse's belly, so as they tried to roll the horse away it was like to break his foot at the ankle.

"Here, take my sword," I said to the man I had spanked, "and use it to cut off that toe."

He reached up and took it, jumping away quickly as my black tried to sidestep and barge into him. His gray eyes met mine over the blade of my sword for an instant and his eyes were full of wonder, and a strange kind of delight, as if we weren't in the middle of a cannonball-strewn field but in a field strewn with flowers for a May Dance.

I smiled at him and said, "Mind you cut off only the toe of his shoe and not the toe of his foot," and he smiled, a bit wickedly, like it was a shared joke of old friends. Almost like he was my brother and we were in Domrémy laughing about the silly rich people that passed through our village. Then he pursed his lips and went to his work.

I moved my spinning mount off a small distance, trying to calm the beast. I paced him in big calming circles.

My black had a habit of trying to barge over and trample men on the ground, or reach out swiftly and bite them. I turned him in loops this way and that way at the trot, watching over my shoulders to see what the men were doing.

The knight was yelling again and the man was striking at his foot with my sword, trying to cut, smash or break away the armor that was trapping him.

Finally, the men all gave a great cry of triumph. The man held sword and toe aloft in a show of pride. His friends all cheered as if the man had defeated a great enemy and not just a knight's foot.

There was a boom and another ball flew across the field. I was further away and could see this one, it struck very near the knight at a low trajectory and bounced away. The men almost fled again, but I rode back in and got their attention.

"You have done good work," I said to the man, receiving my sword back from him. "Now, we have a few minutes before our foe can reload the cannon. We shall free this brave knight of France and we shall take this fort."

As I said this, I turned and looked towards the fort.

A small multitude of French was gathered there, trying to knock in the gates, and more were streaming across the field to join them.

I instructed the men what they must do.

I sheathed my sword, took the black's reins in both hands and backed him close to the knight where he sat trapped.

Two of the men I told to grasp the knight under his

shoulders while at the same time looping one arm each under the barding around my destrier's rear. I had to be careful that.he not kick them, for when I backed him up to them, he thought he was supposed to kick, having been trained to it, I presume, by the Duke of Alençon, and they had be careful not to be kicked, for even though I did my best to convey to the horse that I did not desire him to kick Frenchmen, he still desired to kick anyone that came near us, or strike or bite them.

And I told the knight to spread his arms slightly to give the men a place to grasp him under his arms but not to clamp his arms against his body so hard that he pinched under the steel plates of his armor the fingers of the men who would grasp him.

At the same time as I was using my horse and the men hanging on to the barding to pull the knight free, the other men were to pull the headless horse by its mane, tail and the arson-plate of its saddle in the other direction, trying to pull it up over higher up onto its folded legs so that the knight would slip free as I urged my horse forward. If I had had a rope, I would have made my proud destrier into a plow-horse and dragged the body of the headless one off, but I had no rope.

Soon, the duck knight was freed and the men were exultant. I thanked them all, telling them that it was for men like them that I donned my armor every day.

They started up the cry, *"La Pucelle, La Pucelle!"* and I rode away to see what other good I might do on this battlefield.

As I looked back, I saw the knight pull his sword and begin to hack away at the long pointed toe of his other sabaton. He had said not a word of gratitude to any one of us. At least he had learned what a stupid affectation were those pointed sabatons. The cannon boomed again and the ball struck the headless horse dead-on, splattering the knight with blood and entrails. He tripped and stumbled as he ran away, having not quite completed his modifications. I did not know who he was, nor did I ever find out, but I knew he would survive this and many battles.

For he would die of an eye canker that would grow and burrow into his brain.

But not for many years.

He would be a great-grandfather when this happened, his grandson and great-granddaughter sitting at his side as he perished, tending him with love and concern.

I had to bewonder me if he would have ever told them the story of how *Jehanne, La Pucelle* and a handful of peasants had saved his life at Orléans.

26, A Cloud of Doves

Gilles came across the field fast on the gray warhorse, riding bareback as if he had been born to riding. He had brought my standard, for he knew I liked it with me and had a fear, however superstitious, that if I went into harm's way without it, I should die, or that something terrible should happen. The possibility of dying was only part of the fear, however, for, by dying, I should fail to achieve what I had promised and perhaps that was the terrible thing I feared.

My constant companion looked like an avenging angel as he rode, his golden-brown hair streaming behind him, his eyes narrowed in the wind, the gray horse in full career, and the white banner unfurling behind him.

His beauty made my breath catch in my throat. I could easily have believed that Archangel Michael was riding to my aid. I saw how he rode, with no saddle, no stirrups to give him purchase or aid his balance, and I was proud of him.

He had his strong legs hiked up around the horse's barrel, his bare toes tucked in behind the gray's elbows, and one hand gripping both reins and a thick hank of the gray's mane. In the other hand he gripped the banner-staff, the banner whipping wildly in the air above him, and had the butt of it wedged behind the heel of his foot lest the wind prevent him from holding it vertical.

He was a brave boy to ride into a battle thusly, and a friend to me, and my constant and trusted companion.

I let out the breath I had been holding and breathed in a long slow one, thanking God for this breath, this life, this boy.

Gilles reined the gray to a stop in front of me. The standard swung forward with a rustle of silk and the tip fluttered against my cheek, touching it in exactly the same spot as Michael had touched me upon giving me my sight, the spot that still burned. The black shied from the rustling silk, side-stepping away from it. I spurred him to a stop.

The black reached out its long neck and snapped its teeth at the gray and the gray shook its mane, reared up and settled back down, the boy from Le Moineau sitting easily in place.

"Gilles," I said.

"Jehanne," he said, and we looked at each other.

We actually smiled.

For a moment one could almost imagine that we had ridden out here on a lark. But then a cannon roared and there was a cry of pain from someone struck down, and shouts of defiance and anger, and we were brought back to the fact that we were in the field of death.

Gilles twisted at the waist and looked about us.

To his left were the high stone walls of Orléans, *La Porte* open and pouring forth people like a stream unloosed from a dam. To his right was the main gate of *La Bastille de Saint Loupe*, a large cluster of Frenchmen now rallied in front of it, trying to break the heavy oaken doors with woodsmen's axes.

Archers on the ramparts above them shot arrows and barbs upon them and the men were trying to hide from their deadly range by flattening against the wall. Only a few had shields and held them over their heads, two or three men trying to shelter under a single shield. Knights on horseback were circling their mounts and shouting commands at the footmen and brandishing their swords and maces at the enemy, threatening what they would do to them once they gained ingress.

It looked like a hopeless attempt but the French bravado had returned to a nation that had become heartsick and war-weary. There was no holding them back.

Many were shouting, *"La Pucelle!"*

Gilles looked back at me. His eyes were very blue, reflecting the color of the sky. His cheeks were flushed a rosy pink from the ride.

I could tell his heart was racing for I could see the blood in the veins of his throat, I could feel in my own vessels the pounding of that blood, feel in my own chest the squeeze and release, like a strong fist, of his heart.

His wild, free and wonderful heart, the heart that loved me.

"Gilles," I said, wanting to say something but not knowing how to say the words, the words that were on the tip of my mind.

He cocked his head and his bow-shaped mouth quirked at one corner and I had to content myself with just the sound of his name.

"Gilles," I said again.

There was uproar at the gate. Several Frenchmen were on the ground, struck down by something dropped down upon them, and a knight had been hit by an arrow in the eye-slot of his helm and was in the act of toppling from his horse, and the English or Burgundians were cheering their successes.

The gray rose up under Gilles and tossed his great head, the yellowed mane shaking back and forth.

"Follow me, Jehanne," the boy said. "There is a thing I know about this place."

The gray leapt into the gallop, coursing away across the field.

I followed, the black charging fast to catch up, but the gray was fast when given his head and I could not close the distance. I was watching the great hindquarters of the gray, the flash of its shod hooves and Gilles' hair bouncing on his shoulders, my banner streaming behind him, as we skirted the fort, the sounds of the uproar at the gate receding behind us. We left the tilled field and entered another, where the un-harvested grain of last year stood in tall ragged shocks or lay in thick lodged patches upon the ground.

My black's hooves ripped through the yellow grain, sending a spray of seeds before us and a cloud of birds rose with clapping wings right under us. They were white birds, and gray and rose-pink, and I saw that they were doves, wild doves of the field, a whole cloud of them.

Their wing-beats made breaths of air brush my cheeks, and their wingtips struck notes on the steel of my shoulders, like tiny gentle arrows. A few soft feathers drifted off of them, tumbling down around me like butterfly wings.

The river came into view, wide and green. There was the fortress's flank, the high wall of heavy timber rising almost from the water's edge, and a thicket of willows, and hidden away there in the shadows, a boat-landing dock, and nearby in the wall of the fort, a small dark doorway whereby supplies could be brought within after being unloaded on the dock. I glanced upwards to the ramparts.

No faces peered down at me.

It was quiet and still on this side of the fort and cool in the shade of the trees in the lee of the great fortress wall.

Gilles had reined in near the willow thicket and slid down from the gray.

He leaned the banner against the trees and stepped silently to the doorway. With a smile at me, he placed his shoulder against the wood of the door and levered the handle of the door.

The door swung open.

27, *La Bastille de Saint Loupe*

So, we took Saint Loupe.

It was an easy thing once we knew how to enter.

I rode back to the front of the fort, waved my plumed hat. I don't even remember how it was that I was wearing the hat. I had worn it when riding out to greet the army, for in addition to my banner, it helped people to identify me from a distance.

Had I had it on even as I prayed to Saint Michael?

Or did Charlotte put on me as I left the house, after helping me on with my arm protection? She liked me to wear it, saying it gave me good luck, but that was because she liked the style of it, its low flat crown and wide brim edged with white plumes that curled all around the edges, and bounced gaily with every movement. It was too fancy for my taste, a country girl who had worn straw hats and linen bonnets all her life, but people expected me to dress the part now, of a grand person, and so I let them dress me as they would.

I had worn the hat so often in Orléans, eschewing my helmet which covered me so much that folk could barely see my face and could not see my hair at all, that I was instantly recognized by it. Now, waving my hat and shouting, I attracted the attention of the French who were assaulting the main gate and many of them came at the run.

Gilles showed them the little door and they streamed inside, taking the occupiers by surprise, and after some fierce fighting, taking control of main gate from the inside and flinging it open. The mob of men outside stormed in and we could hear shouting and screaming and the clashing of weapons. Englishmen and Burgundians were flung over the ramparts and French faces filled with elation took their places, peering over the walls.

By this time, Gilles and I were riding back and forth in the open field, he carrying my standard aloft and me waving my plumed hat. Frenchmen were still coming from the city and many were knights and soldiers of the King's army. They followed their countrymen inside and joined in the fighting.

A group of mounted English bolted out of the open gate, they having been preparing themselves to exaunt and make a direct assault upon us, thinking to finish us off, before we breached the fort by means of Gilles' secret door.

They tried now to flee, making a break for it through the throngs of French who had come to my call, and were hacked down by French knights. I saw among these French knights The Bastard and *La Hire* and Xaintrailles, and Alençon as well, and their swords were bloodied and their armor specked as they then rode up to me, raising their visors to peer at me.

They were, to a man, shocked and surprised beyond expression that *La Pucelle* had attacked and taken the

Fortress of Saint Loupe without consulting or including them.

"What have you done here?" The Bastard said through his bared teeth as he approached, his large and hairy face bulging from inside the helm which seemed too small to contain his great head.

He pressed his destrier hard up against mine in that way he had of trying to intimidate me, but my black turned sideways and barged his shoulder against the dark knight's steed, bringing down one great hoof upon the other's pastern, causing the beast to squeal in pain and spring away.

"What have I done here, you ask? I have given France her first victory in some time," I said, though as I spoke the words, I knew it was not my gift but the gift of those who had followed and had faith in me, who had suffered and died on this field, and the gift of the rabbit boy who knew the secret of the fort's weakness.

"You could have spent the King's Army on this small purchase," the dark knight complained. "This fort is not critical to the siege of Orléans."

"This fort is ours now," I said, "and its taking is critical to the lifting of the siege in the hearts of these who took it."

As if to confirm my observation, voices raised in cheers issued from the interior.

"And this is only the beginning," I went on. "We shall take each fortress one by one that surrounds this city."

The killer Xaintrailles smiled his sharp-edged smile at me and blew a hard breath out his flaring nostrils. He was happy because his face was streaked with blood and his hand was wet with it as it ran down over the quillions of his sword.

He liked hearing that his opportunities to kill were about to increase.

"Now, let us go and see what our labors have won us," I

said.

The Bastard frowned, *La Hire* loosed a barking laugh and a string of invective, and the Duke of Alençon smiled at me and gave me a salute with his bloody sword.

We entered the fort as a large body of mounted warriors, first the famous captains and the Duke, then me with Gilles at my side, bearing my standard, and the lesser knights and squires behind. As we rode through the shadowed passage from the gate to the bright interior, I looked at Gilles and raised my eyebrows at him in a question which he could read as well as my unspoken words.

He leaned his head closer to my armored shoulder and said in a soft voice, "I walk out along the river in the evenings sometimes, Jehanne, and I see things."

I nodded.

My approval was in my little smile and the gratitude in my eyes, which he could read as well.

A boy like him, simple and barefooted, could travel under the noses of the enemy and hardly draw a glance. This was a good thing, and a useful thing.

I would think upon this.

Objects were dropping into the courtyard of the fortress from the levels above as Frenchmen ransacked the place. Just off my right shoulder, as I rode out of the shadows into the sunlight, a crossbow dropped from above onto a great pile of crossbows. My horse shied as the thing fell, as it had just missed him by an arms-length.

Two black-barred chickens ran across our path, inches from his front hooves, and next, a man chasing them, his leather apron flapping around his knees.

The black reared and I leaned forward, keeping my balance in the saddle. I heard Gilles chuckle to my left as the staid old gray he rode handled all the commotion in stride, like the old campaigner he was. And commotion there was, for the interior of the fort was a chaos of activity. Men dashed this way and that, checking every space that all the enemy be accounted for. The bodies of dead Englishmen and some of my own countrymen were scattered about.

These were being sorted, the French dead to be born back to the city and the foe to be buried elsewhere. Weapons and supplies were being gathered and piled. The goods would be placed on wagons and brought into the city of Orléans and the fortress itself would be burned after everything of value had been stripped from it.

Someone had presented The Bastard with a group of prisoners, dressed in priest's robes.

The enemy had built this fort around the church and monastery of Saint Loupe and used the labor of the monks to their benefit and their lands to help feed them. The captains were now debating about whether to kill these men as foemen, regardless of their vestments. The opinion of some was that even if these men were French priests they had colluded with the enemy.

I rode over and dismounted, handing the reins to Gilles.

"These men of God will not be harmed," I stated in a loud clear voice.

La Hire turned and laughed in my face.

"They are Englishmen hiding in the robes of priests to deceive us," he said, his language peppered, as usual, with profane words.

I pushed past the big mercenary and addressed the prisoners.

"Who are you men?" I asked.

They said nothing and *La Hire*, laughing again, said, "See, little maid, if they are priests they have all taken the vow of silence, but I think they are English and will not speak and betray their accents."

Xaintrailles, holding his bloody sword, grinned his wolf's grin and said, "I will prick one and make him speak," and he stepped forward.

I reached out my hand and laid it upon his arm.

"Poton," I said gently, "I shall not let you add the murder of these men to the long list of indictments against your soul."

The killer stared into my eyes for a moment, and lowered his arm. He wanted blood, more blood, and he wanted it badly. I could feel his desire for it boiling like water in a closed pot, it was the strongest desire he had, and it was a torment to him not to have it fulfilled.

Yet, he lowered his arm, and looking in my eyes, he said, "As you wish, *Pucelle*." And I knew I had won a victory here that was as great as the taking of Saint Loupe.

I turned and faced *La Hire* and *Le Batârd d'Orléans*.

"These men will be brought to me at the House of Boucher. No one is to harm them. Their bodies are in my keeping. Their souls, like all of ours, are in the hands of God."

And at that moment, looking at all those faces, those faces which turned to look at me, those bodies, ragged and dirty and beaten and bloody, those of the captives and those of the men who held them, those faces and those souls and the deaths that would befall each of them, I thought then of my own soul, my own body, my own death which would befall me as surely as it would come to each of them.

I could see their deaths, every one of them, but I could not foresee my own.

I could not know what would befall me, *Jehanne, La Pucelle*, though all of History now knows of it.

How could I know?

How could I know that I had seen it, indeed, seen it in the flames of my first remembering?

And how could I know that though I kept those captives in my own house, close to my heart, fed them with my own hands from my own board, how could I know that though I protected their bodies, risked my safety to protect them, that they were in fact my enemies, and that they would gain strength under my protection, and that they would escape from my keeping and slip away and join the ranks of my foe?

And beyond that, who knows, but only God, whether they, any of them, would be among the men who, but less than a year from this moment, would drag me from my black, kicking me and pulling me by the hair and smiting me with their hands, the very hands that I had placed bread in, would bring me from my friends and companions into the cage which would be built for me in the fortresses of my enemy?

At that moment, I said, "Their bodies are in my keeping. Their souls are in the hands of God," and I meant it.

Their souls are in the hands of God.

May He keep them, and may He forgive them their trespasses against me.

28, The Cathedral

Our boot heels rang loud as we filed out.

The spurs of the knights jingled as they raked the flag stones.

I was among the men, all the captains of France, all their knights and squires and the pages and followers, the priests ahead of us and the novices behind, with the incense-sensors swinging and billowing pungent plumes of blue smoke that reminded me of cannons, and the droning of the male voices that filled the great vaulted spaces above and around me. I was jostled by the mailled and armored bodies of the warriors, a girl among men.

As I walked, my boots ringing with all the rest of the boots, I was looking at the back of The Bastard, that broad back below the great mailled shoulders, the shoulders upon which could be laid the deaths of so many men and upon which had been laid the hope of all France and from which shoulders that hope had fallen upon me.

I was looking at the heavy leather belt at the small of his

back from which he hung his many weapons, the tatters of his torn jupon which bore his symbols and his colors, now stained with blood.

We were brethren now, he and I and all of this bloody company, for we had been in battle together and had fought our enemies together.

Like it or not, and no matter what I thought of The Bastard, and *La Hire*, and Xaintrailles, and all of them, they were my brothers now. We were warriors together, warriors of France, and so bound one to the other, with bonds stronger than any I had known with my true siblings. We each wore the badge of blood on us, the blood of our foe, the color of our kinship. Though I had shed none, I was spattered with it also.

We had prayed and been prayed over by the priests and now were processing through the stony vaults of the Cathedral to the out-of-doors, where low sunlight slanted between the buildings and lit the stones of the square and where a fountain bubbled water from the River Loire and where my boy stood holding my horses.

I passed between the columns, approaching the doors flung wide, watching the world open before me as the heads of the men in front of me dropped lower as they descended to the street.

The Bastard's head, bared like all of ours, was large, with the skin around his neck rucked up by his gorget and the little curling hairs at the back of his neck sweat-matted and tangled, the hair of his head close-cropped in what the men called a "helmet-clip," and a small balding patch at his crown which I had never noticed. His hair and beard were dark brown with gray creeping in throughout and I realized that despite his bluster and his forceful nature, he was feeling his age.

He was no longer a young man and had been fighting for France his whole life. Still strong, still powerful, still commanding, but getting older every day.

A fighter all his life, still fighting.

I bewondered me if he bewondered him, when, if ever, there would be an end to fighting.

Did he desire an end to fighting?

What would he do if an end to fighting came?

I could not know his mind, though I knew some of his thoughts from time to time, could catch glimpses of them like swimming cormorants winging through deep water.

I knew he bargained with the Burgundians, but why? Did he have friends among them? I did not think so, for he had been imprisoned by them once for two years and his memories of that time were bleak. Had he ever honestly tried to ransom his half-brother, Duke Charles, or did he want the man to remain a captive of the English, that he, The Bastard, might have the rule of Orléans?

He was a cousin and childhood friend of the Dauphin but had been exiled by that King and held for a goodly time in disgrace, though he had been allowed to return to favor in return for war service.

Did he hold any grudge against the King?

What did the dark knight truly want?

The weapons of us all were piled to the right of the door and each man turned and bent to retrieve his own, the sunlight glinting off of plate and maille and sword and dagger and axe and mace and that which each picked up, the hafts and metal sticky with congealing blood and in need of cleaning. The men picked up their weapons and moved off, each to his own place of rest.

The Bastard mounted his steed and rode off towards his house, a few of his companions following him.

I stopped for a moment on the top step and the ones behind me parted and flowed around and past me like water.

I looked out to the fountain and met the eyes of my boy, there holding the reins of both my horses, the gray and the black. The gray was standing stolidly, his eyes half-closed, and the black was lifting his muzzle from the water and turning his great head to look at me, a stream of water sluicing from between his teeth and wetting the stones.

Gilles, holding the gray's reins in his left hand and the black's in his right, looked at me, his eyes conveying all the love that the world ever held and all the joy at beholding me that the hearts of men had ever felt since the very birth of time.

I paused then, took a deep slow breath, and looked at him. He was ragged-looking, in bare feet, and in the same torn and dirty peasant's clothes in which he had run away from Le Moineau to follow the girl who wept across France. I would have to remedy that, find him something better to wear, and some shoes, though I doubted he would wear them.

He liked to feel the earth beneath him or even the stones of the streets.

He was so wild.

Would the world ever tame him?

I would clothe him, as I had fed him, but it would wait just a while. I had a plan and it required he keep his ragged peasant garb a while longer.

I stepped down to the second of three steps and before I could descend to the first, a man dashed across in front of me, holding two squawking chickens in his hands. I recognized him by his flapping leather apron.

He was the same man who had run in front of my horse in *La Bastille de Saint Loupe*, chasing the black-barred hens, and the chickens he carried now were the same hens he had chased then, and he ran right to left in front of me, just as he had run right to left at Saint Loupe as I had ridden under the raised portcullis.

I thought this was a strange thing, but then I realized that life is full of such patterns, repeating patterns, and only God knows what they mean.

But this compelled me to stop short, which caused me then to turn, and turning, to see my confessor, Father Pasquerel, who had come with me from Chinon at the King's request, and the Archbishop of Rheims, sent by the King to oversee the religious needs of my army and to spy upon me, standing upon the top step under the great arched doorway of the Cathedral, the sunlight illuminating them and bringing to my eye the contrast of the rich dark brown of the friar's habit of Pasquerel and the bright colors and gold trim of Regnault's vestments, and the contrast between the men, Pasquerel humble and kind, the Archbishop proud and cruel.

"Father Pasqueral," I said, "I ask you to spread the word among our soldiers to give thanks to God for the great victory this day and to tell them from *La Pucelle* that the angels have said that within five days the English shall relinquish this city and be gone."

The friar smiled and nodded to me, his hands folded in front of his brown robes, but the Archbishop scowled as if I had said something foul.

I said to them, "Tomorrow is Ascension Thursday. I shall not make war nor shall I deck myself in armor. At the first hour after midnight I should like to receive the sacrament of the Eucharist in my chambers at the House of Boucher. You,

Father Pasqueral, shall please to attend me, and I shall remain there alone in deep prayer throughout the day."

De Chartres made to protest, as I knew he would, thinking that he himself should be the one to serve that high office, but I turned from them and stepped off into the street, and reached for the Sword of Saint Catherine which was alone now, leaning in the light against the wall of the Cathedral in its cloth-of-gold scabbard.

I picked it up, the holy relic that was most powerful in France, that sword that would give me all victory, and held it loosely in my hands, letting the Archbishop get a good look at it, and I saw in his eyes that he coveted the sword, wanted it for his own, was jealous beyond bearing that it was in my possession, a simple country girl, and that he would at some time try to get his hands on it, and my eyes met his for a long direct stare before I hung it from my belt and walked away to join my rabbit boy.

Gilles' smile as I approached and the way his eyes glinted, let me know he had seen the look of consternation upon the face of the King's cleric.

"Come," I said, as I took the reins of the black from his fingers, "we have some things to do."

Gilles did not need to say it.

His face told me that he would follow me anywhere.

29, Guyenne

I felt the rough hempen rope as if about my own neck.

They had brought him out upon the wall, his feet right at the edge, and put the noose about his slender neck, tightening it down with the knot behind his ear. The youth's narrow face, capped by a flurry of sand-colored hair that blew about in the wind, the bright blue eyes over-arched by pale yellow brows, his well-shaped mouth, the lips trembling now, were all familiar to me.

Barely had Gilles and I reached *la maison de la famille Boucher* when I had heard the clamor and rode to the English fortifications at *La Porte d'Orléans*, where my enemy Glasdale leered at me from the wall.

He stood, holding the elbows of the lad and shaking him, as if to push him over the edge. The young man with the sandy hair was terrified, his heart pounding and the vessels in this throat blue with the hot desperate blood within them.

I stood below, looking up, the angry bees buzzing in my

head. Ambleville stood beside me, his hands curled into fists.

He was my Herald, my first of two given me by the King. The lad with the rope on him was the second. Ambleville was a solid strong man in his forties, not much taller than me, with short gray-black hair and thick black eyebrows that almost met in the middle. He felt about the lads like a protective father and this one, Guyenne, as his favorite lad of all. He kept a small gang of youths about him, whom he used as messengers and runners, and whom he said he was training for the next generation of royal heralds.

Guyenne was one he had trained, raised as his own son and brought before the King to be made a Royal Herald and given the jupon with the King's badge.

As such, he was meant to have protection under the law, protection against kidnap, ransom or punishment. And yet, these English had taken him captive when he had come to them to deliver the second of my letters.

Now they waved him in front of me at the end of a rope, threatening to drop him from the side and so destroy the young life that was in him.

I knew they would not do so, not because I had faith in their compliance with the law that protected messengers in war-time, but because I could see Guyenne's death every time I looked upon him, as I could see the death of all I looked upon, and I knew it was not now, and not thusly.

Yet, I was angry, so very angry, because I hated the terror that was in the boy, and I hated the evil in men that can so wantonly cause such terror, and for what?

To dishonor me, to flaunt their disregard for me?

What cared I for their disdain?

I was sent of God, I was touched by an angel.

I was not as they thought me, a vain girl, a child of man

that needed their respect.

I did not require their respect.

I required that they heed my message, that they leave this land, that they obey the word of God.

France was not theirs and they must leave.

Now they wanted to play these games.

Terrorize my people and make mock of me.

The English laughed as they shook Guyenne and made him fear for his life. They wanted to see him weep and beg, but he bit his lips and stood upon the edge with as much dignity as he could maintain.

He wore the King's badge on his breast and upon his shoulders. He would not dishonor his King with tears and pleading.

He would not dishonor me.

Glasdale saw me in the crowd below him. "Here is one of your limp fish, Joan! Want him? Come and fetch him!" he shouted in bad French, but using the English pronunciation of my name that makes it sound harsh and cold. He shook and goaded Guyenne even more, smiling at me.

I turned on my heel and pushed my way through the throng of Frenchmen, not wishing to fuel this fire.

Father Pasquerel was behind me, his face grim and his gray eyes sad. He had penned for me the third and final letter that was required to give the occupying forces fair notice to vacate before the final act of war was meted out.

Ambleville was at my side.

He reached for the letter but I stayed his hand.

"I shall not lose you as well, *mon ami*," I said to him.

There was an archer near to me, one among many, but I recognized him as I passed by.

His name was Richard and he had ridden with me from

Vaucouleurs in the small company given me by Squire de Baudricourt. I had not seen him since the day we arrived at Chinon.

Again, life's strange coincidences made me stop and turn.

His face lit up under the dented helmet he wore, in joy that I had known him.

"Good Richard," I said, "take you this message and tie it to your arrow. Deliver it by bow-shot over the ramparts."

He took the letter and wrapped it about the arrow shaft.

"I beg you, try to not kill Commander Glasdale," I said.

Richard smiled grimly but obeyed, shooting the arrow in a high arch that landed well away from any of the English.

"Here is news!" I shouted to Gladsdale, and heard only in response the jeering voices of Englishmen, "News from the whore of the Armagnacs! News from the whore!"

I shook my head as I mounted the black, trying to take the blur of tears from my eyes. They will say I wept at the insults of the foe, that I was a tender-hearted and pious girl who suffered under their foul invective, but that is not why I wept.

My heart was broken by the knowledge of all the killing I would do.

I rode the black back to the House of Boucher, with Gilles upon the gray at my side.

The law was satisfied.

I would have no mercy upon them now.

30, Crossing the River

The dark shape bobbed towards us in the dark.

The morning was chill and the sun had not yet risen to begin burning away the damp mist that hung over the river.

The boatman, his white hair visible like a small cloud floating in the dark and misty sky, stood over me, manning his long rudder, gripping the shaft with hands gnarled and boney.

I lay in the bottom of the boat, trying to not be seen on the chance that someone was watching, yet I lifted my head every once in a while to look about. I saw the dark shape bobbing in the water. It came closer, but was it moving under its own power or by the push of an unseen current? I could not tell.

I thought it might be an otter, out for early morning fishing, the way it shone in the gray light, like an otter pelt wet with river water.

I glanced to the bow where Gilles was lying below the

gunwales like me, and I caught his eye and gestured at the thing, a smile on my lips because I thought it was a playful otter. I saw his eyes find it, his brow furrow in examining it, and his mouth frown when he determined twas no otter.

I turned and looked back at the thing, just as it drew so near as to bump against the boat. I leaned out a bit to see it and recoiled in horror as I saw it was a man, naked, dead, and long in the river, for the skin was peeling away and layers of it fanned out in the ripples on the top of the water.

It floated past us and disappeared into the darkness.

We landed on the south side in a copse of willows on a secret beach which our handy boatman told us was only known and used by loyal Frenchmen, and we had likewise embarked from such a secret place on the north side.

He knew full well who I was, though I was dressed in some of Charlotte's clothes, the most old and ragged of which I could find in the bottom of her wardrobe. I thanked him for his passage of the river and let him know we would be returning in the evening dusk and should hope to find him here waiting with his boat.

He touched my shoulder gently in the way a grandfather would touch his grandchild, and said, "Do you be careful, *Pucelle*, here are many dangers for any French girl, and much more so for you. Do not approach the English too closely or I fear the result." His breath puffed out white in the chill air, and his eyes looked rheumy and sad.

"We shall be careful, I promise you," I said, "as should you, *Grand-père*, for I think you shall have English company today as well," and Gilles and I clambered up the steep bank and found the trail the boatman had told us of, which led westerly along the southern bank of the River Loire towards where the English had their forts.

31, Ascension Day

History tells that I spent the Thursday of May 5th of the year Fourteen Hundred and Twenty-nine in solitary prayer after having received Holy Communion in the wee hours, or alternately, that I received the sacraments, prayed and then spent the day making the rounds of the army, extolling all the soldiers to make confession, receive Communion and pray with me.

I find it strange how all the world seems to know what was in my heart and what I thought, and felt, and how I acted based upon the words of a few who were there, many of whose presence I was not even aware of at the time, and many whose statements were written down long afterwards, when their memories, if they were in fact there, would be faded like an old tapestry left out too long in the weather.

I can tell you with surety that I did not spend Ascension Thursday in prayer, but in spying.

Gilles Le Moineau, my crafty rabbit boy, my constant

companion, and I crept along the foot paths and hidden animal trails of the riverbank, which zigged and zagged among the dense thickets of tall brush, between stands of water trees, and up and down the steep buffs of the valley. We avoided, if we could, the wagon roads where the horsemen of the English army would travel, and we stayed quiet and listened if we heard any human sounds or sounds of horses.

He was dressed in his peasant rags and my borrowed clothes were none so fine, a plain linen dress and pale green kirtle that was fraying at the hem, a woven brown shawl that had seen better days, and shoes that were finer than the rest of my costume, being of a tattered gold braid over worn red velvet. The shoes were mostly hidden by the dress. I wanted anyone that did see us, to think we were simple people, only villagers and inconsequential.

We spied first upon the English in *La Bastille de Saint Jean le Blanc* on the shore adjacent to *Île-aux-Toiles*, the island in the middle of the widest part of the Loire. It was fairly quiet in the early morning, as we sat upon a high bank over the river in a dense patch of arnica, shivering in the chill as the sun crested the earth and cast its first warming rays over France.

We sat there, our legs swinging in time to one another, his leg just missing mine as mine swung forward and his back. I liked sitting there with him, just quietly, timing our legs so that we almost, just almost touched each other.

The mist began to break up and the river came into view in patches and the fort appeared, ominous in its strength, surrounded by gray water.

We craned our necks like curious herons looking for a frog or little fish. Some standards of the English colors snapped from poles on the highest towers. We knew from having been on the river that was always a breeze or a wind in the river canyon.

A few English sentries paced the wall, but they could not see us, or if they did, they seemed unconcerned. We were far enough away, in any case, that the dark green foliage of the arnica, about whose new yellow blossoms some early-foraging bees were buzzing, probably shielded us from view. But as the light grew, and from our vantage point, we could see some new activity beginning in the fort's interior. Men were piling barrels and boxes in the center, and someone's voice could be heard calling out orders. We craned our necks the harder.

"They are packing it up, Jehanne," my constant companion said.

"Yes, they are," I said. "I bewonder me where they plan to go?"

"Most likely to *La Barbacane de Saint Augustin* and thence to *Les Tourelles*," Gilles said. "The loss of Saint Loupe has them feeling like a rabbit soon to be flushed from his hiding hole. They would rather leave before the hunter comes and join the warrens of their brethren, where their sheer numbers will give them courage."

"Hmmm," I said, looking at the face of the boy from the village of Le Moineau, he who was wise in the ways of creatures of the field and of the forest.

Men are not so different from the beasts.

His golden-brown brows made a hard straight line over his eyes which were a green to match the leaves of arnica, and he said, "Yet, strengthening this place would seem a better course than retreating from it, I should think. Were I in command, I would bring several more hundreds here, and some more cannon, for this position sweeps the island as well as the river crossing and the boat landings. There is room here for an army to gain a good foothold. You would think they would want to prevent that."

I smiled at him, which made his eyebrows raise in curiosity and his mouth spread in a grin.

"What?" he said.

"You," I said. And I was proud of him, of his mind, and the way he saw things clearly, as I did, for all that he had said was all that I was thinking myself.

"I bethink me you are right, Gilles. Let us go now and have a look at this Barbican of Saint Augustine."

We slipped from the riverbank and, ducking under the bushes and pushing through the tangled brakes of vegetation, we found a narrow track to follow westward.

32, A Grand Old Oak

The little shoes were soaking wet from the dew in the grasses. Those grasses made a swishing noise as my dress pushed through them where the long stalks leaned inward over the narrow track.

I looked down at my feet as I walked, Gilles behind me, and saw the toes of the gold and red shoes, dark now with dew, moving in and out of view under the equally damp hem of the kirtle. There was an open space, circular in shape, upon the top of each shoe, through which I could see part of my toes, not the toe-tips but the part between the joints. I did suppose it to be an affectation of fashion but I thought it annoying how the holes brought the water down inside the shoes and made my feet even colder and brought little grass seeds down to poke me between the toes.

I was thinking on this when I raised my head to look about us.

The land opened up from a steep place to a bit of a sloped meadow and at the highest point of the meadow stood a grand old tree.

I stopped short and Gilles, who must have also been looking down at his feet, almost bumped into me.

It was a beautiful tree, an oak, with its old dark green leaves shining in the morning sunlight and the new leaves of this year just budding out, and its heavy curving thick limbs creating a high broad canopy above its straight and very thick trunk, and it reminded me so much of the Faery Tree of my childhood that I found myself drawn to it.

I stepped off the little trail and began to make my way through the tall un-trampled grasses of the meadow towards it, hearing Gilles' tread and the swishing of the grass as he followed me.

Halfway up the slope, grasshoppers or locusts began to fly past me from behind and I knew that Gilles could not contain his excitement and was about to run past me and make it to the tree before me.

And he did, passing me on the run, sending the insects before him, and raced to the top of the slope and flung himself down in the tall grass in the lee of the tree.

When I caught up to him, he lay on his back, with a piece of grass between his teeth, and the grass all flattened down under him and oak leaves, old and brown, scattered about him.

He was so wild!

He was so beautiful!

How I wanted to just fall down upon him and let him wrap his arms and strong legs around me and roll me over and over in the grass! And let him take my face in his hands and kiss my cheeks and my chin and my forehead and my lips. And kiss him back, all over his face, all over it, while laughing and looking in his eyes, and then finally, kiss his lips.

Like a girl, a simple country girl, might do with a boy, a boy of her own age and who she might want to marry one day.

Instead, being *La Pucelle*, I did not do these things.

Knowing I could not touch him, nor let him touch me, I lowered myself to the grass at his side, careful to keep a distance of some inches between our bodies. He smiled at me, his smile saying as ever that he accepted these things as a necessary part of being with me and that he wanted to be with me, would always choose to be with me rather than apart from me, and that, difficult and unsatisfactory as it was, it was the price he would pay, and willingly, to be near me and to be my love.

So, we lay there, breathing, letting the morning sunlight play over us and the insects buzz in the grass and the small birds flit between the leaves of the tree above us and a very light breeze move those leaves and cause the light to glitter into our eyes, without our saying or doing anything, other than just be there, as if there was nothing else on earth we needed to do or could be doing.

The tall grasses around us created a bit of a wall and we could see out into the greater world only by rising up onto our elbows and looking out over the top of the grasses.

I did that once and saw the rolling French countryside of the Loire River Valley and the rocky bluffs to the north and the wide winding blue river and the banks of dark green trees along the drainages and giving away in the distance to the dense forests of Sologne.

From here there was no sight of Orléans, or bastille or bulwarks, or battlements, or any construct made by man.

Only God's creation was visible and it was beautiful.

"It is like we are in a country all our own," I said to Gilles and he said, "Whenever I am with you, I am in a new and better country, Jehanne." I smiled at him, because I thought it funny that I had, somehow, a new and better country following me around, as if a country were like a puppy and might follow on one's heels. Of course, it was a new and better country I wanted to make of France, once we had got the English out.

"A country all our own," I mused.

"Oui," he said, "and I never want to leave it."

He got a mischievous look in his face then and gazed up into the boughs of the great oak. He leapt to his feet and, with a smooth high jump, he grasped the lowest branch between his hands and swung his body upwards until he could wrap his legs around the branch and soon, he was climbing up into the canopy.

I sat up and craned to see him.

I was giggling with joy at seeing him rise so high and with such nimbleness.

He is so wild, I thought, would the world ever tame him?

"Come, you should climb, too," he said, beaconing, and I shook my head and said, "Oh no, that is not for me. The back of a horse is as high as I should want to go."

But just at the moment, he turned his head sharply and rose up onto his knees on the rough bark of the limb he was on and, peering out through the leaves, he caught sight of something that he had heard. He lifted a finger to me to silence any words I had been about to say and then he looked down at me and gestured that I had better climb, whether I wanted or not, for men were coming and we knew not what men they were but they were most likely to be our enemies.

I sprang as quickly to my feet as I could, in the gown and kirtle of Charlotte Boucher, and I did as he had done, leapt up and grabbed a branch and, using all of my strength, I pulled myself into the tree.

It was not easy, but fear lit a fire under me, so to speak, and I was in the tree and on a very high bough beside him in a moment. From there, our hearts pounding and the blood storming in our ears, we looked out.

There was a road, as it turned out, that ran along the hills just a short distance from this grand old tree and upon the opposite side of the tree as did our small track, the one we had been following.

A body of horsemen and a body of footmen were making way upon that road, the horsemen in maille shirts, steel gorgets and shoulder-pieces, and helmets with the visors raised up, girded about with swords and carrying long spears, and the footmen in studded leather jerkins and open basinets upon their heads, with pikes braced back against their shoulders and small axes at their belts. The men marched fast to keep pace with the knights, and the knights were talking amongst themselves, though it was hard to hear what they were saying.

They were speaking English, which I expected for I didn't know of any French company that would be abroad in the English-occupied territory in such small numbers. The clopping of their horses' hooves and the jingling of their equipage muffled and broke up their sentences. I caught the words Talbot and Fastolf; names of Englishmen, one a General who had command of *La Bastille de Saint Laurent* to the northwest of Orléans and the other, the most famous war-captain of England, sent here to lead the English tyrant's army to greater victory, against me.

Fastolf was said to be on his way, though no one knew when he would arrive, and he had taken on the power of a myth for all the promise of his coming that never bore fruit.

The knights were laughing as they spoke of these two commanders and before they rode from sight, heading westward towards *Les Tourelles*, I caught another English word I knew. They spoke of "The Maid," and that would be me.

Gilles and I looked at each other. His eyes were lit by a ray of sunlight which found its way through the foliage, and were an amazing shade of yellow-green. I looked and looked into them and found them so beautiful. His tangled curls of golden-brown hair hung all about his shoulders and the light beard fuzz upon his cheeks was glinting in the dappled light as he turned his head and leaned forward to peer after the disappearing English. He braced his slender hands against the rough deep-grooved bark of the tree and bent his lithe body forward, watching them as they went from view and from hearing.

"Could you tell what they were saying, Gilles?" I asked.

He nodded his head, still watching the road. "Fastolf is coming to join Talbot this day. They shall join forces at Saint Laurent. Together they shall smother Orléans like a small fire with a wet blanket," Gilles said.

I smiled. "You hear so well. How is it you hear so well?"

"I have a rabbit's long ear," he said. "Many days and nights in the field and forest."

"What was it they said about me?" I asked.

He sat back on his haunches, shaking a small brown leaf from his hair. His bow-shaped mouth quirked and eyes lowered. He did not want to say.

"What?" I insisted.

He sighed deeply and said, "They said they would then light a small fire under you and cook you slowly."

This made him angry and his brows drew together, and the skin of his face became taut over his cheekbones. He looked away so as not to let his anger show to me or his fear of the future.

"They have to catch me first," I said, trying to make light of it.

His mouth quirked again.

A part of the tree was caught in his hair, hanging down alongside his face, a feathery pollen-covered thing about as long as my finger. It bobbed against his cheek and I reached to pull it off.

He saw the movement of my hand and turned his head abruptly towards me. My fingers struck his face just below his cheekbone and my knuckles froze instantly and an icy wave ran up my arm, through my shoulder and up my neck into my head.

I saw in my mind the waters close over me and bubbles rising and the murk of the river bottom stirring up and clouding my vision and I felt in my body the punches to the belly by something hard and sharp and heavy that drove me downward under the water and held me there, striking over and over until the breath was driven out of me and the river water flooded my mouth and my nose and my lungs.

My head, neck and shoulder struck the ground and the breath was indeed driven out of me and I opened my eyes to look up into the sun-spangled leaves of the tree, the dark gray limbs twisting into the air, patches of blue sky beyond, and the startled face of my rabbit boy looking down at me.

"Jehanne," he said, "are you all right?"

I was all right, now that the vision of his death had left me.

He landed on the earth beside me and bent over, all

concern in his face, but did not touch me, though I could see how much he wanted to.

I drew a deep breath, trying to shake the vision from my mind. That is a long time from now, I reminded myself, a very long time. I stood up, shaking my clothing into place.

"A long time," I said to myself under my breath, "a long time from now."

"What is a long time from now?" Gilles asked. I had forgotten about his long rabbit ears.

"Nothing," I said.

"I hope you don't mean the English threat to burn you," he said. "I won't let them burn you, now or ever."

I wanted to take his hand. I wanted to embrace him, be embraced by him.

But I couldn't.

"No, I don't mean that," I said.

And we walked.

Westward to spy upon *La Barbacane de Saint Augustin*.

33, The Stone Fence

We followed the tracks of the armed company that had just passed, staying far enough back that if one of them turned, we should not be seen.

The day was lovely, the sun now high overhead, warm and bright, and the flowers and grasses bursting with life.

Tiny yellow flowers sprouted everywhere, making the hills golden-green, and little blue butterflies with yellow spots along their wings flitted everywhere, even against our faces.

And there were birds, small ones of every type, both plain and colorful, with elaborate many-noted songs and simple chirps and trills. I looked at my constant companion and he looked at me and we both smiled so broadly as to make our cheeks ache.

We were both thinking it: A country all our own.

But before we knew it, the road dipped, rose, and dipped once more, then snaked its way between two small hills and wound its way down the high bank, where stood *La Barbacane de Saint Augustin,* with its gray walls and arrow-slits, rising from the beachhead.

Gilles and I had not wished to be trapped in the pass with nowhere to escape to, so we had not followed the road between the hills. Rather we had gone off the travelled way and climbed up one of the hills, crested it gingerly and traversed the slope to a place where once had stood a farmstead or perhaps a wayside inn; nothing now but stone foundations, charred wooden beams lying in a jumble, and a fallen chimney.

As we walked reverently past these, we entered what seemed the remains of a stable-yard and some low broken-down stone fences along the edge of the river bank, which appeared to once have prevented livestock from tumbling over and landing upon the river strand. From this sorry place, this lost enterprise, this ravaged home, yet this so-very-advantageous vantage-point, we stooped behind a stone fence to spy upon the English.

The grass was dewy still along the base of the stonework and my feet were wet.

Under my flimsy velvet shoes, I could feel more bits of stone and mortar which lay hidden in the grass, there was charred wood there too, from the buildings that had been burned, and I knew with sadness, that the English invader had laid waste a thriving business and home of a once-happy family. I could see their once-smiling faces and then their flesh-denuded bones, which also lay somewhere under these grasses.

I was distracted by these thoughts but when I looked at Gilles, at his narrowed eyes and the set of his jaw, the way his body bent forward to peer down, his smooth strong hands gripping the rough cap-stone of the fence, I knew that he was taking in all in; the fortress, the way it was constructed, the entrances and exaunts of it, its height and its size, how many men it could contain and what their fighting positions would be.

He was examining the way the high looming walls that were the ruins of the old Convent of Saint Augustine had been used to create a bulwark for The Barbican constructed behind it. He saw the heavy wooden drawbridge spanning the gap between the fort and *Les Tourelles*. And the many arches of the bridge extending north to the city, and *La Guérite du Saint Antoine* and the *Île-Belle-Croix*, with narrow cat-walks going to gun-placements, and men camped on the island, making it look from here like a busy ant-hill.

His quick eyes and clever mind were taking it all in, cataloging each part and committing it all to memory.

No need to discuss it now.

I knew that later, when we sat together in the stable under the House of Boucher, with the warm breath of the gray campaigner huffing down upon us and the animal's great hooves shifting the straw about us, we would discuss what he saw and how he thought it could be used and together with his observations and my tactical thinking, we would find a way to destroy the English hold on the city of Orléans.

But for now, we watched and we saw activity of our enemies and we noticed where the greater strength in men and cannons were concentrated within that construct of towers and forts and walls and walkways.

We saw a changing of the guards upon the ramparts and several groups of riders and foot soldiers leaving and entering by the gate, and we saw a boat coming downriver, the flowing white hair on the head of the rudder-man telling us that it was our friend the boatman, and we saw him draw his craft up under the footing of the central tower of the bridge, where a portal to the inside must be, and men come out, walking down some stone steps, and unload something from the boat and carry it back up the steps and inside.

And we saw our friend push away with a long oar and set a sail and begin to tack his boat back upriver.

We said nothing, but only watched, and Gilles looked at me, with a little smile on his mouth, for he was thinking that I had been right about the boatman having English company this day, and we kept our hands, me my right, and he his left, very close to one another upon the cap-stone of the fence, so close I could feel the heat of him.

And at one moment, we moved suddenly, for we had heard a sound and thought to be discovered.

We moved suddenly, ducking our heads, and our fingers touched. There was that rush of icy cold that raced up through my hand and into my forearm, and I was about to jerk my hand away from him before I should be made to faint as I had when I touched him by accident in the great oak.

But then, to my surprise, the cold retreated back down my wrist and settled into the palm of my hand, where it pooled for just a half-second than dissipated, as if sucked right out of me by the chill of the stone under my hand.

So, the cold having retreated, I left my hand near his, in fact I pushed my hand closer and he lifted his and laid it over mine. We stayed like that for a long time, like two ordinary people. I felt the cold coming in and I felt it leaving through my palm into the stone, and it went no further than the bones of my wrist.

Nor I did not see his death, his watery horrible death and

I did not feel it in my body as I had done before, when it had caused me to topple from the tree.

We looked into each other's eyes.

He was smiling, knowing that we had discovered something.

Something important.

A way, perhaps, to touch each other.

34, A Terrible Encounter

"They have landed some boats in the cove," Gilles said to me. "I could see them from there."

He had gone off a little ways into the trees so that he could have some privacy to attend to a personal matter of the body. Twas a place where a tributary came down to the river from the hills and, though the stream was a small one, trees and shrubs grew thickly all along its length, and its waters emptied themselves into the river within this little cove.

"Show me," I said, and he led me to the place from where he had viewed the boats.

I looked down from the bank upon a tiny cove which was hidden from sight of the fortress by the curve of the river and the jutting headland. Indeed, there was fleet of vessels there; some oar-boats and some pole-barges, and a good pile of faggots, brush and logs. This was a place where men chopped up wood brought down from the little forest, from whence to supply the enemy's fireplaces within *Les Tourelles*.

"Let us go down and take a closer look," I said. "There is

no one about."

We scrambled down the steep trail where I could see men had dragged trees they had harvested. Upon the sandy beach, we examined the boats and barges. Two of the barges were already loaded high with faggots of wood and logs cut into short lengths and split in half, ready for burning. The oar-boats were pulled up on the beach and tied fast against the rising and falling of the currents, their oars shipped and lashed into the gunwales.

There were many footprints and piles of prepared firewood, heaps of useless slash and woodchips, and wedged between the stacked logs there was a large saw and three axes, set there as if to make them ready for when the workmen returned.

"This is another good thing to know about," I said, looking at everything carefully, wanting to commit the details to memory. "We should walk back along the strand and see how this place lies in relation to other landmarks, in the case that we need to return here by another route."

I had the shadow of an idea forming, perhaps placed in my mind by the remarks of the English. There are times, I was thinking, when lighting a small fire is useful.

Gilles grinned his broad mischievous grin at me, mayhap knowing what I was thinking, and headed off down the beach with bold sure steps.

I followed behind him, struggling a bit in my girl-shoes, into which the sand was pouring through the opening on the tops, filling the spaces between my toes. At the end of the cove, the high banks of the river rose above us and left a narrow space between the wall and the waters of the River Loire.

Through this narrow space I followed my rabbit boy,

watching his bare feet powering through the deep sand, flicking back rooster-tails. I found myself admiring his strong legs and the curves of his buttocks through the fabric of his linen trousers, rounded and strong, his little bag, containing I knew not what, dangling there on its strap, the inward dip of his spine at the base of his back, the nubs of the bones all neatly lined up and pressing against his threadbare tunic, resolving themselves into the arch of his upper back, and there, spreading like the wings of an angel, the broadness of his strong wide shoulders, with curls of his tangled hair falling over them.

I followed him and sighed, like a girl would sigh who loved a boy and thought she might like to marry him one day.

A fist came out of nowhere and struck him on the side of his head. He staggered sideways, caught his balance, and was struck again.

I took two steps more and a man appeared into my view, he with his fists up, striking Gilles. He had been behind a jutting rock and Gilles had walked right into his attack.

Beyond him, I could see the opening-up of another small cove and some other men and a couple boys there, bathing in the shallow waters. Two men and a boy were in the water naked, another man upon the shore, pulling on his clothing. Gilles made a sound like a whimper, and I saw him struck again and he went down.

As he fell, he said a single word and I heard that word.

The other man on the beach pulled his arms through his shirt and came running.

I didn't think they had seen me, so focused were they upon Gilles, and now I was hidden from their view behind the other side of the jutting rock.

Gilles was curling into a ball, for now the kicks were

coming, and his hands and arms were up around his head. I heard the blows landing and I heard the breaths of my boy being forced from his body as the kicks landed and I heard the groans that came with those breaths.

They were beating him.

They were beating him badly with kicks and with punches.

I wanted to stop them, to step out and yell something, step out and make them stop, but I was *La Pucelle* and these men were English and though they might not know me, they might indeed know me. I had let enough of them see me, had wanted them to see me, had made myself quite plain to them from inside the walls of Orléans, dressed in battle gear astride my warhorses, I could not now know which among them might recognize me seen up close, even here outside the walls, dressed in lowly clothing.

I was The Maid of France and they were the English, my enemies, and they were the ones who would be glad to catch me and deliver me to Glasdale and to Talbot and to the soon-arriving Fastolf, and if I was caught, the war would be ended and the French would lose the war and the English would be triumphant.

And I would have failed.

And so, while they were distracted, I did what I must. I put my love of country and my duty above the love of my life.

I did what Gilles had said to do, in that one word that he had said before they forced all the breaths from his body.

I ran away.

35, Breathless

I ran and I ran, fast and away.

I spun around, keeping the jutting rock behind me, and I ran back down the beach, in the narrow place betwixt the wall and the water, and I ran as hard as I could, tripping and stumbling in my haste, my shoes filled with sand, and one of them almost flying off of my foot, and I ran away, away, away.

I passed the woodpiles and the boats and I found the trail and I ran up it, scrambling on fingers and toes, falling on my knees, tangling in my kirtle, and getting up, gathering my skirts and running once more.

I reached the top and broke out of the trees and I ran through the meadows, over the rolling hills, kicking little yellow flowers in front of me and scattering thousands of tiny butterflies, which rose in clouds of blue all around me.

I ran and ran until my breath came raggedly through my teeth and my lips were burning and my tongue was dry and my lungs were hot as cinders.

I ran and ran, blind in my haste and in my fear and in

my leaving of you.

In my losing of you.

By the time I reached the great oak and fell into the grass below its spreading limbs, in the same place that I had lain with you, I was breathless. As if, though I drew hard to fill my lungs, though I drew so hard and so many times that my ribs were cracking, that my lungs were expanding so far that my chest was bursting wide open, they were filled but with nothing.

There was nothing, and I was empty.

36, Weeping

When finally I breathed, gasping wracking breaths like a man dragged up from underwater, the weeping started.

This was not the weeping of the girl who wept across France, the silver tears slowly welling and spilling over smooth seamless cheeks, nor the weeping of someone who sees the deaths of all around her and feels the leaden weights of compassion dropping one by one and filling the bottom of her heart.

This was not the weeping of golden tears while making fervent prayers for the damaged lives of innocent strangers, nor the weeping of ebony tears in knowing that one must kill and destroy one's enemy for that they will not heed one's honest warnings.

This was not the weeping over the beauty of the faces of bright angels, the white-light tears radiating from one's eyes and evaporating in air. These were not the melancholy tears of a country girl lamenting the loss of her simple life and overwhelmed by the great destiny of being the savior of her country.

All of that weeping was like breathing, something done without noticing, like a normal function of the body. The weeping that started now was red and bloody, like a violent death.

It began deep within me, in my bowels, and tore me apart from the inside. Rending and savaging, its teeth shredded my viscera and it rose inside me, like a savage beast ripping and tearing through all my organs, breaking my rib-bones, puncturing my diaphragm, until it reached my heart, my fiercely pounding heart, which it ate whole.

What was left of me was flung down into darkness.

.

37, In the Darkness

My heart was fiercely pounding.

Pounding in my ears, the sound like the fast beat of the drum of an oar-boats' time-keeper. And I was breathing fast, wind whistling in and out of my clenched teeth.

I was in pain.

There was pain all over my body, but I was alive.

Alive and surprised to be alive.

Like a hunted and injured rabbit hiding in a dark place, I was waiting, hoping for enough time to catch my breath and let my racing heart come to rest before I must run again. For the moment there was safety; a bit of safety, perhaps enough safety.

I was crouching on my haunches, darkness above me, shadows behind me, light before me. I placed my hands upon stones to either side of the light, felt the stones beneath my palms.

Whose hands were these?

They were mine, but not mine.

I recognized them. Long, smooth, slender and strong.

The knuckles bruised and some blood smeared upon the back of the left one.

I heard a sound and pulled back from the light. Then, hearing only birdsong, cautiously, I went to lean forward, to put my face into the light once more. A jolt of pain arced though my arm into my shoulder, up my neck. My head hurt, and the side of my face, the places where fists had struck. There was pain in my ribs, my left hip, my right side, my belly, my shoulder from kicks and blows. I felt the strap of my bag slide across my bruised shoulder. I touched it; it and its contents were safe.

I was safe.

So I sat on my haunches and I took a moment to breathe and try to relax the pain, to still my pounding heart and to feel the peace of the world, aside from the struggles of men. There was peace; peace and beauty, and the birds and the butterflies and the trees knew it. The insects in the grass and insects in the air knew it.

All the earth knew it, all but men.

Then I put my head out between the stones and looked from side to side. Outside was a green meadow, spotted with yellow flowers and dark trees beyond. There were stone fences ringing the meadow, and I knew I was in a sheep shed, a long low stone structure with a turf roof that was partly fallen in.

I had seen it in the distance as I had run away from the beach after escaping the men who beat me. Sheep had not been here for some time and the stone walls were broken in places. It was one such place through which I peered.

There was no one about.
I had not been followed.
I was safe.
Now I needed to find my love.
I needed to find Jehanne.

38, Out of Darkness

I came from the darkness to the sound of someone approaching, to the swishing of grass around their feet and to a baby grasshopper that leapt before them and landed on my face. I opened my eyes to the blinding sun and someone stepped into that sun and cast his shadow over me, the sunlight haloing around his head as he looked down at me.

It was an angel, with bright light radiating all about him.

I thought it was Michael and I thought that I was dead and taken to Heaven, for I had been sure that my body had been torn asunder and my heart eaten whole and I had perished. But then the angel dropped out of the sun and landed beside me in the grass and I saw that it was Gilles.

His face was bruised and bloodied and one eye was swollen from the punches. He made a little groan as he sprawled in the tall grass next to me, but he was alive.

And I was alive.

"I dreamed of you," I said to him, my mouth so dry I

could barely even whisper the words.

He raised his eyebrows. "What did you dream, my heart?"

He had never called me any other way but by my name.

I smiled, thinking of my heart and how it had been eaten by the savage beast of weeping. It was strange that he should choose this moment to begin to call me by a new name. He waited for me to answer and I moved my tongue about in my dry mouth and got it to moisten enough to speak.

"I dreamed that I was in a sheep shed and looking out through a broken-down place in the wall," I said. "I was hurt and I had been running and was hiding, hoping to get away from the men who had beaten me."

I looked at him and I saw that he was amazed and that everything that I had dreamed had been the way it had been for him.

"I dreamed that I was you," I said.

"You are me," he said, softly, "and I am you."

We were lying on our sides, facing one another, and there was one tall stalk of green grass growing up between us, upon which my eyes kept focusing, and I would have to change my focus in order to see him not in a blur.

I reached my hand down to bend the stalk away and at the same moment he did the same and our hands touched.

His fingertips grasped hold of mine, the grass between them, its seed-top bobbing above our fingers, and for just a moment I could feel his soul, a bright, vibrant joyful soul, full of love of all things in earth, all things of nature, from the dirt and the worms that tunneled through it, to the things that grew from it, the grasses, flowers, and trees, and the warm-bodied creatures that nested upon it, to the birds that flew in the air between the treetops.

His wild soul, that I could see complete and entire, was so beautiful and so filled with joyfulness, that I was for that moment unable to see or feel his death.

But when that thought entered my mind, I drew my hand away, lest that vision come.

"You are so beautiful," I said to him, "so joyful," and saying it, realized that if anything brought sorrow into his life it would be love of me. For I was danger, I was war, I was destruction, I was sorrow.

"I am so sorry," I said, looking at the bruises on his face, the swelling weal over one eye.

He bent down the stalk of grass and looked at me earnestly.

"I am not," he said, "for you were able to run away."

I smiled ruefully. "You are my shield," I said.

"Yes," he agreed. "Yours."

39, Battle Plans

We made our battle plans, Gilles and I, sitting across from one another, our bottoms in the dry manure and dusty straw of the stable, wrapped up in old woolen cloaks against the night's chill, using what intelligence we had gained, what we knew of the nature of men and what inspiration came to us, and my angels, whose glowing faces I could see in the puffing mists that blew from the nostrils of my old campaigner, said nothing to me but only concurred with their eyes, their gentle smiles.

At the house across the city where dwelled *Le Batârd d'Orléans*, other battle plans were being made, around a warm hearth, with wine and meat spread upon a board, and the negotiations and agreements completed that would allow this man or that man to take credit for this part or that part of the battle to come and to leave no credit to The Maid.

I would not be made privy to any of this, but it mattered not, for their plans would not be the ones that came to fruition and their schemes and ambitions would be as chaff on the wind, once my horses were saddled in the morning and my banner unfurled into the air.

I had told my friend, the old boatman, that any boats promised to the English for their use the next day should be withheld and that he should have as many boats and barges, and as many boatmen, gathered before dawn at the secret landing whence Gilles and I had embarked that morning, for I would be bringing a great army to cross the river.

And I had told him that if any messengers came to him with instructions other than these, to disregard those instructions, for they would not be coming from me, unless, perchance, that messenger was Gilles.

It was late, and across the city, the war counsel of the captains had resolved itself into celebratory wine-drinking and feasting, boasting and back-slapping. They could carry on that way all night, pretending to be all agreed and all comrades-in-arms, but I knew that underlying all of that camaraderie there was hatred and jealousy and base desire, bribery and secret plans, and not a little treachery.

Leave them to it, I bethought me.

Gilles walked me to the kitchen door and placed his hand upon the stone of the wall and I laid my hand near his and he lifted his hand and set it on mine and the cold chill death that was to be his entered through the back of my hand, tickled at the bones of my wrists, then gathered in my palm and flowed through my palm into the cold stone.

And I felt the warmth of his life on the back of my hand, the chill of his death leaving the bottom of my hand, and I smiled into his dark green eyes, knowing it to be a good trade.

I gave him my old cloak to add to his for a coverlet.

I did not have to say, *"Bonne Nuit,"* or remind him to

have the horses ready, nor did I have to say that I loved him nor that he should sleep sweetly, for our eyes said all these things.

He closed the door behind me and I went through the kitchen and up the stairs to the room of Charlotte Boucher. Laying myself down naked under the smooth clean covers and rolling over on my side, I imagined myself curled up within the warm half-circle of his body, my legs folded within the strength of his folded legs, my back against his deeply breathing chest, his strong arms wrapped all around me, and my neck receiving the gentle warm puffs of his breaths.

And I slept, so sweetly slept, and dreamed of green fields and wildflowers, in a country all our own.

40, Early, May 6th, 1429

My pages, Louis and Raymond, cried out loudly as I
wakened them in the early hours, demanding that they rise
and arm me.   The whole city was still asleep and so they
wanted to be, they had heard nothing of any intent for *La
Pucelle* to go into battle this day, not from any of the
captains, nor from their squires, men-at-arms or knights, with
whom the boys fraternized every chance they got.   But I
insisted and they got up and, rubbing their faces and whining
like children, they put my steel upon me, did up my buckles
and my billets.   When they were done and had belted my
sword about me, I strode for the door.

"Go back to bed," I said to them, "unless you want to see
a battle."

At that, their pouty faces brightened and they clambered
for their own over-garments and searched for their shoes.

I placed my plumed hat upon my head and picked up my

heavy steel helmet. In my heeled boots I clattered down the steep stairs, made my way through the entrance hallway and pushed through the door to the silent street. In the darkness and drifting mist, Gilles was there as planned, holding the reins of my horses.

Our eyes met. His were a deep sea-green and had a glint of mischievous light in them, like a sliver moon might make upon dancing dark river-waves.

He took my booted foot in his hands and lifted me into the saddle of the black. The horse stood stock still, which was unlike him, as if he knew that the serious work of war was now about to begin.

Gilles grasped a handful of the gray's thick mane and sprang onto his back. He carried my banner furled up tight upon its pole. We galloped off through the sleeping streets of Orléans to seek my army.

I rode into the square before the great Cathedral and circled the fountain. Clumps of men were sleeping along the walls, their gear and weapons piled here and there.

"Warriors of France, awaken!" I shouted.

I pulled the sword of the saint out of its scabbard and held it, the sword that would give me all victory, straight up above my head, the gleaming tip pointed towards Heaven. Men stirred and rubbed their grizzled faces and, looking all about them, finally saw me in the dim light of the coming day.

I spun my horse and rode in a high-stepping trot around and around the fountain.

My destrier snorted and flung his beautiful head, his iron shoes clanging upon the stones with a sound like the hammer of Saint Eloie on the anvil of God, shaping the mettle of men's souls. The sound echoed between the high walls of the

215

square and resounded in the vestibule of the great Cathedral. Everyone was awake now; knights, and men-at-arms, and squires and boys, and all eyes were on me.

"The sun will soon rise upon the day of our victory, warriors of France!" I yelled.

"*La Pucelle!*" a man shouted, rising to his feet, his rough woolen blankets falling about his ankles. *"La Pucelle! La Pucelle!"* others began to shout, until a hundred men or more had risen and, raising their hands skyward, took up the cry. They came forward, surging forward like little curling waves lapping a shore, and made a circle around me.

"Today, I lead you men of France," I said, in a quieter voice, my eyes moving over the crowd, meeting each pair of their eyes, seeing their deaths, seeing their lives, their precious individual lives, seeing the pounding of their hearts. I saw their sweethearts and their wives, the children's glowing faces in their eyes. I saw their homes, both high and humble, their homes built with hands both smooth and hard. I saw their loves, their longings, their desires and their hopes for a better world than this we found ourselves in.

"I lead you men today," I said again, "and we shall go together and make war upon our foe. Our foe shall feel our steel upon their bodies, they shall feel the violence we shall mete upon them, they shall feel our wrath as hot breath upon their necks, and they shall know that we will have our homeland under our dominion once again. We shall pitch our bodies against theirs, our weapons against theirs, our strength against theirs, our determination against theirs and ours shall be the greater."

The men shouted exultantly in one voice and quickly made to ready themselves and each other, donning hauberks and armor and sorting out their weapons. The square filled with other men, come from alleyways and avenues and all parts of the city where they had bedded themselves down, brought to gather to me by the calls of their fellows.

When I marched, I had several hundred at my back.

I reached *La Porte de Bourgoyne*, where Sire Raoul de Gaucourt barred my way, saying it was not yet daylight and he had no order from *Le Batârd d'Orléans* to open the gate before daylight for anyone whether begging entrance or exaunt. This man was the Bailiff of the City and in command of the City Watch, a grizzled old commander and well-respected. He had a small group of his men there to brace me but greater numbers of the men of his command were behind me, ready to follow me wherever I wanted to go.

Behind me were most of the City Watch, plus knights, squires, men-at-arms of the King's army, members of several neighborhood militias, and citizens of the city who would become warriors for France on this day.

I looked up at de Gaucourt where he stood upon the high wall above the gate, torches fluttering in the breeze on either side of him, carving his narrow checks into deep lines of shadow, and said, "I am *Jehanne, La Pucelle*, the Maid of Orléans, and I do not beg, Sir, I command. Open this gate and let us through or we shall tear the gates asunder. In the name of God, I shall pass, and God forgive any man, French or English, who stands in my way, for they make of themselves my enemy."

The Bailiff hesitated and I saw his eyes drift to the growing mob behind me and I could hear the sounds of multitudes of hooves and feet as more entered the open space before the gate and I smiled gently at de Gaucourt for I saw that he had no choice.

The man sighed deeply, then gestured for the gatekeeper

to unbar and swing the gate wide and for his small guard of men to stand aside.

We streamed through the gate in a long narrow procession, close to a thousand men. Once we left the gate and began to make our way over the dark countryside, all were silent and solemn. Nothing but the hooves of horses and the feet of men and the jingle of harness and the soft chinking sound of steel weapons in scabbards could be heard as we went to the secret river landing where the boats would be waiting.

Gilles rode by my side, the gray campaigner stepping out proudly as if he were in a parade. In the hand of my rabbit boy was my standard, still furled, and even without it snapping in the wind, my following grew. I had no captains beside me, no *La Hire*, no Bastard, no Duke, fair or otherwise, no Archbishops.

A peasant brat and a milkmaid led the army of France.

Before we reached the water, two horsemen swept at a canter up the flanks of the procession to join Gilles and me. They rode black horses and were young and vibrant and looked almost exactly alike, with their thick black hair, bright blue eyes, and broad smiles.

Pierre and Joseph Cadieux.

They would not leave my side all that long day.

41, Dawn

We were on the water when the sun rose over the gently-sleeping body of France on the morning of May 6th.

My friend, the boatman, was true to his word and there were scores of boats and barges pulled up all along the shoreline at the designated place and many others lying to in the river and up and down the banks, hiding in the reeds and rushy breaks of the riverbed, waiting their time to come in and take on passengers.

Many of the river boatmen had been told by the English to moor on the *Île-aux-Toiles* and to stay with their vessels overnight so as to be available to the English upon demand, but these men, these loyal Frenchmen, had played the obedient serfs to English rule and had pretended to sleep, but once the dark and silent night had fallen, they had cast off and poled quietly upstream to the secret landing so as to be ready for the French assault at daybreak.

Gilles and I and the two Cadieux pulled our horses onto the first of the flat boats and were poled out into the strong current of the Loire.

As the barge bobbed and dipped over the river waves, Gilles and I stood near each other in between the standing horses, whose great warm bodies swayed back and forth, bumping into us. I braced my hands on the big solid animals, one on the black and one on the gray. It was coming day and the sky was turning from black to slate-gray and the stars were fading.

There was some mist over the river, as there often was. We sometimes passed through clouds of it, cold as an executioner's heart. Gilles looked at me and shivered, he was still barefooted, and wearing only his peasant rags, but had his rabbit-skin hat on his head, the rabbit feet tied up under his chin and the funny ears flopping down. He had one of the old woolen cloaks that was his bed around his shoulders. Faint white puffs were blowing out of his nose as he breathed.

I loved every line of his dear face, the brows that overarched his eyes, the shadows cast by his high broad cheekbones, the sweet curve of his lips, the pale fuzz that grew over his jaws, and the little dimple in his chin. Even in his bruises and with his swollen eye, he was beautiful.

As beautiful as an angel, and I was a girl who had been blessed to see angels, so I was well-acquainted with their beauty.

Reaching out, he placed his hand over mine where it rested on the gray's shoulder. I felt his touch and the death of him that passed though and then went out of me as soon as it entered, pulled down into the body of the big horse.

I looked at our hands, his with the scuffed and bloodied knuckles, with amazement, and I looked at his face and smiled, for it was a miracle that we could touch and that I would feel and see only his life, his life and his joyfulness, not his horrible watery death.

I wanted to reach out and take him in my arms and bring his mouth to mine, to see if I could, while kissing him, keep the death of him channeling out of me through the great living bulk of the horse, and I bethought me it was still dark enough and we were between the big horses, doubtless no one would see us, and just as I thought I might try it, the sun broke over the edge of the world and lit the river and us with a radiant golden light.

We turned our faces towards the light and near us, standing with their matching black steeds, Joseph and Pierre both said, "Ah, so lovely!" at the same moment, just like twins will do. They laughed and I laughed and Gilles laughed and even the bargemen laughed, for indeed it was a lovely dawn and it would be the start to a lovely day if the day proved to be the one in which we defeated the English and chased them from Orléans before that sun would set.

"Let us pray," I said, "that it is the day that we defeat the foe, and that it is a day that few Frenchmen will die."

Right then the boat touched down on the sandy beach of the *Île-aux-Toiles.*

Our war was about to begin.

41, *Île-aux-Toiles*

The island was longer than it was wide and really more of a sand-spit than an island. There were clumps of trees; willows, birch, and larch, and bands of wildflowers and sparse grasses between low dunes. From the island, in the early golden light of daybreak, I could see the high stone walls of the city across the river, the waters lapping at the heavy footings and the towers' copper roofs glinting. I could see, to the west, the nineteen arches of the river bridge, some of them in rubble.

The bridge began at *La Porte d'Orléans*, whence I had ridden out the other day to exchange words with Gladsdale, now closed and barred, and several of the first arches were those that were in ruins, destroyed by the French themselves to prevent the English from crossing and taking Orléans in the early days of the siege.

From the broken arches, it bounded onto the mid-river

island *Belle-Croix*, where stood *La Guérite du Saint Antoine*, the standards of the English snapping high above the ramparts, and there were bulwarks and catwalks all over this island and platforms built to house cannon with which the English bombarded over the city walls.

Thence from the island, there were many more arches joining Saint Antoine to *Les Tourelles*, which stood close to the south shore. Between *Les Tourelles* and the old Convent of Saint Augustine built of gray stones upon the sandy beach, was the wooden drawbridge. And finally, all around the Convent were redoubts, a great Barbican, built by none other than *Le Batârd d'Orléans* last year while I was still tending sheep and milking cows in Domrémy and conversing with angels near *l'arbre de fées*.

How I knew this now when I did not know it yesterday, I cannot say, but I did know it. The knowledge was just suddenly in my head, just as I knew that, despite all The Bastard's efforts in building this stronghold, the English had routed the French in October and driven them into the city, arch by arch across the river bridge until, just before the city gate, the French had destroyed the last arches and let the stones fall to the water, as they retreated inside and barred the gates.

Today, I planned to do the same to the English, corner them in their fortresses and drive them up the bridge arch by arch. Only for them, there would be no safe place to retreat, only the open air and the waters and rubble far below.

Hundreds of my men had now disembarked upon the *Île-aux-Toiles*. The sandy pure-white beaches of the island were awash in a tide of men and horses. One man rode up to me, upon another black horse which he capered and danced in front of me. He wore gleaming armor, all white steel and inlayed with gold. Under the armor, his clothing was velvet and trimmed in the fur of sable.

He raised the visor and I saw the smiling handsome face of the Duke of Alençon.

"My Fair Duke," I said, "*Bonjour à toi.*"

He gave me a little bow and looked about us at the growing army. "*Bonjour, Pucelle.* You have raised quite a host," he said. "Yet I see none of your captains here." He gave an impish smile.

I shrugged. "They will be along presently once they find that the battle has started without them and their army is in the field before they are even out of bed."

Alençon laughed. "*Non,* this is not what they had planned."

"You were at their council then?"

He glanced at me. "Oh, *oui.*"

"How was the wine?" I asked. "And the meat? And there was a small cake."

He paused, his big blue eyes growing wide. "I had none of that cake, but the rest was excellent; wine and meat, and I partook of much of it, today being Friday and only fish."

"Oh, you shall have red meat today, my Fair Duke, and much of it, though it be shall raw and bloody. Keep your sword loose in its scabbard and keep a good watch to your rear, for danger will seek you from there."

He smiled ruefully. "You are a wonder, Jehanne. Sometimes I know not what to think of you."

"Think well of me, my friend," I said, "for I am all good. There is no evil in me. If there ever had been, it was burned out of me when an angel touched me. Right here." I pressed my fingers against the place on my cheek where Michael touched me.

Alençon stared at my face in what might have been reverence, except for that fact that he was a man that held himself unto himself and did not become a follower. He saw the politics in all things and was not swayed by grand speeches about honor, nor promises of riches, nor the rewards of Heaven.

Alençon was for Alençon and he was for adventure and he was, I could see, politics aside, for France. These things I saw in him, I liked about him.

The boatmen had been assembling a floating bridge between the island and the south shore, made of the barges lined up and lashed together. This bridge would bring us right up to the postern gate at the rear of *La Bastille de Saint Jean le Blanc* and avoid the need for a frontal assault upon the great south-facing walls of that fortress. The very boats that the English had been denied for their final flight from this place were now being used to aid our assault against the English now trapped within its walls. Once the last boat was laid in, my men rushed en masse over the bridge and began with axes to break down the heavy oaken gate.

From the walls above, English faces were looking down and the grey-goose-feathered arrows from English longbows began to rain down. Men protected themselves and other men with their shields as they ran across the bridge and, with a great shout of triumph as the gate crashed inward, Frenchmen poured into the fortress.

An arrow struck the sand close by my horse.

"Put on your helmet, Jehanne," the Duke said.

Someone handed me up the helm and took my plumed hat from my hand. I looked down and saw Louis, my page, standing at my side, the reins of his horse looped over his wrist.

I smiled at him, wondering where Raymond was. Then I saw him as well, pulling his horse from one of the barges.

The steed gave a great leap from the boat and landed on the shore; causing the barge to rock back and bump against the one behind it and almost knocking Raymond down. Raymond spun the nervous animal in a circle, jerked at the bridle-bits in the horse's mouth, which caused the horse to fling his head and pull back. Cursing, the boy put his foot in the stirrup, clawed his way into the saddle and rode over towards me, his horse trying to buck him off as he came.

I shook my head.

The boy has no way with horses, I bethought me.

My pages had no armor; only the jupons with the colors of the royal house. They each had a small battle axe and a shield for their arms, given them by the King, a small thing considering the danger they would be in. But they would follow me into battle, untrained boys that they were.

I pushed my windblown hair back from my face and pulled the helmet on, buckling it under my chin and raising the visor, setting it upon its spring-pin. My comrades sat their horses in a circle around me, watching me. There was fierce fighting now in the fortress.

I closed my eyes and the golden sunlight of daybreak reached me through my eyelids and the sounds of fighting came to my ears and images of fighting appeared in my mind. My horse moved under me, stamping alternately each hoof into the soft sand, wanting to be in the fight but respecting the loose rein, and there was a breeze against my face as the chill of the mists rising from the river passed over me.

"What do you see, Jehanne?" asked the gentle voice of the Duke.

"I see men dying," I said, as the tears leaked from under

my eyelids and spilled like liquid fire down my cheeks. "I see men dying that wanted to live. I see little joys snuffed out like candle flames."

I opened my eyes.

Surrounding me on the sand beach of *Île-aux-Toiles*, all mounted upon black steeds like me, bedecked in armor and hung with weapons, like me, were the Duke of Alençon, Pierre Cadieux, Joseph Cadieux. Jean de Metz and Bertrand were soon beside me, their horses as black as mine. Even the horses of my pages were a dark seal-brown, almost black, though I had never noticed that before.

And upon a white horse, whose brown-specked coat was now golden in the morning light, was mounted my angel.

My rabbit boy.

My shield. My boy from the village of the sparrow.

My Gilles. My own one.

They all, save Raymond, stared at me with the same expression; mayhap surprise, mayhap admiration, mayhap reverence, or mayhap, which would please me most, one I might call love.

42, The Shallows

At the same moment that French faces began to appear at the walls, looking down and shouting in exaltation, *"La Pucelle! La Pucelle!"* and waving bloodied weapons in the air, Englishmen began pouring from the front gates and running westward along the shoreline towards The Barbican of Saint Augustine. Some of them were horseback but most were afoot and they struggled on the loose footing of the pebbly beaches and over low sandy dunes clumped with tall bunches of coarse grass.

Alençon made a happy sound and slapped his visor down over his grinning face. His destrier leaped into the air and demonstrated some of his airs. At this, mine did the same. I rode him easily for he was as graceful as a dancer.

The Duke laughed and said, "They are brothers, these two, and trained in my stable. They know all the ways of battle. Let him do as he will this day, Jehanne, and he will slay your enemies for you without you having to do a thing."

I frowned at the thought of killing. "I will kill no one with my own hand."

"So I am to understand, which is why I gave you the best war-horse in all of France."

We rode to the point of the island, where the water parted on either side of it, and splashed our horses into the shallows. The water rose higher and higher but not so high that the horses would have had to swim, which they would be hard-pressed to do with their riders wearing armor. We charged through the river, cold water pouring up and over the striving shoulders of our steeds, and came out on the opposite shore, the great hulk of *Saint Jean le Blanc* at our backs.

In addition to my six companions, all the other horsemen who had unloaded their mounts on the *Île-aux-Toiles* followed me. Gilles unrolled my standard from its pole and raised it, letting it flutter in the river breezes, the white satin and gold threadwork catching the morning sun like fire.

Englishmen were still coming out the gate and, seeing us between the fort and the perceived safety of the Convent, stopped and milled in a circle, drawing their weapons. Some of my men charged them and began to kill them. Other English were past us and running as fast as they could for the Convent. Alençon gave a cry of joy and galloped after them.

My black took off after its brother and Gilles, the twins, de Metz, Bertrand, and my pages, came after me. We splashed into the shallow water of the river beach and ran down the fleeing Englishmen. One man turned and took a swing at me with his sword.

My destrier lifted his powerful left foreleg and struck the man a deadly blow in the middle of his face. He fell back into the water and we galloped after another man, whose back was broken by another blow from my horse. In fact, my steed killed seven men before I even thought to draw my sword. Gilles, meanwhile, rode at my left side, holding my banner aloft.

He bore no weapons but shadowed my every move. He kept the banner always over my head for he knew I had a fear that something terrible would happen to me if ever I went into battle without it with me.

We had cut down the first group of Englishmen that we had come across and, as we galloped further down the river shore towards the Convent of Saint Augustine, splashing our horses through the sparkling waters as if we were pleasure riders out for a jaunt, we saw another group, larger than the first. Pierre and Joseph gave an identical shout of excitement and spurred their mounts ahead.

They were beautiful in the warm yellow light of early morning, two handsome young men in the very flower of their youth and manliness, their armor glinting, their shining swords held high, and the sleek rumps of their black destriers, gleaming wet with water, powering through the lapping river wavelets.

The Englishmen, seeing they could not make the gates of Saint Augustine in time, turned and engaged them, swinging swords and battle axes.

There was a clashing of steel and the grunts of men exerting themselves, the horses screaming defiantly, and the shouts of Alençon as he urged his horse forward to join the fight. Englishmen were falling down in the water and being trampled and pushed under, the water foaming red around their bodies as my knights struck them down.

Pierre and Joseph were fighting in tandem, surrounding

and circling one or two men at a time and dealing blows upon them, crying out triumphantly each time another fell under their alternating strikes. Their excitement was evident in their voices; they had been trained since childhood in the arts of war and had been knighted at age twenty-one, but this was their first opportunity to kill anyone.

My black shook his head wildly from side to side and I let him have his way. He surged ahead, charging towards a knot of English who had gathered back to back, their weapons bristling in a ring of steel. I thought for a moment he might impale himself upon those sharp points in his fever to reach those men, but at the last moment, he wheeled, just out of their reach, and kicked out with his hind hooves, dashing them in the faces and driving them towards Alençon, who had just then stabbed a man in the throat and was casting about for more to slay.

The black horse of the Duke, which was the brother of mine, squealed and cavorted, adding his hind hooves to the slaughter.

Men went down like toys broken by hammer blows.

Even my pages were wielding their small axes, shattering skulls and splitting the helms of those foemen who wore them. Each group of men we ran down, we killed, and advancing further along the beach, more fleeing men appeared.

We were about halfway between Saint Jean and the river bridge and dead men littered our path, bleeding in the sand or floating and bobbing in the shallows.

More horsemen of my command had caught up with us and many of my foot soldiers. The main body of my army was still crossing the river in boats and barges. It was a lengthy task to bring them all over, for they were many and there were but a finite number of boats, which were returning to the north shore as quickly as they could to pick up more. My army was advancing along the shore towards the English forts like a long snake with a growing tail.

My comrades and I were the head of the snake and we were now close enough to the river bridge that we could see the English all along the ramparts of *Les Tourelles*, and even on the walls of *La Guérite du Saint Antoine* and we could see that they were angry, for they were shouting and shaking their fists.

I knew they wished they could fire their cannons at us but all their guns were pointed towards the city and we kept running down their fellows and slaughtering them in the shallow waters of the Loire, as they watched helplessly from their fortresses.

I turned in my saddle, looking this way and that, taking it all in, my heart swelling with the excitement of it all. Finally, after all the waiting, I was waging war, I was driving the English before me, I was raising the siege of Orléans, as I had promised to do so many months before, as my angels had told me I would do. Behind me on the beach, my foot soldiers were hacking at the bodies, letting out their long-pent-up anger upon men too dead to feel it.

A fresh group of English was chased out upon the shore, that had been hiding somewhere in the thickets along the riverbank, and was surrounded on the beach.

Horsemen swirled around them and cut them into pieces.

The riders spun their horses, looking for more, then seeing me, my banner flying above my head, they came on in my direction, three knights with their squires. They drove their heels into their horses' sides, pushed them to great speed, then reined their horses to the stop before me, kicking up sand and water in a spray.

They raised the visors of their helmets and grinned boldly at me, their sword-tips dripping blood. I knew them, they rode usually with The Bastard and I had often heard them in his company laughing at jokes I was not privy to.

One was Gilles De Laval, the young Baron de Rais, grand-nephew of Sir Bertrand du Guesclin, who had been the most famous knight in all of France and a man whose exploits I had heard of and admired all my life. De Rais, seeking the notoriety of his great-uncle, would acquit himself well in the battles to come and would one day be made the Marshall of France and carry the Sword of Charlemagne in grand procession behind King Charles. Yet when I looked at him, black-haired and handsome, I saw not the paragon of chivalry that his great-uncle had been but a man whose soul was like a dim light seen through a small window, glimmering from a room full of terrible yearnings. And of course I saw his death, an horrific one of slow strangulation and painful burning, long and tortuous.

Yet, strangely, I shed no tears for him, as I did for all mortals. It was his victims I felt compassion for, though I knew not who those victims were or would be.

His noble companions were Sir Jean de la Brosse, an honorable man who was to be my companion at many subsequent fights, and a young knight I knew only by the sobriquet Robinet, but whom I could tell was a man of adventure and mischief. All three dipped their heads to me in a sign of respect.

"*La Pucelle*," de Rais said to me, his smile as brightly-polished as his gleaming gold-inlayed armor, "we humbly ask your permission to kill your enemies." He lifted his sword and cocked his head ruefully at it. "Although we admit to having indulged ourselves already."

"Kill as many as you like, Baron de Rais," I said. "They have been thrice warned and thrice have failed to heed me."

Robinet flashed a boyish smile with crooked teeth and said, "So the season is open on all Englishmen? The time for private pardons and secret dealings is over?"

"There never was a time for such things with me," I stated. "I answer only to God and God does not make deals."

Robinet and de Rais laughed and de la Brosse met my eyes with an expression of sadness. I saw there, like a lengthy tome, all the things I did not know and did not care to know.

"And where is The Bastard of Orléans, your friend and commander?" I asked. "Does he not know we are fighting a war? Or did he have other plans for this day?"

De Rais chuckled. "He might be fighting a war with his own aching head this morning for he cracked the seal on many a jug of wine last night. He did have plans for this day but these were not them. I am sure he shall be along presently."

"If you see him, tell him *La Pucelle* gives her regards."

I turned the black's head and cantered off, Gilles and my banner at my left side, for I could see that my companions were at the place on the river shore where the beach narrowed down and where Gilles and I had been surprised by the enemy firewood-cutters the day before and Gilles so badly beaten.

I could not allow my men to ride their steeds through that narrow defile and it was no place to bring an army through.

I called, "To me! To me!" in as loud a voice as I could.

One by one, they each, Pierre, Joseph, and Alençon, de Metz and Bertrand, turned their blood-streaked helmets towards me. I waved the Sword of Saint Catherine in the air and Gilles swirled my banner with the lilies of France, with the names of *Jhésus* and of *La Magdalena*.

My boys, my bloody boys, gave a shout and they reined their destriers about, letting the last few English escape past the jutting rock like rats through a hole.

They, and my pages, galloped back to me, their horses swirling around me in a mass of sleek black horseflesh.

43, A Wound

Pierre and Joseph, looking just alike each other, the black hair plastered across their foreheads as they lifted their blood-dripping visors at the same exact moment, smiled with bright white teeth, with their blue eyes flashing, and began talking at once, telling me about the men who had nearly taken their lives but who they had slain instead.

They spoke at once, using many of the same words, except for each made his brother the hero who had saved his life and then they began to pleasantly argue the finer points, each telling of his brother's prowess and quick skill with a blade.

Alençon watched this with amusement and said, "In my family, brothers try to do each other in, not aggrandize each other. This is a novelty."

I slid the sword of the saint into its scabbard and looked at Gilles. He knew what I was thinking, that he was familiar with this place and the trails up from the beach to the higher bluffs and the best way to approach Saint Augustine. We needed to pause and let more of our army draw up before we assaulted the structures at the end of the river bridge and this was not a proper place from which to stage a mass assault. Gilles sidled his horse closer, with a mind to discuss it with me, and my black shook his mane wildly and snapped at the gray. The gray threw back his head, rolled its eyes, and barred its long yellow teeth.

"Jehanne! Look, you are wounded," Gilles said.

I felt it then, a sharp stinging pain on my left foot. I looked down and saw the slice in the leather of the boot where a sword or axe-blade had passed through. I wiggled my toes and could feel that one toe, the second smallest, was cut almost clean away. Blood was dripping out of the gash in the leather.

Gilles glanced about, thinking to hand the banner off to one of the twins so that he might dismount and tend me.

"No, Gilles," I said, "it is nothing much. And there are things to do, if we are to succeed this day. And this is not now a safe place to linger long."

We would have to gather our forces and approach Saint Augustine upon the broad road and make a frontal assault upon the Convent and Barbican around it. And the enemy knew we were coming now and would be ready for us.

The pleasure jaunt along the beach was over and the hard work of fighting an entrenched foe would begin. But behind me, near *La Bastille de Saint Jean le Blanc*, I had a sizable army and the day was still young.

Also, I had not forgotten the hidden boats and their cargos of firewood and I was thinking now how they might be used.

I reined my horse about and began to ride back the way we had come and my troop of horsemen came with me and the footmen saw us coming back and turned about as well.

My foot was hurting but I would be alright as long I did not need to walk.

44, Attacked

We were about half of the way back to Saint Jean and I was scanning ahead, excited to see how many French had made the crossing, how big my army had grown, when there was a shout from behind.

I turned in my saddle.

The foot soldiers, who had started in front when we first turned back but who had now fallen to the rear because of the faster pace of the horses, were receiving arrow-shots. Several were down, writhing in the sand. Before I knew what was happening, Englishmen appeared above the beach on the bluffs, some on horses, others on foot.

Five of them appeared suddenly behind us and a man in a studded jerkin swung a pole-arm at Alençon.

He barely avoided having his head swept off, ducking just in time as he pulled his sword free from the scabbard. He ducked another swing as the tip cleared and he brought the sword around in a sweeping arch, catching the wielder of the pole-arm across the forehead. Alençon yelled with anger as the man shook the blood from his eyes and swung again, trying to take out the Fair Duke so that he could get to me with his long spiked and axe-headed weapon.

Joseph and Pierre had the other men surrounded and were dealing with them as effectively as they had dealt with many other English that morning, and Alençon, on the second swing of his sword, knocked aside the shaft of the pole-arm, side-passed his horse towards his enemy, and cleaved in the man's head.

Arrows were landing in the sand all about us now and Alençon moved his horse next to mine and stood in his stirrups, trying to protect me from flying death.

We began to gallop. I did not want to leave our French footmen to their fate but I was given no choice; my black matched his brother stride for stride as if Alençon held the bridle, which he did not. I tried to turn the horse and go back but he seemed to be under other orders than mine.

Likewise did all my companions stay with me, Gilles of course, and the Cadieux twins, Jean de Metz and Squire Bertrand, my pages Louis and Raymond, and de Rais, de la Brosse, and Robinet, who had joined with us. There were other knights and their squires also, about twenty-five or thirty strong, and now we were retreating as fast as our horses could run, gathering up my straggling army like the rolling up of a long strip of braid.

Beside me, at the gallop, *Le Beau Duc* glanced back.

I could tell by his eyes that what he saw was not favorable. There were things I just seemed to know, because my angels put the thoughts into my mind, and other things I wish my angels would have told me earlier.

One of those was that, which I knew clearly and suddenly now, from the look on Alençon's handsome face, the garrison to the west, the one called *La Bastille de Saint Privé*, upon hearing the army of France had crossed the river in the early morning (how did they know this?), sent troops to support the English in *La Barbacane de Saint Augustin*.

Those troops had just arrived at the moment my bloody boys ran the last survivors of *La Bastille de Saint Jean le Blanc* through the narrow defile.

Angered by the tales they heard from these survivors, they had called to their fellows inside The Barbican of Saint Augustine, who had watched much of the slaughter from their walls. These English, incited by what they had seen and by the encouragement of their reinforcements, had sallied from their walls, joined the soldiers of Saint Privé, and given chase to us. Now we were the ones being routed, for the river beach was no place to make a stand, with the water to our backs and we all stung out along it.

Our only choice was to fly and try to join our main force at the boat landing and hope we did not get cut off from them. I and my companions had been the head of the snake and now we were the tail. The tail was now in danger of being cut off.

In which instance, it would the head cut off.

Me, *Jehanne, La Pucelle*, being the head.

45, The Dark Knight

But that was not to be.

Our destriers were fast and we caught up with more of our soldiers and knights, whom we then surpassed, and, reabsorbed into the body of the French army, I soon was safe from capture. My party had returned to the shadow of the great Fortress of Saint Jean, where a great host was gathered, some still disembarking, and still the boats went back for more. Breathless and excited, we splashed our steeds back through the waters at the point of the *Île-aux-Toiles*, and came out upon the white island, dripping water and running blood.

My boys, my bloodied boys, surrounded me in a laughing, gasping, smiling mob. Even Raymond now looked at me with love, his little battle-axe running red along its broad edge.

The Fair Duke and the Baron de Rais bracketed me on either side, sheathed their swords at the same moment.

"That was smartly done, *Pucelle*," said de Rais.

"Yes," said Alençon, "more English killed this morning

than at Saint Loupe, and more killed at Saint Loupe than in the six months preceding."

I was about to give them, "*Merci, Beaucoup*," but at the moment, *Le Batârd d'Orléans* appeared in front of me, fully armored but bare-headed, pushing his big ugly horse up into the face of my black. His horse was not wet, nor sweaty, nor bloody, and so it seemed he had just now gotten it off of the boat.

"What have you done here?" he demanded, much as he had done outside *La Bastille de Saint Loupe.*

I was willing to pardon him his rudeness, for he had only seen us routed, he had not seen us killing English all the way to Saint Augustine, but he went on, spitting fury and venom, like a coiled viper. "You foolish girl, you country trollop! You have no idea what damage you could do. You act without thinking! You know nothing of war!"

And so he went, sounding much like my enemies.

Behind him, the faces of my boys had gone from jubilant to furious, as they listened to the great man's diatribe. He was the son of a Prince, albeit a natural one, and the cousin of our King and the half-brother to the Duke of Orléans. He had a well-known sobriquet but I had given him another, secret one. I called him the dark knight. And his darkness was what I saw now, his face, hidden in eyebrows and beard, was dark and menacing as thunderclouds, his mood as dark as a grave. His inner workings, so strange to me, were dark and mysterious.

He was known as a French patriot, a great warrior and a skilled commander, but in my presence, he had seemed only an angry man, an ineffectual man and conflicted. Dark were his ways, and wicked and self-serving at times, but I did not think he was evil. Sometimes fervent, sometimes reticent, he was a man so very difficult to understand, even for me, compassionate and gifted with an angel-given sight as I was.

I let him finish.

He did finally and backed his horse a pace. He looked about and his eyes met the flashing eyes of Alençon, de Rais, Robinet and the other knights. He noted their blood-streaked armor, their missing helmet plumes, their breathlessness and their buoyant demeanors.

Behind him, *La Hire* and Xaintrailles rode up, having also just disembarked. Xaintrailles had heard The Bastard yelling and he had a sneer on his face behind the dark knight's back as he met my eyes with his killer's gaze.

La Hire was grinning as he put his helmet on over his head of wild unruly hair and raised the visor.

"You've had some fun, have you?" he asked de Rais, and the Baron said, "I have killed more English in the last half an hour than I have in a year, and yes, it was fun. You should join us, we were just about to go another round. Weren't we, *Pucelle?*"

"*Merde alors!*" said The Bastard of Orléans and he scratched at his short-clipped hair and he cocked his head to one side and he smiled. "Were we? *Pucelle?*" he asked me, with irony.

"*Oui, Batârd,*" I said. "We were."

The Baron de Rais said, "Jehanne was just telling us we must wait for your arrival and, now you are here, we can put into place the second part of her plan."

"Is that right?" the dark knight said.

"Yes, it is," de Rais said. "You, Bastard, are chief to its success. You are to lead us towards the Convent of Saint Augustine, driving this skirmishing party of the enemy before us. When we reach it, you will take your companies towards the west to kill any English assault from Saint Privé and to discourage Talbot from leaving Saint Laurent and coming to the aid of Saint Augustine and Gladsdale in *Les Tourelles*. Do you like this plan, Bastard, or do you prefer another? You were full of plans last night."

Behind the dark knight, the killer Poton de Xaintrailles chuckled. I glanced at him and he was looking right at me and he nodded his head, his eyes still and unblinking as those of a serpent, and grinned his joyless grin.

The Bastard glared at de Rais and said nothing, just shook his head and rolled his shoulders, straining against the straps of his armor as if his squires had put it on him too fast and not well.

La Hire urged his horse up alongside The Bastard's and put his hand upon the ornate steel pauldron of his commander's shoulder, giving it a hard shake.

"We were all full of plans last night, weren't we?" the mercenary captain said. "And wine. And good food, but our army was gone in the morning and we find it here, already bloodied and blooded. What of it? We are warriors and will fight when and where the battle is! I for one am ready to fight. And it is a lovely day for it! Show me the way, *Pucelle*, and I shall be your battle hound!"

Several of the younger knights bayed like hounds at this and even the dark knight smiled.

46, The March

My army was all across the river now.

We numbered over a thousand but a few hundred of those were men who had never taken up arms. Yet they were staunch and willing to die for me, for France, for their uncrowned King, and their courage was as inspiring as the smell of French wildflowers upon the French wind as we began to march.

The dark knight separated his companies from mine on the shore under the shadow of Saint Jean, and his were several hundred strong and consisted of some of the best knights of France and most fierce foot soldiers in the King's Army, granted him by the Duke of Alençon, its commander, as well as many men of the City Guard.

The Bastard would drive the English skirmishers back to *La Barbacane de Saint Augustin* and then continue west to as far as Saint Privé, if he felt it necessary to block any further assaults from that direction. In the end, he would go as far as Saint Laurent, having terrified the garrison of Saint Privé so badly that they abandoned that place and retreated to Talbot's stronghold.

Alençon gathered his companies into blocks so that we might march with order upon the enemy at Saint Augustine. While this organization was going in, I had a brief discussion with my friend, the handy boatman, wherein I asked him to shadow the army along the shore with several boats and the most skilled boatmen, in the event we had need of them.

I was glad I had made this provision for I would need them sooner that I thought. I had thought to need the boatmen if and when I decided to use the fire-boats, but another situation soon arose where the boats and river-men would be necessary.

Riding with me was Alençon, *La Hire*, Xaintrailles, de la Brosse, all of their squires and the young knights of their following, Pierre, Joseph, de Metz, Bertrand, my pages, and of course, Gilles with my standard. De Rais and Robinet had ridden ahead with The Bastard, thinking the killing might be better, and more immediate, in the fore. We moved out in good order, following behind the companies of The Bastard, who was in the van.

Our companies consisted of knights and soldiers of the King's Army and many men of the city's neighborhood militias, who were good at defending walls but inexperienced at open field battle.

We took the wagon road westward and, passing through the green rolling hills and small forests, I could catch glimpses of Orléans on the other side of the wide river, Orléans with its encircling walls, thirty-four high gate towers, the spires of its Great Cathedral, and the smoke rising gently from its chimneys. I thought of all the families, the fathers, the mothers and their precious children, gathered and cooking their breakfasts over those fires, hoping for safety this day, hoping that the cannons might stop sending soaring murder on the air this day. Hoping this day that their city might be freed from danger, death, and destruction.

We had gone a mile or two and had passed the Grand Old Oak. Gilles, riding the gray on my left side, had glanced at it and then looked at me with a very large smile on his face. The bruises from his beating were large and purple but he carried himself with pride, bearing my banner. Just yesterday, we had hidden in the limbs of this tree as English soldiers rode by, bragging of what they would do to me, and here we were today, at the head of a large army, going to give those Englishmen their chance.

After the great oak, the road meandered closer to the shore and the river bridge became visible as we rode along the high bluffs. I could see the strand below us, covered with the hoof-prints of our horses and littered with the bodies of dead English, some bobbing in the lapping waters. There were little trails that ran from the wagon road down the bluffs to the beach. I could see *Les Tourelles*, many stone arches of the bridge and the Gatehouse of Saint Antoine bounded on either side by the *Île-Belle-Croix*, with the blue glittering waters of the Loire parting around it.

Our destination, *La Barbacane de Saint Augustin*, the old Convent converted to a fort, was not yet visible around the curve of the road.

I turned in my saddle and admired the long snaking line of my army, the knights riding four to six abreast, some with lances jammed in their stirrup boots and flying pointed or squared banners of many colors, and the footmen marching up to ten abreast, in closely-spaced ranks.

Seen from the battlements upon the river bridge, it must have been impressive and terrifying. I bewondered me what Gladsdale was thinking now, as he watched me marching out.

And what was that Burgundian, The Bastard of Granville, thinking now? And the other Burgundians, who had taken bribe money to leave and had stayed nonetheless and who would soon be wishing they had fled.

It was too late for them now, their fate was sealed.

But my army was beautiful in my eyes, my men, my beautiful men, marching to save Orléans, marching to save France. I saw their courage, I saw their pride, and I saw their joyfulness in stepping out with their weapons to do a bold thing.

And I saw, as I always did, their deaths.

Just as I saw this, a gun fired from *Île-Belle-Croix*.

47, *Île-Belle-Croix*

Ten of my men marching just behind me disappeared in a cloud of dust. Before the dust cleared, the screaming began. I could see the broken bodies running blood and the men who survived the shot scrambling out of the jumble of their killed and injured comrades. Then I heard another boom and, looking back, saw that another cannon on the island had fired its shot at us, the black smoke rising from its barrel. That shot struck home and more men in my train died and were broken.

Alençon wheeled his horse and his bright blue eyes met mine. "Some of the guns on the island have been turned upon us," he cried angrily.

"We must march on the quick to get out of their range," I suggested.

La Hire had ridden up to me. "Yes, but even so, they may adjust their guns and from there will use them to break up our assault on The Barbican."

In frustration, I watched as another cannonball fired from *Île-Belle-Croix* killed several French soldiers right before my eyes.

"Alençon!" I shouted. "Keep them on the march; march them double quick! *La Hire*, Xaintrailles, de la Brosse, bring your banner knights, come with me! De Metz, Bertrand! And you, Pierre and Joseph!"

I spurred my horse and rode back along the road until I found one of those little trails and I headed my black down it onto the beach. The boats were there, shadowing us along in the shallows as I had requested. I galloped down to the water's edge and the old boatman with the snow-white hair leaned on his rudder and brought his boat to me.

"*Grand-père!*" I shouted. "We need to be taken to *Île-Belle-Croix*, we and our horses, and if you have some sturdy men who have tools and know how to spike those guns, please introduce me to them. I need a dozen who are no cowards!"

The old boatman said, "No Loire river-man is a coward, *Pucelle*. You may have a hundred if you want them."

"I need only a dozen, *Grand-père.*"

The old man laughed nervously. "The wind is not good for *Île-Belle-Croix* at the moment, *Pucelle.*"

"Never mind the wind, *Grand-père*, never mind that," I said.

La Hire and Xaintrailles, sitting their steeds beside me exchanged glances, and I half-expected them to cross themselves, but, of course, they were not those kinds of men. In mere moments, it was done and barges had been brought in, enough to carry sixteen horses and their riders, and several other boats loaded with able river-men, and the wind shifted just so, filling the sails on the boats.

We pushed off of the strand and bounced over the waves, making way for the island. We were all mounted, which we usually never were when we brought our horses over the river, but I set the example and the men followed it.

My black stood as calmly as the gray as we sailed, and Gilles was beside me, holding my standard unfurled in the wind. The rest of us riders carried long lances with pointed tips and from some of these flew pennons, and the spear-tips glinted meanly in the sunlight. I wanted to terrify the men manning those guns, wanted to make them abandon their cannon before we even landed, for I didn't want to have to kill them to make them stop killing my beautiful men. But alas, as our barges drove up hard onto the sand of the island, the guns were still banging away and the English gunners were still swabbing hot barrels, pounding in charges and rolling balls in.

I spurred the black and he bounded off of the flat boat, his great hooves digging into the pebbled scree and charging up the beach. He burst over the lip of the scour made by the rising and falling water and the first cannon was right in front of him.

An Englishman holding a wet swab was startled, and, using the swab as a pole-arm, swung the black dripping sponge at my destrier's head.

The black reared and kicked the man in the chest, then charged at the other gunners, barring his teeth. He grabbed one man by the throat and lifted him from his feet, shaking him, like a dog does with a rat, until his throat ripped out in a gush of dark red blood.

La Hire and the other knights were on the island also, charging the gun placements with lowered lances, killing

Englishmen and driving them down the island towards the Fortress of Saint Antoine. They ran their long lances into men's backs as they were fleeing and I caught sight of Xaintrailles driving his spear-point through one man's eye as the man folded to his knees and raised his hands in surrender. I saw the killer change his point's aim from chest to eye-socket at the last minute, as if in a game of skill, and his happy grin as he watched the man's head snap back and the spear-point slide back out, gleaming, from the skull as he rode by, pulling it free.

The sight gave me a chill, but then who was I to judge?

My black had killed five men at the first gun, kicking and biting them to death. The final one had fled, getting himself up onto the wooden boardwalk down which they had rolled the guns to their placements and was pelting down it barefooted, the rough wooden planks giving his feet purchase.

I would have let him go, but my black knew better, charging along the edge of the boardwalk until he came abreast with the running man and then thrusting his great head in front of the man's pumping knees, sending him flying onto his face.

The gunner slid about twelve feet along the wood, picking up splinters and leaving a blood smear behind him. When he stopped sliding, he looked up at me with a dazed look on his face, blood dripping from his mouth, where he had shattered several teeth in his lower jaw, and I saw that he recognized me, for my visor was up, a strand of my long reddish hair blowing in the breeze. The black stood over him, as if giving him a chance to see his death coming.

The man said, spitting out blood and bits of tooth, "God-damn."

"Better to ask God's forgiveness than His curse," I said to

the Englishman, seeing his death even as the black dealt it, a blow to the head with the beast's huge left fore-hoof, the iron shoe pulverizing the skull against the solid planks of the boardwalk, the eyes popping out on their blue strings and the tongue lolling out, dropping blood onto the sand.

We silenced the guns at *Île-Belle-Croix*, killing or driving off the gunners and guarding the river-men while they drove iron spikes into the touch holes with their great ringing hammers. English soldiers on the ramparts of Saint Antoine, shook their fists at us and shouted obscenities and *La Hire* and Xaintrailles shouted back and outmatched them with good French obscenities.

History likes to tell how I disapproved of the language and debauchery of *La Hire* and the other warriors and how I railed against them and got them all to change their ways, but the Histories were written by the clerics and Churchmen and the clerics and Churchmen never did understand the fighting man or even the common man. Nor did they care to, their only goal was to bend men to their will, to force God upon them rather than let God enter their hearts gently, like a sheep returning to its fold. Those Histories were but another attempt to bend men by bending the truth. But I remember the truth.

The truth was, I never endeavored to change a man except through example and I saw many a man change that way. The only true change is one a man chooses for himself, not that which is imposed upon him.

When we were done with our work on *Île-Belle-Croix*, we jumped our steeds back up onto the flat boats and our river-men poled our vessels away from the beach.

The wind shifted and bellied our sails and we set off for the southern bank.

48, Crucifixion

The river breeze had dried the salt tears on my cheeks before our boats touched the south bank. Gilles had sat beside me on the gray as I sat upon the black while we made the crossing and he watched the tears course down and he watched them turn to faint white streaks along my nose and down into the creases around my mouth. He knew that they were tears of regret for the pain and horror I had witnessed on *Île-Belle-Croix,* the island named for the sacred cross of the crucifixion, at the pain and horror I had taken part in and that I had been the cause of.

He looked at me in sympathy.

He was the boy who could have stayed in the little village named after a sparrow and hunted rabbits and run wild and free in the field and forests and waited to inherit a turnip farm and married a simple country lass, but who had chosen, instead, to follow the girl who wept across France.

He had said he wanted to watch me save France. Well,

he was watching me, from as close a vantage as was possible, right at my elbow, bearing my standard.

There were times, like now, that I bewondered me what he thought of all he was seeing.

I professed to have such compassion for all living things; I could see their deaths and I wept for them, as I wept for myself, for we all share the same fate, we all are bound together, we all shall die, and yet twas my doing, by my order, and by the hooves and teeth of my own horse that these deaths occurred, these horrible deaths, the ones Gilles was witnessing. The tears I wept for this pain and horror that I was the cause of, the pain I felt, the guilt I felt (though in my mind I exonerated myself of guilt, saying it was the will of God and I was but an instrument of His will), this pain was my own crucifixion.

I was crucified on *Île-Belle-Croix* and I felt every scourge-mark and every thorn, every nail, every broken rib, and all the shock of thirst and inability to breathe and loss of blood of that crucifixion. I took all that suffering on myself to spare the others the guilt, the sin, and the responsibility of what we did here. I was the instrument.

I took the blame.

Gilles saw all this as he watched the tears dry on my face while we jounced over the river waves.

He would have reached out to touch those tears as he had tried to do the first time we stood on the north shore of the Loire together, waiting for the horses to be unloaded, the day I asked him, "What do you have in your little bag?" But he knew now that he could not touch me without me seeing his death, unless there was some failsafe, some stone, or steel, or horseflesh, to draw the power of that vision off like one draws off cream from milk or whey from curd, and we were still trying to figure that one out, so he just watched them dry without wiping them away.

He looked at me with sympathy and he looked at me with a kind of awe and he looked at me with love.

I shook my head and blew out a breath.

How could he love me, watching me rain down death as I did? How could he love me and believe in my compassion for all living beings when he saw more killing in my presence in the past fortnight than in all the years of his entire life?

All committed in my name, at my bidding, and in the cause I had espoused?

That strand of my hair blew on the wind and lay across my cheek. Gilles leaned over and grasped it between his fingertips and carefully moved it back, tucking it under the cheek-plate of my helm. It was reddish-brown, shiny in the sunlight, silky and slightly wavy, like good sheep's wool that has been combed out and is ready for the wheel.

He held my hair gently so as not to pull on it and was so very careful not to let his fingers touch my skin and when he was done, his eyes met mine, a very pale light green to match the color of the water slapping against the planks.

He had never asked me about his death, his cold watery death, which would be a river drowning, in a river like this one, maybe even was this one, and I would not want to have to tell him.

I did not think it possible to avoid the deaths I saw simply by being forewarned, and in any case, his was many years off, when he was an old man, not ancient but old, with graying hair on his temples and gray hair on his chest, and I did not want to talk about it for another reason, the fact that nowhere in his death did I see any sign of me.

I had been gone from his life for most of a lifetime, this I knew.

I did not want to tell him that.

So I let him look at me, with sympathy, in awe and with love. And I looked at him with gratefulness, that he could love me, could believe in me, after all he had seen, all that I had done, that he could and would stay beside me, bearing my banner, and watch me do more. He saw my weakness; the tears that I shed, the guilt that I felt, the burden that I bore and that I felt myself so unequal to.

He knew that I hated killing and would not kill with my own hand, but that I would lead others to kill, point them at those I wanted killed, turn my steed's great proud head in the direction of the enemy and let him kill them as my instrument.

These were my flaws; that I could be such and do so, a killer but innocent, a leader of warriors but no warrior. I was flawed, greatly flawed, but Gilles only saw me as strong.

In his eyes, I was perfect.

In my eyes, under this pure white gleaming armor, with the pure white silk banner of *Jhésus et Maria* flapping over my head, I was full of holes.

I felt every one, like bleeding wounds, like stigmata.

49, Music

We couched our spears and charged up the bluff trail to the wagon road, dipping our points under the overhanging branches of trees.   At the top, in the clear, we raised our spears point-skyward and rested their butts in our stirrup-boots and galloped on.

The road was churned with the hoof-prints and footfalls of many steeds and men and we rode to catch up, through the meadows green with lush grasses and colorful with wildflowers, those same meadows that Gilles and I had called "a country all our own," and the air was filled with clouds of tiny butterflies and the songs of birds.

We were *La Pucelle*, my barefooted banner-bearer and fourteen armored knights galloping in a tight knot towards *La Barbacane de Saint Augustin*, lances and banners held high, to join the siege of the besiegers.

There was no roar of cannon now and of this I was glad. No flying death to kill and shatter my beautiful men, my French soldiers.

We had succeeded in saving their lives, at least for now.

I rode at the head of my party, my heart lightened by the guns' silence, and I reined the black slightly that I might turn and look back at my comrades. *La Hire*, de la Brosse and Xaintrailles were in the rank behind me, their banner knights in ranks behind them, Jean de Metz and Squire Bertrand, and Pierre and Joseph bringing up the rear. All rode with their visors open, breathing the sweet air of Spring.

The faces of these men were exultant. Their joy was as evident as the smiles on their faces. And I could see, they were like brothers, they had made an assault together and though they might not all know each other's names, they were as brothers now. That is how war is, one of the things war is made of; brotherhood.

There was music as we rode, the ching-chinging of the maille-coats and the clink-clinking of weapons and the harp-string chiming of steel upon steel, overlying the percussion of the beating hooves and the soft fluttering of flying banners.

Twas a joyful music, this song of brotherhood, and my regretful heart lifted with its lilting tune.

I came to where the road dropped down betwixt the two round hills and, without slowing, I galloped down through the narrow pass, entering the shadows and feeling the cooler air chill my armor, my brothers following.

We did not fear attack coming out of this pass, for on the other side lay The Barbican of Saint Augustine, and it would be surrounded by the army of France.

50, Assaulting The Barbican

And it was, completely surrounded.

The graystone walls of the old Convent were high with narrow windows through which English long-bowmen were shooting their goose-feather-fletched arrows. All around the building were earthen bulwarks sheltering English soldiers, redoubts made of timber filled with enemy pike-men and elevated fighting positions of archers and crossbowmen and all the way around it, a deep moat filled with water to impede our movement with a draw bridge on one side all pulled up tight against its two great suspension structures.

This Barbican had been built last year by The Bastard and since taken by the English and maintained by them, but of course, all around the Barbican was the filth, trash and detritus of a long occupation.

It sickened me to see it and to smell it and see my beautiful men fighting their way through it.   The gray water of the moat stank of piss and I saw feces floating on the water's surface. Wave after wave of brave Frenchmen were struggling through that foul water, suffering flights of arrows. Those that made it alive charged the redoubts on foot and with weapons in hand, seeking the bodies of their foe, and each wave was cast back, leaving some of their number killed or wounded behind.

I burst out of the narrow pass betwixt the hills, the sunlight striking all over my white harness, making me gleam. Men saw me, turned their exultant faces to me and took up the cry, *"La Pucelle! La Pucelle!"*

I galloped along the edge of my gathered host, my black raising his knees high and thudding his great hooves hard upon the ground, arching his thick neck and tossing his gallant head, his bridle-chains ringing. He saw the army and heard the sounds of battle and he slung his head from side to side against my hand on the reins, snorting with desire to enter the fray and kill men with teeth and hooves.

I steadied him. It was not yet his time.

The men had their work to do before he would carry me into the midst of the dangerous foe.

The best thing I could do now was to be seen.

Be seen by my people to give them courage and be seen by the English to strike fear into their hearts.

And so, I rode my black up and back and all around, calling out to my beautiful men words of faith in their prowess and belief in our cause, for, after all, was not the act of saying it the act of making it true? with Gilles beside me, holding my white lily-bedecked banner high, and, looking up at it, I saw the blue light of Michael's love glowing all around it and my heart, which had been so heavy and so sore on the boat ride back from *Île-Belle-Croix*, now grew light and joyful.

Joyful in the light of Michael's love.

My angel was nigh me, though I could not see his face.

I long had hoped he would appear to me, speak to me, even touch me (though his touch burned), remind me with his touch that I belonged to him. But only his light appeared.

Could my men see his light, or only I?

Pray God, I thought, that his light would be seen, that his light would give strength to the warriors of France, that his light would strengthen the arms of the men as they fought.

Oh, my men, my beautiful men! You men of France, so brave and true!

Be strong, my valiant men! See the light of God!

I watched as more men launched themselves into the waters of the moat, sinking in mud and struggling through the water in their maille and steel-plated brigandines to reach the edge of the high motte on the other side. The moat was an obstacle that was difficult to surmount, what with arrows flying down from the Convent walls. I thought of how they might cross over it, were there planks or logs that could be thrown down over the gap?

I recalled the firewood-cutters then and the piles of slash and bundles of faggots on the beach in the little cove and I rode about until I found one of the militia captains, a big strong man with carpenter's hands whose name was Bernard Josselin, and I told him of this place and he and many of his men went there, shown the way by my rabbit boy whom I dispatched to direct them, while I held my standard and continued to ride, giving encouragement, and stopping to speak to many of the squires, whom I knew by their small pennons were in charge of groups of foot soldiers.

Soon Gilles was back by my side, taking the standard from my hand. He grinned broadly and said, "They are bringing the wood now."

We looked and saw many men, led by Josselin, carrying bundles of brush and tossing them into the water all around the drawbridge and at another spot Josselin directed where the motte on the other side was none so high. And I felt I had done a good thing, one that would help my men, my beautiful men.

But then I heard a sound I did not like to hear and it was close.

My black stopped, skidding on his hind hooves and threw up his head and looked about. He pawed with his great left forefoot, the one that had killed the gunner on the Island of the Cross. The sound came again and, born on the breeze, the smell of burnt powder.

Before I even moved the rein, the black turned and galloped the other direction, knowing what I needed to do; find *Le Duc d'Alençon.*

The black did find him and bore me straight to him, where the Duke and his banner knights sat their horses in a good vantage point to watch the assault and to give orders. I rode up to him and he touched the raised visor of his helmet in a salute to me, as if he were doffing his hat.

"Jehanne, La Pucelle," he said. "You did well silencing those guns on the island. Now we have only to contend with these culverins they have in some of those elevated positions of The Barbican."

"Culverins?" I asked.

"Oui," the Fair Duke said. "Those small cannon there and there and there," he pointed. "Filled with small shot, they scatter at close quarters. Each time some of our men get across the moat and try to assault from certain directions, those guns tear them into little pieces."

At those words, my mind filled with images of my men, my beautiful men, their faces bright with achievement, scrambling up the steep side of one of the deep ditches, emerging at the lip of the ditch, only to be greeted by a blast of one of those culverins.

Iron shot the size of robin's eggs, in a blast of fire, sparks and black smoke, hit them in their faces, necks, shoulders, chests, and bellies, ripping through their living, pulsing, feeling bodies, and tossed them away like soiled rags, like worthless things no longer of this world, though they had been men with wives and families, with great and small joys to live for.

"The Bastard is at Saint Privé," I said to Alençon and it was not a question; I knew the dark knight was there, could feel him there. He had driven the English back, pushing past The Barbican, knowing Alençon would surround it and protect his rear, and killing the enemy as they fled, drove them hard for their fortress, and then assaulted that fortress as soon as he arrived, before the English could even get the gates of *La Bastille sur Le Champ de Saint Privé* fully closed behind them.

Many of the English had not wanted to be trapped in that place, seeing the ferocity of The Bastard of Orléans and his determination, and they had bypassed the fort rather than enter it and others, seeing them do so, had left the fort and joined them in a retreat towards the stronghold of Saint Laurent. The dark knight now had *La Bastille sur Le Champ* encircled and had his men cutting saplings from the nearby woods with which to make scaling ladders.

Alençon said, "Yes, I suspect he is. He followed your plan and, after I took up position here, he assaulted west towards Saint Privé."

I smiled for I saw how it would play out. *La Hire* and Xaintrailles would rein their horses up across from me in just a moment and I would tell them what to do and what they would do would be what needed to be done to reduce those culverins that were turning my Frenchmen into pulp. But first the Cadieux twins would ride up and begin to tell me tales of the other brother's valor.

I heard their horses approaching behind me.

"Sir Pierre, Sir Joseph," I said, "you are demonstrating today that your spurs are well-deserved," and I turned in my saddle to see their beaming and blood-streaked faces, and their surprise that I knew they were coming up behind me.

They wore their faces clean-shaven, which was a popular fashion in France at that time, especially among the young, and they were small men, no taller than was Gilles, who was only a little taller than I was, myself, and they had a youthful innocence and sweetness about them, thus would always look like boys. I thought of them as boys, my bloody boys, and boys they would be, for they would get no older, this I knew, for of course, I had seen their deaths.

So, when they began to talk, telling of each other's brave deeds, I listened, my eyes moving from one set of blue eyes to the other, and I smiled and I nodded, and I said, "You Cadieux men are serving your country well, protecting your King, acquitting yourselves valiantly, and making your father proud."

Pierre and Joseph stopped talking and looked at me and looked at each other and looked at me again and I knew what they had communicated to one another.

"You make me proud," I said to them, for I knew that is what mattered most of all.

Their faces broke into wide smiles and both leaned down

at the same moment with the same hand to stroke the neck of their black horses, which looked so very much alike, I could not tell which was the one I had of the King that I had given to the horseless brother nor could I tell which brother was which.

But at that moment, *La Hire* and Xaintrailles appeared before me and I had to turn away from the twins and direct my attention to the mercenaries and I said, "I have an important duty for you," and I told *La Hire* and Xaintrailles what they must do.

When I had finished and saw *La Hire*'s nod of acquiescence, I looked into the eyes of Poton de Xaintrailles, the mercenary killer, the man who had seen and caused so much death that he cared little for life, and he was smiling, not laughing in his usual broad, open and rude way, just smiling a private smile, and I had a thought of what he might find amusing.

He saw me watching him and he actually flushed a little and reined his horse back and took it a little distance from the group, folding his hands over the saddle pommel, and sat waiting for his friend.

The Fair Duke and *La Hire*, meanwhile, had begun discussing what men *La Hire* and Xaintrailles should take with them and before they concluded their talk, I moved my horse out of the cluster and sidled up next to Xaintrailles.

"You mustn't try, Poton," I said before he was even aware that I was beside him. "That is not how The Bastard dies, so it is a waste of your time to even think such thoughts."

He jerked away from me, startled by my words and by my presence, but more by my words. His eyes, always narrow and blood-shot, were now wide and round and full of terror.

I had never seen him afraid; he seemed to have no fear, for he had no love of life, therefore no fear of losing it, but he was afraid now.

"I do not mean to frighten you," I said. "I mean only to help you and I pray that one day, you will find in yourself a worthy man. A man worthy of friendship, and of loyalty, and of love. Killing *Le Batârd d'Orléans* will not make you worthy of any of those things, no matter what you might think. Plus, you will not succeed, this you may believe of me. His is an old man's death and he is not yet an old man."

Xaintrailles snorted through his narrow nose, as if he did not agree about the age of The Bastard. He steadied his horse, who had felt his tension of a moment before and become restive.

There was more I might say, but I kept quiet, letting the man ruminate on the words I had already spoken.

Sometimes more work is done with a lighter hand.

Finally, he looked at me and his shoulders dropped, the worn leather straps of his armor creaking, and his mouth worked. He let out a breath, as if he was willing to believe that I knew what I was talking about.

"As you say, *Pucelle*," the killer said finally.

"*Merci*, Poton," I said, "believe me, it is better this way," and turned my horse away.

In a little while, *La Hire*, Xaintrailles and their hand-picked men rode away from The Barbican in the direction of *Le Champ de Saint Privé*.

I rode closer to Alençon and said to him, "Order the men to avoid assaults against the culverins. Let us direct our attacks upon the lower bulwarks, those redoubts there, see, where the men are making a bridge over the moat," I pointed, "and the places where Englishmen are concentrated outside the Convent walls. And let the men use large shields to protect themselves and their fellows from the archers in the windows. I saw them doing this at Saint Loupe."

The Fair Duke smiled and gave these orders to his banner knights, who galloped off to tell the commanders of the foot soldiers.

Joseph and Pierre said at the very same moment, "*Pucelle,* what do you want us to do?"

I smiled at their eager faces and said, "If you like, dismount your horses and fight on foot. The presence of knights fighting with the common soldiers is very heartening. They will soon have that drawbridge down and that will be the place for you to enter."

I knew it was safe for them to do this, that I was not putting them in any danger for suggesting it. I leaned forward and surveyed The Barbican, streaming with battling men. "There, do you see the timbered redoubt with the little blue pennon flying upon it? That is where you should go. There is a man there I want you to capture for me. A Burgundian with hazel eyes, which is how you shall know him. Let him stand before me armed. Do not harm him in any way."

The faces of my bloody boys lit up.

All this mystery, all this intrigue. How did I know these things?

In truth, even I did not know how I knew these things.

They soon dismounted their matching black destriers and gave the reins to the pages standing nearby. They checked each other's armor quickly, pulling on the straps and tightening the billets, slapping the various parts as they checked, making the steel clash, and their smiles widened with each slap.

Soon they drew their swords, looked up at me, nodded, and used their sword-blades to swat down their visors.

I heard the simultaneous click of each tiny spring-pin engaging, holding the visors in place, and then the boys were heading into the fray, side by side.

51, *Le Champ de Saint Privé*

The ladders were against the walls and The Bastard's men were clattering up them. The woodsmen who had cut the saplings from which to fashion these ladders had cut extra ones with forked ends and had used these poles to buttress the ladders so that the defenders would have a harder time pushing them away from the walls. The men climbed quickly, filling the ladders with their weight, because they knew from experience that the more men that were on a ladder, the heavier it was and the harder to shove away.

There were less than a hundred men inside *La Bastille sur Le Champ de Saint Privé* and those men knew now that they were going to die, knew that they should have evacuated while they had the chance and retreated with their fellows for the strongholds north of the river. I saw this and knew this and felt this all the way to where I sat my black watching the assault on The Barbican.

I felt the leaden weights of compassion dropping one by one and filling the bottom of my heart. There was nothing I could or would do to change it. These events were set in motion, and I could only watch them unfold.

I wished for the solace of my angels then.

They had been absent from these battlegrounds, though I still looked up to find them beside me in other places, in the stable, in the room I inhabited in *la maison de la famille de Boucher*, in my dreams. It was as if they could not bring themselves to look upon the carnage I had wrought, as if they disapproved and therefore could not look, and yet would not chide me nor judge me, but only let me bear the burden of it on myself without their sanction. And yet, how could they disapprove, since it was they who sent me here?

Could angels be both approving and disapproving?

And how could I ever understand the minds of angels?

I could not. Another of my crosses I must bear.

I would have thought that of all of them, Michael would be here, more than just his light; his Self.

He was the archangel, the avenging warrior angel, one would think he would revel in this, would want to witness it and to lend to this battle his sword of blue flame, his shield of an azure sea, and his cloak of the winds of the world.

Perhaps I had misunderstood him, when he came to me in Domrémy, under the spreading boughs of *l'arbre de fées*, and in the places where I walked with my sheep along the banks of the Meuse, when he told me that I would leave my village and go to war, leading the army of France and that I would dispel the English from our country and make it French again and return it to the rule of a monarch of the *sangrail*.

I had thought that my angel Michael would be with me,

guiding me, teaching me, and protecting me.

I had thought my angel would be with me through it all.

Instead, someone else had been with me through it all, the boy from the village of Le Moineau.

A boy as beautiful as an angel.

I looked at him now, sitting the gray, holding my standard in the breeze that came up off the River Loire. The old gray campaigner looked almost asleep, his great hooves planted squarely and his neck arched and his long face vertical, the lower lip drooping slightly, the yellowing forelock hanging down over half-closed eyes. Gilles sat astride him, a small weight for a steed used to bearing a heavy armored knight all of his life, an insignificant weight.

The old horse might well have been in his stable taking a nap in his stall. Yet if we needed to ride, the gray would wake and be galloping in an instant. My boy sat upon his back, watching the fighting, watching Pierre and Joseph fighting and scrambling through the ditches.

His golden-brown hair was blowing across his brow and falling wind-tangled over his broad shoulders, where the rabbit hat was hanging down his back tied around his throat by the rabbit-foot ties. His cheeks were flushed a rosy color under the dark bruises and the one swollen eye was black underneath it where the blood had settled.

He would have to be angel enough for me, I thought.

No sword of flames, no shield of seas, no cloak of winds, just a boy in ragged clothes, but an angel still.

While all of this was running through my mind; at Saint Privé, The Bastard's scalers had made the top of the ramparts and killed the men who met them there. They had swarmed over, running down the length of the walls, fighting and killing and being killed, and descending the levels by ladders and staircases, until enough of them were inside and enough defenders had been slain that someone reached the bolts on the interior that held the gates closed. These they pulled and swung the gate to, and The Bastard and de Rais and young Robinet rode their horses in.

They swung down from their steeds and the English prisoners were brought before them and while The Bastard and de Rais were sharing a flagon of wine someone had found, for the men were already raiding the storehouse, and were discussing what they might want to do with the captives, *La Hire* and Xaintrailles and their party came clattering in. Robinet had just been handed a flagon and had uncorked it with his teeth and was upending it when the group of horsemen charged in.

Robinet gave a yelp and jerked the flagon down, as he fumbled with his other hand for his sword-hilt, causing a gush of wine to shoot out of the narrow neck and spill down the front of his cuirass, looking much like blood.

All of them laughed, The Bastard and de Rais and *La Hire* and Xaintrailles, and Robinet looked angry, but then cocked his head and shoved down his pride under the gaze of so many senior men.

"Waste of good wine," he said.

"I was going to say, Robin, you've been wounded," said *La Hire*, reining in his horse and dismounting.

Robinet accepted a piece of cloth from a squire and wiped the wine from his armor, tossing the rag away. "I have yet to find the Englishman that could wound me," said the young knight, "and I have been making their acquaintance all day long."

"Your list of friends must be growing then," said *La Hire*.

"*Non,* because I kill them each one as I make their

acquaintance," Robinet said, and pulled on the wine again.

They all laughed, and The Bastard asked after the progress of the assault upon The Barbican. *La Hire*, glancing at Xaintrailles where the mercenary still sat upon his horse, his hands folded over his saddle pommel, gave a subtle flick of his eyebrow towards the ground, indicating that Xaintrailles should dismount like all the others. Xaintrailles stared blankly at him and did not move.

Sighing, *La Hire* addressed The Bastard's question. "The place is surrounded and Alençon's companies are attacking. We had to divert some of our forces to *Île-Belle-Croix* to take out the gun placements there, as they were being used against us at Saint Augustine, but that was easily done."

The men in the storehouse had found some dried meat and fruit and cheese and now brought this out, handing portions first to the captains and then to the men. Xaintrailles watched as *La Hire* and the Bastard and de Rais and Robinet received more wine, and he glanced at the captives all lined up in a row and upon their knees, trembling and awaiting their fate while their enemy feasted upon their stores.

The killer smiled grimly.

There was a time, he would have enjoyed first killing these men in various and sundry interesting ways and then, with their blood still dripping from his hands, he would have relished eating meat and fruit and cheese. Right now, beside killing The Bastard of Orléans, that gloating boasting pig, an act he had promised not to attempt, all he wanted was to fulfill the mission that he and *La Hire* had been send upon.

Had he changed so much in a few days?

What had changed him?

The Bastard spat out a bad part of an apple and asked,

"And what has *La Pucelle* been doing while this has been going on?" He laid a special emphasis on her title.

La Hire lowered his flagon, smacked his lips, and said, "Riding to and fro with her banner and cheering on the men."

"Well, for that she is well-suited, at least," The Bastard said. "I am amazed at how the idiots will follow her, on blind faith. I never had faith, blind or otherwise."

Xaintrailles watched their faces.

The Bastard's revealed exactly what The Bastard was, no mystery there, but something was going on under the lines of *La Hire*'s visage.

Robinet was but a young fool, randy as a goat and lusting for everything; blood, food, wine, women, power, wealth. His was a life led by the nose by things he wanted. He could step right over anything that wasn't one of his wants and never see it. Xaintrailles knew this well, understood it. For most of his life, he himself had been this way.

Baron de Rais was hiding something. He acted as if he agreed with all things The Bastard said and did, but he did not. His dark brows had lowered at the mention of *La Pucelle* and he did not like it when *La Hire* had demeaned the girl's value. So de Rais was in love with the girl. He desired her, but would never act like he did, for that would be beneath him. He was one of the wealthiest men in France and she only a milkmaid, from Lorraine of all places. A God-forsaken wilderness.

And *La Hire*? Xaintrailles was sure that *La Hire* had greater regard for the girl than he would let on, especially to The Bastard. *La Hire* was being subtle, he was working The Bastard, working his way around to the issue at hand. Xaintrailles shook his head and worried at the broken teeth in his mouth, pressing against their sharp edges with his tongue.

Everyone was busy kissing the big hairy arse of The Bastard and stroking his puny cock, trying to make it grow large and stand upright, and no one but a half-pint girl from Lorraine was actually fighting a war.

Well, fuck them. Fuck all of them.

Xaintrailles pulled back on the bit in the mouth of his horse, making it back up.

"Where are you going?" *La Hire* shouted to him, and they all stared at him, with food in their mouths and flagons dropping from their faces.

"I am going back to The Barbican," Xaintrailles said. "Nothing is happening here and over there, the girl is killing Englishmen."

The Bastard snorted. "Well, shit. We are about to kill some right here if you just wait a minute." He gestured with his flagon to the captives on their knees. Xaintrailles looked at The Bastard wordlessly and then cocked his head and looked at *La Hire*.

The Bastard followed his gaze and looked at *La Hire* too.

"What? What is it? Why did you come here anyway?"

La Hire shrugged, then corked his flagon and handed it to a squire. "We need some cannons at The Barbican. They don't have to be very big ones, two or four pounders, but we need to bring maybe four or five guns. Those cowards are using culverins against us and we need to take them out."

The Bastard laughed. "Yes, those used to be our damned culverins! We killed a few English with them last year before Talbot called for re-enforcements and overran us. I could probably tell that girl a few more things about The Barbican and what she might expect there if I wasn't over here at Saint Privé!"

If *La Hire* hadn't said it, Xaintrailles would have.

"Mayhap, Bastard, since you are done here, you should come back with us and tell her these things."

"No, I think not," The Bastard said. "I have a few other things I want to do while I am in the vicinity. I don't get out this way very often anymore."

He walked over and gave a swift hard kick to the belly of one of the kneeling men, who fell upon his back and then rolled over on his side, curling up. The Bastard kicked him again in his head, making his ear begin to bleed. "Take whatever guns are suitable, *La Hire*. Take them all if you want. I am going to clean this place out of anything of value and then burn it to the ground."

He bent over and grabbed the man he had been kicking by the hair and pulled his face close to his own. "But before I do that," he said, looking into the man's eyes, "I am going to have a little hunt. You understand me, English? Going to have a little hunt."

He said the last part in English, and the man's eyes grew wide with fear. He let go of the man, walked over to de Rais and reached for the wine flagon.

He took a long drink and looked up at Xaintrailles, saying, "You should stay, Xaintrailles. This will be a game to your liking."

52, The Game

But Xaintrailles did not stay.

He saw the beginning of the game, sitting his pawing steed and waiting, saw it as *La Hire's* hand-picked company located the guns in *La Bastille de Saint Privé* and wrapped them in slings and ropes and carefully lowered them from their placements and brought them out to the edge of the forest to take stock of them and to decide which should be brought back to The Barbican and which might be best to leave behind, either to be spiked and discarded or hidden and later retrieved for French use.

He watched from a distance as The Bastard's men untied the captives and brought them out of the gate, lining them all up, forty-two in all, some of them bleeding and wounded, but most seemingly hale.

He watched as they turned the men loose and the English pelted away from *La Bastille* as fast as they could run, some of the men helping the wounded and others just fleeing for their lives. The captives ran across the flat open fields that gave the area its name.

He watched as The Bastard and his party of chosen friends passed around a large flagon, drinking from it as fast as they could, trying to empty it, for when it was empty, the first group of hunters would depart on the chase.

The Bastard pounded each of them on the back and handed him his weapon, a spear or an axe or a flail, and sent them on their way, on foot.

These men, some twenty or so, favored foot soldiers of The Bastard's companies, gleefully ran off through the meadows, seeking their quarry, and The Bastard uncorked another large flagon and the horsemen began to drink.

Once this flagon was empty, The Bastard, de Rais, Robinet, and the other knights mounted their horses. They spun and reared them, drawing their swords and clashing them against each other's, and they charged out over the land, armored but helmetless, their voices carrying back to Xaintrailles' ears, calls of excitement and blood-lust, and for a moment, he thought he would ride out after them.

Another voice was in his ear, however; "I shall not let you add the murder of these men to the long list of indictments against your soul, Poton," and so he steadied his horse, who had felt the surge of excitement that had momentarily flooded his veins and begun to prance and sling his head, and he turned his attention to the task at hand, helping *La Hire* to determine the best way to transport these guns to The Barbican.

At The Barbican, I sat my black, and saw these events at Saint Privé as if though the eyes and mind of the cold-blooded killer and I thought to myself, and smiled, if I might help to save one man's soul, if would be this man, Poton de Xaintrailles.

53, Pierre and Joseph

The two young knights ran, their swords upraised, to the edge of the crowd of milling men who had just brought down the drawbridge over the moat of The Barbican. Arrows were landing around them and I saw one glance off the curved crown of one of their helmets.

Of course, I could not tell which Cadieux brother it was for I could not tell them apart while looking at their faces, much less at their almost identical armor. They pelted over the bridge and passed a group of French soldiers who were trying to pull two of their wounded fellows out of danger, clambered over a bulwark of timber heaped all about with piled dirt and stones and leaped into the space beyond, where several English were pushing their long wicked pole-arms into the bodies of every Frenchmen who tried to surmount their bulwarks.

Pierre and Joseph's armor protected them from the long

curved and spiked blades, which skittered across their cuirasses and glanced off their bodies. One man in the back swung his long-handled war hammer over the heads of his comrades, crashing it repeatedly on the top of one of the twins' helms, trying to crush in the steel and thus the skull inside the steel.

As Joseph, or Pierre, or whichever it was, was using his sword to kill his fellows that stood in front of him, the man found himself now exposed and shortened his grip on the handle, trying to jab the long spike that was on the top of his war hammer into the eye-slot of Pierre or Joseph's helmet, to pierce his eye and enter his brains.

But the other twin, upon pulling his sword from the body of the last man he killed, saw this and struck the haft of the war-hammer with his blade, just below the long protective steel shanks of the weapon's head, breaking the handle in two, and taking off most of the man's left hand as well.

The Englishman shrieked, which I could hear above the tumult, and Pierre and Joseph killed him, both at the same moment, their sharpened points of their swords entering his body through his worn hauberk of studded leather.

The two knights in their armor had killed seven skilled pole-arm fighters in less than five minutes, men who, for three-quarters of an hour, had held off the French foot soldiers who had slogged through the moat and had wounded and killed many.

Now the Frenchmen who had witnessed this grew excited and followed Joseph and Pierre over the bodies of these English and began to assault the next bulwark.

There, one of the brothers met a well-armored man-at-arms and the two exchanged sword blows and parries, their swords ringing against each other and clashing upon the steel of helmet, pauldron and cuirass. The Englishman was taller and used his height to lay heavy strikes against the head and shoulders of the Cadieux brother he faced, trying to dizzy him by dint of blows and put him off-balance.

Meanwhile, the other brother was fighting against three English in brigandine armor and basinet helms that were open-faced and had mailled coifs hanging down around their shoulders. These coifs swayed and back and forth in the dance of battle and some of the links were bronzed and glinted in the sunlight. Falchions and small battle-axes were the weapons of these foemen and, while deadly, did not seem to worry my young knight.

I watched in amazement as this young man of my following parried, struck, and feinted, keeping three attackers at bay with only his sword and the small shield that he had pulled from his belt. These battle games were the games he and his brother had played every day of their lives since they first took steps and he still seemed to think it was but a game.

In fact, I could well imagine his smiling face under the visor of his helmet. However, the faces of the men he fought were not smiling. I could see the drawn lips and black teeth of their grimaces. And in their chests, I could feel their thudding hearts, and over all the sounds of war, I could hear those hearts beating the dread tattoo of mortal fear.

Pierre, or Joseph, kicked one of these men in the lower belly, making him double over, and as the man bent, he struck downward into the base of his neck with the metal bosse of the shield, dropping that man to the ground, and then stepped on the back of his head to hold him there. In the same moment, he swung his sword in a cross-body strike that landed under the raised arm of another of the English, who had thought to take his head off with a well-placed blow of his battle axe, and that man was down and gushing blood.

Joseph, or Pierre, brought his sword back into a high guard and faced the last man that stood before him but before the twin could kill him, the man was struck down by the French men of foot that had stormed the bulwark with them, and Pierre, or Joseph, turned his attention to helping his brother.

The man-at-arms, whoever he was, was a formidable fighter and both Cadieux brothers, the one who fought him and the one who now watched him fight, were thinking that under different circumstances, they would have liked to exchange words on the finer points of weapon's play with this man. This thought crossed my mind, as I watched from my vantage, just as it crossed the minds of my bloody boys.

But then the thought passed, for it was not to be, this man would be dead in less than a minute, and I knew, though (mercifully) they did not, that my boys would be dead tomorrow.

Joseph, or Pierre, clambered up the short slope that separated him from his brother and without warning, took his sword blade hard at the back of the man's knee-cop, where the flesh was unprotected, once, twice, and thrice. The Englishman faltered, staggered, tried to regain the use of that leg, but fell sideways, landing on that knee and now, defending himself again two matched knights like a brace of perfectly-trained battle hounds, he began the fight for his life.

The fight was not long.

The brothers, attacking from two sides, laid waste to the man's helmet, now that he had been brought down in height. The crown of it took repeated blows and began to split. The visor, relieved of its anchoring rivet on one side, swung away from the man's face, and for one horrible moment, I saw the man cry quarter, the words forming on his mouth amidst the blood.

But my young battle hounds smelled the blood and they went for the throat.

The man, whoever he had been, was dead at their feet before the words were fully formed.

More French foot soldiers and men-at-arms and even some dismounted knights had joined Pierre and Joseph in the bulwarks and I saw several of the men with large shields sheltering themselves and others from the arrows that were now streaming down upon them from the windows of the Convent, while the Cadieux brothers scanned about the works, looking for the blue pennon I had pointed to and planning their best route towards it.

At that blue pennon was the Burgundian.

I knew not who he was nor what I wanted of him, but I knew he needed to stand before me.

54, The Culverins

In my company there were two men who had great skill with firearms, a Spaniard called Alfonso de Patada and a man the local people simply called Colin the Lorrainer, since he had been born, like me, in that fair province.

These men were made ready to receive the guns with which *La Hire* and Xaintrailles would return from Le Champ, and I dismounted my black for a time that I might walk about with them.

My wounded foot with its half-missing toe had stopped bleeding through the boot, and dirt now caked over the blood, but it pained me and caused me to hobble a bit.

Yet I made my way around with the gunners and listened as they discussed the placements, angles and trajectories of the weapons and how best to destroy the culverins without the culverins being able to destroy us. They could not make final decisions until they had the guns in hand and saw what type they were and what were their capabilities, but I learned much by their discussion which I would remember for future use.

When *La Hire* and Xaintrailles arrived, leading a cohort of men and wagons, the gunners got busy, placing the guns. I remounted my black and rode over near Xaintrailles, who glanced at me and quickly averted his eyes. But in that glance, I saw what I needed to know.

He was beginning to make peace with himself.

"*Tout est bon*, Poton?" I asked him. All good?

"*Tout est bon, Pucelle,*" he said and could not help but look up at me.

Gilles knew better than to be too near me when I was in conversation with any of the great men, but I knew he was sitting on the gray somewhere behind me, beyond me. I saw Xaintrailles' eyes light on him, like a wasp lights just before it stings. I knew what he thought, seeing the rabbit boy.

I knew what he thought but that he would not ask and so I would answer. "He is my friend," I said to Xaintrailles, and Xaintrailles gave a little snort, like he was embarrassed at being found out and also that he thought friendship a waste, or at least wanted to be thought to think that. Or that he thought Gilles was more than my friend only.

"*Oui.* My friend," I said. "Have you no friends, Poton? Is not Étienne (by this I meant *La Hire* for Étienne was his Christian name) your friend?"

Xaintrailles stared at me with the blank expression he had perfected when he did not want to speak, but wanted the other to say more, and so I obliged.

"You and Étienne have fought side by side all across France, from Agincourt to Coucy, in the Vermandois and the Laonnois and in Lorraine. You have celebrated victories and suffered defeats together, taken wounds and cared for one another. In Baugé, you pulled him from the rubble when a chimney fell down upon him and set his broken leg and while he healed, you nursed him. You have never failed to be at his side when there was battle, ready to fight and die beside him, and he has never failed to defend you, nor you to protect him."

I wanted to tell him that *La Hire* would die years before him and he would mourn him the rest of his life, suffering terrible nightmares, waking in the darkest hours of night with his face wet with tears, and feeling a deep gaping hole in his heart which could only be filled by the commission of more dark deeds and self-abuses, and all for Étienne, but I withheld that knowledge.

"Is he not your friend?"

Xaintrailles narrowed his eyes and spat out the words, "Yes, he is my friend, perhaps the only one I can count," and he was thinking, how did she know about all of that? No one alive even knows we fought at Agincourt and we do not speak of that great blow to French honor, that terrible day.

How does she know? he wondered.

I smiled gently at the killer. "Where you can count one friend, Poton, you can count another. Do not fear friendship. Friendship is a comfort."

I saw his eyes flick upwards, beyond me, at the boy who sat on the gray, and his grim mouth quirked a little smile. I worried then, perhaps I had said too much, had I put Gilles in danger, more danger than he already was? Could I trust this man, this man whom I wanted to be able to trust? Or was he a viper and would always be a viper, no matter my desire to see him redeemed?

The first of our small guns boomed then, sending a ball

over the bulwarks with a long shrieking hiss of sound. It struck directly on one of the enemy culverins, killing the man who was loading it and striking the arm from the man who held the hot-match.

The Spaniard gave a shout of triumph and my men began to swab and reload the cannon. The other cannons were almost set and the hour of the culverins was about to come to an end in showers of sparks, flying iron, and clouds of nostril-stinging smoke.

Once those culverins were silenced, my beautiful men would swarm over The Barbican, taking it level by level, and putting the English to the sword as they went. I saw it all as if it had already happened and I knew that before nightfall, *La Barbacane de Saint Augustin* would be ours and that I would make the acquaintance of the Burgundian, whose blue pennon still waved from the highest bastion.

What I was to have of this man, I did not yet know.

55, A Sword, a Sword

"Gilles," I said. "Give me the standard."

I would ride down and enter The Barbican over the drawbridge and would not want to risk Gilles being hurt. He had no armor, no helmet, and though I knew he would not die here, I could not be certain that he would not be wounded.

I was *La Pucelle* and I believed in the will of God, or at least had always said that I believed in the will of God, and was not the act of saying it the act of making it true?

Though I said it and though I believed that I believed it, when it came to it, I had to bewonder me, if God would will Gilles to be wounded if I showed the least disregard for his safety.

Perhaps I was merely a superstitious country girl after all.

Still, to bring him willingly, dressed in threadbare peasant's clothes and barefooted, among so many armored men and men in hauberk and brigandine, helmeted and gauntleted and bearing weapons, to bring him below the arrow-slots and carrying my standard, seemed to invite his being targeted.

I had suddenly known, known! I needed to go, needed to enter The Barbican, but I dare not take him with me.

I could not bear to see him struck down.

Or even frightened.

He stared at me, and I saw his hand tighten on the staff.

"Please," I said. "You shall stay here and I shall go, but I need my standard with me."

It was the first time I hurt him. I saw the blow I struck.

A blow struck with words.

His jaw set, clamping down on what? A word? A sob?

I saw his eyes as they went hard then went soft, like a dying bird. I wanted to take it back then, the words I had said, the blow I had struck on his unarmored heart. But I could not take it back.

"I am sorry," I said, "but you must stay here. I will carry the standard, but you must stay here."

I did not have time to explain more or to try to salve his feelings. There was a timing to these things in war. I knew not how I knew this, but I knew it to be true and that I dare not wait or the moment would be lost. I remembered how I had said to him, "...if we are to save France together..." and he had said, "...you are to save France and I will watch you do it."

I would remind him of this now, only there was not time.

I reached out my hand and he put the staff into it, his eyes so very pale and filled with tears.

My fingers closed on the wood, warm from his hand.

I rounded my horse and heard the silk rustling in the air above me and felt the black shy and leap sideways under me, until he realized that the standard was part of me and that we were moving, moving towards the fight, and then he heaved a great sigh and charged towards The Barbican, the standard snapping in the wind over our heads.

I could not think of Gilles then, or of what he was feeling, watching me charge the enemy, but I saw it as he saw it, as he watched me do it.

We thundered over the wooden planks of the drawbridge, the great iron-shod hooves of the black gauging chunks out of the wood. We surged into the interior of *La Barbacane de Saint Augustin,* arrows striking the ground and thunking into the timbers all around us.

I would be wounded by an arrow but that was not today, so I let them fall around me as if they were flower-petals and worried not about them.

I heeled my destrier around.

He raised his front and spun on his hind, making my banner form a silken circle over my head and I called out, "If you love me, follow me!" and even as I said it, I thought, "except for you, Gilles. If you love me, stay where you are."

At that moment, every French soldier that was outside The Barbican now came within it, over the bridge or over the faggot-filled moat or through the stinking water and slimy mud and clambering over the sides of the earthen motte and scaling the timbered bulwarks. Every French knight that was outside The Barbican now came within, spurring their destriers over the bridge in a storm of horseflesh and steel, like hailstones driven before a gale.

Upon my ears resounded the discordant song of war; the ring of steel on steel, the thuds of blows, the crack of breaking bone, high cries and low groans from the throats of men as they killed and as they died, the screams of the wounded ululating eerily, and the laughter of the victorious, and the fast-coming breaths of my horse as I rode him up the levels of the works, calling for my valiant men to follow me. Foemen snatched at me, their fingers raking at the steel of my quisses, their hands grasping my tassets, encountering the sharp edges of the steel fluting and losing grip, leaving bloody streaks upon the polished steel.

Weapons swung at me, barely missing me.

Arrows fell around me like butterfly wings.

English voices cursed me.

I laughed and rode on. I knew they could not catch me, could not kill me, not today.

And Gilles, on the gray, in his vantage of safety, wiped the tears from his eyes and watched me, watched me.

I wanted to say to him, you see? You see?

Why you could not follow?

This is a storm of steel! And you, you are my rabbit boy, my gentle joyful rabbit boy!

When the hooves of my steed crested that final bulwark, it was over. Before me, when I reined my black to a halt, was the blue pennon and under it, a man standing betwixt my bloody boys. Pierre's and Joseph's visors were up, their eyes like blue wildflowers, and they smiled with exaltation and pride.

The Burgundian's head was bowed and his clothing and armor were un-bloodied. His sword and dagger were in their scabbards on his belt.

I knew not his name or his rank and History never saw fit to remember either.

The battle for The Barbican was over.

Saint Augustine was French again. French again, forever.

"You," I said, and the Burgundian lifted his head and his

hazel eyes met mine. They were mild in appearance, not hateful, nor fearful, but more like the eyes of a man who had known for his entire life that this moment was coming and had only wondered when. But it was not the moment of his death, for I saw his death, and it was many years from now in another fight and somewhere in Normandy, and Xaintrailles would be there to, as he was now, having just ridden his horse up behind me.

"You," I said, and I dropped the reins on the arched neck of my black, and reached out my hand.

The Burgundian blinked those mild hazel eyes at me.

And then he understood. He grasped his sword by the hilt and slid it free of its scabbard and handed it to me hilt-first over his arm. I grasped it, raised it, (I heard my men cheering all around me) and gave it a swing or two. Twas a good sword, well-balanced so as to return easily to the hand, and heavy enough to strike good rending blows. The tip was pointed for the thrust and keenly sharpened to the first hand-and-a-half of its length and the rest was edged stout for parrying and for crushing armor and shattering bones. A good sword, a weapon to take to war, if a man must go.

"It is a good weapon," I said to the man.

"It was my father's," he said, in his Burgundian accent. "And it was my grandsire's, and I think his sire's as well. I am not sure when it came to my family."

I nodded appraisingly, swinging it again.

"It has killed many," I said, for I could see them, their faces going back through the ages. Most were French, some were not, but all felt the same pain, the same agony, the same great disappointment at being killed by it. I looked down at the man and his mild eyes met mine, wondering what I would choose to do with him. I am sure the leering face of

Xaintrailles over my shoulder did not reassure him.

"I am not fond of Burgundians," I said. "I lived in terror of them all my life. Where I live, in Lorraine, they are always coming over the border and destroying villages, raping girls and women, killing children, and burning homes. I hate the sound of their voices."

I did not know why I was telling him these things. I was not proud of my hatred, it was not Christian to feel these things. His hazel eyes were constant and steady, though I saw him swallow.

He would accept my wrath, if wrath was what I choose to mete out.

I had the power. I held the sword.

My black stamped and shook his glossy mane. He was watching the man and would stomp him to death if I so much as thought I wanted him to. I kept my thoughts upon mercy and my body relaxed in the saddle and my horse steadied. I breathed French air and looked all about me.

Frenchmen stood on every level of The Barbican, looking up at me, their weapons bloody in their hands. Englishmen lay dead in every ditch and atop every motte, their bodies strewn like broken poppets over the bulwarks and ramparts. Even in the arrow-slots of the Convert, only French faces looked down. The Burgundian was the only enemy here alive.

I looked down at him and he swallowed again.

"I shall keep your sword," I said. "And you shall go home, to wherever you call home."

I handed the sword back to Xaintrailles. "Poton, hold on to that for me, would you?"

"As you wish, *Pucelle*," the killer said, and I could imagine his grim little smile as he took the weapon from my hand. I looked at the Burgundian again, his hazel eyes seemed full of disbelief and yet of hope, hope that maybe, just maybe there was no trick here?

"Go home," I said to him. "Embrace your wife if you have one and teach your children if you have them. Teach them peace."

I backed my horse.

Behind me, Xaintrailles backed his.

Pierre and Joseph, who had one hand each on the man, dropped their hands and the Burgundian slipped from between them. He walked, a bit shakily, past the warriors of France who had taken The Barbican, down through the bloody bulwarks, past the bodies of his comrades, and crossed the drawbridge.

He broke into a run and, with only the clothes on his back and the dagger on his belt, he ran past where Gilles sat mounted on the gray.

Their eyes met and each wondered about the other, the Burgundian about the bruised and ragged boy on the old warhorse, the boy about the last survivor of the battle of Saint Augustine, whose life I had chosen to spare.

56, Fires

Father Pasqueral was beside me as I dismounted my black. He had been told that he would be a busy man this day and so he had been. He had heard the confessions of many men and given the rites for many men and to him it mattered not if those men were French, English or Burgundian, they were the children of God, and he would try to ease their passage from this life to the next. He understood my tears.

Perhaps better than anyone, even the boy who followed the girl who wept across France. Together, the friar and I sorted the dead, had the English laid in one place and the French in another.

The friends and comrades of the French bore them away, perhaps to lay them in the great Cathedral or one of the small churches. The English remained.

We laid them out, crossed their hands, prayed over them, and I alone wept over them. My tears, the tears of *La Pucelle,* could not buy their way into Heaven. But if my sorrow for their great and little joys snuffed out, their breaths untaken, their mornings unawakened-to, could wash any of their sin away, I would weep for a thousand years.

It was not only my tears I shed in the mud of The Barbican. I shed my blood there as well, stepping on a *chausse-trappe* as I moved from one dead man to the next. The four-pointed little device was one of many the English had flung down at the beginning of the assault, hoping to stab the feet of French attackers. Of all of us who attacked that day, I believe I am the only one to be injured by stepping on one, and that only after the battle had been won.

It was my left foot, the same that had taken the other wound, by sword or battle-axe, in the morning during our pleasure-jaunt on the beach, so I now had a missing half-toe and a puncture wound in the bottom of that foot, and I was seen to be hobbling about, so that everyone knew I had been wounded at *La Barbacane de Saint Augustin.*

History knows only of the one, since only my boys knew of the first wound and their stories were never told.

Since the end of the battle and the departure of the Burgundian I had not seen the boy from Le Moineau. Pierre and Joseph had taken down the blue pennon and had set my banner there on that high rampart where it would be seen by the English inside *Les Tourelles,* and there were a good many inside *Les Tourelles,* which would be our objective on the morrow.

Though I cast my gaze about from time to time, I caught no sight of Gilles or of the gray. I knew that I had hurt him.

I knew not where he had gone.

I was *La Pucelle* and though I might, like a country girl, desire beyond all else to go look for the boy whom I loved and whom I thought I might like to marry someday, I was *La Pucelle.*

I was *La Pucelle.*

All the while I was with the good Father seeing to the dead, others of my company were securing the weapons and gathering up enemy standards and cleaning up the mess of battle and making little fires and burning things they didn't like. There were fires burning everywhere and the smoke was in my nostrils.

I remembered that it begins with fire and it ends with fire, though I could not say how it was I remembered that, who had told me that, or what it even meant.

But there were fires, men burning things that had belonged to the English, men setting small fires and cooking food over them, for it was late in the day now and time for men to eat and refresh themselves. Fires were burning to the west too, towards *Le Champ de Saint Privé*, and I knew that The Bastard was burning English forts in that direction, could see those leaping flames in my mind, feel the burn of that acrid smoke at the back of my throat, even smell English bodies burning in those fires, men who would not be properly and respectfully buried.

I shed tears for the things I could not change, the men whose deaths I could not prevent, and the men whose wrong-doings I could not stop.

It begins with flames and it ends with flames, which of my angels had told me that?

I only remembered that when I first heard it, it had had the ring of truth. I had feared (and been intrigued by) flames all my life.

The only flames that, in my life, I had not feared, were those of the fire in the hearth of Isabelle Romée, by whose warmth I would sleep on those nights I gave up my bed to wandering strangers, for they had been tamed by the hand of my mother and trained to do her bidding, stay in their place and cook our food and warm us and nothing more, and also the fire that burned in the grate of the King at Chinon, for his was living fire of the King chosen by God.

Those fires had given me comfort. No other fire had given me aught but a sickness in my belly, a trembling in my limbs, and stinging tears to blind my eyes, and yet, I knew not why.

The victorious men of France made their war-camp there, at The Barbican and on the bluffs overlooking the River Loire, and all night they would sing and make a joyful sound so that the ears of their foe, those English locked tightly within *Les Tourelles*, the great drawbridge drawn up and the guns aimed outward towards the shore where once they had been aimed city-ward, would hear them and fear their fate upon the morrow. The sun was low to the west, its glorious red-gold light as blinding as an angel of God.

Alençon stepped up to me, where I worked with Father Pasqueral over the bodies of the dead.

"Jehanne," the Fair Duke said gently.

I rose from my knees and rubbed the mud from the knee-cops of my armor with my palms. A lock of my reddish-brown hair blew into my eyes from the breeze off the river. I pushed it behind my ear.

The Duke smiled, as if the gesture reminded him of something, or more like, of someone. He said, "You should go back to the city, have that wound seen to. I dare say you have eaten nothing all this day."

It was only then I thought about it; food, and drink. I had risen that morning before light, wakened my pages and said, "If you want to see a battle, follow me."

I had not breakfasted and the day had gone from one thing to next and it seemed a year ago that I had ridden from the Burgundy Gate.

Yes, I was hungry. Yes, I was thirsty.

Yes, I was tired.

Yes, my foot pained me.

I looked at Father Pasqueral, on his knees beside a dead man. "You, Father, must attend me early, earlier than even you are accustomed to," I said. "And stay close by me tomorrow, as I shall be wounded."

I touched myself where the wound would be taken, pressing my fingers down in the joint between the gorget and the pauldron of my left shoulder.

"My child..." Father Pasqueral began, as he rose to his feet. But I raised my hand.

"It is the will of God," I said, and I knew that what I said was true.

The Fair Duke's jaw dropped, showing the inside of his astonished mouth. He clapped it shut and furrowed his handsome brow. "Jehanne..." he began.

"I shall return to *la maison de la famille de Boucher*," I interrupted Alençon. "Tomorrow, when I return, we shall take that fort," and I pointed to the spires of *Les Tourelles*.

As I rode away, towards the place of the boat landings, the blazing watch-fires of the war-camp were in their hundreds were all about me, like a sky of stars cast down.

57, The Truth, a Lie

The gray was in the deep grass of the meadow below the Grand Old Oak, and I knew the boy would be in the tree limbs. I rode the black through the grass, his feathered pasterns swishing and throwing grass seeds before him. The gray lifted his head from grazing, blew through his nostrils in greeting, and lowered his head again. I rode below the spreading branches of the tree, reined the black to a halt and looked up. The twisting limbs of the tree were rough and ominous-looking against the darkling sky. Gilles was silent and though I knew he was there I could not place him. But I felt his eyes on me, so I spoke.

"It must be the same tomorrow," I said.

He was silent.

There might have been a rustle of leaves, or it might have been the wind only.

"I will carry my banner," I said, "or someone else will, but you must not be near me."

How could I tell him that I would be wounded?

How could I tell him that I would have to place myself right in the thick of the fighting, that many Englishmen would try to be the one to kill me; that I would make of myself their primary target and thus prove my cause, in that they would all try but not be able to kill me?

That I feared he would be hurt in the fighting, that I had not equipped him in any way for being in battle? That it was too easy for unexpected things to happen in a battle and that I did not even fully trust some of the great men, my own men, not to take advantage of the fact that I brought my rabbit boy into danger with me.

How could I tell him that I did not need to have to worry about him on the morrow, when I had so much else to think about? That worrying about him, I might miss something, be distracted and not do the proper things?

So far, I had been lucky.

I had done the proper things, more by guesswork than knowing. Things came into my head, what I called my voices, and sometimes in times of quiet, I saw the forms and the faces of the angels and they spoke quietly to me, with voices as sweet as little brooks of water running to meet the Meuse after the first rains of Spring-time.

But in the Faery Wood, in Domrémy, Michael the archangel had spoken directly to me, with his eyes as bright as the sun, his face like burnished bronze and his golden hair in ringlets to his glowing shoulders. He had drawn nigh me, let me feel his burning light, so bright and strong and powerful and dangerous. He had told me that I must do this, and because he was not to be denied, I had, despite my fear that I was a poor choice for this great undertaking.

But I had thought to have his counsel, the counsel of the

archangel all through it, to tell me how it shall be done, what war was made of, those parts that it is built from, cannons and towers, and swords and halberds, and arbalests and bastions, and what ways to defeat an enemy that had not been defeated in four score years of constant warfare, how to outthink and outfight men who had been born and bred to war and taught it from the cradle. He had counseled me none of these things and I had had to see them for myself, try to understand them for myself.

All Michael had given me was a touch.

A burning touch that was the gift of sight, the gift of seeing the deaths of others before they happened. To teach me compassion, he had said.

But I had had compassion. I had had it my whole life.

I had cared for swallow babies that fell from nests broken by boys with stones. I had given my bed to people wandering homeless in the storm. I had brought forth earthworms from water puddles and loosened the harnesses of tired horses left standing too long in the rain.

Michael said it was the gift of compassion.

Perhaps what I had had was only sympathy.

Perhaps I needed something greater to move my heart, to commit me fully to compassion. If so, that touch bestowed it.

I wept for the lost lives I witnessed.

I wept for the joys snuffed out. I saw the wonder that was their lives, while they were living them, their special, distinct, and irreplaceable lives. There were still those I had not seen, whose deaths I had not seen.

I knew I could not alter the things that were to be, but if I had not seen a death, then that death might not happen.

If I did the proper things, then lives that might be lost could be saved, if they were the lives of people I had not yet seen. So I must not be distracted.

I was still learning on my own what a war was made of, the parts that made a war, and if I paid good attention, heard the voices who put things in my head, and made good choices, then lives would not be lost. I would not see their deaths for they would not die.

But if Gilles went to battle with me and was the target of the enemy for that he carried my standard, I would be distracted. I might not make good choices.

I would be too worried about him, about the safely of one boy that I loved, that I loved above all other people, and might thereby, cause the deaths of others.

These were things I had been thinking.

It had started after the pleasure-jaunt on the beach early that morning, when the English arrows had flown and struck down our footmen and we had had to fight our way free. If I had known more of what war was made of, if I had known earlier that the enemy had marched from Saint Privé, those lives would not have been lost.

I had put Gilles in danger, letting him ride with us.

He could have been struck by an arrow.

He could have been hurt.

Now I would not be able to go into harm's way without that worry. So he would have to stay away from me when I came within reach of the foe.

He was so silent, in the tree.

Only a little rustle of the breeze through the leaves was heard.

"I would climb up there, to see you," I said, "only my foot is hurt and I dare not."

He gave a little laugh then and said, "Oh, Jehanne, do not climb. I will come down."

And I heard him, the sound of his bare feet scrabbling on the rough bark, parts of which fell down into my hair, and the ripping sound of his breeches on a stob.

"Oops!" he said and laughed.

He dropped to the ground, landing right next to the shoulder of the black, which, to my amazement, did not shy away, or try to stomp or bite, but stood calmly and let Gilles put his hand on its glossy shoulder close to my armored knee.

Gilles looked up at me, all love in his eyes. It was almost dark but some light from somewhere was catching on my white harness and glinting off of it and into his eyes.

I had hurt him.

I could see the love in his eyes but the hurt was there too, like a thin layer painted over the underlying landscape of his love. I could never forgive myself for that hurt but I could not, would not, take away its cause. What was hardest for me was knowing that he would never, ever again, be able to fully trust me not to take his joy away.

That is the cost of hurting someone.

"You understand why it must be so?" I asked him and he stood there, most of his weight balanced on his right foot, so that if my horse made a move against him, he would be able to leap away, and he looked up at me and said, "No, I do not understand. I am your banner-bearer. I want to be with you. I should be with you."

I sighed. "You are not my banner-bearer. In fact, the King sent me with one and I have not even used him yet. He is here somewhere. If I need someone to carry my standard tomorrow besides myself, I will have him do it."

Gilles lowered his head, his tangled hair falling over his face.

"I don't want you to be in danger," I said.

He looked up at me then, his eyes blazing with the desire to argue with me, to convince me. "But you are in danger, why should not I be?"

"I am *La Pucelle!*" I said, not with anger but with exasperation.

"And I am... I am..." he started.

I thought he might call himself the rabbit boy as a way to belittle himself, thinking that maybe that is what I was thinking to say to him, that he was only a rabbit boy and had no business in a battle, but he stopped and did not say more.

I bent over, my armor whispering like harp strings brushed by a finger, and I touched his hand. It rested on the great quivering shoulder of the black destrier and it was warm. I felt for only a half of a half of an instant, the chill that would be his death, before the hot horseflesh drew it off and all I felt was the hand of my lover.

My lover who was not my lover, could not be my lover, for I was a girl who was never to know a man. I was *La Pucelle.* Was it fair to tell him he was my love?

He knew it, knew it in his heart, though our talk had always skirted around the edges of it, like the army of France had skirted around the edges of Orleans, finding ways to sneak in past the English lines.

"You are my Great Joy," I said to him. "You are my own one, my best friend, my constant companion."

He smiled at me. Indulgently, it seemed. "You, *Jehanne, La Pucelle,* (and by this he showed me he knew why I felt I could not say what was in my mind) are my heart."

"Yes," I said. "Yes."

"And I am your shield."

I moved my hand from his then and straightened up on my horse's back. The black felt the shift in my body and in my mind and he stamped his hooves, ready to go. Gilles stepped back a pace to avoid being trampled.

My shield. My shield.

Was it possible?

I knew that I would be wounded. I knew I would be struck down but not killed. What protects a man from being killed but his shield? And to protect him, his shield must be struck. Struck but not always destroyed.

Would Gilles be wounded protecting me if I let him stay at my side in the fight? Would he take the brunt of a blow for me? Receive the greater part of it that I might receive the lesser?

"I do not..." I said, using my legs to steady my horse. "I do not want you to be my shield. I want you to be my love," I blurted out.

He smiled then, a big broad smile that captured the glinting early-evening stars and tossed them in my face. "I want that too, my heart. But when?"

I shook my head and took a big breath and blew it out.

"When this is done. When we have won and the King is crowned at Rheims, and the English are chased from France and the Lord of Orléans is home in his city and his bastard brother hands him the keys of the city. These are the things I have promised to do. These are the things that must be done and they can only be done by *La Pucelle,* and I can only be La *Pucelle* if..." and I choked on these words, "...if I do not love you now."

He came closer and placed his hand on the cold hard smooth steel of my knee. "But, when you have done these things, my heart? When you have done them, and I know that you will do them, then you will love me? Then you will marry me and be my lover?"

I began to cry.

Not because I would deny him.

Not because this was not my desire, in fact it was my greatest desire, but because I did not see me anywhere when I saw his death. If I was to marry him and be his lover and his wife, if these things would truly come to pass, why had I been gone from his life for most of a lifetime by the time that he would die drowning in a river, unknown and unmissed by anyone, his body food for fishes and turtles?

I wept for him.

I wept for me.

I wept because I would break his heart by denying him now. I had only one choice and it was a sin.

I would lie to him.

"Yes," I said. "Yes, I will marry you. When these things I have promised to do are done, I will marry you joyfully and love you the rest of your life."

It was doubly a sin for I believed in the power of words. If the act of saying it is the act of making it true, then I lied doubly for I knew it was not true, would never be true. I could not know then why it would not, could not, be true. I remembered that it begins with flames and it ends with flames, but how could I know what that meant?

I had had hints, I had been given clues, but I threw them off lightly like a summer shift and donned a heavier garment.

I would not look at that which I knew, knew! that I would die, and soon. I would not look into that fire and willingly go there. I would not let myself believe it, though I knew, I knew I would not marry Gilles.

I lied and it was a joyful lie and I spoke it joyfully.

I gave myself to that lie and it was the best thing I think I ever said, though it be a sin. And his face lit up.

I could see it in the dimness, like a thousand glowing watch-fires, the brightest, most joyful face in all the history of the world, and for a moment, just one beautiful moment, we were the two most joyous people.

"So we are affianced," he said.

"Yes," I said. "Though I do not think we should tell anyone."

"Of course not!" he said. "We shall wait until your other promises are met."

"Yes," I said, "until then." And then the other matter came into my mind, the matter of his safety. "But you must be safe, my love. You cannot follow me into battle. I need you to watch me do it." He smiled again, his heart light and joyful now.

"Watch you save France?" he said, remembering our first talk. "You shall save France and I shall watch you do it?"

"You shall watch me," I said, "and I shall do it better knowing you are watching me."

I did not want to tell him of the wound; it would worry him and disturb his sleep tonight and, for certain, he would not agree to watch me be wounded if he knew, so I said nothing about it.

He nodded, as if sealing a bargain.

He strode off through the grass to seek the gray.

I could see the rip in the seat of his breeches and a bit of his strong buttocks, but the light was so dim, I could not see much.

I was a little disappointed.

58, Bread and Wine

Gilles and I sat in the kitchen at the House of Boucher.

It was only us and the old cook, who seemed in a better mood than was usual and seemed to like me and my rabbit boy better when the great men were not around and especially tonight, since she had heard the town's excitement that we had taken The Barbican. She had placed a whole roasted chicken in front of Gilles and a trencher of breads and cheeses and some pickled root vegetables and some fruits. I asked for some bread to be toasted and this I ate dipped in warmed and watered wine.

It was my normal meal.

I could not stand the smell of the roasted bird, though I took pleasure in the pleasure that my love took in tearing the hot steaming flesh from its bones and eating it, licking the grease from his fingers. For him it was a great treat to have an entire chicken all for himself.

As for me, the cheese seemed too heavy and the pickles too vinegary and so I only nibbled at them and only because the cook was being unusually nice and I wished to reward her pleasantness. I rarely took more than bread and wine since I had begun my journey from Vaucouleurs, though sometimes fruit was welcome. Perhaps it was some requirement of my mission; that I abstain from bodily pleasures until my work was done.

I had always relished food as a child, there never was enough to sate oneself upon and, so, what was had was savored and enjoyed. But since I first mounted a horse and rode for Chinon, I had cared little for eating beyond what was needful to sustain myself. Wine and bread was what my soul and body needed, perhaps because I was in a state of Grace and required only that which was provided by the Eucharist. I had not thought this through. But the way Gilles looked at me as he ate his fowl and cheese and the other things laid out for our repast, made me wonder.

When my tasks were completed, and my promises fulfilled, would my appetite return? Would I then crave all the pleasures that life had to offer?

The great men, the captains of France, had taken to joking and teasing me about my habits, calling me the wren, the little bird who barely pecks at food and takes tiny little bird sips. The Bastard, watching me eat had one day gripped my arm like a father, squeezed it, and told me I would waste away if I did not develop a more French appetite.

I had not yet wasted away.

In fact I seemed more full of strength and energy each day and all the world could see that I slept less, worked harder, and accomplished more than all these captains put together for all their feasting and indulgences.

I thought of these things and shifted my feet under the table. My wounded foot had been cleaned of blood and wrapped up. The half-missing toe throbbed but I tried to ignore it.

Outside, in the city of Orléans, the folk were celebratory.

Through the little windows at the top of the kitchen wall that brought light and air into the kitchen from the street above, I could heard the singing and cheering of soldiers and citizens alike. I was glad to hear their joy, joy that I had brought to them. Or was it wrong of me to take pride in the joy they were experiencing?

The efforts of our soldiers, our valiant knights like Pierre and Joseph Cadieux and others, the men of the City Watch and the local militias, all who had fought and struggled, all who had perished in the fighting and taken painful wounds, these are the ones who deserved the credit. I cocked my head and listened at the sounds coming through the tiny windows.

Gilles watched me, piling all the little bird bones off to one side of his trencher and reaching for some cheese. He tore a piece off and put it in his mouth, chewing slowly. He had those dark bruises on his face from the beating but the eye was not quite as swollen as this morning, a hundred years ago, when we had risen early and called up the army from its slumbers in the square before the Great Cathedral.

He was joyous, and I knew why.

We had pledged our love, I had promised to marry him.

Everything he wanted was within his grasp, if only he was patient and waited. And the rabbit boy knew how to wait. The forest and the field were his body and his blood.

The earth was patient.

"It is because of you, Jehanne," he said to me.

"Hmm?" I pretended not to know what he spoke of.

"Their happiness," he said.

"It is because they fought," I said. "It is because it was important enough for them to die for it. They proved themselves worthy of freedom today. God helps those who help themselves."

Gilles laughed. "My mother used to say that old saying to me," he said. "I would tell her I agreed and take another piece of bread." He reached for a piece of bread to illustrate.

There was a fire in the hearth that was to one side of him and the warm glow of its low flames made his hair a halo of gold. "Tomorrow," he said, "you shall help yourself to *Les Tourelles*, and I shall watch you do it."

I was glad he had made peace with my decision.

I could ride out with my love beside me in the morning as we had ridden out today, cross the river as we had done today, and join the army that was encamped at The Barbican. I would find a safe vantage place for my boy to watch from, safe and secure and far from the fighting, and then I would join my men, and we would assault the great formidable bastille that was *Les Tourelles*, where six hundred of the best soldiers of the English army were now cornered like desperate lions.

At some time in the day, I would take a fatal wound that would not be fatal.

I would be seen to die, yet I would not die.

My angels would save me, this I knew.

But not before I came to that dark doorway and put my foot across its threshold, leaned my head and shoulders into its unknown spaces to see whatever lay beyond and feel myself drawn through.

It came to me then, that on the morrow, rather than

Gilles being my shield, I would be his, take the blow that would have been his, protect him as a shield. I would be the shield of all of France, take the blow meant for my people, suffer for them, die for them, and be resurrected that they might live.

"What are you thinking, *La Pucelle?*" he asked. He called me by my title for the benefit of the cook who, having provided for us, was reclining upon her cot in the corner and beginning to snooze. I smiled at him, for I knew that if we had been alone, he would have said "my heart."

"I was only musing," I told him. "Girls are allowed to muse." And I thought, how deceptive I have become since I declared my love.

He smiled and shook his hair from his eyes and drank deeply from his cup.

My Great Joy, I thought, looking at him.

My great beautiful boundless Joy. How much more shall I have to lie to you? Add another wound to my stigmata, another sin to my burden.

A knock came then upon the street door.

59, De Rais

He came sweeping in, Baron de Rais, his rich cloak draping his broad and manly shoulders. He was trimly bearded with arching dark brows and long dark lashes over blue eyes as pretty as Alençon's, and like the Duke, had barely embarked into what would be the third decade of his life. The young Baron's smile was confident with his knowledge of himself, yet I knew that there was much inside him that he was years away from knowing. He was born of a family in whose blood ran that of all the greatest and most noble families of France and he was wealthy beyond all imaging and had married great wealth as well.

He was all pride and power, had never known want or hunger or been deprived of any luxury he wanted, and in his gleaming eye, in the place that lay beyond that blue sky-like shine, gestated a horror yet unborn.

He had a hat and swept it off, its trailing ribbands

sweeping crumbs upon the floor that would be gathered up at midnight by the mouse in the wall, who sat waiting now, its long whiskers twitching at the smells of roasted bird and ripe cheese.

De Rais was out of his armor and wearing elegant clothes in tones of russet-red and dark-earth brown broidered with gold thread and edged with pleated braids of saffron-yellow and deep forest green. Lovely colors, I thought, and ones that made me want to like him, though I knew he was not a good man and one I should not like.

There was a matched dagger and sword girded about his narrow hips on a wide belt of brown leather with raised metalwork of beaten bronze and copper. The scrollwork of the weapons' hilts was gilded and set with red gems that shimmered in the firelight.

Standing before me, he gave a little bow, also intended, I believe, to make me want to like him, for the great men did not bow to me and only the Duke of Alençon ever doffed his hat to me. He had run some pungent oil through his black hair, perhaps witch hazel, and I saw Gilles' nostrils flare at the scent of it.

"*Jehanne, La Pucelle,*" he said to me, in a very formal way.

"Baron de Rais," I said.

Behind the Baron's back, Gilles, who had been all languid and relaxed but a moment ago, was now on alert, his back straight and his eyes bright, watching de Rais like a hawk watches for another movement in the grass. He had quietly moved his trencher to the side, laden with its gnawed bones and bits of crust and nibbled ends of roots. His hands were laid flat upon the wood of the board, as if awaiting orders.

I noticed all this, but made no indication that I saw it.

I said, "Would you like to sit, my lord? Shall I waken the

cook?" and I smiled at the Baron, meeting his brooding gaze and trying to ferret out his future there. De Rais pursed his lips and looked at the table as if he might indeed consider sitting, but apparently thought better of it, and shook his head.

"*Merci, mon ami*, but no," he said. "I have come to deliver a message from the captains of France, who have been in a council of war. They have chosen me as their messenger boy."

He winced, as if it were a slight, but I could see it was all feigned and that he had offered to come see me and to bear this message and that he wanted to see me, liked to see me, and wanted something of me, and what he wanted from me was not grace, and not a healing, and not a blessing, which is why many people wanted to see me, thinking I could bestow these things, which, of course, I could not.

"Ahh," I said, and thought to appear unconcerned by dipping myself some more wine, and then I leaned further forward and poured more into Gilles' cup as well, meeting his pale green eyes. This was my way of saying, to Gilles, "Watch this man," and to de Rais, "This boy is my companion, my friend, and my trusted confidant." Gilles gave a tiny nod and lifted his cup to his mouth, looking over the rim at me.

The wine was watered, spiced, and warmed in a lidded iron cauldron that the cook had placed in the center of the table, with a ladle for dipping.

De Rais gave a sigh, dropped his fancy hat onto the table and threw his leg over one of the benches, seating himself opposite me and beside Gilles, straddling the bench like a horse. He reached for an empty vessel, banged it upside-down on the table to knock out anything unwelcome that might be within it and set it right-side-up. I filled it for him.

The Baron swirled the wine in his cup, sniffed at it, and took a draft. In his lowered brows, in his smooth high well-formed forehead with its little peak at the center, I saw, as he drank, the prayerful supplication of his soul to a wicked god. When he sniffed the wine, it was the coppery scent of blood I smelled and I felt the beat of his heart increase in tempo until his limbs tingled with the thrill.

I looked then, through the downward gaze of his bright blue eyes, under his lowered lashes, into his cup. With my mind and his eyes, in the depths of the dark red wine, I looked, and what I saw was not mulled wine but the warm and clotting blood of children murdered. His ears, which seemed my ears, heard their wails, their screams that were like the shrieks of fawns being torn apart by wolves, horrible sounds unheard except by his ears and the huge heavy stones of his castles and a few of his closest companions. And I could hear also his own excited exclamations, his groans and grunts of bodily pleasure, and feel, as if in my own body, his consuming arousal striving towards satiation.

I threw my head back then abruptly, and shook off the seeing. A wave of nausea swept over me then and I opened my mouth and gasped for breath, forcing back the desire to purge myself. I had seen it, heard it, felt it but even seeing it, hearing it, feeling it, I knew it had not happened, not yet, these children were un-conceived, these notions as of yet unformed in his own dank brain, and yet I could know them.

Gilles had watched me watching de Rais.

I felt his eyes on me.

Looking at his face, his braced body, his widened eyes, I knew that he had seen that I had seen, that he knew that whatever I had seen was something horrible, something evil. He glanced sharply at de Rais, who was emptying his cup, draining the final drop as if it was the last thing he would drink in his lifetime.

It would be good if it was the last thing he would drink in his lifetime, if that wine were poison.

There were some men, I was thinking now, who would be better dead, for the harm that they will do alive is too great a burden for the rest of humanity to bear, and we should not have to bear it. This was such a man and yet I knew that to kill him would be a sin, if it was even possible to kill him before his time. Who would take on that sin, or attempt it?

And on what account? My tales of evil yet undone?

Evil as of yet not even imagined by the one who would commit it?

Gilles might, if I told him what I knew.

But how would my gentle joyful rabbit boy kill a man?

I dippered Baron de Rais another cupful, wishing it was poison. That he would drink it, deliver his message, and stumble out into the celebrating city, to be found dead in the morning in some street or alley. I could then claim I had not seen him; that he had not delivered whatever message the captains of France wished me to hear, and I could do as I liked on the morrow without having to defy them, for I knew I would have to defy them, and would by defying them, win back Orléans from the English before the end of the day.

And if he were found dead, the un-conceived and unborn children of my country would, like wildflowers on the hillsides and birds in the trees, live and grow without fearing the building tempest of his madness, the base desires of his demon nature, his violent exploitation of their physical innocence.

As if on cue, as if knowing that I was contemplating committing the sin of murder, Father Pasqueral entered, coming in through the interior door from the house above, where he had a tiny room in the highest floor of the house between the gables.

He seemed shocked to find de Rais with us but greeted the Baron politely. The friar sat on the bench beside me, wrapped his fustian robes about him as if chilled, and I poured him some wine and handed him a loaf of bread, which he tore in half and half again with his fingers, fingers which this day had made the sign of the cross upon the foreheads of a hundred dead and dying men.

When I turned again to look at the Baron, his brooding gaze rested on the face of my rabbit boy, looking at him as if he had never quite seen him before. What I saw in his expression raised the fine hairs at the nape of my neck.

He stared at Gilles with a mix of responses, one of which was physical desire, as he marked upon the beauty of the boy with his fair face exemplified by the light and shadow of the fire in the dark room and his strong lithe body and his golden-brown curls in a jumble on his shoulders. His other emotion was a kind of childish jealousy, two-sided.

De Rais was jealous that the boy loved me and would therefore never be persuaded to leave me for another lord, not by promises of favors nor enrichment nor even love, and he was also jealous that because I had the boy as my closest friend and confidant, that he, Baron de Rais, would never be able to insinuate himself into my life in that role, for this was what he desired of me and perhaps more.

He was a man of power seeking more power and he would seek it in every avenue that he might walk and under every stone he could turn. His thoughts were that I had power, though truly the only power I had was vested in me by God and nothing of my own making or control.

"My lord?" I said, wishing to draw his attention away from Gilles. "You had a message for me?"

He turned to look into my eyes then and I saw them. Innocent young boys. Beautiful tender youths. Girls in their virginal purity, sweetly growing into ripeness. They were there in his dark heart, their futures fettered to his.

At the same moment that I spoke, he spoke as well, saying, "I have a collection of relics of a religious nature I would like to show you one day, *Pucelle.* They are in my favorite home, Tiffauges; it is a lovely place and a fitting reliquary for these wonders. I even have a crucifix crafted of pieces of the True Cross."

He glanced at Father Pasqueral, whose hand had stopped halfway to his mouth with a piece of bread. "You may come as well, friar," said de Rais congenially. "I have many learned men in my circle. We study and debate the scriptures, and my library at Chantocé Castle, at Anjou, where I was born, will one day be the finest in France, better even than at Poitiers or at Rheims. I have illuminated texts there that are most rare and precious and I am still collecting, and I am hiring skilled artisans to repair the bindings and enrich the covers with silver and gold. It is my life's work, to come to a greater understanding of God and to be His servant in good and varied works."

Father Pasqueral put his bread in his mouth and chewed slowly. As the friar set his hand on his lap, I saw his fingers trembling.

Gilles' eyes had narrowed and flicked from de Rais to me and back again.

I had asked the Baron a question which he had ignored or had not heard over the ardor of his own voice, his own barely-contained passions. I asked again, "My lord, you have a message for me?"

De Rais said, "I wish to create colleges where young men may study the word of God. Where the great questions of our existence may be explored."

"An admirable calling," Father Pasqueral said, without much enthusiasm.

De Rais sighed and turned to me. The firelight gleamed on his oiled hair. He looked sad and wistful, almost like a lost child. My heart actually did feel pity for him then, a man of two parts, trying to be whole but forever riven in twain, like a condemned man torn apart by horses.

"They have held a council," he said.

I nodded. "They have their councils and I have mine," I said. "And from what I have seen so far, my councils have had the better record."

The Baron gave a nervous chuckle. "Well... the captains bid me tell you," he said, "that they have decided the gain we made today against the foe was well enough for the now. We shall enjoy our victories. The city is well-provisioned, the threat of *La Bastille de Saint Loupe* is alleviated, we have control of *La Porte de Bourgoyne,* therefore a free flow of goods to the city, and the English are tightly holed in *Les Tourelles*, which means that we may starve them out. The English remaining at Saint Laurent and the other bastilles to the west are terrified and will not make trouble."

I sipped my watered wine and stared at Baron de Rais, adopting Xaintrailles' trick of waiting until the other became uncomfortable and said more than they intended. And soon he did.

"Granted, Saint Loupe was your victory which is the only reason we have not to fear that stronghold any longer. Saint Augustine, today, was your victory as well. And the thing the

English are terrified of is you, *La Pucelle*. But, that being acknowledged, the captains believe we must now await reinforcements from the King. We should not press our luck too far."

I managed to keep from laughing. I did not want him returning from his message-bearing mission to tell tales on me. Inside, I was seething with rage. They thought it was luck that had brought us this far? Luck?

It was ludicrous that they should think it mete to wait now when we had the English in our grasp, just requiring us to tighten our fist and squeeze the life out of them. What kind of men were they? What kind of captains, warriors and commanders were they? If they were the best France had to offer in this, her most desperate hour, no wonder she had been defiled and brutalized, plundered and exploited, for four score years.

This was why I had come.

This was why the angels spoke to me.

To me and no other.

If they thought that now I would sit upon my hands and wait, they did not know me. There had already been far too much waiting for me since I left Domrémy, waiting my life away when I had been told I had a finite amount of time to achieve what I had promised to do. Was the act of saying it the act of making it true?

Yes, but one had to do the thing as well.

"Very well, my lord," I said. "You have delivered your message. I have heard it."

De Rais nodded his handsome head.

"Have you a message for the captains in return?" He asked, with a hint of a smile. He wanted to know what I would say to them, for he expected something provocative that would be of great amusement when he brought it back to The Bastard and the other great men, that would keep them stirred up and in debate all night, and he might sit there and drink and watch the show.

"No message," I said.

He sat there a long moment in the silence that I had left behind my words. Neither Gilles nor Father Pasqueral gave a twitch of movement, nor spoke, nor heaved an audible breath.

In the tiny recess in the stone wall, behind the slab table where they butchered the meat, the mouse stretched its tiny limbs and stroked its whiskers and readied itself to venture forth in search of the chicken bones and crumbs that it knew were there, somewhere in the great beyond.

De Rais pushed his cup to the center of the table, placed his fine hands upon the board. There were several rich rings upon those hands, gleaming with gems. He pressed his palms down and rose to his feet, swaying a little, and grasped his hat by the brim.

He looked down at me, broodingly.

"Something more, my lord?" I asked.

He fingered his hat with the long ribbands dangling onto the floor.

"There is a prophesy," he said, and glanced furtively at the friar. "An ancient one that is said to be from Merlin. That a virgin girl will come from the *Bois Chesnu*, the Oaken Wood, and will restore France to glory..."

"I put no faith in such things," I said, abruptly.

"There are others," the Baron, insistently. "Many of them. I have a record of them, who said them and when, and the exact words that they said. I have them in my library. They all say that this virgin will accomplish things no man can accomplish, by virtue of her purity."

I smiled inwardly, though the Baron's intense gaze made me nervous. I was thinking, perhaps if the motives of men were more pure, they might then accomplish more, but I said nothing.

"Imagine," de Rais went on, dreamily, "what such a girl could do, what she might achieve, if she put her mind to it? Anything might be possible."

I gave him nothing more than, "That anything would have to be the will of God," and smiled mildly.

He sighed and stood swaying in his fine shoes for a moment. "I bid you good night, then," he said, and with a flourish, swept his hat up upon his dark locks and tugged it firmly onto his head.

"*Bonne nuit,* Baron de Rais," I said. "Thank you for your work today, in the name of the King and in the service of God."

"That was my pleasure," he said, and I remembered his gold-inlayed armor splattered with blood, his dripping sword. It <u>had</u> been his pleasure, but then, it had been the pleasure of all my bloody boys, my bloody men. It had even been my pleasure, the excitement of charging down the beach, running the foe before me.

My face flushed at the memory of my own exaltation.

He smiled broadly then, perhaps thinking I blushed at his gallantry, like a simple country girl might do before a noble knight, and cocked his head almost shyly like the youth he must have been but a few years past. A charming youth, all good looks and wealth and refinement, destined for greatness in a great family, with all the delights of the world at his fingertips.

He adjusted his cloak over his shoulders, and, levering the door latch, stepped out into the night. When the door had closed behind him, I heard Father Pasqueral let out a long-held breath.

I looked at the good friar. His face was ashen, as if he had seen a ghost.

He met my eyes and said, "There is something about that man that affrights me and I am a man of God, and should, being saved, fear nothing."

"He treads close to the edge of something," I said, "when he knows he should stay to the middle path where it is safe-going. He puts body and soul in peril because it is only in peril he feels that he is alive. He seeks for forbidden boxes to reach into, hoping to pull out objects of power."

Why I said this, I do not know, yet Father Pasqueral nodded sagely and said, "I fear for his soul, Jehanne. But the power of Our Lord to redeem a man is great. It is never too late for redemption, at least, that is, until death."

I looked at Gilles then and could see that he saw in my eyes that I believed it was already too late for Baron de Rais, that his terrible sins, though not yet committed, could never be purified; they were too heinous.

Like Father Pasqueral, I believed in Absolution, counted upon it in fact, though in my heart of hearts, I felt that there were some things that should never be forgiven.

And thinking this, I had to wonder, what kind of Christian was I, truly?

60, Transportation

His breathing was deep and steady and on his breath was a hint of the roasted onion he had eaten for our supper. He lay upon his side in the straw of the stable, the two old cloaks drawn up over his body, and the staid old gray warhorse standing watch over him. From time to time, the gray would lower his great head and place his lips behind the boy's ear and puff warm breaths of air through his nostrils, making the curls of Gilles' hair move.

He slept, soundly, which he would not have done if I had told him of the morrow's wounding, and I was glad of that, that I had not told him, though now I had to bear that fear alone. My foot throbbed and made it hard to sleep, for me, in the warm clean bed of Charlotte Boucher, between the smooth fine sheets where I ran my legs up and down, feeling the caress of fine linen.

Since I could not sleep, I thought of him, and thinking of

him, transported myself to where he was and so watched over him, much like the old horse, though I could not nuzzle his neck. He was wearing the new dark brown breeches I had gotten for him, to replace the old ones he had torn descending from the Grand Oak. These were of better stuff, thicker, warmer, and more durable, and had buttons at the knees where the old ones had had strings that Gilles never tied.

The buttons were bone and carved with little boar's heads and I think Gilles liked them for he had examined them closely and smiled when he saw what they were.

I had gotten him stockings too and shoes of leather, though he had seemed much less interested in them than in the boar's-head buttons. These I could see, shoved under a rail and half buried in the straw, and there, I thought, they would likely stay. A shirt and a new tunic were next, I thought, as I watched him slumber, but he was slow to take to new things, unless the old were utterly destroyed, and so I would wait just a bit.

It was almost midnight and I had not slept and Father Pasqueral would be with me early to spend the hour of the Eucharist with me. I would spend the dark hour before dawn in adoration of *Jhésus* and pray for His company in keeping watch with me in my own tiny Gethsemane.

And Gethsemane was what it felt like, to me, a simple country girl, far from her native sphere, pushed beyond her bounds of normal experience, and made to take herself into harm's reach, and knowing... knowing! she would be harmed, the time and the very place.

I wanted to say, "Take this cup from me. Do not make me to drink."

I thought upon Our Lord then and wept for Him, biding

that time alone in the garden, with His men slumbering nearby, knowing it was not them who would be scourged, suffer, and die on the morrow, but Him. "Could you not keep watch with me one hour?" He had asked.

I would keep watch with You, Lord, for You keep watch with me. You are my light and my salvation. You are the Glory and the Hope.

I thought of *Jhésus*, Whose face I had never seen but in my imaginings. I thought of Michael, His mightiest angel, whose face I had, whose face was cherished and precious to me. Michael, bright angel, my guardian and my guide.

Where were you now? Have you forsaken me since I fell in love with the rabbit boy?

I would not think that angels would be jealous, prone to petty hurts and peevish angers as are we mortals, but then many folk believed in a jealous God, so why should not His angels be so?

I wanted to say, "Lord *Jhésus*, if You see Michael, tell him I shall always love him, that loving that dear boy from the tiny village of Le Moineau does not diminish the love I have for my bright angel of Heaven," but then I thought, how silly, how childlike, how like a simple country girl to think matters in Heaven are anything like matters here on Earth. I was too small to have a true understanding of such great things.

All that was of importance to God, *Jhésus*, and Michael was that I do my duty to Them and to France, that I fulfill my destiny as a page of Christ. How I felt in my heart about a boy mattered not at all, so long as I did nothing that jeopardized my mission and I would not. I was *La Pucelle* and would remain *La Pucelle,* so long as it please God.

At least, I hoped that that was true, that my feelings for Gilles and my thoughts about him, did not make me unworthy to be *La Pucelle.*

Father Pasqueral would come in a few hours. I had a big battle before me on the morrow. I should leave off these worries. I should let the oblivion of sleep take these cares away and, in dreaming, find respite in green fields and wildflowers. I rolled over to my side and placed my hand on the scabbard of the Sword of Saint Catherine, which I always kept beside me, even in bed.

My fingers traced the soft nap of the velvet at the edge of the beaten-gold throat of the scabbard.

There was a man in Orléans, whom, after Saint Loupe, I had asked to make me a stout scabbard of leather, which he had done. Better in battle, the leather did not seize upon the blade when I drew it, but for bed, I liked the soft one.

Silly, I know, but I am but a girl after all.

I touched the sword with the five crosses, the sword most powerful in all France, the sword that would give me all victory.

Saint Catherine, I prayed, as I did every night, my hand on the sword, help me be strong enough, pure enough, and virtuous enough to wield this sword to victory, for the glory of God.

And then, as I did every night, I thought upon the sleeping boy in the stable below, imagined him asleep in the straw at the feet of my warhorse, pictured him there in his living skin, with his strongly pulsing heart, and his warm blood surging in his vessels, and his lungs breathing in and out and in and out, and transported myself.

And transporting myself, I gently kneeled and lay down and rolled over into the curve of his body, felt his arms come around me, pulling the ragged cloaks over the two of us, and his strong thighs in their fine new breeches against the back of my legs, and his man-part which I had never seen (and could only imagine) warmly between us, and his slow steady breathing on the back of my neck. And I was being held by him, his body touching my body, cradling me tenderly, and there was no horrible premonition, no cold dark death, just a man and a woman holding and being held, warm and alive.

And in a little while, I felt the gentle touch of the gray's fuzzy lips and his gentle puffs of warm hay-scented air in my ear.

And in a little while, I was asleep, sweetly asleep.

61, Capsized

When the quiet tap of Father Pasqueral's hand came upon the door of the chamber of Charlotte Boucher, I had been deep in dreams. I had fallen asleep, in my mind, in the arms of the rabbit boy, and had drifted in visions of green fields and yellow wildflowers buzzing with insects in a warm French sun.

But in the night, my dreams had changed and I was sleeping to the sound of water splashing against gunwales and the sound of oars dipping into the river and the slap of wavelets against wooden hulls. Men were on the move in the night; they were slipping the river currents and pulling towards *Les Tourelles* from downriver.

On the Loire, they passed the burned-out ruins of *La Bastille de Charlemagne* upon the mid-river island which The Bastard and his companions had burned the day before in their frolics. They had left Saint Laurent in the darkest hour of the night and taken to the water in boats they had kept for themselves on the north shore, pulled up and chained to trees.

There were many boats, in the dark. I could not count them all in my dreams, pushing against the flow, filled with men in full armor and heavily-weaponed, coming to the aid of the English inside *Les Tourelles*.

As I dreamed this, my heart began to pound, for I could see a danger to my men, my beautiful men, that they could not see. The men of France were bedded down and sleeping soundly on the banks of the Loire and in The Barbican, without fear of attack, and now, I could see, a threat was approaching them.

These English were many.

I heard, in their minds, the voice of Talbot telling them to go help Gladsdale. Most of these men were against the idea, thought it folly, but would not defy their General. Some were of the belief, still, even after the past few days, that all Frenchmen were weak and foppish and they relished the chance to get a blade at the throat of one and were happy of any opportunity. There were some very young men in the boats, only boys in truth, excited and apprehensive but eager to prove themselves men and warriors, and these I felt especially sorry for, for I knew they were all to drown.

Would drown before they became men and warriors.

And even as I knew it, I saw it happen.

One boat after another filled with water and, as the men began to panic, pulling off their helmets and using them to try and bail the water out, they flipped, spilling men and boys into the Loire.

Why these boats, kept safe on the north shore in English-held territory and guarded day and night, would suddenly all fail, as if they all suffered the same fault of construction, and why, as the occupants were bailing the water from them, they should flip, as if overturned from below, I could not say.

But I had to bewonder me if it was my doing, that seeing them coming, and seeing a threat to my men, and not having any way from *la maison de la famille de Boucher* to warn them, I had caused the boats of the English to capsize and fling them all to their deaths, dragged under the waters by their heavy armor and gear.

Or was it the will of God, and are not all things the will of God?

And then the quiet tap of Father Pasqueral's hand came upon the door of the chamber of Charlotte Boucher and I awakened, shivering with the chill rush of river water pushing into the closed armors and padded hauberks of those men, feeling the splash of cold water over their heads, and my ears ringing with the sounds of their terrified cries.

And when the friar entered, I pulled on my chemise and slipped from the bed, with the Sword of Saint Catherine in my hands, and knelt upon the hard floorboards to speak my confession and be forgiven and receive the blood and body of Christ and keep watch with Our Lord in the Garden of Gethsemane.

62, A Wicked Man

De Gaucourt again tried to bar my way at dawn, this time with more men and many whose faces I recognized as being in the service of The Bastard of Orléans. I had even greater numbers behind me than I had had the previous day at this juncture and this was even without the many that were encamped upon the south side of the river in and around The Barbican, keeping guard upon *Les Tourelles* that the English might not make a break for it.

It was therefore senseless for de Gaucourt to even try to stop me, though I believe the man was under much pressure from the great men who had determined to let the English starve in the towers while waiting for the King to send more soldiers. Knowing the English, who still had a huge garrison at Saint Laurent and other bastilles to the west and north, and knowing our King, I personally could scarce believe that any sane man could consider this a viable strategy.

I sat my black before *La Porte de Bourgoyne* and looked up at the drawn visage of Raoul de Gaucourt with the side plates of his helmet strapped tightly against his cheeks and his chin protruding between them and the chin moving up and down as he chewed on his tongue. I waited a bit for him to get a good look at the army at my back.

"Open the gates, Bailiff," I said mildly.

"I have orders to keep them closed, *Pucelle*," he said.

I smiled inwardly at the use of my title, knowing that he was no more committed to his course than he was yesterday and probably less.

"Sire de Gaucourt," I said, pleasantly, "look, it is daylight. No need to keep the gates locked." Behind the high wall the first light of the sun broke in the east.

"The gates are to remain locked all this day, by order of *Le Batârd d'Orléans*," said de Gaucourt. "Any attack upon the English today is forbidden."

"Are you not a wicked man," I said, "if you do the bidding of The Bastard, whom, in this instance, you know to be wrong? These warriors will march and they will have victory as they have had before, it is the will of God. Are you not a wicked man if you stand against that which is the will of God?"

He was not a wicked man and, in a moment, as I knew he would, de Gaucourt caused the gates to be flung open, and as I knew he would, for he had donned his armor and his helm, he mounted a horse and joined my company, and as I knew they would, the men that had stood with him, men sworn to the service of The Bastard of Orléans, marched with me upon the English in *Les Tourelles*.

63, Agincourt

My banner was still flying over The Barbican and so I rode without it and Gilles rode beside me, with nothing in his hands but his reins. And Joseph and Pierre, my pages Louis and Raymond, de Metz and Squire Bertrand, my banner-bearer Jean de Aulon, whom I had found, and de Gaucourt and all the warriors of my army who were not already in front of *Les Tourelles* having spent the night there, the ones who would follow were I to shout, "If you love me..." were all riding behind me.

We had crossed the river in the same place, in the same manner, as yesterday, and I had said, as we disembarked from boats and barges and mounted our horses, "Tonight we shall return by way of the river bridge!" and the soldiers had cheered.

The great men, The Bastard, *La Hire*, Xaintrailles, the Fair Duke, de la Brosse, Robinet, and de Rais, and the others, whom I called the captains of France, were not with me, although Alençon joined me before the others did. They all would join me before the morning was long gone, finding that the army had again slipped its fetters and enjoined battle before they woke.

This would be the decisive day and the bloodiest day since Agincourt, but the victory would fall into the hands of the French, as Agincourt had fallen to the English.

Let them use their longbows this day.

On this day we would redeem ourselves.

64, We Meet Again

He appeared before me.

The same man I had seen behind the fist that struck Gilles on the side of his head at the narrow place by the jutting rock on the river beach two days ago.

Seeing him there, I knew, as I had suddenly known many things, that he and his fellows had been working at the woodcutting place yesterday when, on our beach jaunt, we warriors of France had suddenly appeared, driving English before us. Not making the gates of The Barbican in time, these men had fled into the trees on the trails they knew well from their work.

They were hiding there, hoping to reunite with their brethren and avoid their enemies. We were their enemies and twas their foul luck that they happened to be right in our path.

We were at the canter through the forested area that the wagon road traversed and I was enjoying the feel of the black beneath me, behaving himself, moving at a comfortable rocking gait, all high-arched neck and flowing mane, his breaths coming from his deep chest at a splendid steady rhythm and his shod hooves pounding the road, hitting muddy patches from the light rain that had fallen after midnight and spraying the mud out from his strides.

Behind me, the men were strung out in ones and twos with their armament making happy music.

I rounded a bend and he was before me, standing in the road, his sword freshly drawn at the sound of our coming. Other men and boys were with him, the same as were with him on the river beach, the English woodcutting crew, and they turned and ran.

The man who had first struck Gilles looked up into my face and his eyes widened, knowing me for *La Pucelle*, and he raised his sword, which was old, bent at the *forte*, jagged at the *foible*, and nicked all along its edge from parrying better blades. He swung for me, trying to sidestep the great destrier that bore down upon him, but my black anticipated this move, knowing that the man, being left-handed, would sidestep to his right, and the horse veered that way and plowed the man with his pumping knees and went over-top of him.

I saw the man's face change as he saw this happening to him and it was a look that recognized his own death coming.

I remembered that death now, had seen it that brief moment on the beach when he had stepped out from the jutting rock and struck Gilles in the side of the head.

I had seen him sidestep from the rock and strike my

rabbit boy with the same move that he now used to sidestep and strike at me with his ancient battered sword, and at the time, I had seen him go down beneath something like a great wave of blue with little sparkles in it, like a river wave when the sun shines through it and glimmered atop it, and being upon the river bank, I had thought his death to be washed away in the river.

But now I knew that the blue was not water.

The man's sword flew from his left hand into the brush at the roadside and his right hand clasped around the barding at the chest of my black, broad blue barding with tiny glimmering *fleur de lys* upon it, grabbing ahold of it as he went down before me.

He held on, dragging, being pounded by the hooves, and his left hand came up and grabbed ahold. The knuckles of both his hands were scabbed from the face-and-body blows those hands had dealt upon the person of my love.

The man's face was etched with desperation as he held on and I felt, by looking in his eyes and the way they winced, every strike of the black's knees on his ribs and lower body and every stroke of the black's hooves upon his legs and feet, breaking the bones and bruising the flesh, before he could not hold on any longer and his hands released and he fell away, to be trampled further by the army of The Maid.

I turned in the saddle and watched him being overtaken by a wave of blue, for most of my men wore some blue, the color of France, upon their standards or jupons, and the glimmering of their armor and weapons was like sunlight on water.

He went down beneath that blue wave and was not seen again.

Ahead of me upon the road, the other English men and

boys were running, like a covey of grouse will do before a group of horsemen, and they ran and ran, glancing over their shoulders in terror, until one of them found an opening and sprang into the trees and then another leaped away to the opposite side and, one by one, they scattered off the traveled way into the woods. My boys gave a hoot and reined their steeds after them and I heard them crashing through the trees and shrubs seeking the runaways.

I did not want to watch and so I rode on at the canter, the limbs of the oaks and beeches swinging past my face and the overarching boughs with their tiny new leaves beautiful in the early sunlight. I heard the sounds behind me and tried not to hear them.

But I heard the hoof-beats of the gray and knew my constant companion was there, always there, always my banner-bearer whether he carried the standard or no.

And so I turned to see.

His golden-brown and tangled curls bounced on his shoulders and his bare feet were tucked in behind the gray's elbows, the dirty toes curled up with effort. His buttocks in their new dark brown breeches rose and fell upon the gray's broad back, getting covered at the seat with white horsehairs, and his old torn and soiled linsy shirt under the equally torn and soiled brown tunic was open at the throat and the strings that were to tie it closed were streaming back. The funny rabbit hat had fallen from his crown and hung upon his back, the little paws dangling at his throat.

He was beautiful, as beautiful as an angel.

A ragged angel he was and he was my love. He was my own true love.

We rode on like that, in the beautiful woods, in the beautiful morning, in a moment like pure Joy, in the moments before the battle, and behind him, one by one, my boys, my bloody boys, came back up onto the road with their swords dripping red, and I smiled at Gilles, a bit ruefully, and he smiled at me, knowing what I saw behind him, and I turned my face to the fore and we rode on.

65, Butterflies

My standard still stood planted upon the highest bulwarks of The Barbican.

I rode right in over the drawbridge and cantered my black up and up the dirt and timber levels to the top and there, beside my standard, sat upon his back with the banner on its pole fluttering slightly in the light breeze. The chill was rising off the water and mingling with the warmth coming from the sun in the east. It was a wondrous sensation, cold and warm coming together on my face and hands, the cold steel of my harness slowly warming on receiving the touch of the sunlight.

From here I could see well our task at hand: *Les Tourelles*, an ominous four-towered structure that guarded the way onto the long river bridge of stone arches, a wide heavy drawbridge spanning the water to its stout gates. This drawbridge was, of course, drawn up snug and tight and before it lay an expanse of moving water of some two wagon-lengths between the gate and the landing on the shore. From the lapping waters rose high the walls, made of mortared smooth brown stone, arrow-slitted and topped by a crenelated rampart, with the looming towers at the four corners.

All along its walls, the faces and weapons of determined English warriors were visible.

They saw me there and all English eyes turned and gazed on me. So I sat my destrier and let them see me. One hand upon the high pommel of my saddle and one upon the hilt of the Sword of Saint Catherine, above me the gold-fringed edges of my standard catching the morning sunlight, I let them see me.

My visor was up and my face was in the sun.

I closed my eyes for a moment and prayed to my angels.

Let them please to watch over me this day, let them please to be with me in my trial of pain, let them please to give me strength to bear what must be done. Let them please to keep my love safe, safe on his vantage place where I had left him, behind the broken-down stone fence on the bluffs where first he and I had spied upon the English at *La Barbacane de Saint Augustin.*

I thought of him, watching me.

My enemies on one side and my dearest love on the other, watching me, and I kept my eyes closed and I leaned my head back, the weight of the heavy helmet making my head fall back easily, and I let more of the sunlight hit my face, and I breathed deep.

Oh, to be alive!

Every such breath was a gift.

Every moment spent alive and lacking pain and suffering

was a gift. I knew what a treasure my life was.

I knew about the little joys.

I knew about the Great Joys. I wanted to have them all, the great and the small.

I wanted to live, to take one breath after another and feel each one. I wanted to feel each beat of my heart, each surge of blood in my vessels, each tingle of excitement in my limbs. I wanted to see all the beauty of God's creation, His wondrous world.

I wanted to know all the pleasures that a human body was capable of, for God created them, these bodies. Made of bone and blood and muscle and sinew and organs, with the humors mysterious and marvelous coursing through them, and senses of sight and sound and smell and taste, and an extraordinary mind full of notions and ideas, God had created them and given them these capabilities.

I wanted to live in mine and experience all of its wonders.

I wanted to share mine with a certain wonderful boy, a man really, but whose heart was that of a boy's and would be that of a boy's forever, I was certain.

I wanted to love him, joyfully, as a woman, with a woman's body and a woman's mind, but with the heart of a girl, forever.

How I longed for this!

I opened my eyes and saw the English watching me from their high walls. My eyes beheld the task before me, this daunting task. I let out a long breath and drew another, sweet blessed breath.

I wanted more than this.

I wanted to live.

But first this.

This must be done and then I would see what God would

grant me. I wanted to live.

I would beg God that I might live. I would beg my angels to intervene on my behalf that I might live. I wanted so to live!

I wanted to marry the boy who sat watching me from behind the broken-down stone fence.

Mayhap I would.

Mayhap flames were only flames and would lie tame within our hearth, baking our bread and boiling our soup and warming the beds of our children and giving light and comfort to our nights.

Mayhap my fears were for nothing.

But first this.

I raised my arms high into the air, my palms open to the sky. I heard a collective gasp from the throats of the English opposite me upon the ramparts and I opened my eyes. The breeze had picked up and my long silken banner flapped against the blue sky. All around it fluttered a cloud of tiny blue-white butterflies.

There were hundreds, perhaps thousands of them, making a shimmering cloud over my head and all around me, and many had lit upon the fabric of the banner, covering parts of it with a shimmering sheen of pearl blue. The English were shouting in their harsh tones, their guttural speech, pointing their fingers at me and crossing themselves.

I looked closely at the standard, seeing the tiny bodies of the butterflies pushing against each other and crawling over each other. Their tiny curled tongues were out and they were sucking at the silk, drinking the water of the morning dew from the tight weave of its strands.

Thirsty butterflies and a damp standard!

And the English were terrified!

I threw my head back and laughed. The ways of nature in its lovely simplicity were beyond the understanding of superstitious men.

They saw only what they wanted to see. They were shouting now, calling me witch and enchantress, claiming that I exercised dark powers.

They did not see me.

I was anything but dark.

My heart was full of light, full of love.

I reached out for the pole of my standard, lifted it high in the air with the butterflies all around it. With a leg to the side of the black, I spun him easily about and we went slowly down the levels of The Barbican, the black prancing in place and arching his neck handsomely, the butterflies all around us, some of them landing on him and drinking the salt moisture from his glossy hide. I kept laughing, feeling little butterflies tickling my face with their fluttering wings, and the English called curses upon the witch, and my Frenchmen, seeing me coming, called blessings upon their page of Christ, their *Pucelle.*

As I reached the lower level, the sweet voices of my angels came to me. Saint Catherine and Saint Margaret, their voices like running water, told me how it would be done. They told me when the standard with the lilies of France and of *La Magdalena* touched the ramparts of The Turrets, the fort would be taken.

And I laughed more, and more joyfully.

Pounding over the drawbridge of *La Barbacane de Saint Augustin*, I handed the standard to my banner-bearer, Jean de Aulon, where he sat waiting on his dark bay horse. His young face was alight with awe as he took it from my hand and rode behind me in a cloud of butterflies. I glanced up to the bluff, to the broken-down stone fence in the tall grass, and the face of the boy who peered over.

I had felt the hard thud of jealousy in his heart as de Aulon took the banner.

But I also felt the swell of pride that filled that heart, the flush of hot love, and the stretch of longing. And in his mind, the lightheadedness of wonderment.

Now, I would call a council and we would begin.

66, Council

I sent a man to the city to summon the captains to me.

Alençon arrived before the rest, as he was already on his way, and brought with him, to my surprise, a man called the Lord of Gamaches, who had once insulted me in front of The Bastard, telling him that he would excuse himself from council and take the role of humble squire, not experienced war-chief, so long as The Bastard allowed me, a peasant brat, to play at being a commander.

I thought this funny at the time, first because Gamaches never did excuse himself from the role of a captain of France, in fact loudly and consistently opposed me at all times, and secondly, because The Bastard never had given me much credence as a commander and so why should Gamaches complain that he did? But at any rate, here he appeared, at the side of the Fair Duke, and bowed his head solemnly in greeting to me.

In a short time all the great men were with me and I said, "That stronghold will fall into our hands this day and we shall ride into Orléans by that bridge before nightfall."

I pointed my finger northwards to the city. "Captains," I said, looking around into all their faces, "we will move our guns into The Barbican and place them in offence of *Les Tourelles.* I shall speak with de Patada and The Lorrainer about their exact placement."

I searched for the Scotsmen, Ogilvy and Crichton, one the Constable of Scots in France and the other a Commander of Scottish men-at-arms and longbow-men. The Scots had long been our allies and Scotsmen had fought in France against the English and Frenchmen had fought against the English in Scotland for generations.

"Our Scottish archers should take the high ground there," I said and I pointed to the place I had sat my horse with my butterfly-spangled banner and the tiered levels just below it, "and use their bows to pick off the bowmen and arbalest-men of the enemy. They should begin this vital work now," and as I finished this sentence, Crichton bowed and left.

I looked into the dour eyes of The Bastard of Orléans, and saw, even in his silence, a hint of his defiance. "We will build more scaling ladders, since we have not enough, and, once we begin, I want to assault the walls from every quarter where the water isn't running too fast and deep. There are trails into the woods there," and I pointed, "where saplings grow tall and straight, and on the beach below there, are piles of stripped saplings already de-limbed and stacked. The man called Bernard Josselin knows where they are." I looked at all of them, seeing in every set of eyes, if not fully those of The Bastard, a grudging admiration and acquiescence. "We will need men, hopefully men who can swim, to stand in the water and hold the bases of the ladders when the time comes for men to climb and we need other men with large shields to protect these men so that they may do this duty."

I saw nodding heads and eyes behind which the thoughts were running as so which men should be selected for these things.

"But before we launch the assault against the walls," I said, "we must make preparations. We bombard the walls and kill as many as we can before we enter. We make things uncomfortable within the stronghold. I have some ideas on how we may do that." I was thinking of the boats on the beach. "And we taunt them and invite them to open the gates, lower that bridge, and meet us on dry land."

La Hire's eyes lifted from where he was picking at a scab on the back of his hand and he smiled.

"Yes, *La Hire*," I said, "I think you and Poton and your mercenaries are the perfect ones to do the taunting. You have the right vocabulary for the work." Xaintrailles smiled his killer's smile and slapped the steel-clad shoulder of his friend.

"De Gaucourt," I said, "once we have begun the assault, I think it mete that men of the city should join us from the north side. Can the arches of the bridge be spanned and a timely attack led from Orléans?"

The Bailiff, his narrow face braced by the side-plates of his helm, nodded vigorously. "Yes, *Pucelle*, it is possible."

I nodded at him. "Well, you of all men know the workmen who can build it and you have your garrison of City Watch. Attacked from both sides, the enemy will either be caught between hammer and anvil or they will lower the bridge, open the gates, and try to come out. Either way, they will be destroyed or forced to surrender. It will be harrowing, it will be long and arduous," I said. "There will be times we think it cannot be done. But I tell you, before the day is done, we will go in."

They were all on my side now.

I could feel in their hearts the growing confidence, the eagerness to do as I had said, to believe what I said.

Only The Bastard held a small hard rock of dissention stuck at the center of his chest, though his mind was working over ways that he might voice it or trying to decide if he should or no. I turned to him.

"We have The Bastard to thank for this opportunity today," I said.

He looked up. "We do?" he said.

I smiled. "Of course. You were the one who, just yesterday, cleared the English from *La Bastille sur le Champ de Saint Privé.* You are the one who burned *La Bastille aux Île de Charlemagne.* You are the one who chased them all the way to *La Bastille de Saint Laurent* and humiliated Talbot in his own fortress by defecating on his road in sight of his walls."

The big man blushed at this, wondering how I knew and in truth I did not know how I knew. "And, are you not the one," and this I knew also, though I had not known when I wakened from the dream of it, "who found their hidden boats and split the seams which caused them to capsize in the night?"

The blush rose to his ears, exposed by his helmet-clip, and dissipated.

"Yes, *Pucelle,* that was all my doing."

He had stumbled upon the boats while hunting the captive English. The boat-guards had been run off, fleeing through the woods and fields like the captives to escape the

French hunters. In fact, one captive, the very one he had beaten so viciously in Le Champ, had pulled himself under one of the boats to hide. The Bastard, having chased him thus far and lost sight of him, and having seen the boats, dismounted and took his sword to the seams of the lapped planks, driving them in until his blade found the body of the hiding man.

As a man of Orléans, he knew boats to be valuable, and so he had made his damage repairable. These were French boats usurped for English use, destroying them would be wasteful. That being said, it was more fun to stab into the boats seeking the fugitive than have to wait for help to flip the big boats over. And it was much more sporting.

"So," I said, "you took the fight to the enemy in their holds yesterday and because of that, we may attack this fortress today without concern of a flank attack. And so, I say, all things being in place, God now wills us to proceed."

I thought The Bastard was happy now, the rock of dissention dissolved like a lump of crystalized honey. All the captains seemed happy, eager to move. Only Poton de Xaintrailles held back, not liking that I had given The Bastard so much credit when The Bastard's exploits yesterday had been purely self-indulgent and vengeful.

But Xaintrailles was shrewd enough to know why I said the things I said. He knew I had to play these men's pride like a pennywhistle and get them dancing to my tune.

I caught his eye and the little shake of his head and the quirk at the corner of his cruel mouth.

We do what we must, Poton, I wanted to say, you know that.

67, As I Said

It was done as I said, cannon shot like a heavy hailstorm, arrows like flocks of birds. *La Hire* and his mercenaries before the walls, brandishing their weapons and exchanging words with the English between the booms of the guns. The Bastard and Alençon had mustered their companies of knights and men-of-foot upon the rolling hills in colorful ranks in plain view of the enemy inside *Les Tourelles*. Elsewhere, other men were constructing what would be a forest of long ladders.

On the other side of the river, the townspeople were building a structure over the broken arches of the bridge. They laid on every old beam, plank and wagon-bed they could find, pinned and lashed together.

Each carpenter was a captain, each shopkeeper became a laborer, each laborer a craftsman, and together they built a bridge. And with them were the militia-men of the city, who were, many of them, carpenters, shopkeepers, and laborers, their weapons laid by and their hands full of pegs, nails and rope.

On the walls of the Gatehouse of Saint Antoine, Englishmen looked with alarm upon the work. They shortened their cannon range and fired a few shots, but the balls, strangely, went wide and struck the walls of the city and fell into the river and the French workers laughed and made obscene French gestures and carried on.

I sought out my boatman friend and asked him for the bravest of his river-men.

"All Loire river-men are courageous, *Pucelle,*" he said, with his usual pluck, his white hair billowing about his head in the breeze, his ears red with the chill off the waters.

"I have no doubt of that, *Grand-père.* There is a thing that needs doing, which only Loire river-men can do," I said, and told him what it was.

And within an hour, three boats from the woodcutters' beach laden with slash and firewood were landed at the arch below *Les Tourelles*, where Gilles and I had observed English receiving goods from the boatman on Ascension Thursday. The small door on the footing of the arch was forced open with prizing-bars and the brush and wood carried inside. Debris from the riverbank; rags and rubbish, old leather harness and the bones of cattle gathered from around the English fortification were all taken within as well while the English, under assault, were unobservant.

Kegs of tar were taken in, the material drenched and lit afire. The river-men rowed away while the black foul smoke rose inside, filling the passageways and towers of *Les Tourelles.*

I saw the smoke begin to reach out through the lowest

arrow-slits first and men pushed their heads out, trying to get air. At the same time, the townsmen finished the bridge, picked up their weapons and rushed *La Guérite du Saint Antoine.*

68, *La Hire*

The mercenary captain stood on the shore within arrow-range of the walls, calling for Gladsdale to come and speak with him. Each time that an English bowman drove a shaft towards him, he laughed and danced aside, and Scottish archers on our side had a chance to kill an Englishman.

I sat on my black with Alençon, Pierre and Joseph Cadieux, de la Brosse, de Metz, Squire Bertrand, Gamaches and de Rais, with my banner-bearer de Aulon beside me holding the shaft of my standard that it stayed over me all the time. The day had warmed and the butterflies had flown away to the fields. I envied them their brief, simple, and beautiful lives.

I wished to be in the fields myself, with Gilles, in a country all our own.

But first this.

We watched with interest the actions of *La Hire*.

He had left a great space before the drawbridge and placed his men far back leaning on their weapons. Smoke was rising from within the walls and pouring out the windows and men that we could see were coughing, but still they were sending shafts down, their aim blurred by the smoke in their eyes, trying to kill *La Hire*.

"Come out and fight us, if you be not craven," *La Hire* shouted. "Or are you mice to hide within your burrow?"

"He is bold," Pierre said at my elbow. Or mayhap twas Joseph.

"Indeed, he is," I agreed.

"I like a bold fellow," said the other twin.

I smiled at the twain of them, handsome boys with their glossy black hair and bright blue eyes. "You are both as bold as *La Hire*," I said, "and not near so unpleasant to be around."

They smiled back at me and turned their faces again to watch the mercenary captain.

La Hire was not a big man like The Bastard, but he was strong and very broad at the shoulders. His hips were narrow and he had a perpetual limp but it did nothing to hinder his graceful movements while dodging arrows. He was armored in his perfectly-fitted but somewhat battered harness, whose embellishments were battle-scenes etched into the steel and darkened by time and wear. He stood before *Les Tourelles* helmetless with his long bedraggled brown hair hanging to his shoulders and his drooping mustache framing his taunting mouth.

"Would you not like to be out of that mousetrap you have made for yourselves?" he hollered. "Would you not like to be out in the open air, where you may breathe and have room to run, or to fight?"

Several arrows streaked down and like a miracle, *La Hire*

avoided them all. He had seen the flower of French chivalry slain by such arrows at Agincourt, witnessed the airborne slaughter of hundreds of armored knights, and he wanted to show these English that he did not fear them, that Frenchmen were no cowards, and that this day would be ours.

I, watching him dance his dangerous dance, did not fear for him, for I had seen his death. He could dance under English arrows all day long and not be killed here.

Down inside the pillar supporting the arch where the river-men had piled the brush and debris, something new caught fire and a roiling black column of stinking smoke issued forth, rising high above the towers and pouring from the tops of the slit windows.

Gladsdale appeared on the wall just above the drawbridge. He peered through one of the crenellations.

"The Ire of France," the English commander said sourly, in French.

"You don't look glad to see me, Gladsdale," shouted *La Hire* in English, emphasizing the "glad" in the man's name.

"No, truly," Gladsdale returned, with dry sarcasm, "tis always a joy to see you."

"What are you boys cooking in there?" *La Hire* asked. "It must be English cooking. I hear you fellows overcook everything. This dish seems to be burning."

Gladsdale waved a bit of smoke from around his face.

"No, no cooking. We are just preparing to burn a witch."

I shifted in my saddle, hearing this, and the black, thinking we were moving, began to toss his head. I reined him in and tried to relax into my seat to calm him, but he was agitated now, sensing my unease, and wanted to charge and stomp some people to death. I took my hand from the reins and stroked his neck and he dipped his head, the bridle-chains jingling, and worked his tongue against the bits.

La Hire was laughing jovially. "A witch?" he said. "You have got yourself a witch?"

Gladsdale shook his head. "We know where she is. We haven't got her yet." He raised his head and looked right at me.

La Hire saw this and nodded, saying, "Ah, well, why don't you come on out and get her? It looks rather uncomfortable inside, a bit hot and stuffy. Nice clean breeze out here."

I smiled at mercenary's use of my word; uncomfortable.

Down below in the arch staircase, the fire reached a fresh pile of slash and detritus soaked with tar and the sound of crackling and popping could be heard. Black oily smoke rose in bilious clouds and Gladsdale began to cough.

When he stopped, he said to *La Hire*, "Mayhap we shall at that. Give me a minute," and he disappeared.

Joseph and Pierre both looked at me with a questioning expression. I was surprised at this, myself, and then not so surprised. Alençon gathered up the reins of his black, the brother to mine, and said to de Metz, Gamaches, and de la Brosse, "Do not let them near *La Pucelle*."

Everyone readied themselves, locking down their visors and getting their horses well in hand.

De Rais said, before closing his helmet, "There is not an Englishman in France will get close enough to Jehanne for her to smell their stinking breath, not while I am alive."

I knew then how it would be.

I had seen parts of it already.

The long slow lowering of the wide drawbridge, its heavy solid thunk onto its landing, the relaxing of the chains that lowered it. Then a breathless moment and the wide gates of *Les Tourelles* began to open. We watched, knights and mercenaries, and waited for the English to pour out. Everyone gripped their weapons and rolled their shoulders, ready for a fight.

But nothing happened.

A bit of black smoke trickled out over the lip of the opening and snaked its way up the masonry above it. The sky above *Les Tourelles* was black with smoke and the cannons had ceased their firing. There was an unnerving silence.

"Where are they?" Joseph or Pierre said, muffle-voiced inside the helmet. "Why don't they come out?"

I knew the answer, though I would not speak it. They want us to come in. And they know if they wait long enough someone will try and come in.

I leaned forward and my horse was moving before I touched my spurs to him. De Aulon, taken by surprise by my sudden movement, lurched his mount forward in a rush to keep the standard over my head, and the boys came right after him, taking up position on my left and behind me while de Aulon was on my right.

The others, the Fair Duke, de Metz, Bertrand, de la Brosse, de Rais, Gamaches, and others fell in behind, some twenty of us all together, and the companies in ranks behind us on the hill shifted their feet and watched and looked towards The Bastard, who held his horse tight-reined and frothing at the mouth.

I cantered down into the open space that *La Hire* and his mercenaries had kept. I knew as I approached that *La Hire* was about to move, as did Xaintrailles who had joined him at his left side, a shield on his arm. And sure enough, *La Hire* pulled his sword in his right hand and lifted a small axe from his belt with his left and, turning to look at his men ranged behind him, raised these weapons into the air, with a shout on his lips.

The shout died there as he saw me charging down, the mounted knights behind me. I rode straight for him, my black lowering his head to bite, and both *La Hire* and Xaintrailles leaped out of the way.

If the mercenaries went first, it would all be different.

God and His angels only knew how that would change things.

I wished that I could change things but I was afraid to try. What if my tampering with what was to be threw a shoe into the works and destroyed everything?

I had seen it, seen it each time I had looked into one pair or the other of those blue eyes, those bright blue eyes the color of cornflowers, the pretty eyes of my boys, my bloody boys. Joseph and Pierre would die here, within the minute; that was how it was to be.

For that to happen, I had to be the first to cross the drawbridge.

69, My Bloody Boys

I pulled the Sword of Saint Catherine and raised it high.

I shouted, "*Au nom de Dieu!* In the name of God, let us go boldly! Bravely! Let us go!" And I slapped my visor down.

I heard the joyful cries of the Cadieux twins behind me.

"Boldly! Bravely!" they echoed me.

I heard the whisper of their swords leaving their scabbards and I heard the thudding hooves of their horses, and quieter, but still heard, was the thudding of their excited young hearts within the encircling cages of their rib-bones and the encircling protection of their armor, their armor that was no protection against what waited beyond that open gate. I charged for the bridge, spurring my horse who needed no encouragement.

I spurred him, hard in the flanks, raking my rowels over his ribs. I spurred him, mayhap, to punish myself, to punish my black as an extension of myself, my instrument of death and destruction. I might have spurred him hard enough to make him bleed but twas I that felt the wounds, another scourge-mark, another spear to the side, another wound to my stigmata. But the horse acted as if he felt no wound.

He leapt joyously ahead, as if he lived for no other purpose but this, to carry me forward.

To carry me.

And we went.

His mane flew back into my face like a clamor of rooks taking flight. I leaned into the wind, hearing it whistle through the eye-slots of the visor, feeling it against my eyes. The bridge was there, I turned my head enough to focus through the narrow slots. I steered him for it.

His great hooves roared upon the wood and I felt the structure bounce under our weight. The others came onto the bridge too, their horses' hooves added to the roar and the timbers flexed under us. Two and three great surging strides and I saw the open gate, the black space beyond that was the portal through the wall. Then I saw barred light upon the stone flags and realized the portcullis on the opposite side was down. For a moment I thought we should crash right into it, but a band of light appeared and quickly widened.

The portcullis was being raised.

There was the yawing mouth of the big cannon.

Then the fist of God slammed into me, or so it felt, a concussion that might have cracked my bones had I not been in full harness. Fire flew through the port and sparks and particles pelted my armor like thrown pebbles. The sound knocked all hearing out of me save the ringing of a bell that would not stop. The black was rocked back on his hocks and I nearly was thrown off but for the high back of the saddle and the fact that I had been leaned forward so far. I was in a cloud of hot and sulfurous smoke.

I could not breathe and I could see nothing, hear nothing but the ringing. My black was spinning and rearing beneath me and I held my sword in one hand and the reins in the other and tried to settle him.

Thank God I had not dropped my sword!

There was movement in the smoke and I saw English faces. They were streaming forward, going around the big cannon, rushing into the dark portal. Their leering faces told it, they wanted to catch the witch. I reined my destrier about and gave him the spurs again. As I turned, I saw the things I had seen in the eyes of my beautiful boys.

The horrible things I had seen and known would come to pass. Oh, such horrible things!

There on the heavy timbers of the drawbridge lay the large bloody pieces and steaming piles of organs that had once been two black horses, one that I had had of the King and one that a knight in the service of the Duke of Lorraine had given his eldest son. Having two sons but having only one horse to give, he had given it to his eldest son, Pierre, who had been born three minutes before his other son, Joseph. And scattered among the pieces of the horses were other pieces.

Of bloody flesh and stark white shattered bone, a small broken shield and twisted plates of polished steel, a hand still in its gauntlet, and scraps of fabric, much of it blue, a shock of glossy black hair, the pieces that were all that remained of my boys, my beautiful boys, my bloody bloody boys.

Alençon was there, on his rearing black horse that was the brother to mine. I saw his eyes in the narrow slice in the steel that was his eye-slot, eyes as blue as the Cadieux brothers' eyes had been, saw them see the English that were behind me, coming for me, and he touched my horse on the neck and charged away and my horse followed, as if Alençon had his hand on my bridle, though of course, he did not.

The others were ahead of us and the horses clattered off the landing of the drawbridge onto the sandy shore and we raced away thinking they might load and fire that great gun again. But they did not.

The English retreated inside and the outer gate closed and in a moment, we heard the portcullis slam down.

But try as they might, they could not raise the bridge.

The great wheels inside were turned, the massive iron chains tautened but the bridge could not be raised. The weight of two dead horses and two dead men was too great a weight for the apparatus to move. Seeing this, the men of France cheered.

The men cheered and The Maid wept.

I kept my visor down that they would not see my tears.

70, Vantage Place

The boy I loved and wanted to marry someday watched all of this, his eyes filled with tears. Those eyes that were a color that is beyond color, more like light of varying degrees, dark and gray as slate, or as yellow, light and clear as clover honey, or as blue as a summer sky, or as green as new leaves on the limbs of the birch, those eyes, those beautiful eyes, filled with tears when he saw what happened on the drawbridge.

And I had to bewonder me, what did he think, watching me lead those boys to their deaths?

They were our friends.

They had been his friends.

Though knights and sons of knights, they had been kind to him, where most looked through him as if he were furniture, or in the case of de Rais, looked at him as something pretty and tantalizing to be used and used up.

Pierre and Joseph had laughed and joked with him and looked into his eyes when they told their stories. They had been good men and Gilles had watched me, knowingly, lead them to die.

I wondered, what did he think of me, watching me do this? How could he love me?

I took good men and threw them at my cause.

I shattered their bodies against these walls I believed I needed to surmount and I climbed over them, using their flesh and bones as a foothold for my ascension.

The boy from the tiny village of the sparrow, whose tender heart wept at the necessity of slaying rabbits, watched me killing his friends, and wiping the tears from his eyes, leaned over the wall to watch me prepare to lose more men their lives. He saw me, my visor covering my face, raise my sword and signal for The Bastard. The ranks of the dark knight's men on the hillside, row upon row, in jupons the colors of meadow flowers, stirred like a wind running over a lush field.

The boy who had followed me across France because I wept for the lives of others and cared for every small joy snuffed out like a candle flame, watched me as I turned, and with my sword, give the order to de Patada and Colin to resume the bombardment, sending winged carnage over the ramparts to strike unseen and unknown men.

He must have watched in wonder, or in horror, as I gave these orders, having just seen what I had just seen, done what I had done.

How could he love me, instrument of destruction that I was?

The boy whose heart was wild and free and who had never dreamed he would ever leave the fields and forests of his birthplace, but did for love of me, watched me with my sword beckoning for the men with the long ladders and the men with the large shields to bring those things to bear upon the smooth high stone walls.

The boy who could have stayed at home and waited to inherit a turnip farm and married a simple girl from his own village, watched, from his vantage place far from home, as the great assault began, ranks of soldiers marching in to fill the space around The Barbican, between the bluffs and the water's edge and the looming heights of *Les Tourelles*, hundreds of men with their weapons waiting to climb.

His gentle eyes, those eyes that were a color that is beyond color, those eyes, always gentle, watched as a forest of ladders was laid up and men were like ducks in the waters of the Loire, struggling to hold them against the shifting mud and running currents, under turtle-backs of shields and a rain of rocks and barbs. And he watched other men clambering like monkeys and falling like sparrows in a freeze, splashing in and either struggling or floating there in the sparkling river whose blue water was running streaks of red ribbands towards the sea.

And since we had the drawbridge, the boy who inexplicably loved me watched as I called for more men to bring a log as a battering ram against the closed gate and saw how those men slipped and stumbled over the slick blood and parts of men and horses that they must step over in order to try the strength of that barred gate, over and over, with all the might of their sinews, over and over.

The boy, who loved the sounds of birdsong and the wind in grass and the chuckling of creek water over shifting pebbles, covered his ears against the deafening thunder, cracking stone, thuds and shouts and the shrieks of slaughtered mortals.   He loved the blue sky and the scent of pollen on the air but this blue sky was painted black with smoke and reeked of sulfur and it was because of me.

I saw it all through his eyes and through my own, through his from his vantage place and through mine in the midst of it and strangely, also from above, as if through the eyes of an angel, but that view was silent and veiled as if looking through vapor.

If it was an angel's eyes, I prayed it was Michael's, for that would mean he was here, keeping watch, lending his strength.   But I could not tell if it was Michael, I did not feel the heat of him in the gaze, did not feel anything, but only saw.

And I realized, perhaps it was the gaze of God.

72, Raymond

While he had his ears covered and was watching me so carefully, they came up upon him, so that by the time he saw them, they were very close. He sprang to his feet and saw Raymond first, with his cohort with him. They were the pages of some of the great men and one was in the service of the dark knight, but Gilles did not know his name.

They spaced themselves in a circle around him with the broken-down stone fence, the wall that had once been built to keep livestock from the edge, and the lip of the steep bluff, behind him. He recognized this tactic right away, being a hunter.

Give your prey nowhere to run but into greater danger and you will have him, either by our own hand or by the danger they must flee into.

The result was varied, depending upon the prey.

Rabbits cower, stags leap, and boars fight.

Gilles was not a boar.

"*Bon après-midi*, rabbit boy," said Raymond, running a hand through his unruly dark hair. He was in a jupon of the colors of royal pages, only it was dirty and torn and covered with horsehair and splatters of blood, and he had his little battle axe hanging in a frog at his belt. I could see Raymond through the eyes of my love, and the other pages with him, in their various colors with their youthful faces and mischief in the corners of their mouths.

In Raymond's eyes was more than mischief, he had a hatred in him and annoyance and disdain and a jealousy that was new-blossomed.

The hatred was deep-bred with his cruelty, which was why he could not get along with horses, and had been built into him, block by block, in his childhood.

I could see this, though Gilles knew nothing of it and wondered at this boy, why he should be so.

Raymond's annoyance at Gilles was because Gilles was better than him at some things and his disdain was that Gilles was a peasant and beneath him yet was better than him at some things. But one thing Raymond now knew he was better at than Gilles, had known it since yesterday, was killing people with a small axe. He fingered that axe now, and saw Gilles' strangely-tinted eyes, devil-eyes he thought, drift to that axe.

The newly-flowered jealousy was because Raymond, after yesterday, after the beach jaunt, had a whole bright new picture in his mind of The Maid.

He had thought her a peasant and beneath him, and wondered at the wisdom of the Dauphin to place him, the son of a Viscount, in service to a milkmaid, but having seen her pulling her sword and charging down the enemy, smashing men to death under her destrier with aplomb, having seen grown men and knights of renown riding with her and doing damage to the foe and laughing with her afterwards, his mind had painted her with all new colors, vivid and exciting, and he thought, mayhap in her service, if he acquitted himself well, he might soon be squire, then knight, and if things went a certain way and she pleased the Dauphin, he Raymond, son of a Viscount, might then be considered a good match for her, and she would have wealth and renown.

He had seen her once almost naked when they were on the road from Chinon and had to camp and sleep in the open. She had no women to help her dress and undress and change her garments so she had tried to do it all herself, but having men's clothing and not knowing much about how to handle the ties that held the hose to the pourpoint, she only got it half-undone and had to kick and wriggle to get out of it, pulling off her underclothes with the over.

Her body was as comely as any maid he had seen, smooth-skinned and white as duck's down, her legs long and straight and her breasts the size and shape of ripe apples.

Her face, when happy and not all drawn in prayer as she often was, was pretty enough, and her eyes were big and pretty as a cat's. Her hair was neither fine and straight nor curling and girlish but somewhere in the mean betwixt the two and was a color that not quite red. He was glad it was not all red, for that was a color he thought belonged to witches and wanton women.

He had seen the way she looked at the rabbit boy and he had heard The Bastard of Orleans say that he would be grateful to anyone who would discourage the rabbit boy from continuing to follow Jehanne about like a little irritating dog, so there were two reasons to be rid of him.

And, Raymond was thinking, here he had made it easy for them, and unexpected things happen during a battle and people got killed and no one was looking, they were all fighting a battle and not paying any attention to what might happen to a peasant brat watching from the bluffs.

All of these things Raymond was thinking.

Looking at him though Gilles' eyes, I could see these thoughts all running like a fountain in my page's mind. In the flurry of battle, I could not do anything about what was transpiring on the bluff, barely had time to even glance and see the boys standing there half-obscured by tall grasses and the broken-down stone fence. But I could see it through Gilles' eyes, the boys crowding closer, threateningly, and trying to drive my love back closer to the edge.

Gilles braced himself, watched the hands that were near the weapons. Only Raymond had a real weapon that he could see, the boy in the service to The Bastard had a long knife on his belt and the other lads, if they had anything, he did not see them.

He knew that if they intended to kill him, they would want to do it in such a way as to have it appear to be no one's fault, most likely by having him fall, but the height here, though enough to injure a person, was not certain to cause their death, so perhaps they might try to smash his head in before causing him to fall. The axe would serve, if Raymond used the back of it, not the blade.

A chosen leap over the wall and a scramble down that steep bluff would be better than having his skull smashed in and be thrown, but a leap would be a leap of faith and Gilles had no faith that it would end well.

He searched their eyes, looking for their intent, their seriousness. Raymond, he could see, was most serious, he had found that he liked killing people and would like to continue doing it as long as he could say he had a good reason and no one could say his reasons were unjustified.

The others were just up for a bit of self-made excitement, as the life of a page was mostly waiting to be told what to do; bring me this, do that, hold my horse. But Gilles knew that people are like animals; most animals will follow a strong leader and most animals will be afraid to go against a strong leader. These boys had already left their duties to follow Raymond here to confront him.

Gilles kept his eyes soft, not wanting them to see the preparations he made for his self-defense if it came to that. His left heel was pressed against the stone on the base of the fence, deep in the grass, and the right slightly away from the fence and his weight evenly-balanced on both. Under the soles of his feet, he felt broken stone and the charred pieces of wood from the burned-up buildings that had once been here.

He wondered if any of these things might make a weapon if he needed one.

In all of his life he had never owned nor needed a weapon, he had hunted rabbits with string and broken their slender necks with his bare hands and done the skinning and butchering of them with his father's knife at home. But in the past few days, he had seen many weapons and how they were used, he knew what he might expect of one used against him.

He had no weapon.

He had no skill at fighting.

He had only one thing that the pages did not seem to be considering in any way. Past them, in the long waving grass, near the pile of rubble that had once been a house or a wayside inn, grazed the gray horse. The old campaigner snorted and swished his tail and ripped mouthfuls up and chewed them, once in a while lifting his great head and looking about. Gilles wondered, if he were to call or whistle, would the old horse come to him?

Would the old horse, maybe, fight for him?

"*Bonjour*, Raymond," he said politely in answer to Raymond's greeting.

Raymond sneered at him and spread his feet, hooking his thumbs in his belt. "Rabbit boy," he said, "we have been talking it over. We have decided it is time for you to leave. You have no purpose here, you are just in everyone's way."

Gilles looked from one face to the next.

Mayhap they simply meant to run him off, scare him badly and run him off like the timid peasant they believed him to be. He met each pair of eyes, wanting to see, like looking into an opening in the forest, what was beyond.

Would each of these boys commit to violence against him? He was older than most of them, was older than Raymond, though Raymond was big, having been well-fed all his life, on better than fare of rabbit and turnips, but age meant nothing to those born to superiority. The oldest and wisest man was treated like a child if he was a serf before a lord.

A few of the boys looked away from his gaze, looked at their hands or at the ground or at Raymond.

Gilles saw then, which way he might run, for sometimes a cornered rabbit might get past right between your legs.

But that was not to be.

For, at that moment, the moment wherein Gilles was deciding whether to be a rabbit or a stag or try, perhaps with the help of the gray horse, to become a boar, there was a definite and sudden change in the sounds of the battle, a sudden strange hush, and then a clamor of voices, shouts of alarm, and English voices yelling something about the witch, and all of them turned towards those sounds and the boys all rushed to the broken-down stone fence and looked down.

73, Wounded

The bolt struck me with such force it knocked me down.

One moment I was on my feet reaching to steady a ladder that had begun to slide sideways, as it was being pushed by Englishmen high above on the ramparts, and the next I was on my buttocks on the hard wood of the drawbridge, sliding in the congealing horse blood and slipping off the edge into the water.

My armor instantly took me like a stone to the bottom.

The cold water closed over my head.

All sound ceased save for the gurgling of large air bubbles boiling up from inside my cuirass. Tiny ones fizzing out of the fabric of my gambeson. Bubbles bursting on the surface.

The mud was slick under my hands and feet as I tried to rise. The spaces between my fingers filled with slick dark mud and gritty particles. Clouds of stirred-up silt rose before my face.

The water chilled everything but the shaft inside me felt like a red-hot billet from a blacksmith's forge, driven in my flesh. It burned from my shoulder to the top of my heart.

Strong hands grabbed me and pulled me up and I rose screaming out of the water, for one man had me by the elbow-cop of my left arm and his heave upon it drove the bolt further in. He thought I had simply slipped and fallen but when he saw the fletchings of the bolt, he released my arm and grabbed instead the faulds at the back of my cuirass and, with the other man, hoisted me through the water toward the shore.

I was a small weight for them even in full kit and they hauled me out like a fish and laid me out on the sand in the lapping wavelets.

Mere moments before, I had been with Alençon and de Rais and Gamaches. We had been riding by where the men on the drawbridge were bashing at the gate with the ram. I looked over and saw that a party of men was reaching the top of the ladder nearest the bridge and the two men closest to the top were Jean de Metz and Squire Bertrand.

The English were striking de Metz with axes and using forked poles to push against the ladder. It began to move and Bertrand grabbed the edge of a stone and held fast. The men holding the ladder in the water below were slipping and struggling to hold it. I swung down from the black, almost fell as my foot caught in the stirrup, and ran up the landing and onto the drawbridge.

I tried not to look at the bloody pieces as I stepped over them to reach the ladder.

I did not want to recognize any part of what had once been my friends, nor think about Pierre and Joseph and what

I had done to them.

I reached out and took the wood of the ladder into both my hands and pushed against it, halting its sideways slide. It took all of my strength to hold it and the English above me saw me there and pushed the harder.

My boot-heels began to slip in the congealed blood on the wood of the drawbridge. Gamaches appeared next to me and then de Rais. I could see Alençon was holding their horses, as the great men had all left their pages far back from the battlefield, and de Aulon had my banner, flapping over the Duke's head. Gamaches and de Rais reached to help with the ladder and I could hear excited English voices above me on the wall, voices saying, "The Maid! The Maid!"

The thought ran through my mind, here are at least two Englishmen who do not think me a witch, for they are referring to me by my title. I looked up to see the faces of these men.

That was when I saw the arbalest.

It was a wicked-looking weapon, large and ungainly in the hands of the brawny man who held it, with cranks on the side to pull back the heavy cord, bending the steel prod, and its short thick barbed bolt waiting in the grove, ready to fly, bringing death on the wing.

I felt the force first more than the pain.

It drove me down hard, my legs falling out from under me and my seat hitting the wood of the bridge. Then the pain caught up with the momentum of the bolt and a deep searing agony tore me in two. Then I was sliding in the blood and guts of the horses and men, and then I was under the cold water. When the two men dragged me and laid me on the sand, I was dazed and confused, trying to catch my breath, choking up water, and not sure where I was.

There were men leaning over me whom I recognized and men whom I did not. I saw all of their deaths, however, and all their deaths seemed to go in and out of focus and weave together into one death, one great terrifying, undeniable death, unassailable death.

It was a death you could not defeat.

You could not chase it down a beach and strike and strike and strike at it and make it retreat before you, leaving you joyous, breathless, and alive. You could not surround it and assault it wave by wave, kill and conquer it.

It was not defeat-able, you could not win against it, nor could it be bargained with, you could not bribe it off or negotiate a peace with it. It was the ultimate foe.

I saw all the deaths, it was the gift of the angel that I had never wanted, the gift to see it clearly and not be able to turn my eyes away.

I, of all people, had to see the deaths and not turn my eyes away. It was my death, the death of us all, for we all are mortal and we all shall die, whether we consider ourselves English, Burgundian or French, partisans of the King of England or of the Armagnacs, of any nation or of any religion, there was no turning one's eyes from it.

One had to, in the end, simply take the hand of it and walk away with it like a child.

A powerless child.

The point was at my heart. I could feel it there and feel it killing me.

The faces and the voices of the men whom I had recognized and the faces and the voices of the men whom I had not all receded now and all that was left was the point at my heart, that burning red-hot bolt.

It was my death, after all, and it <u>was</u> by fire, but the fire was inside me, not without. It was consuming me from within, not without.

A few minutes before I had seen through many eyes.

My own from the midst of the battle, the eyes of the rabbit boy into the mind and thoughts of Raymond, and through the eyes of God high above, or if not of God, then of a colder Michael.

Now, my awareness was narrowed down to a single point, that sharp point of the barb at my heart, or in my heart, or at it and worming its way in, a flame licking its way to the core. All else was darkness, but for that fire.

All else was silence save for the frenzied pounding of my assailed heart.

So because there was nothing else, I went towards the fire, pushed into its searing heat, to see what lay beyond.

The fire went from red-hot to white-hot and I pushed into it and what had been the pounding of my heart became another sound, a rushing, roaring sound which filled my ears painfully and then mercifully faded to a whisper, and beyond the sound and the heat and the pain was a soft and silent nothingness. It was a relief to enter it and see, as if from a distance, a single welcoming point of softly glowing light.

As I looked, it seemed as if the point of light was not light only but a face illuminated by light, by the light of candle-flames, and the face was not a face but the reflection of a face in water illuminated by candle-flames, and I studied that face as I would a stranger's.

But it was not a stranger's face, it was my own, my child-face, reflected in the still waters of the font at our little church in Domrémy, round, with a pointed chin, large catlike eyes, and a lip that trembled with fear or with wonder or with something else I have never been able to adequately name, but which has filled me since my earliest remembrance.

I could not tear my eyes away from that face, though my Father's hand urged me to follow Him, and I wanted so to take His hand and go with Him, walk away into the welcoming darkness and forget all that had happened, all the horrors of it and the loss, and all my flaws, and be born again, clean.

But in the end, I could not go, for I could not tear my eyes away and, finally, I saw why.

It is not my own face that I saw, but yours.

74, You

I would have to leave you one day. This I knew.
But not today.

75, My Angel

And you would have to let me go, one day.

But not today. You would not, could not let me go today.

You came flying in on angel wings. Great, powerful but ragged angel wings. You came flying in and lifted me up in your strong arms and bore me away.

And I felt your arms come around me and I felt you lift me and I felt my head fall back and the heavy steel helmet fall from it, and my eyes opened, just a little, and I looked up and saw your face, your face as beautiful as an angel's.

Some sounds came back to my ears then.

Voices I recognized and didn't recognize, and the sounds of battle, the splashing of water, and the whinny of a horse, and shouts in English, shouts of terror, shouts of "Michael, Archangel!" and "Saint Michael!" I smiled and closed my eyes.

The English thought you looked like an angel too.

They had seen you appear, your youthful body astride a

pure white horse. They had seen you fly through the air, carried aloft by your steed of vengeance, your golden hair like a glowing halo about your head. They had seen you part the battle before the hooves of your mount, casting Frenchmen to either side, and they had seen dukes and knights of renowned stand aside, letting you through to raise me from the ground.

They had seen the angel bear me away before they, the English, could crank their arbalests and pierce my fallen body again and again.

Men see what they want to see, not necessarily what is real. Anyone who thought my old gray campaigner looked like a pure white horse at his age must be half-blind with terror. They thought they had killed the witch and feared demonic retaliation, or if they were wrong and had slain the page of Christ, they believed God's wrathful angels would appear to punish them.

They saw you, probably through clouds of smoke and the blasts of cannon, swoop down from the heavens on a flying horse, though in reality you and the gray had leaped over the edge (the quickest way to reach me and a leap of faith, for certain) to scramble in billows of dust down the steep bluff, the staid old warhorse so sure-footed and strong that he bore you safely down, his hocks flexed under him and his huge hooves peeling the soil like a sharp knife.

They saw this white apparition and the beautiful golden-haired youth astride him, fresh and young and unarmored, an angel of Heaven certainly, swoop in and carry me away.

And inexplicably, they had seen white butterflies in the air above us as you bore me away and a blue light around my standard as de Aulon raced on foot to keep up with you, the long pole in his hands, tripping and scrambling, trying not to let it fall.

76, Multitude

I was being born.

Not born into a new life, clean, but born along the ground, born by the strong arms of my love, born away from danger.

I felt as if I were skimming along the surface of the ground, seeing through my half-closed eyes the blue sky with its pure white puffy clouds break free of the smudge of smoke that had obscured it, and a bird of the field flitted across my view and a blue-white tiny butterfly seemed to follow me, lilting through the air above Gilles' head.

My love's curls hung down over much of his face and the little rabbit paws of the ties of his singular hat bobbed before my eyes. The strings that were to tie his linsy shirt closed at the throat dangled before me and just beyond those was his chin with a little dimple in it and the soft stubble of his not-yet-man's beard glinting along his jaws.

My right arm was thrown up over his shoulder and I could feel the muscles of his back with my fingers, and in my mind I pictured wings sprouting from those muscles, great powerful wings that lifted and carried us far away, me and my love.

Far away to a country all our own.

Gilles bore me away, but not to that country.

He bore me and the others followed, and when he found a safe place far from danger and the noises of the fighting, he laid me gently down. It was betwixt the rows of once-cultivated trees, walnuts maybe or chestnuts, my vision was too blurred to tell, but the trees were overgrown and almost as wild now as a forest, and grass grew lush and green and cool between the rows, and the light coming through the limbs and glittering upon the leaves was lovely. He lay me down and looked upon my face.

The color of his eyes was beyond color, more like light of varying degrees. I had seen them dark and gray as slate, and as yellow, light and clear as clover honey, as blue as a summer sky, and as green as new leaves on the limbs of the birch. But now in the neglected grove of nut trees on the edge of the battleground with the spangled sunlight illuminating him, burnishing the planes of his face, accentuating his perfect lips, his high cheeks, his strong brow, and beneath that brow, those eyes were a clear gray-blue and as sweet and soft as the gaze of a rabbit as it hides from sight under a berry-bush.

The others were around me.

I could hear their voices, see their movement as they crowded and bent to peer down at me, but my eyes were only for him, my Gilles, my shield, my own one, my Great Joy, my angel, my rabbit boy. And as I looked up at him, with his halo of golden-brown tangled curls framing his face, the sunlight seemed not just to illuminate him but to emanate from him.

It was a bright golden light and as I looked, it seemed to grow brighter, becoming almost white, and then I saw the others. Not the other men but the other angels.

There were all around him, and beyond him, their faces forming a circle all around his face, and another circle beyond the first and another circle beyond that one, angel faces, all beautiful and bright, glowing with love, each one different. Some were male, some were female and some I could not tell, or they were of neither gender.

Among them were two whom I did know, the ones I called Saint Catherine and Saint Margaret, and they both did smile at me, knowingly, and I did feel their love for me, for I had done as they had asked of me. I had obeyed God's command and I had done as Michael had told me I must when he told me that I must travel away from home and leave my mother and my father and friends behind and journey with strangers far into the land of our enemies.

I looked for Michael's face among these angels. I searched every face, my eyes streaming tears at the brightness that surrounded them. I wanted to see Michael, he who had told me that the truth must be fought for and that I must lead the men who would do the fighting, that I was the only one that could lead them and whom they would follow, bearing the truth with them for all the people of the world to know.

Twas a duty, he had said, that I could not shirk, for I alone was born to do it, and I must do it for *Jhésus*, and *La Magdalena*, and *Maria* the Mother of God, and for the truth to be known. And that truth was, that Charles the Dauphin of France, he whom I called the King, bore within his veins the blood royal, the *sangrail*, the blood of the Kings of France, and the greater truth was, that the *sangrail* was the blood of *Christ Jhésus* and His wife *La Magdalena*, from Their union and passed down through Their children through the generations, for after the death of *Jhésus*, His wife had come to France and here Their progeny had grown and flourished despite the Church Militant's attempts to destroy It and to destroy all who believed in It.

This was the truth.

This was the secret truth that I had shared with the Dauphin before the living fire in the King's grate at Chinon. This was why I had promised that I would see him crowned King of France in the traditional place at Rheims and why it was the will of God that Charles be King.

I had promised Michael that no matter what I had to sacrifice, this thing would be done. I looked for Michael's face, hoped to see it, prayed with tears streaming from my eyes that I would see it, the beautiful face of that most powerful and most dangerous of all God's angels, but I did not see him in this multitude.

One by one, the angel faces slipped away into the light, the light that faded from white, to gold to pale blue, one by one they disappeared, even Saint Catherine and Saint Margaret, one by one, until the only face in the light was the face of my Gilles.

Not an angel, but a boy as beautiful as an angel.

77, Healed

With my own hand I pulled it forth, the bolt that had dealt me that mortal wound, struck me hard and forced its length into my body until it pricked my very heart, the short stout barb that all the English and most of the French would say had killed me.

And it had killed me, or at least was killing me, when the multitude of angels pressed around me, and one angel in particular drew me back from the edge of that place from whence there is no returning. He looked upon me now, all love in his eyes and a tear running down each side of his nose, and he watched me as I pulled it forth. I felt every fraction of an inch of it as it came out and a gout of hot blood followed it, spilling over my armor.

He took the bolt from my hand and I saw his shoulder move as he swung his arm back and slipped the bloody thing into his little bag, his little bag that he never let out of his sight.

I smiled, thinking, *finally, I know at least one thing he has in his little bag!*

Then the silence that had muffled my ears broke and the clamor of voices was heard; men talking all at once, and shouts in the distance and a rumble of horses' hooves and the prayers of Father Pasqueral behind my head, where he was kneeling, sprinkling holy water on me.

De Rais was suddenly in front of me, elbowing Gilles aside and bending his handsome face to within inches of mine. "Jehanne, I have a potion. Guaranteed to close all wounds," the Baron said, in a low voice that bled of desperation, or like a lover's pleas. "Let me anoint you, I beg you, *Pucelle*."

"No, Baron de Rais," I said, my voice unaccountably calm. "I need no salve but God's love. Nor do you, nor ever shall, though you will not believe it."

He clamped his jaw and sat back on his haunches, so very disappointed.

Pasqueral was asking me questions, asking me if I accepted Christ, if I confessed my sins. I turned my eyes upwards to look at his face as he knelt behind me, as close as he could get for the press of bodies surrounding me.

"I do, Father," I said, "but I am not dying. I have been close to that place, close enough to see into it, but I have returned. Now, there is another place I must return to. The foot of *Les Tourelles*. Help me to rise, you men."

There was argument and discourse but I insisted, and finally Alençon and Gamaches lifted me. As soon as I stood, my head swam and I bent and spilled the contents of my stomach upon the lush grass; it was but yellow fluid only, not even bread and wine for I had had none this day. The dark blood was congealing upon my steel and I debated whether to remove it or leave it there for the English to see, but before I could decide, Father Paqueral was using his fustian robes to wipe me clean. De Rais pulled a piece of silk from within his vambrace and, as if he were assisting, wetted it with my blood and quickly stowed it again.

I met Gilles' eyes through a gap between men.

He was standing with the gray, the large animal's head held between his hands, the gray's eyes closed under the stroke of his fingers. I smiled at him and he smiled at me, a smile so sweet that I wanted to taste it, lick it from his lips and savor its honey. What thoughts from the page of Christ!

What desires from the virgin who would save France!

But they are real.

They are what I thought.

They are what I felt.

History is a stodgy chronicler. History knows not what is in our hearts.

78, Surrounded

The men of the city were now at the back door of *Les Tourelles*. They had stormed over the bridge, chasing every Englishman from Saint Antoine before them, killing many as they fled. Now they were on the back side of The Turrets, causing the enemy within to face to the rear as well as the front, fighting a two-sided defense. I appeared near the drawbridge, close by the place where I had been struck down.

I heard the cries of dismay and astonishment from English throats as they saw me alive and standing before them with my banner unfurled and flapping over my head. Upon the high walls, men were crossing themselves and calling upon God to save them. Clouds of smoke were still billowing out of the windows, as the river-men had brought more faggots and trash and were tossing it into the stairway below the fortress.

The face of Gladsdale appeared on the rampart above me.

He coughed and spat a glob of phlegm down. His face was black with smoke and soot.

"How is it you are still alive?" he asked me, his ragged voice thrown hard at me like a stone.

"Tis the will of God," I shouted over the din, "that I live and that I stand before you. And that I see the English out of France."

He laughed. "What does God care about our little spat?"

"God sees the fall of every sparrow," I said, because that is what Father Guillaume had always said to me in the tiny church in Domrémy, whenever, as a girl I had gone there to pray for guidance in all the petty concerns of childhood, and later, for solace against the great and terrible fears of growing up, growing up in an occupied country with enemies on every side.

Gladsdale looked disdainfully down at me. "God is fickle then. He has suffered us English to be here fourscore years, blessing our enterprise, bestowing rulership of this country upon our Kings and now suddenly, He has thought better of it? Come now, Joan, you are not a stupid girl."

I paused then, chewing my lip.

His argument could not be turned aside with a simple platitude. He smirked at me and bared his big white teeth in his soot-darkened face. "It is all politics, girl, it has naught to do with God! You are a game-piece just as am I! We play our parts and fool ourselves that it is for the greater good, that God has put His blessing on our works, but it is just a game, not a holy calling. We are fools, you and me, our lives mean nothing except to ourselves. Yet here we are!"

What he said unnerved me.

I was glad no one else seemed to be able to hear it, his men and mine were doing battle on every side. He had called us game-pieces. Hadn't I said something to that effect to the English soldier at *L'avant-poste de Saint Pouair,* the one whose wife's name was Lizzette?

I thought of the Dauphin, the man whom I would see crowned King of France. I thought of death by fire, standing here in conversation with a man who had threatened me with it, and could not escape the fear of it, or to wonder how, if I did all the things I had promised to do, that would ever, could ever, come to pass. The image of that fire burning in the King's grate still rode before my eyes. Where once it had comforted me, now it worried me.

Could I put my trust in King Charles, a mere man? I had had dealings with many men since leaving my country of Lorraine and I had been able to trust very few. Men, I now knew, even men of the *sangrail,* were only men. In fact, of them all, it was the men of no name and of little power whom I seemed to be able to trust the most. Gilles, a peasant boy, and the Cadieux brothers, bless them, poor knights who had to borrow a horse, and the hundreds who threw themselves against the weapons of our foes so valiantly but whose names I would never know and History would not remember.

Was I but a playing piece in the games Kings play? Was Gladsdale?

The difference between me and him was that I saw angels. They spoke to me. They commanded me.

It was not the Dauphin, nor The Bastard, *La Hire,* Alençon, or any of the great men who commanded me. This Englishman could believe he was only a game-piece if he wanted, but I was not.

I straightened my shoulders and shouted up to him, knowing as I did so, that he would never heed me. He would not save himself.

I had seen his death.

Yet I was bound to say my lines.

"Well, you have played your part for your King, Sir!" I shouted. "If it is but a game, you should not have to die for it. Has there not been enough blood spilled? Put down your weapons and open your portcullis and come on out. Save the lives of all these men of yours who have served you so well!"

He shook his head. "I cannot do that, little girl."

"Why not?" I asked. "If this is a game, not a holy calling, why should you die?"

He coughed in the smoke for a long while, then said, "Because I have honor, Joan. I cannot surrender to a mere girl. Besides that, my people will remember you as a witch and I cannot have my name besmirched forever by handing my sword to a witch." He ducked back behind the wall then, and I did not see him for some hours.

79, God, the Mercenary

Men were fighting, men were dying. It seemed to go on forever, and my prayers, which I voiced from time to time within the closed casque of my helm, were loud upon my own ears but seemed to fall deaf upon the ears of God. I was on foot, my black held by my page Louis far from arrow-range, near where Gilles waited with the gray, watching. I tried to be everywhere that I was needed, to be seen and to inspire, and to help where I could be of help.

I rushed forward to help an exhausted man to his feet. I soothed another's wound with cool water. I bowed my head with Father Pasqueral over the slain body of another. I waved the sword of the saint in the air with my good hand, while the standard with the lilies of France, held by de Aulon, fluttered over my head.

I called to my men, my beautiful men, my soldiers of France, and encouraged them to fight on, fight hard, fight for the glory of Charles.

I encouraged them with all my being, but I could see they were faltering.

Assaulted from every side and in thick clouds of smoke, the English held out.

"They are a foe to give a warrior pause," the brusque *La Hire* said at my elbow.

I lifted my visor, hearing the latch-pin engage, and glanced at *La Hire*'s grizzled face, which was streaked with dirt and sweat and blood. Some of his long hair was plastered against his cheek, a strand of it caught in the corner of his mouth.

"They are indeed, my friend," I said. "Why do they continue?"

I could not understand the mind of the defeated enemy who would not surrender, when this was not their homeland they were dying for.

The mercenary captain shrugged his broad shoulders, making his battered armor creak.

"Pride?" he said, uncertainly. "Or fear of Gladsdale, should they drop their weapons? Who would be the first to stop, to say to his companions, 'we should give up'?"

"There must be many within," I said, "who would like to give up and save themselves."

He nodded.

"What would you do, *La Hire*," I asked, "were you one of those?"

He laughed. "I would find a way to kill Gladsdale without anyone seeing me. Then I would convince the rest to join me in surrender. I would find a way to make it out of there alive. And then, mayhap, when times were better, I would fight again." His eyes rested on me for a moment. "That is what *La Hire* would do, if *La Hire* were English and inside *Les Tourelles.*"

I looked around me. The battle raged and beyond the turrets of the fortress, the many-arched bridge leapfrogged the river waves to the great gates of the city. Beyond the city walls, cook-fire smoke rose from chimneys and the day-to-day business that had transpired was being wrapped up. Over there, families were preparing to sit down to supper.

Close by, men were in mortal combat, spending their last energy in killing and dying, while other men industriously pulled bodies from the fray and stacked them out of the way like cordwood; English here, French there, tidying up the battleground for the continuing business of bloodshed.

Others waited beyond the danger. Idle knights mounted on horses, watching and waiting, yawning and stretching, and their servants and pages holding their horses and their standards and handing them wine-skins and rounds of cheese.

Beyond them, the field and forests were the same, still and peaceful, the small animals and little birds living their tiny lives, just as God had intended. If I ignored the sounds of fighting, the clashing of weapons and the shouting, I could almost hear birdsong. There was cannon-fire no longer, men were too busy trying to kill each other at close quarters, or else the powder and shot was exhausted, or else gunners were collapsed fatigued against their guns. I thought about what Gladsdale had said about God.

"Do you believe in God, Étienne?" I asked suddenly.

The mercenary coughed, or mayhap twas a laugh. He glanced over his shoulder where, I could see, Xaintrailles was standing, both hands resting on his sheathed sword, perhaps listening in on our discussion, perhaps only waiting for *La Hire* to get back to the more interesting pastime of battle. *La Hire* shifted from one foot to the other, the huge rowels of his spurs jingling.

"*Oui, non?* Do you?" I prompted.

He laughed again and this time it was clearly a laugh. "There have been times, moments, I truly believed in God, and even called out His name. Loudly."

Behind him, Xaintrailles laughed. I looked from one to the other and did not see the jest.

"Yes, really?" I said. "Tell me."

La Hire shook his head, and his cheeks turned red. "I believe, *Pucelle*, in the things I can see and touch," *La Hire* said, in a quieter voice meant only for me.

"So, you do not believe in God?" I said. "Do you not see God in the works of His creation?" I was thinking of the fields, and the rivers, and forests, and the sky, the buzzing lives of insects, and the feathered flight of birds and the surging blood in the bodies of beasts, and the song of river-men plying their oars.

I thought of the boy with the golden-brown curls and of his strong lithe body, his gentleness with horses, and of his love for me. "Is not this world a miracle that could only be created by God?" I pressed.

While I waited for him to answer, I watched the struggling soldiers before us and noticed one, a boy with an open-faced helmet and a small shield on his arm and a little ax, running to and fro using his ax to split the skulls of any Englishman he saw fall from the walls. His dark hair stuck out from below the helmet and he wore the colors of the King. It was Raymond.

"Is that not your squire?" *La Hire* said, changing the

subject.

"My page, Raymond," I said.

"Seems he has decided upon his tasks for the day," Xaintrailles broke in.

"He is not a very good page," I said.

"He seems a good little killer," Xaintrailles observed.

Is that how you started, Poton? I wanted to ask him. But I was more interested in *La Hire*'s belief or non-belief in God. I looked up at the mercenary captain's face expectantly.

He looked at me and sighed. "If this world is the creation of God," he said, "then God is more of a mercenary than me."

Xaintrailles showed his broken teeth in a smile. "God is more a mercenary than *La Hire*," he said. "Now there is one for the scribes."

I turned to Xaintrailles then. "And you, Poton," I said, "what is it that you believe in?"

The killer looked surprised that I should ask. He gave a curious little tilt of his head, much like the falcon I often compared him to in my mind, and said, "Why, Jehanne, I believe in this," and he slid the steel of his sword out of its scabbard until about a hand's length of its blade glinted in the late afternoon sunlight, "and in this," he said, holding one scarred and calloused hand before his face. "These are what I depend upon. These are what I can trust." He turned then and walked away, as if to say to me and to *La Hire*, that there had been enough talk.

La Hire watched him go.

The mercenary captain sighed and looked down into my face. There was a trickle of sweat that ran down from inside his helmet near his forehead and made its slow way down his cheek into the whiskers on his jaw.

"I will tell you something, *Pucelle*," he said. "I may not

have believed in much in my life, and God not much at all, but I have come to believe in a slip of a girl from Lorraine. There are things..." and here he paused and worked his tongue around in his mouth as though he was very thirsty, and he probably was, "...things... that you..." he said. With a gauntleted hand, he swiped the strand of hair from the corner of his mouth and shook his head.

"*Oui*," I said, to spare him. "*Oui*, I know."

He coughed. "So, in any case..." he said, and gave me a nod and walked after Xaintrailles.

I watched him go, his brown-patina'd armor clanking as he moved and his leg with the slight limp leaving a mark on the ground behind him. He caught up with Xaintrailles and I saw them meeting up with The Bastard, de Rais, Alençon and Gamaches and all of them falling into conversation. I stood there with only the silent de Aulon beside me, holding my standard, and I watched Raymond bending over a fallen English man-at-arms, stripping the body of some of its armor and weapons.

He had almost gotten the hauberk off the man when a ladder-full of Frenchmen was levered off the wall and crashed down, barely missing him. All the men tumbled together, with the broken pieces of the hastily-made ladder, and some of them scrambled up and some of them lay there on the ground, and the English on the walls sent down bolt after bolt to pierce their bodies. Raymond ran with the rest, tripping and stumbling, carrying what he could of his spoils, and his little ax running blood. He was laughing like a madman.

It was like a bad dream, one I could not wake from.

A dream of God as mercenary.

How do I end this? I wondered. How?

Then I remembered something. A dream.

I had told it to my rabbit boy. Like most dreams, it had faded from my memory, like a weak dye under a bright sun.

But Gilles would remember.

He remembered everything about me.

80, Remembered

I found him with the gray behind the broken-down stone fence. He smiled to see me come to him, all love in his eyes. He remembered the dream, as I knew he would, and told me how we were enveloped in the flowing white fabric of the banner, how it encircled us and we caught glimpses of each other as the silk billowed and blew in the wind with the lowering light of the sun shining through it, making our faces pink and golden.

Our hands were on the shaft of it, all four of our hands, mine, then his, then mine again, then his again. Our hands were touching and we were laughing with the joy of it, the joy of our touching each other.

But someone else's hands were on the shaft of it too, below ours, big strong hands and dirty, with broken dirty fingernails, and metal half-mitts that came only to the first knuckles, and no, we weren't laughing, we were shouting. We were pulling and tugging at the shaft, trying to pull it free of the big hands.

We were caught up in the banner, finding and losing each other in its undulating folds until, finally, we got it free of the big hands and the wind snapped the fabric free of us and the banner streamed out straight in the wind, and the sun streamed into our eyes, blinding in its brightness.

And I shouted something, loud and clear, and my voice was the only voice that was heard, and then there was a great roar of voices.

81, The Standard

As I had passed them on my way to find Gilles, *Le Batârd d'Orléans* had addressed me.

His great gauntleted hand, the same one he had once pounded Gilles upon the head with as we rode toward Orléans, had gripped my elbow-cop, pulling me to a stop and he had glared down at me.

"It is no good, *Pucelle*," he had said. "The men have thrown themselves at those walls all day. They have not eaten, they have not drunk. They are done, finished. We are packing it in for the day. Maybe tomorrow or in a day or two, they will have the strength to go on. Or if we get reinforcements from the King."

I looked from his face to the faces of the other captains of France. They all seemed to have the same words upon their tongues, except for *La Hire* and Poton de Xaintrailles, who would have fought on until daybreak and beyond if I had said to do so. De Rais's blue eyes were boring into mine. He licked his lips as he looked at me, as if he wanted a taste of me. Alençon looked weary and sad, as if his faith was faltering with the energy of the soldiers. Robinet smiled insolently, looking as if he wanted to return to the city and drink wine and eat meat and tell about all the Englishmen he had met this day. De la Brosse, de Metz, and Gamaches were there also and looked stoic and tired.

My impulse was to chide them for cowards and laggards, to turn, draw my sword and charge the walls, showing them how it was done.

But I remembered my purpose in seeking my rabbit boy, and I thought better of it.

I touched the steel gauntlet of The Bastard and looked up into his dark serious eyes. "I understand, Bastard. Let the men rest, bring them back out of danger, let them eat and fill their famished bellies. I will pray. I will return to you in a quarter of an hour and we will decide what to do. All of you, call back your men, and take a rest."

The Bastard was about to say a word, but de Rais broke in. "Jehanne, you are going to seek the counsel of your angels? May I come along?" His eyes were ravenous. He was desperate to see an angel.

He would have to find his own, I thought grimly.

"I am sorry, Baron," I said, "they will not appear to me unless I am alone," and I turned and quickly walked away. I climbed the narrow path from the road towards the bluffs above, my armor whispering soft secrets to my ears as locusts buzzed away from my feet.

I had taken my helmet off, closed the visor of it, and

placed in the hand of my banner-bearer de Aulon, and asked him to hold it for me and to wait there for my return, with my standard in plain sight of the enemy. Without the weight of it, I felt lighter and happier. The breeze coming off the river was cool and pleasant as it whipped through my sweaty hair and blew the reddish strands of it all around my face as I climbed the little trail.

I reached the heights and saw Louis with the black grazing a distance from where Gilles sat on the stone fence, with the gray contentedly nibbling grass beside him.

He rose as he saw me come to him, all the love that ever existed on God's earth shining in his eyes, and as we talked, below us the men, my beautiful men, my soldiers of France, came to the calls of their commanders. They left the place of fighting, bringing their dead and wounded with them, and they sat and lay and rested and fed themselves and passed the water-skins and the wine-skins and many of them fell instantly into sleep, their weapons laid on the ground at their sides. Father Pasqueral made his quiet way among them, touching each one gently and tending to the wounded.

From the ramparts of *Les Tourelles,* smoke rose lazily blotting out the light of the sun, and casting a strange orange hue over all. Englishmen propped their elbows on the stones and gazed down, wondering if it was over for the day. In the far distance, in the new silence, I heard the voices of river-men singing. Though it was a sound of the Loire Valley since the very first Frenchmen had plied the rivers on boats, the songs of men who pulled at oars, who liked the cadence of song to time their strokes, I had never heard it until this morning.

They would not sing under English rule.

They were singing now because the French were winning.

My boot-heels were skidding in the soft dirt as I started back down the narrow trail after speaking with Gilles and I almost tumbled. I caught myself with my hands, grasping the tall grass. As I righted myself, I heard a shout and a flurry of movement.

Looking, I saw de Aulon struggling with a large dark-haired knight over possession of my standard. The big man had jerked the pole of the standard out of my banner-bearer's hand and given him a shove which sent de Aulon sprawling, my helmet flying from his hand. I raised my eyes from this small scene to the larger one and I saw that the army had picked itself up from the ground and was forming loosely into marching ranks. The Bastard had mounted his horse and without waiting for me, had begun to muster the men to retire from the field.

Damn his eyes! I thought, and then wondered when I had learned to curse. But damn his eyes, The Bastard was leaving and taking my army with him! I started to run down the slope, trying not to slip and fall in my armor.

But Gilles had seen also, and taking the more direct route straight down the bluff where he and the gray had gone when I had been struck by the crossbow bolt, he landed upon the strand in a cloud of dust, burst from it and was racing in his bare feet across the battleground, leaping bodies and shattered shields and broken ladders, running straight for the knight who held my standard.

I skittered and slipped my way down the trail and, reaching the bottom, I ran for the man also. Gilles was there before me and grabbed ahold of the shaft. I passed de Aulon, who was picking himself up from the ground. His face, seeing me, was contorted in distress that I should think he had abandoned his charge and he began to speak, but I

413

passed him before the words left his mouth.

As I neared, the long streaming banner whipped around me, enveloping me, the late light of the sun glowing through it, beautiful, golden and blinding. I raised my right hand and pushed the folds aside as I tried to find my way to the center, to the pole. I caught a glimpse of Gilles and lost it again in the creases of white silk that rustled and fluttered around me. I fought my way through it, reaching and my hand found the wood of the shaft and my fingers closed around it.

There were other hands grasping, pulling, jerking the pole this way and that. I saw Gilles, and he saw me, and for an instant it seemed we were the only two people there, our hands on the pole, and our faces lit with joyfulness. But then the standard billowed up, revealing the big knight.

He was tall and broad, with curls of black hair that framed his face under the steel of his open-faced helmet, and his eyes were startling; the deep gold color of honey under heavy dark brows. He was a handsome man in a rough way, with several thick scars on his strong chin and a gap-toothed smile. He saw me and pulled the pole against his armored chest.

"Come, *Pucelle*, it is time to go," he murmured in the accent of the Basques, "Captain says we have done all we can here today."

Gilles and I had all four of our hands on the banner-pole and we leaned back, pulling the top away from the knight, the wind caught the fabric and it snapped out straight over our heads, the edge running across my cheek so fast it felt like a burn, like a burn from an archangel's touch.

I was shouting, my voice clear and strong above any other sounds, and what I was shouting was, "It is ours! It is ours! We shall take it! Now! We shall take it! We shall take it!"

At that moment, as my shout faded into the sky, I heard a roar like a thousand unleashed mastiffs.

The men of France, who had but then been forming themselves into ranks to retire, spun upon their weary legs and charged for the walls of *Les Tourelles*, pulling their weapons from their belts.

The Basque released the standard pole into the hands of my rabbit boy and Gilles stood there in the golden sunlight, holding the banner over my head.

Its length spread out in the breeze, snapping like a whip, and then the very tip of it tickled the stones of the wall of the fortress, and I remembered what Saint Margaret and Saint Catherine had said to me, early that morning, *that when my standard touches the ramparts, Les Tourelles will be taken, it will be ours.*

82, Ours

They were unstoppable.

Ladders went up like a thousand lances pointed skyward in an instant. They crashed against the stones and men scrambled up them, scaling even the broken and loose-runged ladders as if they were broad staircases. Frenchmen poured up and over the ramparts, the astonished Englishmen weeping like scared children as they were forced back and cut down. The great captains and their mounted knights, seeing this, flung themselves from their saddles and ran, armor clanging like bells, to the base of the ladders, shoving soldiers aside to take their places on the ladders, and up they went as well, climbing like silver monkeys.

I winced as I watched Alençon and The Bastard, Gamaches and de Rais, thinking the rungs would break under their weight, but the ladders held, and they gained the top, and whatever Englishmen were still alive fell under the cutting blows of their swords and axes.

I could not see it, but my page Louis, standing on the bluff holding the reins of the black, who was snorting and prancing, striking the ground with his hooves, could see the men of the city, with de Gaucourt at the fore, break through the gate at the rear of *Les Tourelles* and run screaming into the inner courtyard, their hammers and rudimentary weapons swinging over their heads.

All was chaos within, weapons clashing, and thuds and the sounds of human voices in fury and agony, in exaltation and in terror.

Les Tourelles, the bastion of the English, was flooded with French. The English that had dwelled there were leaving, but not the easy way I had offered them.

Gilles and I stood side-by-side, the standard with the lilies of France flying over our heads, and de Aulon standing a short distance from us, my helmet under his arm. We watched as the portcullis was cranked open.

They were coming out, the last English were coming out.

A new fire was burning. The river-men had planted a boat filled with burning faggots and tallow-soaked rags under the drawbridge. I had not seen them do this and, seeing the thick black smoke billow up from it, I wondered why they had done it.

It was all out of my hands now; I could but stand and watch it happen. When I saw the portcullis raise and the last of the Englishmen come running through, I knew why. It was the death I had seen Gladsdale suffer.

And there he was, in his smoke-blackened armor, his sword in his hand and a shield strapped on his other forearm.

He came through, looking this way and that, blinking in

the smoke. He was standing in the place where Pierre and Joseph had died, where I had stood when I was struck by the bolt, and his feet were slipping in the slime of blood and horse guts.

He took a step or two, tripping over the horrible things that lay in piles on the planks. His eyes were wild, like those of a tortured lion, and he staggered, falling to his knees and clambering up again, and his boots rang upon the broad planks. His visage was contorted by fear, his helmet gone, having been struck off by someone, and his face was badly bruised. Smoke and flames were reaching up through the gaps in the planks at his feet, and other English, heedless for their commander, were pushing past him, barging into him, turning him this way and that. He acted like a man blinded. Or like a drunkard that cannot tell up from down, forward from back.

Tears sprang to my eyes as I watched him.

Maybe they were only from the black smoke that shifted on the breeze and came into my eyes, or maybe they were because I hated to see yet another man die right in front of me, even a man who had threatened me with rape and fire. But I had spoken to him, one human being to another, and I could not hate him as perhaps I should.

In another world, perhaps we would all be friends, we French and we English, perhaps we would live in peace with one another, defend one another, love one another. But not in this one.

Was God a Mercenary?

Was God blood-thirsty, like Xaintrailles?

Mayhap this was God's plan for all of us, after all, to kill one another.

But why?

83, Fallen

"Gladsdale!" I screamed.

His head came round and he saw me there.

For one long minute, his eyes stared into mine. But it was not a minute; it was a mere second, or less than one. I spread my arms.

"Come to me! Run this way!" I thought I could save him, but that was nonsense.

God was a mercenary, and God had chosen this moment for that man's death. I knew this, knew this! after all, I had seen it, but still I thought I might change it. Me, *Jehanne, La Pucelle*, thought I might change God's mind.

I was a silly girl. Why should I think I could change God's mind?

I had not even given God the chance to change His mind

and not kill my friends, my boys, my beautiful boys.

Should I have tried?

Should I have asked God to spare them, to be merciful, not mercenary?

I brushed the tears from my eyes. "Run, Gladsdale, run! Save yourself!" I screamed.

Gladsdale did run.

He saw me, my banner streaming, and he dropped his sword and tried to fling the shield from his arm but could not for it was tightly strapped on. His boots rang hollowly on the boards that were burning from underneath, and he side-stepped to avoid a place where the fire had burned clean through and flames were shooting skyward with showers of orange sparks. Some other men, heavy in their armor, were running past him and the bridge suddenly disappeared from under them all.

With a sound like the laughter of God, timbers and planks and men and armor and hunks of dead horses, and pieces of slaughtered friends, and all the detritus of our little spat, dropped away from the foundation and hit the water below with a great hissing Splash!

Water sprang from the riverbed and the black smoke belched upwards and the white steam rose, joining the clouds, and what was left was a churning mass of shining waves, bobbing floating blackened wood and sinking struggling men, the wood drifting off down the river, and the men dragged downward by the steel upon their living bodies.

I turned my face away and flung myself against my rabbit boy.

He wrapped one arm about me, the other holding the pole of the standard, and I did not care about the cold death that pinged against the steel of my cuirass, trying to gain entry, as I pressed my armor-clad body against his. His hand slid up my back-plate, past the steel of my encircling gorget, and his fingers curled around the back of my head, combing through my hair, and he pressed my face against his neck and jaw and his soft tangled curls.

For one most blessed moment, I was filled with such sweet joy and I inhaled a long breath and relaxed against him, smelling the forest and the sunshine in his hair.

Then I exhaled and a cold relentless death swept into the void and all went black.

84, Rejoice!

The first sounds I heard were men rejoicing. They sounded far away at first but then as I came to my senses, they sounded very close.

They were shouting for King Charles, and for France, and for *La Pucelle*. I opened my eyes and saw Gilles kneeling beside me and de Aulon standing over, my helmet under his arm, holding the standard. Father Pasqueral was there too, kneeling on my other side. The friar was smiling broadly, though his eyes held a residual concern.

"It is over, *Pucelle*," de Aulon said, brightly. "You have done it!" The face of my banner-bearer was lit with orange light from the setting sun and his eyes were full of admiration.

I looked to Gilles.

He was on one knee, his hand upon the steel of my quisse just above the knee-cop of my right leg and the steel was pinging softly from his touch, though no one but me could hear or feel it. Our eyes met for a brief encounter like a secret kiss, and I smiled.

They helped me to rise, and soon I was encircled by cheering men.

85, Return to Orléans

It took some time, but the men were able to patch together a bridge from timbers of The Barbican's bulwarks, enough that we could bring our mounts across and ride in triumph over the river bridge and into Orléans as night fell, as I had promised we would.

The city was joyful and all the bells were ringing so loudly that the black's ears were pinned back against his skull as he carried me through the streets and he ground his teeth against the clangor. Everywhere, people were calling my name and throwing favors, trying to touch me or my horse.

It was all I could do to keep him from stomping them to death as they streamed alongside me as I rode, their hands reaching, reaching, their hands patting his shoulders, trying to pull strands of hair from his glossy mane, their happy faces upturned to me in adoration.

My black, my demon-horse, as I sometimes thought of

him, was learning, reluctantly, to tolerate people touching him without him be allowed to kill them.

All along the way, folk invited me to stop and rejoice with them, the poor, the merchants and the wealthy alike. Politely, I declined. All of Orléans wanted to feast and make merry but all *La Pucelle* desired was to sleep.

Gilles had faded into the background of all this excitement, as he so often did, and when I arrived at the front of *la maison de la famille Boucher,* dismounted the black and made to go inside, he and the gray were nowhere to be seen. I imagined they would soon be in the stable, in their stall, resting. I thought of Raymond, his hatred and his jealousy, and hoped Gilles would be safe.

But before I went inside, I saw Raymond, wearing his blood-splattered royal jupon, in the company of the knights and squires of the great men, and, by their demeanor towards him, it seemed he had earned a place among them. If all went well, in the excitement being with his new comrades, he would forget all about the rabbit boy.

In my chamber, I was relieved of my armor by Louis, who then went down to see to my horse, and Charlotte and Madame Boucher came to bathe me and dress my wound.

On my shoulder just below my collarbone was a circle of darkened flesh the size of my fist, with a hole in the center which had been made by the bolt of the crossbow. It did not pain me much, though I could not raise my arm, and Madam Boucher anointed it with oil from the olive, took a long piece of linen and bound the arm to my side. I was dressed in some of Charlotte's fine clothes and brought warm wine mixed with water and a plate of beef roasted in its own juices, which I could not touch, thinking of the brindled ox on its knees in the streets of Orléans.

I drank the wine and lay back upon the bed.

I could not sleep as there were voices and commotion below the window, so I rose at one point and stood looking down. All the great men were still there, standing in knots and talking, their gestures and movements suggesting they were recounting the action of the day and their encounters with the enemy. They laughed and passed the wine. One man stood slightly apart and gazed up at me in the window.

It was de Rais, his eyes glinting in the light of a torch someone held.

He had an expression of wonder and of awe, as though he gazed upon the face of his Lord, or perhaps with the same expression that I had when I gazed at the face of Michael.

Michael.

Would I ever gaze upon his face again? I bewondered me.

Where was my archangel and why had he forsaken me?

A chill ran down my spine, looking at the Baron looking at me. I had a sudden thought that I had been forsaken by an angel whom I adored, and was now, myself, adored by a devil. I did nothing to invite this man's attention, yet he seemed obsessed.

What would the outcome of his interest be? To what ends would it drive him?

Thankfully, Robinet and Gamaches soon approached him. They conversed a moment and the three of them went off together in search of celebratory opportunities. The other great men, as well as their following, also dispersed into the city and I returned to bed.

This time I slept.

I dreamed of Gilles standing in a silent forest, watching with sad eyes a struggling rabbit twisting in one of his snares.

86, The Confessional

Privately in my chamber in the early hours of the new day, Sunday the 8th of May, Father Pasqueral said the Mass and administered the Holy Communion to me and heard my confession. I asked him why he wept. He knew that in the confessional, he was to listen as God's representative on earth and was not to have human feelings about what he heard.

And yet he wept.

The friar shook his head and would not meet my eyes. He took the edge of his fustian sleeve and wiped his eyes but the tears ran on.

"Why do you weep, good Father?" I asked again.

He sniffed loudly and smiled with embarrassment. "I weep for you, Jehanne," he said. "At the heaviness of the burden you bear."

I was worried then. "Can you not grant me Absolution,

then?"

He looked into my eyes.

"Oh, I can indeed," he said. "But I know however much you are absolved by God, you are not absolved by yourself, and that is why I weep. My office cannot bring you peace."

I had told him about Joseph and Pierre, and my leading them into death even as I knew of it waiting for them there at the mouth of the cannon. I told him about Gladsdale and how it had been to watch him die, like a tortured, blinded lion turning in circles looking for a place to run. I told him too, of the men on *Île-Belle-Croix* and how it had been to hear skulls shattering under the hooves of the horse I rode. How it was to send wave after wave of good men to their deaths over a wall of bristling weapons when I wasn't even sure, as I was doing it, if taking that wall was more necessary then their lives, their individual precious lives.

I had said it was necessary.

I had said that it must be done, repeated it so often, and the act of saying it was the act of making it true. Or was it?

Was it really?

I told him all of it.

And of how I had begun to doubt God.

I told him of my conversation with *La Hire* and my thoughts afterward. Was God a mercenary?

Did God take pleasure in this bloodshed we committed in His name? If not, why was it God's will that we commit these acts?

And if it was God's will, God truly was more of a mercenary than the famous *La Hire!* Or of the equally famous Poton de Xaintrailles!

Was God redeemable, like I hoped the mercenary Xaintrailles was?

How was it that a simple country girl like me, who knew nothing of the world, could even contemplate that God was not redeemable? Surely this was blasphemy.

All of these thoughts were blasphemy! And if they were blasphemy, could I be absolved? Or would I burn in Hell for thinking them? And the very thought of burning, even as I said it, made me tremble, as it ever did.

What about me? Blasphemous thoughts aside, I was more guilty than any man among them, though I never killed with my own hand.

Was I, the bloodless mercenary, the one who led them to these acts yet never struck a blow, was I redeemable?

All these tumbling thoughts, they tumbled out in the confessional.

"Oh, my dear child," Father Pasqueral said, "it is not blasphemy to question your faith. Every man of faith has doubts. You are delving deeper into the mysteries of God and with that comes many questions. How can we understand the mind of God? When we can barely understand our own minds?"

"We cannot?" I guessed.

"No, we cannot," he said. "Though some men profess to, but that is their own lack of humility. You must leave your heart open to God and try to do what is right. Let God's love guide you and ask His forgiveness when you falter. Try not to think too much. Free your mind and let your heart lead you. Try not to let your thoughts devil you."

At the word devil, I shuddered.

Where, for all of my life, in the innocence of my youth, I had felt the nearness of God and seen God in all things living and inanimate, now, here, in the midst of this war, I had seen and felt the presence of evil more strongly and almost continuously. Aside from those times when I was little that the Burgundians had roared over the hills and terrified the villages, I had lived feeling as though I were held gently in the cupped hands of my Lord.

Now, I felt I was surrounded on all sides by men I could not trust, by horrors I could not rid my eyes of, and by the confusion of good and evil embracing and melding into one object.

I was beginning to doubt that good and evil were separate and distinct entities.

Like *La Hire* and Poton de Xaintrailles, evil men, killers who sold their swords to he who paid the highest, yet good men who now, in their own stilted way, had pledged their belief in me, their loyalty to me. Like my black, a wicked beast who reveled in slaughter, yet protected me and carried me out of danger.

Even my white horse was not white, but a muddy gray, and old, and no longer beautiful, and the angel-boy on his back was ragged and poor and had secrets he had never shared with me.

For all the certainty that had brought me here, all the way from Domrémy, to end this war and drive the English from France and see the Dauphin crowned King in Rheims, for all that certainty, only one thing was I now, truly, certain of.

Gilles loved me and I loved him. That was my reality. That was my truth.

Where had all my other truths gone?

Father Pasqueral was silent and watching my face. He had said, "Try not to let your thoughts devil you," and here I was, letting them do just that.

I nodded and said, "Yes, good Father, I shall try."

The friar pursed his mouth as if concerned about something. "And it is best not to speak of your doubts to, say... the Archbishop of Rheims? Should he offer to counsel you or want you to confess to him?"

I gave a little laugh, though it was unseemly in the Confessional. I thought of telling him that the Archbishop was the last person I wanted to discuss anything with, especially God. Much less make confession to. I was afraid he would try to pry from me my belief in *Maria La Magdalena,* and her children. My standard bore the words *Jhésus et Maria,* but it was for *La Magdalena,* not the Virgin Mother, that I had had it written there. Perhaps Regnault already suspected it, or perhaps it was my own thoughts deviling me. Little did I know then how much Regnault would try to undermine me in the future, yet I disliked and feared the man, as much as I disliked and feared Baron de Rais.

The Archbishop was seeking to open dark boxes also.

I would avoid him as much as it was possible to do so, but he would prove unavoidable.

As would the Baron.

"I have nightmares, Father," I blurted suddenly, not knowing I was going to say it.

He cocked one dark eyebrow.

"Yes," I said. "I see war and destruction and the waste of lands and homes and the burning of fields, the rapine of children and the torture of small animals. I see deaths most horrible. I dream them before they happen and then I see them happen in actuality."

I would not tell him I see the deaths of people in my waking state, every day, every person, that I could see his even as he kneeled with me here, now.

Tears sprang anew to the friar's gray eyes, and he said, "Of course you dream these things, Jehanne, how could you not? They are all around you."

He would not say that he had nightmares too, his mind replaying in sleep all the things he had been forced to witness, but I knew it to be true.

"Yes, but did you not hear what I said?" I demanded, too loudly, too desperately. "I dream them and then they happen just as I dreamed."

Tears ran wetly down the man's face now and he bowed his head to me in what seemed like reverence. I waited and when he raised his head and gazed at me again, I saw something in his expression I had not noticed there before.

I could only call it awe.

He said, "You are a saint, Jehanne. You are a prophet. These things happen to such people."

Father Pasqueral wiped his eyes with his sleeve and before I could speak more, he said the words and made the sign of the cross and I was absolved. He stood and drew me to my feet. We had been kneeling upon the hard wooden floorboards with the Sword of Saint Catherine, cross-hilt upwards, for our altar. I sheathed the sword and lay it in its red plush scabbard upon my bed. The friar found the cup of watered wine I had not finished the night before. He offered me some and he drank the rest, setting down the cup.

"There is something I want to ask you, Jehanne," he said and took the stool beside the bed.

I sat opposite him on the edge of the bed and asked him what it was.

"Gilles," he said.

I cast my gaze to my hands folded on my lap.

The good friar went on. "He is not your page. He is not

your squire. He has no official role that I can see."

I glanced up then, meeting his kind gaze. "No, Father, he has not."

Father Pasqueral swallowed and moistened his lips. "You have never mentioned him in the confessional." My brows must have narrowed then, for I could see how my expression caused the friar to draw back his head a bit and examine my face.

"There is nothing about Gilles to confess," I said. "Not unless a person's feelings for another person are a sin."

"Love is not a sin, Jehanne, it is a gift of God."

I nodded. "We love each other," I said. "We have done nothing sinful. We hope to be married, when... when... this is over..." and saying the words, I felt a leap of joy in my heart at the prospect and at the same time the thud of dread in my stomach.

It felt like another lie, and lying was a sin, and I had not mentioned Gilles in confession, and I should have, I realized now, for I had committed a sin with him, not by lying with him, for I had not, but by lying to him.

I had told him I would marry him. Yet I knew I never would.

But did I really know it?

There were moments, like when I sat on my black on the highest bulwark of The Barbican yesterday morning, with the little butterflies all around me and my standard covered by their simple and innocent beauty, where I believed it was possible. What did I really know for truth and what was simply fear?

Only time would tell if it was a lie, and in any case, saying to the friar that Gilles and I were affianced was no lie. We were. We had pledged to marry, and we would marry, if it was God's will.   And I hoped now that God would forgive me for thinking Him a mercenary.

I looked into the serious face of Father Pasqueral.   His brows were cocked inward, making a steeple in the center of his forehead.

"We are betrothed, Father, and until I am free to marry, we are friends."

He looked at me a while longer and his brows settled into a straight line again.

"After all," I said, feeling a blush come over my face, "I am *La Pucelle*."

Pasqueral gave a single nod.

"Still?"

I smiled and nodded.

"Still."

The friar rose, smoothed his robes, and walked for the door.   He stopped with his hand upon the latch and turned to look at me.

"I believe you, Jehanne," he said.   "And I wish you and your betrothed every happiness."

And then he was gone.

87, Maille-coif

It swung out over the void, its bright silver and bronzed links jingling as it swayed. I leaned out over the ramparts of *La Porte du Renard*, de Gaucourt on my one side and the guard-captain of the Renard Gate on my other and many other men with us, looking to the west. I could not wear my armor this day, for my wounded shoulder could not bear the weight of it, and so I had been garbed in a padded hauberk of blue and gold and the maille-coif placed over my head and shoulders.

My hair was plaited and a light linen cap pulled over it, between my hair and the tight links of maille, yet a lock of my reddish-brown hair was trailing in the breeze over my cheek and tickled the spot under my right eye where the finger of the archangel had once touched me, giving me the sight that was the gift of compassion.

I leaned out and could see what I had been brought here

to see; the hundreds of Englishmen who had come out of their various forts, the ones the foreigners had named London, Rouen, and Paris, and had set fire to them as they departed, and how they were now forming themselves into ranks of battle across the vast fields. They were organizing themselves into fighting blocks of pike-men, swordsmen, archers and knights, with their banners fluttering above them in all the colors of their leaders and their weapons gleaming in the morning light as the black smoke rose into the blue, cloud-painted sky behind them.

"They invite battle," said the guard-captain at my elbow.

"Yes," de Gaucourt said, nervously. "There are still very many of them."

"Yes," I agreed. "They are many, but they have destroyed their lairs and have nowhere to retreat to, so they have decided to make a stand. If we fight, it shall be to the death, and shall be for once and final."

De Gaucourt licked his lips. His narrow face was pressed even narrower between the cheek-plates of his helmet. "What will you do, *Pucelle?*" he asked.

"I shall go down," I said, standing upright and taking my hands from the wall. "I shall go out and whoever wishes to come with me may come."

I saw the tiled roofs of the tower of Michaut-Quanteau and the Bannier Tower behind him against the sky, the flags of France once again flapping from their heights. The proud towers and the worried face of the City Bailiff were a study in opposites. I placed my hand upon the vambrace of his rusted armor and held it there for a moment, looking up into his somber eyes.

"Come, Raoul," I said, to cheer him. "Come with me and say farewell to your unwelcome visitors."

And I clattered down the stone steps that led in a gentle curve down to *La Rue du Renard,* where mounted men were gathering and where Louis held the reins of the black and where Gilles was sitting on the gray, looking almost as worried as the Bailiff. Louis legged me up into the saddle and I gathered my reins, the black snorting and jumping about, eager to go. De Aulon was near me, holding my standard over my head, spread and snapping in the breeze, *Jhésus et Maria* gleaming in the sunlight and the red borders around the golden *fleur de lys* bright-red as blood.

I turned and looked at the faces around me. All were there, *La Hire* and Xaintrailles, *Le Batârd d'Orléans* and all his knights and squires, Alençon, Gamaches, de la Brosse, de Metz, Bertrand, their faces serious and determined. De Rais and Robinet arrived, looking unwell from the night's revelries.

"Our guests wish to give us their thanks before they take their leave," I said in a loud voice. "Shall we go and receive it?"

There was a great roar of approbation, from the throats of the horsemen as well as from the multitude on foot who were still pouring into the space before the Renard Gate.

Before the din died down, Gilles' hand was on the bridle of the black and he was leaning in. "Jehanne, my heart," he said quietly, close by my ear. "Please do not go. You have your wound."

I was shocked, I must say, or surprised, that he would think my wound would matter. That he would think that after all that had gone before, all that I had been through, that there was danger here for me, now. I looked into his eyes, a dark yellow like the straw in the stable of the gray, and said, perhaps a little harshly. "I am *La Pucelle*, I must go."

He would not take his hand from the bridle and the black shook his huge head and pinned his ears, almost pulling Gilles from the back of the gray.

"I am coming with you," said the boy from Le Moineau.

"You are not," I said firmly, thinking of the armed and angry multitudes that faced us across the field. "You may watch, from there," and I pointed where he should be to watch me force the English away from Orléans.

The black shook its head violently, jerking the bridle from the rabbit boy's fingers, and snapped at the gray, backing the other horse off.

And I rode, the maille-coif rising and falling heavily like the mantle of the Lord upon the shoulders of the page of Christ, its music gentle on my ears amidst the thundering of many hooves, and left my love behind.

88, The Lord's Day

It was a Sunday.

I would not attack, would not display aggression on a day of worship, yet I assured my captains that if the English attacked us, we would surely fight them, defeat them, kill them all, and so we stood, arrayed in our battle gear, ready for battle if battle was given, our ranks of warriors and knights opposite their ranks, and both bristling with polished arms, our standards snapping in the wind. Our populace was with us, having streamed out the gate behind us armed with crude weapons and tools, eager to get a final lick in against the foe that had oppressed them for so long.

We waited.

Behind me, high on the city wall above *La Porte du Renard,* stood my rabbit boy, his eyes burning a hole in my back. His heart was hurting, his gentle, loving heart, and I could picture him, his full lips slightly pouted, the lids half-closed over his bright eyes, anxious breaths flaring his nostrils. I wanted to look at him, I wanted to be with him; I wanted to say that I was sorry.

And yet, I was *La Pucelle*, had to be *La Pucelle*.

Jehanne might say to him that she was sorry, but *La Pucelle* could not.

I could not give him Jehanne until I was done being *La Pucelle*.

And only God knew if that would ever come to be. Only God knew if this page's mantle would ever leave my shoulders.

La Hire, beside me, said, "*Merde!* Let me go and provoke them!"

I turned to him and gave him my most disapproving face.

The mercenary captain's lips pursed. He knew I hated his cursing in my presence and he reworded and spoke again. "By my staff..." and here, Poton, on his other side, laughed and shook his head, his cruel eyes meeting mine like I was missing some private joke, "...let me go out and speak to them."

"I know well enough how you speak, *La Hire*, and that your words will not be civil enough to be my emissary, especially on a Sunday."

"How about me, *Pucelle?*" Poton said. "Tell me what to say and I shall say it. I promise you." I looked past *La Hire* to Xaintrailles and saw the mirth playing at the corners of the killer's mouth, though he tried to look as innocent as a lamb.

I laughed then, which surprised them both.

"I bethink me not," I said, "as I need the two of you here, if for nothing else but to keep me entertained while we wait to see what these English intend to do."

"We are your entertainment now?" *La Hire* said. "Is this

a demotion? Poton, I think we have been demoted."

I was about to say something when I heard a commotion, a stirring in the ranks, and voices of the assembled men of France rising in inquiry. Underlying it all was the sound of a single horse galloping. I turned my eyes to the fore and saw the figure of Alençon, in all his splendid garments and shining steel, upon his black destrier which was the brother to mine.

He had left the ranks and bounded his horse into the open field between the two armies.

There, he was putting the horse through its paces, cavorting in place, rearing on its hind legs and lashing out with its fronts, leaping into the air, kicking out behind, kicking out in front and behind in the same leap, galloping obliquely and changing directions, side-passing, and then spinning in circles and stopping in an instant, then moving out again in a long-legged lofty trot, the Fair Duke's dark red cloak flowing out behind.

Xaintrailles said, "If we are entertainers, Étienne, I think we are outmatched."

On the other side of the field, English archers were seen to raise their bows and their gleaming bodkins flashed in the light as they moved them back and forth, sighting upon the moving figure of Alençon.

"He has the same idea as us," *La Hire* said, his usually-brusque voice softened by admiration. "The gallant fool will get himself killed to provoke them to start a fight."

My breath had stuck in my chest. A hush came over us all and I felt the army of France stiffen and brace for a charge. The black blew out a hard loud snort and gathered himself against my rein, ready to surge forward. But at that moment, a call from the other side rang out over the distance.

The English bowmen, as one, lowered their bows and the gleaming bodkins went dark.

That voice, was it the voice of Talbot? Or Fastolf?

Whoever he was, he had told them not to loose their arrows. He had told them not to be the ones who started a fight upon The Lord's Day, and so, there would be no fight.

So, for all their readiness to finish this thing here and now, my captains of France, my beautiful men of France, my brave people who had survived siege and starvation and had lived through bloody battle after bloody battle wherein so many had been slain and many more had been maimed and given terrible wounds which would hinder them for the rest of their lives, my fine French people would have to stand here, curb their rage, and watch the enemy leave.

They would have to let them go, because they must, because it was the proper thing to do. Because it was The Lord's Day.

And my rabbit boy, that boy as beautiful as an angel, he who was charged to watch and bear witness to what I did, and who would one day watch my final act on earth and take the sight of it, years later, to his watery grave, that boy, high on the ramparts of *La Porte du Renard,* heaved a great sigh of relief as he watched them turn away from us and begin the long slow march out of our sight, down the road toward Meung-sur-Loire and on to their other holdings in the Loire Valley, where in time I would meet them again.

89, Lost is Found

Once the English had departed and the dust of their passage had risen in the wind and joined the smoke of the fires, I gazed across the empty space to where the Duke of Alençon sat his now-still horse. Beyond him, from the shadow cast by the smoldering ruin of what had been the enemy fort called London, a small figure emerged. I watched as the man stumbled, fell, staggered to his feet, and walked slowly in our direction, weaving.

My black leaped into the gallop without my even touching his sides with my spurs.

Alençon reached him before I did and dismounted before his destrier had even halted.

When I arrived and lowered myself carefully down, my wounded shoulder making it hard to dismount, the man was cradled in the arms of *Le Beau Duc* and I heard his weeping.

I stepped over and knelt beside them.

Guyenne turned his face to me.

The young man's beautiful face was black with bruises, and his teeth, once so fine and straight, were a jumble of broken stubs and jutting out at all angles. He had rope burns on his slender neck and a dislocated shoulder and a few of his fine long fingers were broken. His sandy-brown hair had been crudely shorn and there were bloody scrapes along his scalp from the blade that had shorn him. He still wore his royal messenger's jupon, but it was torn and dirty with holes burned into it, soiled with human filth, Guyenne's own waste.

"Oh, my brave man," I said.

Guyenne tried to smile, but could not. His jaw was so badly beaten that he could hardly open or close it. "I told them nothing," he managed to say, his words as broken as his face.

"I know," I said. "You wouldn't, not matter how much they hurt you."

And the royal herald begin to cry again, long jolting sobs that made him shake in Alençon's arms.

I stood and looked north, to where the English army had disappeared.

I was sorry I had let them go.

90, Threads

I don't remember everything.

Some things are seen as if in dream, or as if witnessed through the eyes of another.

Sometimes it is as if smoke is in my eyes and I squint and blink the tears away and look again, and do not see what it was I thought I saw.

Some things are grasped as if they are threads and I go to pull them, hoping the whole will be revealed, only to have it slip through my fingers and I have to try again.

Sometimes I pull and only a tiny part of it comes free for my scrutiny.

One thing I remember about the day the English went away, was sitting in the chamber of Charlotte Boucher, a single candle flickering as the day's light had left the windowpane, and pulling threads from a red cap. A piece of brown fur lay off to the side. I had torn it from the edge of the red cap and laid it there because I knew the person to whom I would give the cap could not pay the taxes upon the ownership of the fur and would be punished for having possession of it.

This person would one day be punished by some great man for some other, not-yet-committed trifling act, and would die for it, as unfair as that might be, but I could do nothing about the future, I could only effect the now.

And so I tore the fur from the cap and set about removing the threads that had held it in place. Outside, in the day turning to night, were the sounds of a city in celebration. The bells had been ringing since the last dust of the English had dispersed in the air over the fields and people were singing.

But an hour before, de Rais had come to the door of *la maison de la famille Boucher* and had asked to speak with me. He had been drinking and I had said, as politely as I could, that I would only speak with him when he was sober. He had lowered his gaze from mine, perhaps in shame, and said he would then return upon the morrow. But tomorrow, I had known, when he returned, I would not be here. Before he turned to go, I had asked him for the cap he was wearing.

It was a fine one, woven of the softest warmest wool, and dyed a deep red, with a band of thick dark fur. He had met my eyes with such a look of gratefulness that I felt suddenly guilty at giving this man I despised such hope and he had swept it from his head and laid it across my outstretched hand with both of his as if it were an offering to the altar of a powerful god.

"Anything you desire of me, *Pucelle,* is yours," he had

said, and silently slipped from my doorstep.

I turned the cap in my hands now, pulling the final threads from it, making a little pile of threads upon the tabletop. They looked like a heap of tiny blood-red worms, kinked and twisted.

When I slept that night, I dreamed of places I had never been.

They were places in the north of France, cities and towns that I had yet to see, yet I saw them clearly as they were, and knew their names, Jargeau, Beaugency, Patay.

And Rheims, the cathedral there, where I would see Charles crowned, I saw that too, in its glory.

And I saw also my tender love, my rabbit boy, his glowing eyes full of sorrow, his gaunt visage, and old bruises healing on his face, and wearing clothes so ragged they hung on his thin frame, and he stood in a shaft of light in a clearing in the forest, a meadow, a meadow that was home to him. And he looked across the meadow and saw a slender tree, sprung upwards from its string, and a dry and desiccated rabbit hanging from it, hanging by its hind feet and it was only bones and pieces of fur and had been hanging there a very long time.

I dreamed of my plumed hat, ragged and faded, the fine ostrich feathers reduced to curling shafts with just a bit of fluff left upon them, held in the hands of Charlotte Boucher, here in this very room, as she turned and turned it in her hands, hands wrinkled and aged, with tears running down her cheeks like little silver fish.

And I dreamed of de Rais and his evil unborn, and the future that awaited him in the towers and dungeons of his haunted mind. I dreamed of *Le Batârd d'Orléans*, of his arrogance and his power, and I wondered, still dreaming, what deeds they would drive him to do. I dreamed of Alençon in his beauty and his goodness and faith in me and wondered where it all would lead him.

I dreamed of Pierre and Joseph, spurring their steeds and shouting, "Boldly, bravely!" and I remember where I had led them, and I saw them die, over and over again, and I wondered, dreaming, if they were in Heaven, and if there truly was a Heaven, and if people like us truly went there.

I dreamed of King Charles, the Holy Blood coursing in his veins, and the heat of his living fire and of the wind swirling it, making the flames dance this way and that and I wondered which way that wind would finally blow that fire, and whom it would finally burn.

I dreamed of Raymond, my page-boy, of his hatred for the boy from Le Moineau, and wondered what dire actions that hatred might cause him to do.

I dreamed of all of them, the men who surrounded me, all of them, even Guyenne, his face all hail and handsome again, and their faces circled about me, near to me and going back, back, back until they receded from my view, and the light that bathed those faces was not white, nor gold, nor pale blue, but a rosy red as if thrown by the dancing flames of a fire burning down my world.

Not the faces of angels, but of men, men in all their shining ambition and their bloody attainments, their bright flatteries and their dark deceptions. Their secrets and their plans, their loyalties and their betrayals, their failures and their falsehoods.

One by one the faces of the men disappeared, one by one, until the only face in the light was the face of my Gilles. And the light had gone from rosy red to golden. It shone all around his head and his curling hair.

Not a man, but a boy as beautiful as an angel.

As I awoke, I tried to grasp hold of the dreams, but like threads pulled, they slipped from my fingers, or like threads, only a tiny part of them came free.

91, The Boatman

Gilles was by my side in the bottom of the boat. Wavelets slapped the planks close by our ears. Their sound was like that of an otter's tail when it lashes the water's surface as it swims.

It was a joyous sound; a music to sing by.

We lay back so that none might see us, and the air from the river was cool upon our skin. I looked up and saw the boatman above us, leaning on his rudder, guiding the boat across the rippling currents.

His white hair, which normally fluttered all around his head like a cloud, was now contained but parts of it jutted out from under the red cap that he wore, which covered his ears against the cold breeze skidding over the water.

He sang as he plied the boat to the other shore, an old

song of the river boatmen, a song that had not been sung under the rule of the English.

His rasping old voice was a beautiful sound; the sound of freedom.

92, The Sound of Freedom

When we got to the place where the Grand Old Oak grew, we found others there.

We had gone running down the narrow trail, Gilles' bare feet pattering on the dirt path and kicking seeds from the tall grass before him. I had followed, joyfully, running after him in my simple boy's clothing and wooden shoes, my hair bundled up in a brown hat. I was trying hard not to tread upon the tiny grasshoppers that, stirred up from his passing, had landed on the trail before me and so was hopping to avoid them, my eyes to the ground.

Every once in a while I would look up, seeing the crown of the huge tree, trying to tell how far we were from our destination. But just as we reached the place where the narrow trail opened up to the open space where the oak stood at the top of the small hill, Gilles stopped suddenly in front of me, and I almost went straight into his broad back.

Laughing breathlessly and looking up, I saw what had caused him to stop. Two young girls were in the meadow, their long skirts and kirtles hiked up and tucked into their belts so that they did not trip on them, and all about them, their long slender necks bent to the grass, were large white geese.

The girls held smooth sticks, using them to keep the geese from straying into the wooded and brushy areas, and they looked up from their work upon seeing us appear. They were singing a song of May, a song of birds and the sowing the seeds, and the sunshine and the rains, a song I too had sung as a carefree country girl, and the sound of their voices was the sound of freedom. Their song stopped when they beheld us.

One of them called to us and beckoned.

Gilles tucked his head shyly and waved in negation.

The other girl laughed and called also, spinning in a circle playfully, like an otter will in water, trying to entice us to join them. I wondered at this behavior, and then I realized they thought we were two handsome young fellows, me in my boy's attire and Gilles with his beautiful face and golden-brown curls. Gilles waved goodbye to them and sped off down the trail, his bare feet flying and his hair bouncing on his shoulders.

I followed, casting a longing glance back at the great oak, under whose shade or in whose boughs we had hoped to enjoy the day, alone and unrecognized. I followed my rabbit boy, trying hard to keep up with him without flinging the wooden shoes off of my feet.

He was like a rabbit, so swift and sure.

So certain that he knew a place for us, a place where no one would seek to find us.

And I followed, so joyfully followed.

Given freedom, I would follow him anywhere.

93, A Country All Our Own

The sheep shed was there, in its lonely place, the forest surrounding it and the high grasses of the field grown up all around it, even on its roof. It was low and long, built of stones now lichen-covered and obscured by tall un-grazed grass, with an opening at each end just barely high enough for sheep to enter. Beneath the grass, its top was a thick thatch, and it blended into the meadow as if it were part of it, just a hillock in the landscape.

If one did not know it was there, one would never see it and the people who had known it was there had been gone a very long time.

Gilles dropped down and crawled inside.

I followed him, watching his strong buttocks in their new brown breeches with the boars-head buttons at the knees, disappear into the cool darkness.

How I wanted to reach out and touch him!

Then I was in beside him and recognized from my dream the space inside, dimly-lit, with a smooth dirt floor, hard-packed from the hooves of sheep now long dead, and the light coming through the hole in the wall where the stones had tumbled, leaving a little window from which to see the outside world. I sat cross-legged and peered through the window and saw the yellow flowers in the verdant grasses, with the insects buzzing happily to and fro, and the dark belt of trees that surrounded the meadow.

"So beautiful," I said, and turned to look at him.

He lay back upon the floor, his hands up behind his head, making for it a pillow. His eyes in the dimness were like dark green slate and he looked at me as if he would be content to look at me this way forever, until the last breath left his body, and he would lie in this repose, with his view of me in his eyes until the last stone of this sheep shed tumbled down to cover him.

"Yes, beautiful," he said, his eyes fixed on mine.

I sighed. "You are," I said.

"No, you," he said.

I smiled, wondering if I said, "No, you," how long this game would go on. Probably until his last breath, for he would never concede.

"I wish I could touch you," he said.

"I wish you could too," I said.

"But if I touched you, even a little bit," he said, "I think I might not be able to stop touching you."

I sighed again, so full of longing that my breath quavered as it came through my mouth.

"If you touched me, even a little bit, I think I would not

want you to stop," I said, "and then... then..." but I wasn't just thinking about not being *La Pucelle* anymore, about how I needed to be *La Pucelle* so that I could follow the English north and defeat them at Jargeau, Beaugency, and Patay, and drive them from Paris, and... crown the King... no, I was thinking about his death, that cold slippery death and how I hated to have to see it again, feel its icy coldness again, succumb to its deep darkness again.

I bewondered me then; when all this was over and I had done all that I had promised to do, and if, God willing, I might live and Gilles and I might marry, I wondered if, when we touched, I would still see his death.

Or might not the archangel Michael, having seen that I had done as I had promised, take back his gift from me, and leave me just an ordinary girl, an ordinary woman, once more?

"I know," he said, thinking of *La Pucelle*. "I know, but still I wish I could."

"Mayhap I could touch you," I said, reaching and putting my hand over his thigh, just inches above it. "Mayhap there is a way," and I looked about for something, a stone, perhaps, that might draw away the coldness, as had happened before. Gilles looked at me, a spark of surprise and delight in his eyes.

He laughed, a bit nervously, I thought, and said, "Too bad there is no horse in here with us."

"Yes, they are nice and big and warm," I said, feeling my face flush.

He patted the floor beside him.

"Lay here, Jehanne," he said. "Close beside me. You don't have to touch me. I would like to feel your touch, of course I would. I long for it, but I want it to be when I can touch you as well, in all the ways I want to touch you."

I looked into his eyes, so mild, as soft and gentle as the rabbit who hides from sight beneath the berry bush. The whole world resided in his eyes, all the things he loved; the sounds of birdsong and the wind in grass and the chuckling of creek water over shifting pebbles; and me.

Oui, I resided there too, that me that was simply Jehanne, a girl who loved a boy and wanted to marry him one day. I would reside in his eyes forever and ever.

So I lay down beside him, so close I could feel the heat of his body and smell his scent. I could smell the forest on his skin, the sap of trees, the very greenness of leaves, the juice of roots deep in the earth. I could smell the tang of meadow grass, the perfume of wildflower, the powder from the wings of butterflies, and the sunlight that was forever caught in the tangles of his hair.

He is so wild, I thought.

Would the world ever tame him?

I wanted the world to leave him as he was, so wild and free, so pure and good, so gentle and full of joy, but I knew the world was already changing him. I knew that loving me and having followed me from Le Moineau to Orléans was already changing him.

I knew, to my great sorrow, that continuing to follow me, the girl who wept, across France, to Rheims and beyond, would change him even more. He would never again be the boy from Le Moineau that he had been the day I first saw him under the beech tree on the road outside of Tours, a boy only concerned with the contents of his precious little bag.

I called him a boy, but in truth he was surely a man. The events he had seen and been part of since he had decided to follow me had made him a man and his eyes had not yet seen the worst of it.

They gazed at me now, those eyes, those beautiful eyes that were a color that is beyond color, but were, in this dim place, as dark as slate.

No, they had not yet seen the worst.

He took a deep breath and let it out slowly and closed his eyes, as if he knew what I was thinking. As if he did not want to see any more, but only to remember the things that were beautiful and that brought him joy.

A shaft of sunlight, tiny and straight as a sword, without warning, cut through a hole in the thatched ceiling of the sheep shed. It illuminated his high cheeks and strong brow, burnished the planes of his face, accentuated his perfect lips, and struck spears of light from the curls of his hair.

It took my breath away, his beauty, but I wanted to see his eyes, those beautiful eyes that were a color that is beyond color. I wanted to see the sunlight play in them, see what color they wanted to be at this moment.

I wanted to say, "Open your eyes; look into the light."

But he kept them closed, and slowly, ever so slowly, I moved closer to him and pressed myself against him. He rolled to his side and his arms came around me and he pulled me gently into the curve of his body, his strong man's body with its strong man's parts, all of them, and I turned my head to the side and my ear was against his shoulder and I heard the forceful thudding of his heart, his heart that was that of a boy, and would be that of a boy forever, I was certain.

He was my rabbit boy and would always be my rabbit boy. He would always be my constant companion, my love, my own one. My angel of angels.

He was my Great Joy, though only I would remember him. When all this was done and History had had its way with all of us, he would be forgotten, but not by me.

He wrapped his graceful limbs around me, so warm and comforting, and I pushed back against him, wanting to just lie in his arms forever, and I felt the rushing of his hot blood in his vessels and the wind of his breaths entering and leaving his body, and they were also my blood and my breaths, and I heard his deep murmur of my name and his smile in my hair which was like music.

Then, I could ward it off no longer and the icy-cold began to seep into me from the heat that was inside him.

I let the darkness take me.

And then the silence.

The End

ABOUT THE AUTHOR

Amy R Farrell is, among other things, an historical re-enactor who engages in non-choreographed full-armored, full-contact Medieval Combat with real steel weapons at Renaissance Festivals and Medieval Tournaments, under the sobriquet Dame Armsmere De Ravenglass.

The writing of this novel was greatly facilitated by a little Appaloosa horse named Emmy, may she gallop the Elysian Fields in joyfulness.

If you enjoyed this book, check out Amy's other publications at www.armsmerepress.com

(Passion, Book Two of The Love Affair of Joan of Arc
will be available sometime in the future)

461

81738697R00281

Made in the USA
Columbia, SC
08 December 2017